THE
SANDOVAL SISTERS'
SECRET
OF
OLD
BLOOD

Sandra Ramos O'Briant

This is a work of fiction. Names, characters, places and inci-dents are either a product of the author's imagination or are used fictitiously. Any resemblance to actual persons, living or dead, events, or locales is entirely coincidental.

Portions of this novel appeared previously, in different form, in the following journals: "*The Devil at the Dance*," in La Herencia, vol. XXXV, Fall 2002, (Gran Via, Inc.), and was subsequently on-line at LatinoLA.com. "*Of Nuns and the Demimonde*," FriGG (summer, 2004). "*The First White Woman*," appeared in The Copperfield Review, (Fall, 2004).

Printed in the United States of America

ISBN: 0615615104
ISBN-13: 9780615615103

1. Sisters–Latinas–Santa Fe, New Mexico 1848–Fiction. 2. His-tory–Santa Fe–Mexican American War–Fiction. 3. Hispanics–Santa Fe, New Mexico–Fiction. 4. Witchcraft–New Mexico–Fiction. 5. Mexican American War–Texas–Fiction. I. Title.

First Edition
14 13 12 11 10/10 9 8 7 6 5 4 3 2 1

Library of Congress Control Number: 2012935461
La Gente Press, Los Angeles CA

No Statue of Liberty ever greeted our arrival in this country...we did not, in fact, come to the United States at all. The United States came to us.

Luis Valdez

Some memories are realities, and are better than anything that can ever happen to one again.

Willa Cather

My mother told me the Sandoval history, and what she didn't know, she made up with each telling. This is for her.

Contents

Contents

1

The Secrets

"All that praying and what does Teresa leave me? Daughters!"

Oratoria, *1850*
The Sandoval History:

ESTEVAN HAD NO time for Alma and Pilar and left them completely in my hands. I taught them to read the Sandoval diaries and to keep their own. The latter you have before you; what we wrote during the innocent time before the war years, and an accounting of what happened when we lost love and land. We wrote as we lived through the events, and we wrote what we remembered later. Which are the more true, the memories then or those simmered over time?

The diaries afforded an extensive education all on their own, one that included many generations and the experiences of both men and women, but my sisters and I also studied history and languages, including English. We were the Sandoval sisters to the world, even though I first entered their compound a barefoot slave.

Estevan had traded for me—a bag of flour for a ragged peasant girl of five—after I had been captured by Apaches in Mexico. He brought me to this high mountain desert, to Santa Fé, the City of Holy Faith, as a wedding present for his bride. I became doña Teresa's favorite, who was sixteen and far from her family in Mexico City.

1

She taught me to read and to cook, and christened me Oratoria because of my skill with languages. When I came to her, I spoke only the native language of my village, but the Sandovals spoke the cultured Spanish of their Castilian ancestors. Because of their overland trading expeditions, they also had a command of English, and a smattering of French, as well.

I rode to Santa Fé in the back of a wagon loaded with reeking buffalo skins. It was the last wagon in a caravan of six. It rumbled along and I stared out at where I'd been: lost in a savage wilderness. A whirlwind of dust kicked up by the wagons made me cough and my eyes water. They watered more at night when I felt the most alone.

One man cooked for all the others. He shoved a plate of food at me every morning and night, but he and all the other men ignored me. Estevan commanded them, and I feared him. I didn't know what lay ahead and began to forget the life I'd left behind.

Another day wore on and I continued my vigil in the back of the dead buffalo wagon, but shouts and whistles from the men signaled something new. Crawling over the skins, I peeked out the front. The land was flat, but in front of us a huge wall blocked our way. A double gate swung open, and men and women appeared. Women! I pressed my face into the bison fur beneath me, afraid I'd imagined them. Looked again. The women were laughing.

A large house lay behind the gate, and Estevan entered it. The other men remained outside the compound unloading the wagons. One of the women led me to a trough from where the horses drank and motioned me to get into it. I sat in the water and stared at all the comings and goings of the people in the compound. After the woman scrubbed me and gave me a change of clothes, I entered the Sandoval hacienda. Estevan frowned down at me, but a small woman, a girl really, laughed and stepped around him. She knelt in front of me and squeezed my shoulders.

"She's mine," Teresa said.

She took my hand, and wonder replaced fear as Teresa led me around my new home. There were many rooms and unfamiliar objects, but Teresa taught me what she knew. She was lonely, patient, and talkative. I learned her language fast, and thus began my immersion in the Sandoval mysteries.

"My father was eager for me to marry a rich man, even if his family was disreputable," she told me. Rich in land granted to them by royal decree centuries ago, the Sandoval luck remained strong and they had increased their holdings in the usual way: through marriage, gambling, theft, murder, and prayer.

"I don't understand why they choose to live on the undesirable side of Santa Fé," Teresa said. Many months had passed since I'd joined the household, and we often sat together in the library. She looked up from the Sandoval diary she'd been reading, a leather-covered tome, its pages scribbled in fading ink. "We could build to the north, around the plaza, where the other ricos live." She returned to the book. "It's their own contrary decision to live here. Our old Spanish blood makes us stubborn . . . and different. It says so right here."

Of course, I didn't understand about the blood when I first came to live there.

"Old blood marries old blood," doña Teresa said.

She was a cousin, also a Sandoval, although from a poorer branch of the family, and her children with Estevan would bear the rare Sandoval y Sandoval surname. Some celebrated the joint mastery of the name, while others feared the awakening of dark powers for which the Sandovals had always been suspect. Not only had they acquired wealth in a desert frontier, they had survived Indians and epidemics while others perished.

They could read, too, and their home was sumptuous with white marble pier tables, Brussels carpets and wood floors. This, while many New Mexicans lived in one-room adobe hovels alongside their goats. To make matters worse, they were handsome people. All good reasons to fear and respect them.

"My mother told me to ignore the gossip and concentrate on being a dutiful wife," doña Teresa told me.

This meant cooking, managing the household of servants and never criticizing her husband, her adored one, who left her alone while he caroused in town. Oh, to be sure, Estevan made love to his wife, loudly and often. All the rooms opened onto a large central patio, so the entire household heard him. But not a peep escaped from Teresa, who conceived and miscarried one baby after another. And then, even the pregnancies stopped.

It would be ten years before she was able to bring a child to term, and in the interim I became her pupil, her plaything, and her daughter.

Many of the books in their library were written in Latin, and Teresa arranged for the priest who had baptized all the servants of the household to tutor me. Like all the others, bought and paid for, the baptismal record listed only my first name. Had they asked for a last name, I could not have given one. I no longer held a memory of my former life. To their credit, Estevan and his father did not begrudge the childless Teresa's affection for me, and if anyone else thought it unusual, they said nothing . . . to the Sandovals.

Over time I became the sole expert on those forgotten tomes. Since I'd also shown a talent for cooking, Teresa had a desk made for me and moved to a corner of the kitchen. It set next to the patio doors so the light was good all day. I could cook and read and stare out at the birds.

"This is yours, Oratoria," she said, waving her arm toward her gift. It was smaller than Estevan's unused desk in the library, but not so tiny that I've outgrown it. Delicate floral carvings, painted turquoise and red, graced the locking doors underneath the tabletop. A shelf above the desk held a few of the diaries. She handed me two keys. One was large and unlocked the doors, but the second key, tiny and delicate, was for a secret compartment concealed behind the shelves below.

"My mother said a woman must have a secret treasure," Teresa said.

She encouraged me to read the ancient diaries of the Sandoval heiresses, said to contain delectable recipes guaranteed to whet a husband's appetite and keep him at home. The recipes were there, but so were their fears and ecstasies, their seductions and adulterous affairs. The diaries were cookbooks of love.

I transcribed the recipes and Teresa made her choices. The savory aromas and tasty dishes I cooked assured don Estevan's presence at supper, but he usually left for town when he'd finished, and did not return until the morning. Sometimes he remained away for days. Teresa turned to prayer. She filled the niches in the hacienda with santos and set up altars in every room.

Making our household rounds required a stop before each martyr. I followed her, kneeling and making the sign-of-the-cross when she did. I mumbled fervent prayers for God to make my benefactress fruitful. Teresa drank teas made from foul-tasting herbs guaranteed to make her womb fecund. She sought the advice of a bruja, a witch, who instructed her to smear honey and lard on her nethermost region and mount her husband from above. I held Teresa's hand while the witch spoke and felt her pulse quicken.

"I read about doing that in the diaries. It sounded foolish," Teresa said. "I'll ask Estevan's permission, of course."

The bruja drew her lips back and showed her teeth—not a smile, more the kind of mirthless leer I'd seen on Estevan's face when he'd been drinking. This witch was not what I'd expected. She was young and plump, not the toothless, desiccated old woman children were told to avoid.

"Yes, *ask* Estevan," the bruja said, speaking as if she were talking to a child. She held out her hand to receive the coin Teresa had promised.

The prayers continued, as did the teas, and honey and lard were hidden beneath her mattress, but there was no sign of a pregnancy. One day, Teresa led me to the library.

"How do I keep him home all night, Oratoria?" She glanced at my bare feet, but ignored my transgression for the moment. "The Sandovals know about such things. The recipes for charms are here, but we must be careful. Not all of them are for love. That is why la gente fear us." She pulled two books out at random, handing me the thickest. "Ah! Providencia Sandoval. She had three husbands. She must have been beautiful, or a talented cook . . . or a knowledgeable lover." Teresa raised innocent eyes to mine. "She may reveal something, or nothing. One never knows with the Sandovals." She opened the book in her hands. "I'll read this one. Epiphenia Sandoval was known to be pious. Almost a saint."

She left me in the library, thumbing slowly through the diary of a murderess. If Teresa had read Providencia's recipes for poisoned pie, instead of Epiphenia's directions on proper self-flagellation, who knows how the Sandoval history might have changed? The charms and formulas devised by lusty and daring wives were beyond my ken. They awaited the true hand of a blood Sandoval.

The secrets of their line were revealed in those journals, entire lifetimes recorded. A community of blood, the curtain drawn aside, allowed my voyeuristic peek. Human dreams had been written in archaic Spanish, and terrible sins described in faded brown ink on whisper-thin paper. The entire spectrum of love was examined: practical jokes and puns, recipes for desperate wives and artistic poisoners, centuries of words put down for those who followed.

"What does Providencia advise?" Teresa asked one day when I was reading.

My head snapped up and I stared at her, confused, pulled out of the intrigues and conquests of that formidable Sandoval. "You must keep his seed," I said. The lie sprang to my lips easily, though Providencia's advice had concerned pleasure only. "When he spills, hold him tight within you. Clench your womb."

Teresa's face brightened, and she nodded. "Yes," she said, no doubt already planning to ask Estevan's permission. "Yes, this makes sense. Thank you, my lovely, for wading through her diary. It is by far the weightiest." She kissed the top of my head, and turned to leave, but not before she kneeled and signed before the altar. I continued reading.

The Sandoval blood was not mine, but I felt their stories had been written for me, my fate intertwined with theirs. The ancestral voices rang true in my ear. Their ecstasies and petty misfortunes became my catechism; they were now my family. Perhaps my improvised advice worked, for Teresa became, and remained, pregnant. In her joy, she took me to the priest and had me baptized again. This time she added Sandoval to my name on the Church rolls, a precious gift, usually earned only after years of dedicated service.

My fervor renewed, I studied the diaries and wrote what I learned in my own journal. I cooked for the family, and was a loving daughter. Then, a true daughter of the blood was born in 1827. I watched Alma come into the world. I was also there, three years later, at the delivery of Teresa's second daughter, Pilar.

"Take care of your sisters," Teresa said, as she lay dying from birth fever. "And try to wear shoes."

And just like that, I became Oratoria Sandoval, the elder sister.

Before Teresa was in the ground, the whole town arrived to pay their respects. Instead, they witnessed a drunken Estevan destroy the altars his wife had set up. He tossed the wooden saints and rosaries into a bonfire he'd started in the yard.

"All that praying and what does she leave me? Daughters!" He spat on the ground.

Estevan's drinking friends laughed, and said, "The Sandovals have no fear of God."

Their laughter gurgled to a choking stop, as if their throats had sobered up before their minds. They crossed themselves and hurried away, followed by the other townspeople, who cringed at their close brush with such satanic activity. A few uttered prayers for us, the motherless Sandoval sisters, shaking their heads, sure that we were doomed to perdition.

My sisters became my life. I read the diaries for guidance and learned that in every other generation of Sandovals, the burden of old blood, thick with family secrets, flowed into one person's soul. The truth of the blood made itself slowly known, and that individual's destiny was cast. Past recipients of the Sandoval secrets had become wily political raconteurs, owners of vast land grants, goatherds, or insipid priests. Tradition held that the blood flowed solely to the Sandoval males, but it was suspected that an occasional dotty old aunt hoarded secrets.

Estevan Sandoval thought *he* was the chosen one. He was lucky at cards, and always bet on the fastest horse in a race. But he was an ordinary man who'd had a few good hunches. It was his daughter, Alma, who inherited the telling blood. At fourteen it thickened in her veins, and saturated her senses with its heat. Ancient memories unraveled and revealed themselves to her. I had only to lean close to Alma to hear:

7

"Hidalgo Sandoval, sadist and hypocrite, in the year of our Lord, 1484, puts to the rack seven Jews and confiscates their property," she might begin. "He disembowels a crone who practices midwifery, and takes her virginal daughter by force. He keeps her as a mistress and loves her deeply, though she continues her mother's line of healing arts. Providencia Sandoval, murderess and cook, 1563, poisons three husbands with ground castor beans. A recipe book written by her is treasured by generations of Sandoval women. Jesús Sandoval, swindler and incidental murderer, 1735, salts a mine in the Manzano Mountains with gold, and sells it to his cousin. The cousin later kills his family and himself when he discovers that he has squandered his fortune on an empty hole in the ground."

It would go on, a continuous reel, like the player piano in the parlor. When she reached the end, she would begin again. With each recitation a new secret would be added to the never-ending list of Sandoval sins and misjudgments. Her lips moved incessantly, as if in prayer, and the people of Santa Fé, la gente, thought she recited novenas for the repose of her mother's soul.

The caballeros sang Alma's praise: "What a prize your daughter is, Estevan, so beautiful and pure." She was the most obedient of daughters, and read the Sandoval diaries as if they were parables, unlike Pilar, who laughed at the ancestral stories.

She called the diaries lies, and made jokes, and ran wild, doing as she pleased, even secretly riding her father's stallion bareback. But she wrote in her diary like all the Sandovals who came before her. Pilar was a handful, but her father ignored her completely, focusing his attention on Alma, the daughter of marriageable age.

2

A Dangerous Time for Gringos

"Are the Texans coming here to fight a war?"

**lma,** *1841*
Santa Fé:

RIDERS APPROACHED OUR outer gate, and rang the bell hung there. A man shouted, "Estevan, the Texans are two hours away. ¡Vámonos, compadre! Come on."

Oratoria told us to stay out of the way, but Pilar and I gaped at the men who entered. Resplendent in gold epaulets and braiding, Governor Armijo's hat even had a feather in it. The sun glinted off his sword when he waved it in the air, adding to his majesty. Several ricos surrounded him, a few in blue and red uniforms, but most dressed for their usual work as merchants, ranchers and farmers. Even so, they looked and sounded angry, and carried many weapons. The Texas Santa Fé Expedition had traveled from Austin to Santa Fé with twenty-one ox-drawn wagons and more than three hundred merchants, teamsters, and soldiers. It was 1841—a dangerous time for Anglos in Santa Fé.

My father called out orders as his horse turned in a tight circle, its eyes bulging with tension. He posted men to the torreón, the tower built into the thick walls surrounding our compound, and called to others to mount up.

"Shut the gate and bolt it," he commanded Oratoria.

Squat and solid, but still imposing, Oratoria waved him on with the back of her palm, as if he were an annoying gnat. A flick of her head, and Pedro, our foreman, came out of the shadows and bolted the gate. Papá was usually too drunk to run the hacienda, and left it completely in Oratoria's hands. She stood barefoot in the dust, something she would not allow Pilar and me to do. My elder sister examined the yard, the buildings, and my sister and me with a critical eye.

"Bloody business," she said. "Innocents to the slaughter."

"Papá is an innocent?" Pilar asked while picking at a scab on her elbow. Scratches, scabs and scars from her play—much too rough for a scrawny eleven-year-old—covered her sunburned skin. I petted my black cat, Concha, swollen in the last stages of pregnancy.

"Not Estevan," Oratoria said. She slapped Pilar's hand away from her elbow. "The Texans."

She walked toward the house, issuing orders, as usual. The day was warm, and she wrapped her fringed rebozo around her waist. "Alma, make a birthing box for Concha. It should be warm, a place where she'll feel safe."

I gritted my teeth. Not only was I already fourteen, but Concha had been a mother before. We were both experienced.

"Why are the Texans coming here?" I asked her retreating back.

She whirled around. "Why are wars usually fought, Alma?"

I'd given Oratoria an opening for another history lesson. Sweat trickled down my chest and I pulled the high collar of my shirt away from my neck. "For stupid reasons—land or religion," I said, begrudging her each word. No matter how hot the day, Oratoria insisted I wear uncomfortable, tight-bodice dresses she claimed were suitable for a young lady. Yet, like many women in Santa Fé, she wore short-sleeved blouses tied loosely in front, and no corset whatsoever. She said it was practical and comfortable and the sun could turn her no browner, whereas my fair skin freckled. As if she read my mind, Oratoria scrutinized my face and my hands. She would soon tell me to put on a hat and gloves, or retreat indoors to our library. The preservation of my paleness was a high priority in our household.

"Are the Texans coming here to fight a war?" I asked.

"They're coming here because they think they own us," she said, and shook her head. "They claim all this land from Texas, across the Rio Grande, up into Santa Fé, and beyond. They want to command the trade on the Santa Fé trail."

"I heard Papá say the best thing Mexico did for New Mexico was to open up trade with the gringos." Spain had kept foreigners out for two hundred years, but the rich managed to bring worthwhile items for their own use into the city.

Oratoria gazed toward the Sangre de Cristo Mountains, named Blood of Christ by Spanish explorers, their snow-capped peaks visible above the twelve-foot adobe wall surrounding our hacienda. Her hair hung in neat braids, and her face was the placid sea of flawless brown I'd known my whole life, but Oratoria's outside said nothing of what was inside.

She was the only one of us who'd read *all* the Sandoval diaries, those monstrous Spanish histories dating back for centuries. She said they were the source of our power. Like their authors, she reserved all her emotion for the biting edge of her words.

"Time will tell," she said. "But many think the Texans will try to take advantage."

"So Papá will fight for Mexico?"

Oratoria still stared at the mountains, as if they revealed the dictates of history. "Think about it. Who is the stronger ally? Mexico, who speaks our language and shares our religion, or the Texans, insisting we speak English, regarding us as little better than Indians?"

I winced at her words. It was true that Texans, more so than the gringos from the States, made no subtle distinctions. They came here and reduced everything and everybody to a color. Brown homes and people, it was all the same to them. When they saw my fair skin and dark eyes, they thought me an oddity.

"Must have white blood in her," I heard one Texan say when he saw me. Then they stared at Pilar, brown as a pine nut from playing in the sun, and called her a mongrel. "That one must be her mother," he said, meaning Oratoria. It wasn't the first time I'd heard this. La gente whispered the same thing.

Oratoria shrugged and softened her tone. "The Texans fought hard for their independence from Mexico, and they both want our land. We're caught in the middle." She gave Concha a stroke from the top of her head to the tip of her tail, and went into the house without another word.

Papá returned long after Pilar and I were in our beds. I heard the excitement in his voice when he spoke to Oratoria and Pedro. Governor Armijo's forces had captured the entire Texan Santa Fé Expedition, despite the soldiers and brass howitzer that accompanied the "traders." They planned to march the prisoners 2000 miles to Mexico City. He asked Oratoria to set out provisions for him and six of his men; we were not to expect his return for several months. I listened for him to ask about Pilar and me. But his sole concern was for his new horses, which still needed to be broken in.

"Send word to don Geraldo," he said. "He refused to ride with us, so he will be at his ranch, and he knows horses. It will give him an excuse to visit. I want him to see Alma."

See me? Don Geraldo had seen me dozens of times at church. No further explanation came from Papá. Doors crashed open and closed, followed by the rumble of men's voices, and the snorts, neighs and hoof-stamps from the horses. A resounding slam of the boundary gate and the click of the bolt that locked it announced their departure. Silence. Papá hadn't checked on us, or said goodbye.

The next morning, a restless ache bloomed in my chest. A hole had opened up, a vacuum of expectation. Something was about to happen.

3
Spanish Lessons

"Are we talking horses or daughters here, Sir?"

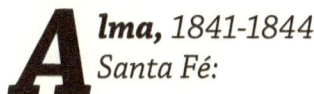**lma,** *1841-1844*
Santa Fé:

Two DAYS LATER, I went to the barn to check on Concha, and found a young Anglo cowboy lying on a bed of straw next to her birthing box. Two kittens suckled. He stroked her gently, and she graced him with her happy mother-cat expression.

"There you go, little mother, push it on out," he crooned to her.

He jumped up when he saw me. "Beg your pardon, Miss, I thought you were Pedro." He snatched his hat off his head, and blushed clear up to the roots of his short brown hair. He shaved, but he wasn't much older than me. I stopped staring at him and concentrated on Concha.

"Name's Bill Pollard. Don Geraldo sent me over to break in some horses. This here your cat?" He waved his hat toward Concha. Her eyes glazed over with another pain, and I knelt to pet her. She kept her adoring gaze on the cowboy. "She sure is a pretty little thing. Always been partial to cats myself," he said in his easy-going drawl. "Guess I better get back to work. No hablo mucho español. Perdone, señorita. Grácias. I don't speak much Spanish." He blushed again, and turned to leave.

"Were you here when the first two kittens were born?" I asked.

"You speak English. Well, that's just fine." He seemed relieved. "I got here for the last kitten. The white one. Anothern's on the way." He knelt beside me as Concha delivered another kitten. She purred loudly through the entire process. "Her purr-box sure is getting a workout," he said. I faced him, and was startled by the color of his eyes. They were a bright blue-green. Almost turquoise.

It was my turn to blush. I focused all my attention on Concha, who was about to deliver another kitten. This one came out legs first, and couldn't get its head out. She tried to reach around and pull it out, finally turning in circles with the kitten hanging limply from her backside.

"Lay on down, mama-cat," Bill said. "Miss, if you'd stroke behind her ears to calm her down, I think I might be able to help her out." He placed his thumb and forefinger on either side of her opening, pressing down and in. With two fingers of the other hand he delicately grasped as much of the head as he could, and rotated the kitten. One more push from Concha, and it was out. The kitten didn't move.

"Is it dead?" I asked. Concha licked the mucus away from its nose. Still, no movement. Bill picked up the little wet thing and put its whole snout into his mouth. He blew hard. We examined the kitten; tiny bubbles appeared on its nostrils. He gave it back to its mama. She began licking again, and it squeaked.

"You did it!" I smiled. For the briefest moment, we gazed at each other.

This time Bill looked away first. "Works with horses," he said. "Guess I better get back to work. Nice meeting you, Miss–?"

"Señorita Alma María Sandoval *y Sandoval*," a voice behind me announced. Oratoria. She glared at me, hands on hips. "You are wanted in the house."

Embarrassed, I held my hand out to Bill to show him I knew how Americans greeted each another. "Nice to meet you, Mister Pollard. Thank you for your help with Concha."

"Yes, ma'am . . . urrr, Miss . . . I mean, señorita Sandoval," he said, sneaking a wary glance at Oratoria. He took my hand and shook it. "Pleasure was all mine."

I marched past my sister without acknowledging her, holding my head high. Outside, I skipped into the house. Just as I thought—no one waited for me. I ran straight for the mirror, and said, "Pleasure was all mine." I began a thorough examination of my features. My hair was long and black, with a bit of wave. My fair skin excited admiration in some circles, but I took no joy in it. My gaze strayed down to my chest with satisfaction. Even in my school uniform, my bosom was ample for a girl my age. *Godey's Lady's Magazine* always showed full-figured women. I angled my torso slightly away from my reflection, peered over my right shoulder, and lowered my voice trying it a different way: "No, Mister Bill Pollard, the pleasure was all mine!"

Over the next month, Bill Pollard broke in my father's horses, and Oratoria kept him busy around the ranch. If Oratoria and I visited the poor, bringing baskets of food from our garden, Bill volunteered to carry them. He hoed her garden, slaughtered and skinned any animal she asked him to, and tagged along to Sunday mass.

Inside La Parroquia, the main church near the plaza, we took our place at the front. Oratoria stood between Bill and me, stolidly ignoring our glances at each another. Pilar insisted on sitting next to Bill. He copied her movements, standing, kneeling, awkwardly crossing himself, moving his lips as if he knew the Latin responses to the priest, even following us to take communion.

"You stay!" Oratoria said, holding her small hand against his chest. Pilar giggled, and Bill stepped back fast and bowed his head to hide his confusion.

After Mass, la gente watched as he helped us into our wagon. Much could be made of the Sandoval sisters and a young, handsome tejano.

"Their tongues are wagging so hard, I can feel the breeze," Oratoria said as we drove out of town. We laughed, but she sat glumly staring ahead.

We reached the hacienda, and Bill helped her down first. "There is more work to be done," she said sternly, and then, softly so only we four could hear, "you were meant to be here."

Bill was seventeen, and already he'd had a big adventure. He'd sneaked off and followed his older brother, Edward, and joined the Texan Santa Fé Expedition. He discovered Bill had tagged along when they'd been on the trail for several weeks.

"You left home? Without telling anybody?" Pilar asked. My sister and Bill were grooming one of Papá's stallions together. Pilar was his shadow whenever Bill worked with the horses. And what was my excuse for being there? I was the pretend chaperone.

"Well, I told a couple of my friends," Bill said, with a mischievous grin, "but my folks had already said no."

He was a good hunter so the expedition bosses let him stay. Indians were a problem and the caravan took a few wrong turns, causing them to run short of provisions. On the day they were rousted by Armijo's forces, Bill was a day away from them, packing antelope meat from a successful hunt. He ended up at don Geraldo's hacienda where he was told the entire expedition had been captured. A few men had been killed, including Bill's brother.

"I was gonna follow them, but don Geraldo said I'd get myself killed, too," Bill said. "He's a good man, don Geraldo."

"An *old* friend of my father's," I said. He was ancient as far as I was concerned. "He stayed home when the expedition came."

Bill shook his head, smiling to himself. "Not cause he's old, cause he's an independent thinker. Lucky for me, otherwise I might never have met you young ladies."

"We're not ladies," Pilar said. She gave me a disdainful once over. "At least not me." Horse lather and her own grime covered her. I wore a new dress and sat up straight on a chair Bill had carried for me from the house. "And I never want to be."

I shot her my narrow-eyed mean look, but she ignored me.

"What's it like where you come from?" Pilar asked.

"Pollard's Corner's got the best bottomland in Texas."

"It's named for your family?" I asked.

"Pop started the town. Built the biggest farm. He's a small man, but strong as an ox. Always gets what he wants, but he met his match with Momma." He shook his head. "It's near a river, so there's plenty of fresh water. We have a wharf where smaller boats put in."

"They fell in love?" I asked. Pilar rolled her eyes, threw the brush into a bin, and left the stable.

"Did I say something wrong?" Bill asked.

"I did. Pilar thinks romance is silly. Besides she's probably meeting Monique and Stinky down at the swimming hole."

"The *secret* swimming hole? Are they safe?"

"They've been going there since they were seven," I said, twitching my shoulders, impatient and selfish, unworried that any harm could come to my sister or her friends. "Tell me about your parents falling in love."

Bill's smile faded. "It doesn't always happen that way. Pop was nigh on forty-five when he married Momma. He scrimped and saved, living in his bachelor shack until he owned eleven nigras."

"Nigras?" I repeated, trying to say it the same as him, *knee-gruz*.

"Negroes. Slaves," he said.

I'd seen one black man in my life, a muleskinner on one of the wagon trains heading for Chihuahua. It hadn't seemed as if anyone owned him. Bill stared hard at me, a curious mix of pride and dread in his expression. He was telling me his family was wealthy. But he used a language and legal tender strange to me. Both Indians and the Spanish took slaves, but over time they were absorbed into the villages and families who took them: like Oratoria.

"So what happened when he finally got his eleven . . . slaves?"

"It meant he was rich enough to go after the most eligible girl in the area, Bertha Mae Hamilton. She'd turned twenty, and was full of hell-fire. Still is. Do as she says or she'll take a switch to you. Don't even think about running, 'cause she'll catch you—runs fast as a fox." We laughed. Slaves had nothing to do with my life in Santa Fé or with the dizzying rush of heat I felt whenever I was near Bill.

New Mexico had enchanted him, and so, it seems, had I.

Papá didn't return for six months, and for that half-year Bill and I spent as much time together as possible. Oratoria was lenient in her own irritable way and allowed Bill and me more time alone than was considered proper by the ruling families in Santa Fé. But who would criticize the Sandovals openly? No one dared. Some of la gente called us witches and said we'd gotten rich by bargaining with the devil. We'd heard the whispers as young girls, seen people cross the street when they saw us coming. Even from a distance we could read their fear.

"Old blood can do that," Oratoria said.

But who could blame the people when I'd wandered around whispering to myself the same as a lunatic? I'd been in the grip of ancient memories, reciting a list of family secrets that stretched back for centuries, repeating them as if I said a rosary. I'd developed an eccentric reputation in Santa Fé, even for a Sandoval. I wasn't sure if the memories were from an unknown part of my mind, or if they came from reading Sandoval diaries when I was much too young. Oratoria had not censored their comedies of love, just as they had not been withheld from her.

The memories would visit me fully formed, and I would speak in the formal tone of the diaries no matter how mundane my activities. One day while working alongside my sisters in the kitchen, one such memory unfolded: "Faustina, another excellent Sandoval cook," I began, "prepared hearty and flavorful meals for her large family of aunts, uncles and cousins, who lived together in the family hacienda." Oratoria nodded and continued to roll out tortillas. Pilar's job was to sort the beans, removing rabbit turds and twigs. I sliced squash and onions.

"Her husband," I continued, "was a rotund and unimaginative old man, twenty-five years her senior. He loved his wife's artistry in the kitchen, but neglected to show his appreciation in the bedroom. Time-and-again after having eaten heartily at her table, he would later mount her from behind; his full stomach was more comfortable in this position. He'd complete a few quick strokes before farting or belching or sometimes both to signal he was finished, and collapse next to her, falling into the blissful sleep of the innocent. Often, sleep would overcome him so quickly and thoroughly he'd fail to notice Faustina still kneeling beside him, her naked bottom in the air."

Pilar snorted. "Did she really say her butt was in the air?"

"Alma speaks the truth," Oratoria said, holding her rolling pin like a baton and punctuating the air in tempo to her words. "Faustina wrote that when the breeze blew through the open window she could feel the cool air moving the tendrils of her hair down there. Her husband snored beside her. Of course, she could not maintain that elevation indefinitely. Yet, she yearned for that airy contact, that ghostly touch upon her bottom, its gentle caress so promising. When she was alone in the hacienda, and the breeze was right, she would bare herself in that position, the only one she knew, tantalizing herself further." Oratoria grew quiet, and the sound of rolling pin on board resumed.

"It's no wonder she fell in love with her husband's nephew, Alonzo," I said.

"Let me guess," Pilar said, "it didn't work out?"

"Alonzo was part of the military expedition sent by the Spanish to map New Spain, so he was seldom able to visit. The first time they found themselves alone, they kissed until their lips were swollen. They could barely eat their food that night and lucky for them because the others got food poisoning."

"Faustina's sister-in-law had prepared the ill-fated supper," Oratoria said. "It sealed the fate of the lovers with each other, and that of their hapless relatives with their own miserable bowels."

"Uh-oh, this story is getting ripe," Pilar said, laughing and slapping the table so hard the beans jumped, the bad and the good mixing.

"You make more work for yourself, Pilar," Oratoria said. "Faustina's lesson is one you should learn."

Pilar pressed her lips together to keep from laughing, and began separating beans again. "What happened next?" she asked.

The words tumbled out, the story a torrent of lurid portraits in my mind. My skin felt hot and my voice trembled. "That meal sent everyone but Faustina and Alonzo careening into the outhouse or the bushes, grabbing their stomachs, while shitting out their insides. Ignored by all, alone again, they made love. Faustina lost herself in her lover's eyes as he entered her."

"She discovered the joy of face-to-face lovemaking," Oratoria said, with conviction. My sister had never even been courted. Pilar and I glanced at each other, eyebrows raised. "She describes the sensation in great detail in her diary. The next time Faustina was on her knees with her husband behind her, she devised a method to insure another rendezvous with her lover." As if we'd rehearsed it, Oratoria stopped, and I began where she'd left off:

"Faustina called her recipe to loosen the bowels La Entrada," I said, "for it was similar to a military expedition. She created a sauce that hid the laxative, and ladled it onto the plates of her relatives, but first she whispered to her lover which dish to avoid. Te de sena, senna leaves, produced a mild upset, and usually not until the next day. Faustina needed something fast-acting and violent, a reaction so severe that each person would be stuck to a chamber pot or outhouse for a long time." My breathing became shallow and sweat ran down my cheek as I struggled in my mind alongside Faustina to find the right elixir. I jumped when a warm and floury hand was laid on my shoulder.

"She consulted the old women in the village," Oratoria said, her voice low and soft. Her eyes probed mine, bringing me back to the here-and-now. "The viejas advised her well, describing cebadilla, the fuzzy plant called deer's ears. Faustina learned the hard way that great care must be taken with this plant, for more than half a teaspoon of the first year's plant can be toxic." Oratoria squeezed my shoulder. "It's quite useful for killing head lice as well." She returned to her tortillas, satisfied I was not lost in Faustina's life.

"Well, did someone die?" Pilar asked, poker-faced.

"Oh, yes, they all died. Eventually. Of the usual misfortunes—old age, snake bites, childbirth. But not that night, nor for many nights thereafter. They would become ill, and Faustina and Alonzo would have their ecstatic moments alone, their passionate moans unheeded by the household who were clenching their guts and groaning. The two lovers would have to pretend that they, too, had been stricken. And Faustina would care for her family, making them a tea of cardo santo.

"She kept meticulous notes on her experiments, and became an astute herbalist, her cures eagerly sought, especially in the area of gastric disturbances. No one ever suspected what she'd done, but Faustina suffered remorse anyway. Not at her adultery, but at the suffering she'd caused her cousins. All for the sake of lust."

I shook my head, willing such a fate would never visit me.

The day I met Bill, these obsessive recollections stopped. If lessons of life were to be learned from the Sandoval diaries, I recognized them only in retrospect, after my fall from grace. My thoughts focused on him and when next we would meet, when next we would touch.

"Cómo se dice, how do you say?" Bill pointed to his nose. We played the game of student and teacher often.

"La nariz," I said, and tapped his nose. He pointed to his mouth.

"La boca," I said, and touched his lips. He ran a calloused thumb lightly across my bottom lip.

"A kiss?"

"Un beso." I leaned forward to accept my reward. His lips were soft, his tongue demanding. My diary fell off my lap, and he stopped, breathless. He tensed up and surveyed the area around us.

"No one is here," I said.

Bill shuddered. "Your father'd have my hide, and no telling what Oratoria'd do if she caught us." He picked up my diary. "You're always scribbling in this thing." He opened the book, and laughed. "It's in Spanish. Am I in it?"

I moved the bookmark separating the first third of the book from the rest. "These are the stories I remember from my ancestors, from their diaries. But I've stopped writing about them."

"And the rest is about us?"

"All about us."

I didn't explain to Bill that my diary was not unique. He knew my ancestors were educated and moneyed, but not that they obsessed over their diaries, and recorded each virtue and misdeed in their lives. For entertainment, they chose romance or religion, or managed a twisted mix of both. They hoarded their silver or frittered it away, but they wrote it all down. It was what we had always done.

Papá came home from Mexico, and he wasn't happy to find a Texan on his property. But when he saw Bill working with the new horses he'd brought back from Mexico, he changed his mind, and Bill stayed on another three years, until the spring of 1844.

In all that time, Papá never suspected a thing. A man's man, he left the women to get along as best they could. He enjoyed Bill and their talk of horses so much that he often invited him to join us for supper. Bill was deferential to him, and maybe he felt Bill was the son he never had. Perhaps he never thought of it at all. Papá lingered on the ranch and didn't stay in town for longer than one or two days at a time. It became more difficult for Bill and me to be alone together.

Our meetings became urgent, fired with secrecy, and bolder each time. We no longer started at the beginning and warmed slowly in each other's arms, but began where we'd left off when last together. Our bodies' marked the spot, and sent our hungry hands and mouths there with a mindless fury.

Bill pulled away. "Alma, we can't . . . I can't keep doing this. Let me talk to your father. He'll listen to reason."

"He respects your work with the horses, but . . . but what if he says no? What if he makes you leave? It's too dangerous. Wait a little longer. Please, mi amor."

I was almost eighteen, and most girls my age had long since married. A few families approached my father regarding their sons, but he didn't consider them equal to the Sandovals. He held out for the day when don Geraldo would notice me, and notice me he did. Papá's insensitivity was limitless, it seemed, for he asked Bill's advice.

"Diós mío!" Papá said. "When it rains, it pours. A rich widower has called upon me to ask for Alma's hand in marriage." Bill bent his back to the task of shoeing a stallion, so Papá couldn't see his face. But he told me later he felt a shock pass through him.

"What are you going to do?" he asked Papá in an offhand manner.

Papá rubbed his chin whiskers. "Tell me, Bill, if you had a prize mare, would it be better to breed her to a young stallion, or would it make more sense to place her with an aging stallion—one with a proven lineage?"

Bill faced Papá. "Are we talking horses or daughters here, Sir?"

Papá shrugged. "I have it on good authority the old stallion is still active, yes, with that dark temptress, Consuelo." He winked at Bill. "What if this stallion is old, but virile?"

"What's in it for the mare?"

"The same as always." Papá seemed surprised at the question. "She produces offspring. If she lives, she produces more. He is old, and his property adjoins ours. Eventually, he will die. Her progeny will hold title to a vast area of land. Yes, I think Geraldo Quintana is the way to go for Alma." He clapped Bill on the shoulder, as if he were thanking him for his sage advice, and left the stable.

Bill was tight-lipped and angry when he told me of my father's plans.

22

"Geraldo Quintana? He's as old as Papá!" I had always been the obedient daughter, but now it felt as if a giant stood on my chest. I feared my father and I loved him which made my fear greater.

I went to the library to consult the diaries, but sat there in a mindless panic. My eyes traveled over the pages, but the words did not penetrate. No memories surfaced to give me guidance. I didn't confide in my sisters. My world no longer felt safe. It was no longer mine.

My love for Bill overrode my fear. "I want to be with you forever," I said.

We escaped to Texas four days later.

4
Child's Play

"I never want to get married."

Pilar, *1844*
Santa Fé:

It STARTED AT the swimming hole on the day Oratoria walked to the plaza.

Our secret place lay on a slow bend in the river that was shaded by tall oak trees. A rock outcropping was a convenient diving spot, as was a fallen tree trunk further downstream. We'd tied an old rope from a sturdy branch that curved over the rock, and spent hours swinging out over the water and dropping into its chilly depths. Sometimes we'd hear riders on the trail behind the trees, but no one ever bothered us here.

Papá wouldn't have approved, but he never noticed anything I did. Oratoria was too busy running the house now Alma was gone, so she didn't ask any questions. Alma had known me and my best friends, Monique and Stinky—his real name was Angel—had been swimming here since we were seven. She didn't want to join in the fun, being too ladylike, but she'd watched us strip off our clothes and run screaming into the water many times. Alma could always keep a secret and she'd never once told me not to do anything I wanted to try. Like riding Papá's stallions in the dark.

"You miss Alma, don't you?" Monique asked that day. I'd climbed up on the rock and held the rope, but got lost in my thoughts.

"I forget she's gone, and then I think of something funny and want to tell her, see her try not to laugh."

"Where did she go?"

"Texas. She left a note saying she loved me especially." A shiver ran through me remembering Papá's fury. "I don't know what she wrote to Oratoria or Papá."

I did an imitation of a bull, head lowered, pawing the earth to show her Papá's reaction when he read her letter.

"He said Alma was worthless now, no better than food rotting in the sun!"

"Will he go after them?"

"He slammed out of the house and went to town to drink. He hasn't been home since."

Monique frowned. I knew she worried about me. "You've got Oratoria, and you've got me," she said. "And the diaries."

I rolled my eyes. Oratoria had turned to those ancient journals, as if they could tell her Alma's future. I'd read a few. Bunch of whiners and schemers, if you ask me. I like creatures who are half this and half that, in myth's and biblical stories, not in my flesh and blood relatives.

"Oratoria says Alma will be back," I said. "She said I should be happy for her." I swung out and dropped into the river, my sorrow erased by using my body, each stroke upward into the light pure joy.

The day seemed no different from all the others at the swimming hole. Monique waited while Stinky and I worked hard tying a newer, and stronger, rope around the tree branch. I felt like a trout in the water, and on land I wanted to fly through the air like a hawk.

"Let's see who can swing the farthest out into the river!" I challenged them, knowing Stinky's heavy bottom made him drop right off with a huge splash, and that Monique was afraid to let go of the rope.

She stood naked on the bank, fists on hips and elbows sticking out. "No fair, Pilar, you've been practicing!" She pushed her blond curls away from her face.

Her mother was a full-blooded Mescalero Apache, but Monique's skin glowed tawny, like too much milk in coffee, so her father must have been Anglo. No one knew who he was, and her mother wasn't telling. She worked at the mission orphanage where Padre Jacquard taught all the orphans to read and write French. He tutored me and Alma, too, and that's how I met Monique.

I just always knew Stinky. He really did smell bad, but he lived on a pig farm so he had a good reason.

He and I lay on our backs in the water, squirting mouthfuls of it into the air. I turned over, took more water into my mouth, and sprayed him squarely on the side of his head.

"Hey, you sneaky rat, I'll get you for that!" I swam away from him and climbed on the bank with Monique. She stared at the water.

"Don't be afraid to try," I said.

She pressed her lips together, and marched over to the big rock where we anchored the rope. Monique pulled it between her legs, took a deep breath, and swung out over the water. She didn't let go and the rope returned her to the rock where she stood trembling.

"Forget it," I said, "let's dive off the log."

Stinky heaved himself out of the water, gasping. I gave his front a quick gander. When he swam, Stinky's private parts folded up under the shadow of his fat belly the same as a flower at sunset. He was more fidgety than usual and kept looking over his shoulder at the opposite shore.

"Something moved over there," he said.

"I don't see anything," I said, and shoved him into the river. He laughed and kicked water at me.

Monique launched herself again, but slid down the rope into the water, despite the fierce grip of her thighs. She didn't come up right away.

I ran into the water just as her head popped up. She limped out crying, an ugly welt from rope burn on the inside of her right thigh. It ran near her crotch almost to her knee.

"That hurts, I bet," Stinky said.

Monique sat on the mossy bank to check her leg, and Stinky and I knelt beside her. It wasn't cut, only bruised bad. I was shocked to see hair at her cleft, so blond you'd hardly notice it. She had puffy nipples, too, and kept crossing her arms over them when we played rough. I personally never wanted a bosom. I'd seen what Alma had to wear to keep hers in place.

Before I could stop myself, I said, "Alma has a salve that will help." Then I remembered my sister was gone. "Oratoria knows what to do."

"My papá has a special medicine for pigs," Stinky said. Monique and I stared at him, not believing he'd bring up pigs at a time like this. He wouldn't give up. "Well, it works miracles." He peered over his shoulder again. "Did you hear something?"

We studied the trees on the opposite bank. "Somebody's probably on the trail," I said.

"Doesn't sound like horses," Stinky said. "More like whispers."

Monique stamped her foot. "I don't care who's there!" She was in one of her moods. "Show me again how you do the rope, Pilar." She'd keep at it till she did it. I dove in and got the rope for her.

"Keep your eyes *open*," I said. "You have to see where to let go. Open your hands *and* your legs at the same time. Remember, feet first in the water."

The cold water helped Monique's hurt leg, and we spent the afternoon taking turns on the rope swing. Stinky stopped checking the trees across from us and Monique learned how to drop into the water. Later, we dressed and lay on the rock, which was still warm from the sun. Nothing moved except the river next to us, and the clouds overhead. A fish slapped the water and a breeze started up, rustling the treetops. In the distance, I heard a horse neigh, a hawk scree.

"When we grow up, our husbands will be handsome and we'll live near each other," Monique said.

I snorted. "Yours will probably be short and fat and keep you in the kitchen rolling hundreds of tortillas. I never want to get married."

"You have to. God says so," Stinky said. "All people get married and have children."

"Uh-uh," I said. "What about priests?"

"Even some of them are married," Stinky said, and we laughed. "Well, what will *you* do?"

"Raise horses. And you?"

He hesitated. "Nobody'd call me Stinky if I was a priest."

"You'll always be Stinky to me!" I tickled him until he jumped off the rock.

We talked and laughed until we got too hungry. Oratoria would be back from the plaza and she always brought home a tasty treat. I promised Monique I'd take Oratoria's salve to school the next morning. We said goodbye, but not before each of us took one last look at the opposite shore. Nothing moved.

5

A Sister for a Sister

"Witches do not ride broomsticks on moonlit nights.
They prefer stallions."

Oratoria, *1844*
Santa Fé:

I AWAKENED IN the night and heard Pilar's soft tread in the hallway. I
knew she would put her boots on outside. I followed and watched her
lead a stallion from the stable. She'd put a bridle on it, but no saddle.
She led it out the gate and into the desert. Wrapping my rebozo tightly
around me, I rushed to the torreón, from whose height I could see girl
and horse in the moonlight. The men posted there nodded, and left me
to my vigil.

The horse was big, and at fourteen, Pilar was still thin and small.
Delicately, almost as if she were lifted by magic upon his mighty back,
she swung herself up and straddled him. She leaned forward, grasped
his mane, and off they rode. Each exhaled mist into the cold night as
they followed the moon's bright beacon into the desert. Her hair and
the horse's tail streamed behind so they no longer seemed separate.
They were one, and I shared her joy, her freedom.

A freedom destined to be short-lived, since Estevan had offered her
to don Geraldo as a replacement for Alma. Geraldo did not immediately

accept the proposal, but promised to consider it. In the meantime, nothing was said to Pilar. She could remain a child for a moment longer.

The Sandoval histories would keep me occupied until Pilar got home. I was anxious to finish reading Eulalio Sandoval's diary, the hapless founder of the New Mexican branch of the family. He had arrived in Santa Fé in 1695, not as conquistador; no, Eulalio was not a hero. His family owned land in Spain and Mexico and had the usual business interests that always turned into gold for the Sandovals, but he had no particular talent, except one. He was a great lover.

He specialized in other men's wives, which was what landed him in the distant outpost of New Mexico. He wrote: *Always choose a married woman known to have had previous indiscretions. She is less likely to fall in love.* His philosophy didn't play out as he had planned for it was not the angry husbands, but their wives who sent him to Santa Fé. His jilted former lovers had requested his immediate removal. Strings were pulled, favors exchanged, and Eulalio was assigned the task of helping to settle the remote northern frontier of New Spain, a semi-arid valley dominated by pine-covered mountains. He was told it was for the glory of God and the Kingdom of Spain. As a consolation, he was given vast land grants of what was deemed a barren and heathenish land, a sagebrush mesa territory dotted with piñon, oily green mesquite, prickly pear cactus, and Indians unhappy at his arrival. A land virtually without women, at least of the sort he was used to.

His other words of advice to future Sandoval adulterers: *Each of us wishes to feel unique. Discarded mistresses feel the same ire, as if they had attended a ball wearing identical gowns. Be ever vigilant: keep your present and past lovers apart.*

I put Eulalio's diary on my desk, and opened the kitchen door to the morning air. The rising sun pinked the brooding Sangre de Cristo Mountains. Cottonwood streaked the dark pine forest where it grew alongside frigid streams flowing from hidden lakes. Pilar would be sneaking home soon; she was already later than usual. I hugged my rebozo around me, and pondered the vagaries of fate.

Eulalio came here and built an empire. If he'd stayed in Spain, no doubt a jealous husband or a possessive lover would have killed him. I was an ignorant Mexican peasant. If I'd stayed in my village, I might have died giving birth too young, or after too many children. If the Apaches had not kidnapped me and sold me to the Sandovals, I wouldn't have learned to read and write, and I wouldn't be setting down the Sandoval history. And if Alma had not run away with her young Texan, Estevan would not have offered Pilar to Geraldo in her stead.

At the sound of the gate creaking, I stepped quickly back into the kitchen, first making sure it was indeed Pilar returning from her midnight ride. We each had our secrets, and one of mine was to allow Pilar hers.

The day grew hot while Pilar and her friends were swimming. A new wagon train was expected at the plaza, and I walked there to buy an iron pot, a rare and precious metal in New Mexico. I'd promised my sister I'd bring back a sweet treat for her, too.

The sun held dominion in a clear blue sky, but thunder rumbled behind the mountains. The scent of piñon and cedar swept down on a moist wind. In the distance, a dust devil held a tumbleweed at its peak, tossing it in an airy dance. If I'd taken the buggy, I would have missed the performance. The Santa Fé River meandered along the edge of the town. I paused before crossing a bridge, and saw a red-tailed hawk in a dead cottonwood tree scanning the terrain behind me. He took flight and circled prey I could not see. I walked on, turned a corner before entering the plaza, and halted: a caravan of twenty wagons had arrived, and a riotous scene lay before me.

"¡Los carros!" shouted women, men and boys, all anxious to get first pick of the goods as they were unloaded.

Filthy teamsters yelled, "Aiiiie, aiiiie," and waved their sombreros at the horses, cows, mules and oxen, herding them into nearby corrals. The uneven wooden wheels of carretas, pulled by tiny burros, clackety-clacked on the street. Wandering pigs, goats and stray dogs added to the uproar, and the smell, of Santa Fé.

Cottonwood trees planted in front of the Governor's Palace provided shade for butchers to hang mutton, and under the covered porches of the Palace, bakers and fruit vendors displayed their produce. Grapes, plums and berries were in peak season, but we had our own orchards. Indians brought in venison and wild turkey. I'd once seen the carcass of a grizzly for sale, and bought the fatty parts. Bear grease was useful in herbal remedies; it made hair glossy black, and it lubricated everything from a baby's rump to carriage wheels.

Other shoppers waited for the wagons to unload, and the men never failed to nod their heads and smile at passing señoritas walking elbows linked, who often as not returned like-for-like. The men slapped their own thighs with dusty sombreros, or threw their arms around each other's shoulders in jubilation. A fandango was held the night the caravan arrived, and the men and women sized each other up. Enterprising Santa Feans had set up stalls to sell food and drink to the new arrivals, and the spicy smell of tamales and chile rose above the heat and dust.

All was movement, except for two figures at the edge of a narrow passageway. They stood in stark contrast to the pandemonium around me. Consuelo Benavides wept, and the young man standing next to her pounded his fist into the palm of his hand. She laid her head against his chest.

The young man gestured toward the river, turning in my direction. Short and muscular, his bearing older than his sixteen years, I recognized Juan Quintana, Geraldo's only child. After his mother died giving birth to him, Consuelo had nursed Juan, the milk springing from her childless breasts. Thus, began her reputation for magic and charms. Women came to her for amulets to ensnare a loved one, or for the putrid philters to rid themselves of an unwanted child. But she was not alone in dabbling with wish giving. La gente gossiped about the Sandovals, too. Everyone knew the forces of good and evil constantly swirled around us.

Consuelo was not a great beauty, but her dark allure attracted many men, young and old. She had come down from the mountains, and worked for various families, including that of don Geraldo and his last wife. Nothing else was known about her past. Consuelo knew how to work leather, softening the skins to the most pliable texture. Like all the mountain people, her ways were peculiar. She was secretive about her work, once taking a knife to the throat of a young servant girl who spied on her.

Consuelo stayed and cared for little Juan, but when his son reached his sixth year, Geraldo hired a tutor, and then another to replace the first. And another. Juan was disrespectful and lazy. He teased the servants and fought with their children. He pilfered brandy, kicked dogs out of his way and rode his father's horses mercilessly, ruining one mare about to foal. The people shook their heads—dogs and servants were one thing, but mistreating a horse was a sin. As a last resort, Geraldo sent the boy to a seminary in St. Louis before his eleventh birthday, arranging passage on a caravan returning East. Both Consuelo and Geraldo were at the plaza to see him off.

"I hate you," Juan had shouted at his father. Consuelo touched his shoulder and he wept in her arms. Geraldo stormed off amidst the stares of the people.

And Consuelo? After Juan left, she moved to town and plied her leather trade. Geraldo was seen leaving her home more than once in the ensuing years. When Juan moved back to Santa Fé, he visited her often, as well. She was the only mother he knew.

Now, Consuelo and Juan's roles were reversed, and she wept in his arms. He pointed to the river I'd crossed, the river where Pilar and her friends swam. He dropped his hand and stared at me, his legs apart, his fists clenched.

They stepped apart. Consuelo started toward me. Juan held her back, but she jerked her shoulder free. He stared at us for a few moments and then blended into the crowd.

Her black eyes were swollen, the softness of tears replaced with a malicious gleam. La gente called her la turka, because of her dark skin and fiery temper. Losing Geraldo would not be good for her love charm business. "Ah, Oratoria, you catch me crying for a man," she said. "But you wouldn't understand, would you, virgin that you are?"

"I escaped slavery once. Why chance it again? I see you are already consoling yourself with the son."

She laid a hand on my arm, digging in her nails. "Your sister is a child!" Her voice cracked. "You can't want this. Help me, Oratoria. I can do many things . . . with your knowledge we could stop the marriage."

I wrenched her hand away and rubbed my arm where half-moons from her fingernails turned blue. People stared at us. A scene between suspected witches was frightening, but too good a match to pass up. Old blood against new blood.

"The decision is not mine. Or yours."

Consuelo lowered her voice. "You Sandovals think you can take everything. You'll suffer. I'll make you pay for what you've stolen from me!"

I left her standing there, but I could feel her eyes burning into my back as I made my way through the caravan. I couldn't shake her stare, and felt chills along my neck in my walk home, as if a giant lizard on my back flicked out its angry red tongue.

Pilar returned home from the river, her fingers wrinkled and her ears cleaner than usual. I made no comment. She slept deeply that night, and did not hear Geraldo Quintana arrive and cement the deal with her father. They sat around the kitchen table, drinking brandy, each well-satisfied. His ranch bordered Estevan's and would strengthen the land grant on both sides. I moved between kitchen and table, listening and serving the men.

Don Geraldo's wealth was in land and horses, and he had traveled widely in his youth. He'd also buried three wives, their deaths each time due to childbirth. With one son, and no daughters, his home needed a woman's touch. Estevan drank too much and passed out, but don Geraldo remained clear-eyed. He rolled a cigarillo.

"Join me in a smoke, doña Oratoria? Estevan will not be much trouble tonight." When he smiled, dual creases fell from dimples on either cheek, outlining a square, strong jaw. The dimples were youthful and disarming, the kind that can make a plain woman beautiful and a good-looking man dangerous. But his manner was respectful—I sat, and took the cigarillo.

"Pilar is very young. I am very old." At forty-nine, his hair touched with white, Geraldo was still an attractive man. With this marriage, Estevan had planned a life of quiet servitude for his daughter. She would attend her husband in his fleeting years of vigor and care for him in his dotage. I was interested to hear what Geraldo planned for his young wife.

"I saw Pilar and her friends swimming today," he said, "she's a wild one."

I remained calm. "Did they see you?"

"No. We didn't stay long." He pulled smoke into his lungs, and released it up into the air, pursing his lips below a neatly trimmed mustache. Don Geraldo's conduct was subtle; it reminded me that I was a woman.

I put my cigarillo down. "How did you know she was there?"

Geraldo flicked ash into his hand. He smoked, in no hurry to answer. "My son. He knew."

"I saw Juan today at the plaza. He spoke with—"

He held up his hand to stop me, and smiled again, the dimples flashing, his attitude mischievous. "Tell me, doña Oratoria, is it true what la gente say about the old blood of the Sandovals?" He glanced at the diaries on my desk. "Is it true that all Sandoval women are witches? Are *you* a witch, Oratoria?"

I mimicked his gesture by inhaling deeply, but choked on the smoke. Geraldo got up and brought me water. He stood over me as I drank, and I caught his scent—smoke and leather, horse and the Santa Fé night. I gestured for him to take a seat again, noticing his stomach was still flat.

"You forget, I am not a true Sandoval," I said, my voice a feeble squeak from the coughing. I held the cigarillo, but avoided the smoke spiraling from it. "Tell me, don Geraldo, is it true you keep a woman in town?"

"Aha! You try to change the subject, but I'll answer you truthfully. Yes, I take my pleasure in town. Now, you answer me: I've seen you studying the herbals at your little desk. You sense many things—"

"It is you, don Geraldo, who must not change the subject. Casual dalliances with many women are customary, I think, for a man without a wife, but I have heard about one specific woman—Consuelo Benavides. Your son was not alone today. He spoke with Consuelo."

Geraldo studied the glowing tip of his cigarillo. His eyes were light brown, the creases next to them the deepest wrinkles on his face. "She nursed Juan after his mother died. They're still close. He will soon leave for Mexico to work with his mother's family. They own mines."

"Consuelo is not happy you chose another."

"I never considered marrying Consuelo."

"She is not from an old family?"

"No, but I never lied to Consuelo. We never spoke of a future together. I loved each of my wives, and except for the first, I chose them." Like many men, don Geraldo failed to perceive danger in a woman who loved him.

"And your son? He must realize a young wife will produce new heirs. He took you to the swimming hole hoping you would change your mind."

Geraldo smiled sadly, nodding. "He and Pilar met only once, but he made a point of finding out about her. He accosted that son of a pig farmer—"

"Angel?"

"He told Juan they'd be swimming today. Her play was raucous, unusual for a girl. Many would condemn her for that. But what concerned me more were her playmates. The girl, Monique, is a half-breed, and the other is rich in pigs. You must admit they're not the best playmates for a Sandoval daughter." He didn't mention they swam naked.

"Pilar chose them, took them under her wing. She protects them. And as for Monique, they are inseparable, especially now that Alma is gone."

Geraldo leaned forward, resting his elbows on his knees. "And the French priest, Jacquard, is he Monique's father?"

I shrugged. "Many children have been left at the mission door. All the children at the orphanage bear his name. Only Monique was born there."

"To the Mescalero squaw?"

"Yes, two years after she began housekeeping for Father Jacquard. It's true his hair is blond. It's rumored the Apache drugged him with mescal. Priests are hard to come by, so no one complains. But such rumors can do harm. See how your son hoped Monique's taint would change your opinion of Pilar?"

"I've made my decision." He stubbed out his cigarillo on the heel of his boot. "I'll share my thoughts, doña Oratoria," he said. "No harm will come to Pilar while she is with me. I am the best man, probably the only man, for someone like her."

"As you say, she is young and willful."

"I'm willing to wait, to risk waiting at my age, for two more years to pass so we may marry. Can you help me gain her love?"

"Pilar cares for little but her horses and Monique," I said.

He smiled, flashing clean, square teeth. "She'll have both, to her heart's content and forevermore." Geraldo ran his hand through his dark, wavy hair, turning white at the temples, the mature accent above the dimples below. Irresistible.

"You ask about witches. You listen to rumors," I said. "Take heed: witches do not ride broomsticks on moonlit nights. They prefer stallions."

6

The Back Road to Texas

"A Mex is a Mex, if you ask me."

Alma, *1844*
Pollard's Corners, Texas:

BILL AND I married at a small mission church. But for the wooden cross above the door, we would have passed it by as just another adobe hovel on the road. Inside, a stooped, old man swept the dirt floor. He stopped and peered up at us, one eye gone and the other bleary beneath grizzled eyebrows.

"Welcome, children," he said. "It's a fine day for a marriage."

Bill and I knelt in the dirt and became man and wife. A strange silence overtook me. I could see the padre's lips move, but I couldn't hear his words. I made the sign of the cross and Bill gave me a timid kiss. He shook the padre's hand and gave him a coin. We didn't have much to say to each other the rest of the day, but that night we spoke our love at last, and consummated the words with our touch.

I didn't think of Pilar or Oratoria; I was much more concerned about what Papá might do if he caught us. We kept to the seldom-traveled trails, most not much wider than the sturdy wagon we'd taken from the ranch, but we met no one. I drove the wagon, while Bill either rode alongside, or sat next to me, his horse tied to the back.

Bill grew quieter as we headed into Texas, but I figured he was just on guard. And maybe he was, for Indians roamed the area, and skirmishes with Mexicans had been increasing ever since the Battle of the Alamo. They had captured San Antonio twice, the last time two years earlier. Then, the Texans took Laredo at the border. And the year before, in 1843, another expedition planned to capture Mexican wagons crossing territory claimed by Texas on the Santa Fé Trail, but failed when American troops arrived.

The air became humid and hot, the surrounding countryside more lush, as we traveled near the center of Texas. Bill's troubled mood continued throughout each day. But at night he was my gentle Bill, fired by an urgent passion that matched my own.

One night I asked him if he was happy to be returning home. He took his time answering. "Things been different, I could've lived in New Mexico forever. Still wonder if we shouldn't of holed up further south, till your Pa got used to the idea." His skin was ruddy in the firelight, making his eyes appear phosphorescent, like a cat's. "But I've seen your Pa with a shotgun before. He's a hothead."

"I don't think he'll ever get used to losing don Geraldo's land."

He nodded in that slow manner of his. "Your pa and my ma would make a fine team. Land and money are everything to them." The lines and shadows on his face deepened. "She's . . . it's going to be different from what you're used to."

"That's what I've been hoping for," I said, and moved next to him to snuggle into his arms. Their warm comfort soothed the thudding in my stomach, the signal I should delve deeper, ask more questions. I rushed to console my love, his worry about the future more important than this warning. "Your mother will be happy to have you home."

"I'm hoping for the best, but Ma likes things her own way. I'll work hard to get us our own place. Trust me, Alma."

After almost two months of steady traveling, we entered a country lane with a dense canopy of oak above our heads, and came upon a Y in the road. At the intersection sat a black man examining his foot. He wore tattered overalls without a shirt. He was powerfully built and so black and shiny he looked polished.

Bill signaled me to stop. He rode up alongside the man, who remained bent over his foot. Bill's hat shadowed his eyes, but I could see the muscles of his jaw tighten. "You got a pass, boy?"

The black man nodded fast, but kept his head bowed. "Yassuh." He patted a pocket in his overalls. "My feets is troubling me some. Skin's bleeding, suh."

I started to get down from the wagon. "I've got ointment that might help. It's in the back."

"Stay right there, Miz Pollard!" Bill said, his voice a deep, mean rumble.

I sat with a thump, as if I'd been shoved. Not only had I never been called by my married name before, but he'd never spoken to me in such a manner. Turning back to the black man, he demanded to see the pass. The injured man stood, balancing on one foot, and retrieved the item from a pocket, handing it to Bill. He bowed his head, never once looking directly at either of us.

"Says here you belong to J.P. Trigg over to Bastrous County. What you doing way out here, boy?"

"Mr. Trigg own land all along here, suh. He sending me to fetch Josiah. She my wife. She was loant to his daughter crosst the river to help wit a birthing." With the slightest edge of pride, he said, "She a house nigger."

"Miz Pollard, fetch me some of your medicine and I'll hand it off to the boy." The growl was gone from his voice, replaced by a cold mastery.

I dabbed salve on a bit of white cloth, and came abreast of Bill's horse. Bending, I reached for the black man's leg. "Lift your foot, please."

He didn't move, but peeked up at Bill, who had flushed crimson. It wasn't the shy blush I'd grown to love, but an angry blood red. I straightened up. "Wrap this around your foot to keep the dirt off it," I said, holding the bundle out.

"Take it!" Bill said. "And take this, too!" He threw down the paper, and wiped his hand on his shirt.

"Thank you, ma'am," the black man said, bending to pick up the pass. His palms were a pale rosy-pink. When I didn't move, he added, "I best

40

be on my way." He limped off into the shelter of the thick brush, disappearing from view. Bill turned his horse away, rode a few paces off, and stopped, his back to me.

"Bill?"

"Get in the wagon," he said, his voice now flat. "If we push, we can make it by nightfall."

Later, we stopped alongside a creek to let the horses rest. We didn't speak, and Bill rolled up in a blanket to take a nap. I sat by the creek with my journal. Two hours later, when I heard him stir, I hadn't written a single word but the date.

"Let's get going," Bill said, in the voice I recognized. He got in the wagon, and I followed him, eager for the comfort of his lanky body sitting next to mine.

We started up, but hadn't gone far when I laid my hand on his arm. "We've had our first argument, and I'm not sure what it was about." He didn't answer immediately. When he did, his words rushed out in a torrent of feeling.

"You're going to want me to explain things to you. I can't. The people here . . . they don't ask why. It suits them just fine. You've never been around niggers. But you got to learn the right way. You got to do as I say!"

He stared straight ahead, his profile sharply etched with self-righteous fury. He reminded me of a marble statue, a heartless replica of himself. Tears blurred my vision of him. "We'll be different to each other?"

Bill pulled up on the reins, and took me in his arms. "Behind closed doors we can be the same as always. I promise you once we get our own place, we'll be Alma and Bill again. But, you're going to have to accept certain things around here, to get along. So we can all get along."

"I will! I love you so much." We held each other for a long moment, letting go only when I pulled a blanket from under the seat.

Bill smiled at my intent, a sparkle in his turquoise eyes. "I guess it won't matter much if we pull in later, since they're not expecting us anyway."

We spread the blanket on the grass next to the road. I lay down out in the open, fully clothed, and lifted my hips, sliding my skirt up, watching him.

41

"Alma," he said, his voice raw. "Alma," he repeated, his voice a grateful whisper in my ear as he entered me. "Alma," he said again and again, each redemptive stroke a prayer that nothing would change.

We arrived at the Pollard homestead at close to one in the morning. A two-story white clapboard house with a pitched roof shone eerily blue under the moonlight. A pack of dogs with identical markings greeted us. An old man in an undershirt and long drawers stood on the porch holding a shotgun. He fumbled a pair of wire-rimmed spectacles with one hand, the gun secure in the crook of his elbow, but pointed in our direction.

"What's the bad news?" he asked.

Bill laughed and jumped off the wagon. "I swear you was wearing the same underwear when I left outta here. I suspected as much and brung you a new pair, Pop."

"My boy, my boy!" He leaned the shotgun against the porch rail and threw himself against his son. Bill caught him up and whirled him around. They didn't look a bit alike. His father was short and wiry, while Bill was over six feet.

"Who's this?" He peered into the darkness at me.

Bill came over and helped me down. "This here's my wife, Alma."

Poppa Pollard inspected me from head to foot. For the trip I'd worn the comfortable full skirts and loose blouse of New Mexican women. My hair hung in braids, again as a concession to travel. I pulled my rebozo up around my shoulders. I'd brought along a small valise of fashionable dresses, and silently cursed myself for not changing.

"Well, son, you've done it now. Gone off and married a Mex," he said, disappointed. "Does she speak English?"

Bill squeezed my hand. "She's pure Spaniard, and speaks English better'n you, Pop, and French, too." He put his arm around me.

Poppa Pollard's expression changed from crestfallen to tight-lipped acceptance. "Well, hell, ain't no Frenchies here. A Mex is a Mex, if you ask me. Come on in. Momma Pollard ain't to home. She's off visiting my sister in town, but she'll be back at first light."

We stayed in Bill's old room. He and his father sat talking in the kitchen all night, and I fell asleep to the murmur of their voices and the tang of tobacco smoke wafting up the stairs. I slept long in the deep feather bed, and awakened with a gasp.

A woman stood at the end of the wrought-iron bed, staring at me. She gripped one of the posts so tightly her knuckles blanched. I squeezed my eyes shut. Opened them again. She was now over at the window, drawing the curtains aside. A wash of light flooded the room, and I squinted at Bill's mother. In a hard, sculpted way, she was breathtaking. Her eyes and hair were dark, the slightest bit of white at the temples, but her skin was still fair and smooth, and roses dashed the sharp ridges of her cheekbones.

"Mrs. Pollard?"

"It's past nine in the morning, my dear. Do you always sleep this late?" She walked out without waiting for an answer and spoke to someone in the hall. She came back in, closed the door and sat at a table by the window. A knock at the door. "Come in," she said.

A light-skinned Negro girl carried a tray of coffee and biscuits, and set it on the table. She left, her head bowed like the black man on the trail. Mrs. Pollard poured herself a cup, and stared at me above the rim as she drank. "People are going to say we resemble each other, dear." She didn't sound pleased, but smiled, nonetheless. "You're quite light for a Mexican, aren't you?"

I scooted out of bed, my nightdress sliding up. She stared at my thighs. I hurriedly put on a robe. "I'm usually up by five, but we got in so late. I guess I was tired."

"You're not with child, are you?" she asked, no pleasure evident in her expression. She poured me a cup of coffee.

"No," I said, surprised at the question. "At least I don't think so." I blushed and busied myself stirring cream into my coffee.

"Bill tells me your family is quite well off. That's good news, at least. We'll need to contact your father. Let him know you arrived safely. I'm sure he's worried sick about you." She got up and went over to a chair, picking up with two fingers the clothing I'd worn the day before. "Peasant clothes," she said. "Poppa mentioned you were wearing these, but I didn't believe him. They're not suitable for Pollard's Corner, my dear. Is your father sending another wagon with your things?"

I felt my face grow hot again, but rushed to explain. "I'm not sure how happy my father will be to hear from me. I married without his permission. I was betrothed to another—an older man, a much older man."

An angry frown distorted her beauty. "My son neglected to tell me that part. An older man, you say? A rich, older man, no doubt? You should have obeyed your father's wishes. I did!" She dropped my clothes and clenched her fists at her sides. "Bill should have obeyed me. He could have stayed here and married the richest girl in this part of Texas! But no, he had to run off and marry the first . . ." She caught herself, touching two fingers to her lips. "Dear me, I am a fool. Don't pay any attention to me. It's such a shock, and you and Bill are such naughty children."

She sat at the table again, and poured more coffee, which she didn't drink. "Let's see what you brought in that little valise of yours, so I'll know what we need to order by way of clothing for you."

I pulled out three outfits: one a rust-colored calico day dress, which gave me some color; a royal-blue Sunday satin with a short jacket; the other, a red silk evening dress with matching petticoat, all badly wrinkled.

"Lovely, my dear. Let's see the calico on you, then I'll have Pinkie iron it while you have your bath. You do want a bath, don't you?" Her sugary concern told me she wasn't sure my kind bathed.

I nodded, my thoughts turned inward: *she doesn't want me here, she thinks Bill married beneath himself.*

"Yes, ma'am," I said, but didn't move. The last thing I wanted was to undress in front of this woman who despised me.

"Don't be shy. I'm sure you have nothing to hide."

Embarrassed, I stared at a wall and dropped my nightclothes. Snatching up the dress, I stepped into it as quickly as possible. I could feel her studying my body.

"Is this suitable?"

She lifted the coffee cup to her mouth, but not before I saw the curl of her lips. "It'll have to do for now, dear."

7

Half-Breeds and Pedigrees

"I don't know much about love between men and women . . . I want to learn from you."

P*ilar*, 1844
Santa Fé:

THE DAY AFTER she hurt herself on the rope swing, Monique wasn't at school. I wanted to stop at the rectory to check on her, but Papá had told me to come straight home.

"Let's go check on her," I said to Oratoria, who always came to fetch me. "We can give her the medicine you made."

"Your father is waiting for you."

"He'll never notice if we're late. Monique never misses school, maybe her bruise got worse." I stopped walking.

Oratoria stared at me as if she were listening to me speak when I hadn't said a word. "Did anything else happen at the river yesterday?"

I wondered about how much to say to her. Oratoria could turn a common sound into a ghost story.

"Monique and Stinky felt maybe someone was watching us."

"Did *you* hear or see anything?"

"Maybe bushes rustling, which could be anything. Who would be interested in us?"

She took my hand and we walked. "Once we get home, I'll go to the rectory and check on Monique. Give me the salve."

As we got closer to the compound, I heard the high-pitched neighing of horses coming from the paddock down the hill. At the top of the rise I got a good view of the corral next to the stable. My father and a group of men examined the horses inside: two immense, black horses did a mating dance. I squeezed Oratoria's hand.

"Go to them," she said.

"But, Monique—"

She stopped me with a fierce hug. "I'm going there now. You are not to worry. Your father . . . ." Oratoria clung to me a moment longer, shocking me into silence, and then she turned me by the shoulders toward the paddock. I dropped my books in the dirt and ran down the hill. Without stopping, I leapt onto the corral fence and stood on the lowest rung. The stallion pawed the earth and snorted when the mare trotted past him.

"These horses are royal, Pilar," said a soothing voice at my shoulder, "descended from the stable kept by the King and Queen of Spain. Their pure equine ancestors claim mightier ancestry from the royal courts of Arabia." I looked up into the smiling brown eyes of don Geraldo.

"Are we buying them from you?"

"They are priceless, a breed I brought here many years ago. The female has not yet come into her season, but soon, very soon. If you can ride her, if I see you can handle her, I will make you a present of her foal. How does that sound?"

"Oh, yes, *yes!* Can I ride her *now*, please?"

Don Geraldo nodded to his groom, who led the mare out of the corral. He lifted a heavy sidesaddle onto her back. I let out an exasperated breath, disappointed. Don Geraldo bent forward and whispered, "You were happy and now you're not. What is it?"

I glanced at my father, who showed his teeth in a fake smile. He expected me to climb some steps and seat myself on the uncomfortable sidesaddle. He'd let me take a few delicate turns around the yard, and return to the steps, where I'd be helped off the horse. He'd expect me to offer the men coffee and leave. Don Geraldo was still eye-level with

46

me. He had honest eyes, like Alma's. I signaled him to follow me, and moved a few steps away.

"You see, don Geraldo . . . I . . . I want to use a real saddle." I peeked around Geraldo at Papá again.

Don Geraldo glanced over his shoulder at my father, who gave an encouraging nod in our direction. "I see," he said. "You've done this before?"

"Many times, even bareback on my father's stallion but he—" I clapped my hand over my mouth.

"Doesn't know, nor would he approve. Pilar, if you have this skill, I think you should be allowed to use it. I'll speak to your father." Papá scowled at me after listening to don Geraldo, but gave a curt nod.

The mare was saddled, and don Geraldo held out his hand. "From this day forward, señorita Sandoval, you will ride a horse in whatever manner pleases you."

"Oh, thank you!"

I didn't wait for the steps to be put in place, but swung my right leg up and over, full skirts bunched around me. My father turned away, as did the other men. All except for don Geraldo, who gazed at me with a happy crinkle-eyed expression that didn't involve the lower half of his face. A groom brought another horse for him, and we headed into the countryside. Alone.

He said, "Her name is Scheherazade, from the Arabian Nights. Have you read them? No? We'll read them together. I think she likes you almost as much as I do."

Don Geraldo was easy to talk to. I don't know why I'd never noticed before. He wanted to hear all about me, and our horses, and the kinds of things I like to do, which brought me back to horses. He told me about my betrothal to him.

"I asked your father to let me tell you," he said. I slumped in my saddle. He was nice, but I hadn't changed my mind about marriage.

"I will never force you to marry. For the next two years, until you are sixteen, you can change your mind at any time. If you decide against the marriage, I will handle your father. I'll say the decision was mine, break the contract, and pay the penalty."

"Papá would be happy then," I said. "He could keep the money *and* marry me off to someone else, unless . . . unless I ran off like Alma." Papá was so eager for Quintana land he'd sent me off without a chaperone. If don Geraldo wasn't such a gentleman, no telling what could have happened.

"You've heard nothing from her?" he asked, his voice softening. I shook my head. "You must miss her very much."

"Yes, more every day, but Oratoria says she's safe. She says Alma will come back."

He nodded. "Alma is following her heart, and I think you should, too. You might enjoy being married to me. It might be fun. But first you must learn to call me Geraldo."

Marriage still didn't sound great to me, but being on top of a magnificent Arabian horse felt good. Two years of riding her would be fine. "Tell me more about the Arabian Nights," I said.

At sunset, we arrived back at the hacienda to a major commotion. Father Jacquard was with Papá and Oratoria.

Oratoria took my hand. "Monique is missing. No one has seen her since she left for school this morning."

The men silently exchanged glances. I never cried, and didn't want to start now, but the tears came anyway.

Geraldo spoke first. "Pilar, is there a place Monique might go if she were upset?"

"Monique would come here! We don't have any secret places . . . except where we swim." My heart thudded its way down to my stomach. "But she might be afraid to go there alone because we heard noises yesterday. Whispering."

"Ah," Oratoria said. She looked at Geraldo, but said nothing.

"Maybe a bad man was there," I said. My throat tightened. I'd heard women whisper about rape. They spoke of the pain, and of the shame. I begged the men to find her. "Maybe he got Monique. It could have been me." Oratoria took me in her arms.

"I know where to go," Geraldo said. "We'll need lanterns. Estevan, you and Father Jacquard follow the crossroads path to the teacher's home. Pilar, you stay here in case Monique shows up."

"No! I want to go with you." My father started to speak, but Geraldo raised his hand. Our horses were still tethered outside and the two of us set out to search for Monique.

We found her sitting on the big rock we used as our launching point. She held the rope tightly and didn't look at us. Geraldo stood behind me, holding a lantern high so we could see her better. Dressed for school, her white blouse was torn and dirty. Her legs were tucked up under her full skirt; it was wet and clinging to her.

"Monique?" She flinched when I touched her, only licked her swollen lips. A thin stream of blood flowed from under her skirt and down the rock into the river. My tears began again, choking me, scalding my cheeks.

"Who hurt you?" I asked. She let me take her hands. On her bare shoulder, I could see a human bite mark.

"He saw us swimming," Monique said.

"Oh, Monique, it's all my fault! I should have believed you and Stinky."

She patted my hand, the barest touch. "I tried to wash," she said. I pulled her gently to her feet, but her legs wobbled.

Geraldo dropped the lantern and caught her. "Get the blanket from my horse. There's a flask in the saddlebag," he said.

The brandy made her gag. "I hate that smell. He made me drink."

"Who, Monique? Do you know him?" Geraldo asked.

"No," she whispered, "but he knew me. He knew all about me."

"Did he say anything else?"

"He said all Indians loved liquor." She stared dreamily at Geraldo. "Especially half-breed bastards like me."

Monique slept in his arms during the ride home, as he carried her to my room, and even as Oratoria and I undressed and bathed her. Another bite mark scarred her thigh, the bottom arch revealing a gap in a perfect row of teeth. Her cleft was swollen and red, stitches were needed lower down. Monique continued to sleep and the blood continued to flow.

Her mother arrived and sat by her bedside. She whispered a soft guttural Apache and French in what I knew was a long, unbroken confession of love.

The doctor left Monique's bedside and joined Papá, Geraldo and Father Jacquard at the table for coffee. Although unmarried, at thirty-two Oratoria could have joined the men, but she stayed close to me. She knew I was afraid for Monique.

The men laughed and smoked and drank more coffee. I scrutinized their expressions and waited for one of them to ask the doctor about Monique. He was his usual jovial self. My sister and I stood aside, holding hands. We listened to every word and noted each gesture. These men were our protectors. They would catch and punish the bad man who hurt Monique.

The doctor nodded at Oratoria. "Sure is good coffee, ma'am. Need it right about now. Been up since before sunrise tending to new folks in town—outbreak of dysentery. New religious folks, padre, bit of competition for you." He winked at Father Jacquard.

"Doesn't anyone care about Monique?" I blurted out.

"Pilar! Go to your room," my father shouted.

"I won't! Who did this horrible thing?"

Papá's scowl slid from bored to mean. I'd embarrassed him. He started to get up, but Geraldo laid a hand on his shoulder. I was grateful he was here.

"The most savage rape I've seen," the doctor said, not to be upstaged. "Fellow wasn't satisfied with deflowering the girl, he wanted to hurt her."

Papá spoke up again. "This is not appropriate–"

"I've already seen the blood. I know what happened," I said. "Who did this to Monique?"

"We'll find him," Geraldo said.

Papá shrugged.

"Odd thing was the bite marks," the doctor said.

"Could be anyone," Papá said.

"Naw," the doctor said. "Know anyone hereabouts with a big gap in their bottom teeth? Fellow left a perfect imprint on that gal's flesh."

Geraldo slammed his cup down. The color had drained from his face, as if he were going to be sick.

The doctor raised his eyebrows. "I won't report it to the sheriff, unless you want me to."

Geraldo said nothing, the slightest tilt of his chin the only sign he'd heard.

The priest moaned. "It's my fault. My sins led to this." He raised his eyes to the men as if seeking absolution. "It will happen again. Men will take advantage of a beautiful half-breed female. She will always be at risk." He wiped his forehead with the back of his hand. "They will say she has nothing more to lose." He tried not to sob, his cheeks tightening into a grimace. He tapped his heart three times with his fist. "Pardonne moi, pardonne moi, pardonne moi. My little Monique, forgive me."

Geraldo stood; anger had replaced his concern. I looked from him to my father, who I could count on for nothing. The one good thing he'd done was promise me to this man.

"Strengthen up, Jacquard," Geraldo said, "for the sake of the young girl in there who must hold her head high." He stared into each man's eyes. "Say nothing of what has passed this day and night or you will answer to me. Father, please come with me. A hard task is ahead of me."

I fell asleep that night on a pallet next to Monique, and didn't hear Geraldo's return or his conversation with Oratoria. When I woke up the next morning, Monique still slept soundly. In the kitchen, Oratoria sat at the table drinking a calming tea. Her eyes were red-rimmed and puffy.

"Have you been crying?" I asked. I'd never seen my sister weep, and my own tears welled up at the thought of hers.

"Sit down, Pilar. Geraldo asked me to speak to you."

I remained standing. "He found him?" I knew I could count on Geraldo.

Oratoria gestured to the chair opposite hers. She poured me a cup of tea, and refreshed her own. "He and Father Jacquard rode directly to Geraldo's hacienda when they left here last night."

I grabbed a tortilla and sat. "He probably needed something from his home, maybe a gun."

Oratoria spoke so softly, it was almost a whisper. "He went home to confront his illusions."

The house was dark. Geraldo lit a candle, and grabbed a riding crop from a tabletop. Father Jacquard followed him to a room where the only sound was of loud snoring.

Juan lay spread-eagled on his back. His shirt was open, and he was naked from the waist down. An empty bottle of brandy lay on the floor next to him.

Geraldo held the candle close to his son's scratched and bloodied face. He moved the candle slowly along the length of his sleeping body. More scratches were etched into his chest; dried blood covered his private parts. Geraldo handed the candle to the priest. He pulled down Juan's bottom lip to reveal the gap between his teeth.

He struck Juan across the cheek with the riding crop. He jerked awake. His father beat him across the genitals.

"You haven't changed a bit!" he screamed at his son.

Juan wrapped his arms around his head, and tucked his legs up. "She was nothing!"

Geraldo swung the lash across his son's shoulders. "She's a child!"

"And you want to marry a child! A tramp who swims naked with half-breed bastards." Juan's face was shiny with sweat and tears. "How can you expect me to accept a harlot into my home?"

"It's not up to you to decide what is acceptable in *my* house," Geraldo said. "Get out." He pointed the riding crop at the door. Juan scrambled on all fours, grabbing clothes and running out of the hacienda. They heard his horse galloping away.

"I've raised a monster," Geraldo said, sobbing, "help me, Father." Padre Jacquard laid his arm around Geraldo, and the two men sat on the bed and wept for their children.

I sat in stunned silence across from Oratoria. "Juan is told to get out of his home. That's it? That will be his punishment?"

"It's not enough, I know, but it's more punishment than many men receive."

I beat my fist on the table until my knuckles bled, and cried again, but this time my tears were righteous. Oratoria came around and sat next to me. She stroked my hair. "Put your love toward Monique, who still has much healing to do. Juan is don Geraldo's only child. Think about what this knowledge is doing to him."

"If Juan didn't want his father to marry me, why didn't he attack me?"

"He's a coward, Pilar. He picked the most vulnerable person to vent his anger. We still have Monique. Geraldo has only you."

We learned later that Juan had gone to Consuelo's home. Neither was seen on the streets for over a week, and her windows and doors were kept shut though the weather was warm. La gente said smoke billowed out of the chimney carrying noxious odors, and they swore a low unbroken sound, almost a moan, came from the house, morning, noon and night. Then, Juan rode out of Santa Fé. The smoke stopped. The moaning ceased. The doors and windows stayed closed.

"I'd understand if you didn't want to have anything to do with me, Pilar," Geraldo said.

"I don't blame you, Geraldo. You stood by me and Monique when we needed you." For the first time I saw the age in him, not so much in the lines on his skin, but in the haggard way his flesh hung from his cheekbones. "Where did he go?"

"Juan went to his mother's people, in Mexico. A marriage has been arranged. He's never to return."

"Perhaps he'll change."

Geraldo kissed the inside of my wrist. "Perhaps," he said. "Perhaps."

A month passed and Monique's body healed, but she wasn't the same. She refused to come back to school. She didn't want to leave my bedroom, and spent hours praying before a statue of the Virgin Mary the padre had sent over.

She decided to become a nun. Father Jacquard arranged for her to join a convent in New Orleans run by French nuns. They housed and taught a number of Indian and colored children, and did many good works. Then Stinky followed through on his threat to become a priest and moved to Taos to study with Padre Martinez. It seemed as far away as New Orleans.

"Everyone is leaving," I said to Monique.

"What a twist," she said. "A half-breed nun and a pig-farmer priest, and you the one who never wanted to marry will be the old married woman with a dozen brats." She laughed, and I was pleased, but my insides were in a knot that twisted tighter when I thought of Monique leaving.

Finally, I got her to venture out of my room for a short walk around the compound.

"Monique, if you want to be a nun, stay here and do it."

She peeked without enthusiasm into the garden at the blazing white daisies. "I need to be away from here so . . . so I can think."

No matter what I said or did, Monique insisted she had to leave Santa Fé. It hurt that she didn't want to be with me. She wasn't just quiet; she was silent, as if her own voice scared her. She often didn't answer when I spoke to her. Monique had gone so far inside herself she couldn't hear or see what was around her.

I couldn't stay indoors all the time so Geraldo and I rode every day. His mare grazed on our paddock, my foal growing inside her. We talked about the buying, selling and breeding of horses, and of their many other noble qualities. We read The Arabian Nights. And we spoke endlessly of Monique. Geraldo became my staunch supporter in my plans to convince her to stay. He tried to persuade Father Jacquard to influence his daughter. "I should have sent her away long ago," was Jacquard's morose reply. Geraldo rocked me in his arms when I wept.

"Monique doesn't seem eager to return to her own home," Geraldo said one day while we tended our horses. It had become a shared event for us after each ride. I brushed them, my shoulder and cheek pressed against their great heaving flesh felt warmed and comforted. "She seems content to remain here, in your father's home." He paused to stretch. "Perhaps she would stay if she didn't have to return to her home, for she must know she can't stay in your father's house indefinitely."

"Where can she go?" I asked. He stroked the horse's rump, and stared at me. "Maybe she could live with you?" I said. "Then I could visit all I wanted!"

Geraldo laughed and leaned against the horse. "Ah, if it were only that easy. La gente would never approve, and your father would kill me. But there is one way it could work."

I searched for clues in his eyes and posture, as if this were a game of charades. "Well, how? Tell me!"

"If you would marry me, Monique could live with us forever, but—"

My eyebrows shot up. This seemed the perfect solution. Why hadn't I thought of it before? I opened my mouth to speak, but he raised his hand to stop me. "But there must be more, Pilar. There must be love."

A shiver crept from the back of my neck all the way to the top of my head, prickling my hair. It shot its way down again and radiated outward to my arms and legs, and I became aware of my body in a new way. Magic potions are said to work the same way. I'd heard Oratoria and Alma discuss them many times. The diaries said they amplify sound, color or smell as lovers discover each other. My breath became shallow, my heart pulsed in my ears, and all I could see was Geraldo. He was passionate and optimistic about horses and life, the same as me.

"I don't know much about love between men and women, Geraldo, but we're friends." I looked him in the eye. "I want to learn from you."

It was the same as the first time I took flight on the rope swing. I'd never done it before, but I knew I'd be good at it.

I couldn't wait to tell Monique.

"It's no good, Pilar. You're only fifteen and I . . . I don't belong. I never have. I don't want you to do this for me."

"I like him. We would get married sooner, instead of two years from now, and he said we wouldn't have to do anything."

"You mean you wouldn't have to let him put it inside you?"

"Well, yes. We wouldn't mate." I cleared my throat. "He doesn't even want me to have babies unless I really want to. Geraldo is a very nice man. He likes me the way I am."

Monique shivered like she'd sucked on a lemon. She recited in a dead tone, "Babies are good. Men and women mate and have babies. Lovers seem happy when they touch." She shivered. "Enjoy your don Geraldo, but without me."

"You said we'd never be apart, Monique. Don't give up so easily on your dreams. Don't you remember them?"

"They're another girl's dreams. Someone I barely recognize."

"They're not just dreams. We could make them real. Please don't go, Monique."

"I'm not safe here, and you're not safe with me here. It's the best thing." I didn't feel my tears until Monique patted my cheeks with a handkerchief. She began to cry, too. We hugged each other. "Please leave me alone about this. Please, please, please."

There was so much pain and sorrow in her voice, and I saw her fear, too. I finally understood I couldn't fix this for her. Monique would have to learn how to deal with her loss on her own. Love and hope for my friend loosened the knot inside me.

I gave in. I let her go.

8

Passing Good

*"You as white as B.B., Miz Alma. Make
the most of it, girl. Passin' is good."*

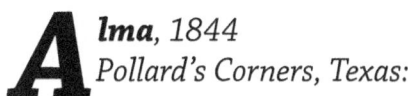**lma**, *1844*
Pollard's Corners, Texas:

MY MOTHER-IN-LAW STOOD next to me, her arm hooked through mine,
a dainty, lace-trimmed handkerchief in her other hand, waving goodbye to her departing husband and son.

We'd been in Pollard's Corner two weeks, and Bill and his poppa
spent most of each day away from the house. Since we'd arrived, Bill
had reached for me across the bed once–a sluggish coupling thick with
controlled silence, dense with complicity. He seemed uncomfortable
in his own home.

Now he was off to inspect cattle up for auction, and would be gone
for almost a month. I'd begged him not to leave me behind.

"It'll be a chance for you and Momma to settle in, get to know each
other." Bill took me in his arms, and kissed my forehead. "I know she
can be tough, but she'll come 'round. I'm doing this for us, sweetheart.
I'm working as hard as I can so we can have our own place."

Bertha and I stood together anchoring the homestead as our men
rode off. We stood in that pose until they were past looking back at us.

Then, she wrenched her arm from mine and stomped off into the house without a word. I felt as if I'd been struck, but I told myself I should have expected it, that over time it wouldn't matter, and soon Bill and I would have our own home.

I held that vision in my head and went over to the garden to pull weeds, busying myself outdoors to avoid the turmoil reigning inside the Pollard home whenever the men were gone. Pinkie, the servant girl I'd seen the first day, hurried from task to task, her head bowed and shoulders hunched, yet she never failed to provoke Bertha's ire. Bill might call the slaves negras, but Bertha called them niggers, and her lip curled when she said it.

The sun was overhead, and I was hot and thirsty, but I didn't want to go inside. My skin pinked; I'd forgotten to wear a hat and gloves. No breeze stirred the air. The cackle of chickens wandering in the yard and the distant yapping of a hound were a faint backdrop to my labor.

The sound of breaking glass shattered the peace. My head snapped up, and alert, like a doe sensing danger, I listened. A sharp smack, skin-against-skin, charged the air. I stood, uncertain whether I should run into the house, or farther away from it. Another smack. Another, and another.

"That's enough, Miz Pollard," an authoritative voice said. Chiding, the same voice continued, "You'll wear yo'sef out, B.B., and you still got the church lady meeting in town. I'll take care o' this clumsy chile. Pinkie, apologize to Miz Pollard fa breaking her jar. These the jars she use fa the preserves!" I rushed indoors to meet the owner of the voice, the voice that could stay Bertha's hand.

"I's sorry, Miz Pollard," Pinkie said. Everything stopped for a moment as we all took one another in. I was sweating, out-of-breath, and my hair had come undone. Bertha had her fists on her hips, glaring at Pinkie, whose nose bled down the front of her dress. Between the two of them stood a short Negro woman. Crosshatched lines etched into her skin didn't match the vigor of her movements. She was rotund, but in a solid, efficient way, and she looked right at me, something Pinkie never did.

Bertha leaned against the drainboard and giggled. "Surrounded by 'em. Niggers and fools. Fools and Mexicans. What next?" She waved a limp wrist, sweeping us all in together and bent forward, laughing harder.

"Yes, ma'am, it sho do seem ta be yo lot in life," the woman said. "The good Lord picked you outta the crowd fo a reason. Glory be! He work in mystery's way, don't he?" She placed her hands on Bertha's shoulders, turning her around. I knew enough by now to be shocked by her touching my regal mother-in-law, but Bertha's compliance was equally unnerving.

"You best get a move on, B.B. You wearing that new hat o' yours? I sho do like that hat." Bertha leaned into the old woman, still chuckling, and they walked out of the kitchen. I stared at the door as if it might explain the incredible scene I'd witnessed. Pinkie's sniffling brought me out of my reverie. She picked up the shards of broken glass, and blood dripped from her nose onto the floor. "Pinkie, leave it for now. Sit over here, and lean your head back."

I pulled out a chair for her, got a rag to wipe her face, and lifted her legs onto another chair. She started to object, but her nose bled more. "Lean back, Pinkie. Do as I say, please."

I swept the glass, and was on the floor wiping up the blood, when the Negro lady returned. She looked first at me bent over my task, then at Pinkie sprawled on the chair. "What going on here?"

"L.B.?" Bertha called from the top of the stairs, "Is that girl cleaning up her mess?"

"Yes, ma'am, and mopping up the floor good, too!" she yelled over her shoulder, then hissed at me, "Git up offa there, girl! Don't you know nothing? Sit down at the table. Pinkie, get her coffee." And she was gone again.

"How does you take yo coffee, ma'am?" Pinkie asked as I sat.

"I prefer tea. I keep the herbs over here, out of the way. I'll put water on." I started to rise, but Pinkie held up her hand to stop me. A light dash of freckles across her broad nose blended in almost completely with her medium-coffee skin.

"Please, ma'am, lemme do it," she said. "I's already in big trouble." The sound of the buggy at the front of the house carried back to us. Bertha's light tread on the stairs, her last-minute adjustments of her headgear in front of the hall mirror, and the rustle of her taffeta dress were distinct. The front door closed, and the horses clip-clopped off. Pinkie and I exhaled, unaware we'd both been holding our breath. We smiled at each other.

"I's most grateful fo yo help, Miz Alma," she said, setting the tea in front of me.

"Anyone would do the same." She raised her eyebrows. "Is the other lady your mother?"

"Lady?" Her doubtful expression was replaced by a smile. "Oh, you mean L.B. No, she not my mama, unless helping deliver you into the world counts. In that case, L.B. be the mama to half the county, white folks included. She delivered Miz Pollard, I hear tell."

The door opened behind me. L.B. stood with her hands on her hips. "What you hear tell, ain't what you oughta tell, Miss Pinkie. Get yo behind outta here. Go shake out the beds, and don't get no blood on nothing. You hear?"

"Yes, ma'am." Pinkie scurried out of the room.

"More tea, ma'am?" L.B. asked me.

I nodded and she poured more hot water into the teapot. "What does L.B. stand for?"

She inspected an iron pot Pinkie had washed earlier. "Everyone round here know L.B. mean Little Bertha, you might as well know it, too. You is Alma—whole town know B.B. got you hid away out here. How old might you be, Miz Alma?"

"Almost eighteen," I said. "You call Bertha B.B. If you're Little Bertha, that must make her—"

"Big Bertha," she said, deadpan. "White man's joke." L.B. didn't smile, but she didn't appear unhappy, either. "I was brung as wet nurse ta her when her Mama passed. I was sixteen, my own boy still at my teats."

"Does your son work here, too?"

She was quiet a moment. "He was sold off when he was eight ta the Triggs downriver. Weren't no more babies fa me. Only B.B."

"They took your child away from you? *Sold* him?"

"I's they property, and he came from me, so he they property, too. Same as a calf from a cow, or the foal from the mare. Same difference to them. Not all white folks willing ta do the same so early, but Bertha's daddy, he give her whatever she want. She want me all to herself."

"Then you *are* her mother," I said.

"Shush, now, girl." She swiveled her head and took in our surroundings as if someone might be listening, but she didn't seem frightened. "Lordy, Miz Alma, some things ain't never said." She studied me. "Ain't there no black folks in New Mexico?"

"I'd only seen one before we got to Texas."

"Who do the work then?"

"Most folks do their own work. They have gardens and raise sheep or goats." I began to warm to my subject, speaking rapidly, "My parents bought a young Mexican girl whose whole village had been wiped out by the Apaches, and named her Oratoria, but she's family now, like a big sister. She manages the whole household." My throat tightened because I held in tears. Homesick tears. I whispered my next words, "Especially now that I'm gone."

L.B. nodded. "Um-hmm, um-hmm. New Mexico sho do sound like the land o' milk and honey." She shook her finger at me. "Mark my words, Miz Alma, colored's be there fast enough if the New Mexes take a notion ta grow more cotton."

"You still get to see your son?" I asked.

"Just got back from a visit. The Triggs treat my boy fine, and Josiah keep him straight. She his wife."

"Trigg...umm. I've heard that name before. First black man we met on the way here said he belonged to the Triggs. I don't know his name, but he's married to a woman named Josiah who's a...a house *nigger*." I whispered the last word and felt my cheeks burn.

L.B. laughed and slapped her knee. "That my boy! Lamarr his name. Praise the Lord! All the Negroes in Texas and right off you meets my boy, Lamarr. Must be a sign." L.B. cupped my chin. "Look at the pink in those baby cheeks o' yours, Miz Alma, cause o' that word nigger. You is something else, all right. You is going ta need all the help you can get wit B.B., and I's the person ta do it. I can see that right now."

She had wide-set eyes, with a golden-brown hue that reminded me of the soft, dry hills around Santa Fé. A wave of loneliness washed over me.

"Why is Bertha so mean? I think she hates me."

"B.B. hate most women. Hard fa two women in one house, and she the Queen Bee. Best you set up yo own hive, girl." L.B. patted my hand, and smiled down at me. One of her front teeth overlapped the other, but it had the effect of giving her a sassy, youthful appearance when she smiled. Even her wrinkles fell into jolly ellipses framing the center of her face.

"What should I do?"

"Well, first thing, you got ta get outta the house. Go ta church." She thought for a moment. "You ain't Baptist, is you?"

"Catholic," I said. "But my family isn't religious. We go to church so people won't talk about us not going." I felt the heat in my cheeks again.

"Same as most folks round here. They wants to hear the talk, not be the talk," L.B. said, her voice filled with conviction. "You needs ta go ta church. Be seen. Do all them good deeds the church ladies work so hard at. If you get in the buggy of a Sunday, Bertha ain't going ta haul you out. She play sick, stay home, the church ladies might swing by fa a visit. Meet you anyways. Whatever happen, you got ta hold yo head up high." She cupped an elbow in one hand while she tapped a finger on her cheek. "Mexes ain't too poplah round here, but I guess you knows it already."

I drew my breath in sharply, but L.B. stopped me with a shake of her forefinger. "You as white as B.B., Miz Alma. You could pass fa her daughter. Make the most of it, girl. Passin' is good."

9

The Fourth Wife

"That was an interesting way to kiss."

 **ilar**, *1844*
Santa Fé:

WITH ALMA, MONIQUE and Stinky gone, my summer would've been empty if it hadn't been for Geraldo. His courting me caused only one problem: Oratoria insisted I wear women's clothing. She suggested the cinched-waist styles popular in the East, but I preferred to dress the same as her: full skirts that fell to my calves, and short-sleeved, off-the-shoulder blouses. She wanted me to wrap a rebozo around my neck, but I tied it around my waist.

Geraldo arranged it so we were alone most of the time. He showed me how to kiss and for once, I was a good student and returned like-for-like. We played kissing games which weren't so bad. His lips tickled my eyelids, my earlobes, and my neck. Geraldo didn't demand more, which was fine by me.

One hot day as the horses grazed nearby, we dozed in the shade of an old cottonwood tree. We'd spread a blanket and feasted on roasted corn and beef rolled in tortillas. A nearby spring tasted sweet, and the gurgling of the water lightened the air. Geraldo kissed the inside of my elbow, but this time his tongue drew a cool line up my arm, stopping at my neck where he bit my earlobe, not so hard that it hurt, but a strange mix of hard and soft that felt good.

"Umm," I heard myself say from somewhere deep inside my throat.

"You are very salty, querida." He nuzzled my neck again, and whispered, "I want to try something new." I turned my face to him, curious and willing. "Open your mouth a bit," he said, his breath hot against my skin. His tongue stroked my lips, probed deeper, and my mouth sent its wet message to my nethers. He stopped.

Barely opening my eyes, I whispered encouragement. "That was an interesting way to kiss." I tilted my chin up to be kissed again.

"Did you like it, Pilar?" He laughed and obliged me.

In my first letter to Monique, I peppered her with questions about the convent and whether she'd made any friends, to describe a typical day, and if the nuns were nice. I worried she spent her days in hard work and solitude. I wanted to tell her about Geraldo and the kissing, but it didn't seem right, her being chaste in a convent and me headed in the opposite direction. So, I concentrated on my good news, the birth of my beautiful filly, Scheherazade's foal, the first equine birth I'd witnessed. I told her Geraldo had promised a honeymoon in New Orleans. We'd see each other soon!

She didn't reply.

Winter arrived and an early snowfall made travel to school difficult. Besides, I preferred my own pursuits. Geraldo and I met daily, for wintry rides when possible, but it was our time together on the hay in the frigid stable which proved to be the most educational.

We kissed, pressing our bodies together as we lay under a blanket I kept there. On our sides facing each other, his leg thrust between mine, and my leg thrown over his hip, I pulled him to me, all thought gone, my body moving as it pleased. Low sounds of yearning, unbidden and surprising, came to me.

I rolled on top of Geraldo and straddled him, but our heavy clothes got in the way. He unbuttoned his coat and I did the same. I kissed him the way he'd taught me. The way I wanted. I ground my pelvis into his, rubbing, rubbing, pulling my skirt higher until only my drawers and his clothing remained between us. I sat up, my head thrown back, moving against him. A musky scent enveloped us, its aroma adding to my pleasure.

Geraldo's eyes told me he wanted more, but softness was there, too, a vulnerable edge to his desire. It seemed as if he wanted to lose control, but feared its loss, and this made me feel a power I hadn't known before.

He held my hips with one hand and slipped the other under my camisole to tweak my emergent nipples. It hurt, and it felt good. I wanted his mouth on them, his hands, his hair, all of him to touch all of me, and all at once. His hand slid down my stomach. He spread his fingers, his thumb kneading the soft mound of flesh cushioning my pelvic bone. Through half-closed eyes we watched each other. I rotated my hips, urging his thumb lower. My pelvis ached toward it, begging his thumb to press there, to rub there. Lower, softer, wetter, around and around, it arrived at the source and I ground my cleft on him, and he massaged me in rhythm to my movements and the sounds came, the sounds exploded from me as the heat gushed downward.

I knew from the diaries this pleasure was rare.

I kissed Geraldo with lust. I kissed him with gratitude. I kissed him with a love so deep, I knew it would never end.

10

Summer's Kiss, Winter's Embrace

"Yearning...Deceit...Joy...Denial...
rages through the Sandoval line."

O ratoria, 1844
Santa Fé:

PILAR AND GERALDO rode into the snow-covered desert daily, and spent hours in the freezing stable. I sat at my desk in the kitchen and worked on the Sandoval history. Distilling the diaries into one volume allowed the hours to pass peaceably while I listened for my sister and her lover to return.

The diaries from which I culled the history were stacked carefully on the shelf above my work area according to era. We had few rules in this household, but my sisters were forbidden to disturb my desk. When I finished a diary, it was returned to its place in the library. Alma and Pilar were free to read them, or not. Only one journal was locked away. My early introduction to Providencia Sandoval's chronicle of her sexual activities *and* her prodigious command of poisonous recipes had not inspired in me a desire for marriage. Who knew what effect she might have on my sisters?

I heard the intimate crunch of Pilar and Geraldo's feet on snow when they crossed the yard from stable to house. Their laughter trumpeted in the snowy night. They paused to kiss one last time outside the kitchen.

I closed my book and rose to greet them. Passion-flushed face, her coat unbuttoned, my sister seemed impervious to the weather. The aura of their happiness flowed over me along with the frigid air from the open door. It snapped me awake and into the present. I had a living, breathing Sandoval, and her betrothed, with whom to contend.

"Pilar, you're dripping wet. And *you*, don Geraldo . . ."

He smiled sheepishly. "Oratoria is right. Run and change into dry clothes immediately, querida." Pilar laughed and ran from the room. Her footsteps echoed across the inner patio.

I came right to the point. "Her blood has arrived. It wouldn't be good for her to become pregnant while still so young."

Not an accusation, but a concern I felt comfortable broaching. Pilar wasn't ready to be a mother. "The youngest mothers experience the most trouble bearing children."

Geraldo paused in taking off his coat. A snap of kindling in the fireplace made us both jump. "I've lost three wives to childbirth," he said. "I do not intend to lose Pilar." He hung up his coat and sat at the kitchen table, unsmiling. "Are there herbs we can use?"

I poured coffee into the cup I'd set out for him. "Plants work sometimes for some people. You should ask Consuelo. She deals in love charms and herbs to enhance or diminish fertility. Was pregnancy a concern with her?"

"Consuelo was pregnant when she came to work for me. Her child was stillborn."

"Ah, the milk, this explains her milk! And her attachment to your son."

Geraldo nodded. "After that, she said she could no longer have children."

The wind surged and outside a bucket was knocked to the ground. We both cocked our heads to listen. No other sounds ensued, which meant neither one of us needed to venture into the cold and dark night.

"La gente say her milk arrived because she has a gift for the miraculous."

"She's one of them," Geraldo said. "She does no harm." He shifted uncomfortably in his chair and looked toward the door. The bucket now rolled around the yard.

67

"But does she have the will to do harm?"

Geraldo answered my unspoken question. "Consuelo will not be a problem."

The wind gathered force, surrounding the hacienda with its steady moan. "The wind hums," Geraldo said. "A stormy serenade."

"You're welcome to stay here tonight, Geraldo."

"You trust I won't violate Pilar?" The merest smile jumped from one corner of his mouth to the other in a fight to break free.

"You tease me," I said, and attempted a smile. I had ground yet to cover. I pointed with my lips toward my desk. "The diaries say barriers can prevent conception–honey and mud, an orange sliced in half and placed within the womb." Geraldo crinkled his nose. I continued: "Abstinence is always effective, but it takes a god amongst men to follow that course . . . or so I am led to believe."

"I'm no saint," he said. "I loved my wives, but I was a young man, selfish and uninformed. Penetration, the young man's dream, is not all there is to lovemaking."

I lowered my voice. "But, surely it is uncomfortable for a man—"

"A divine hardness that makes me feel like a boy again. I was a slave to it then, hurrying through life's little pleasures, always seeking relief." He took out the makings of a cigarillo and began to roll one. "No more. You needn't worry about Pilar."

"Ah, Geraldo, what a rooster you are!"

We laughed together, each for our own reasons. Geraldo was happy with himself and I was happy for Pilar. I put aside my long held beliefs regarding men. He'd thought it out and had a plan; I not only wanted to believe him, I wanted to believe *in* him.

We sat quiet together and listened to the storm which had dropped all pretense of a hum, and settled into a howl. The wind found its way down the chimney and sparks flew. The room was already smoky, but Geraldo lit his cigarrillo. "What do you hear from Alma?" he asked.

"Nothing. She fears Estevan. He's always drunk, but usually not here. He never mentions her." Out of politeness I asked about his son.

Geraldo's face darkened. "Juan is married now. They're expecting a child." He was quiet for a moment. "I'm sure Estevan would not turn Alma away if she returned with a child."

"She listens to the rhythm of young love now, but the old blood is strong within my sister. It will guide her back to us when she is ready." I glanced at the diaries again. "Yearning and fulfillment. Deceit and retribution. Joy and withering denial. It's all in those pages. It rages through the Sandoval line." I poured coffee for him and tea for me. "The diaries predict the Sandoval line will diverge."

"Marriage produces a new mix."

I shook my head. "The name continues but the blood is not ours. I was the first recipient, but not the last."

11

Pollard's Corner

*"When you're asleep, do you ever dream
about making love with a man?"*

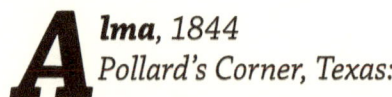**lma**, *1844*
Pollard's Corner, Texas:

ON SUNDAY I asked Pinkie to iron my blue satin to wear to church. I got up early, bathed, and sat in front of the window drying my hair, when I heard shouts from the kitchen. I ran out onto the landing, where the acrid smell of burnt cloth reached me.

I rushed down the stairs to the kitchen. Pinkie stood in one corner, her head bowed, her arms crossed tightly in front of her. Bertha held my blue satin up, examining it. She clicked her tongue. "Tsk, tsk, Pinkie, I've told you before to put a cloth on top of fabric like this!" She turned the dress for me to see the brand of a hot iron burned into the center of my beautiful dress. "Such a shame, my dear, I so wanted to introduce you at church today. Oh well, another day, I guess." She handed the dress to me, and left the room.

"Oh, dear," I said, hiding my disappointment. I'd been looking forward to this day all week.

L.B. came in holding a basket filled with ears of corn. She sniffed the air and found the source on my ruined dress. "What happen in here,

70

Pinkie?" Shifting the basket to her hip, she went over to Pinkie and raised her chin. Pinkie's eyes brimmed with the need to tell.

She leaned closer to both of us, whispering, "I's in here ironing. About done, too, when Miz Pollard comes in. She stare at the dress like it be a rattlesnake. She come over and hold down my hand on toppa the iron. She have fire in her eyes. I's so scared. I's real sorry, Miz Alma."

"I'm not angry, Pinkie. If I had more time, I could probably fashion a patch from the extra material in the hem, or from the jacket. I'll just wear my calico."

"Oh, Miz Alma, it still soaking. I's goin ta finish wit it while you gone today."

L.B. had been leaning against the sideboard, deep in thought. "You got a fancy red petticoat, don't you, Miz Alma? It look to be a skirt to me. Hand me that dress."

I ran upstairs and got my red petticoat. L.B. performed sewing magic. She cut the burned part of the dress out and bunched the remaining fabric in the front center, then tied a satin ribbon around the knot of material. She wove more ribbon through the knot creating an exotic blossom in the center of the dress. About eighteen inches of bare space was revealed below the blossom in an upside-down V. Hence, the red petticoat. It was striking, and made me wish I had a parasol with alternating red and royal blue stripes to match.

L.B. worked fast, humming and smiling to herself all the while. "Miz Alma, run up and finish getting ready. I'll come up wit yo dress!"

Cakes for the bake sale at the Church were loaded into the boot of the carriage, and I waited for my mother-in-law, who came out of the house happy as any hunter who has tricked her prey. She pulled on gloves, and didn't notice me until she was abreast of the carriage. For once, she was speechless.

"L.B. stitched up my dress! I can come, after all."

Bertha tucked an invisible strand of hair up inside her hat. "L.B., aren't you the clever one," she sang in her high-pitched imitation of good will. She got into the buggy, and didn't say another word on the ride into town.

The bell tolled as we rolled to the front of a clapboard building with a steeple and a cross atop it. Townspeople milled around in front talking and laughing. When we pulled up, the chatter stopped and everyone stared. I sat on the side closest to the church, but turned to Bertha for her to lead the way. She sat stiff and unyielding, a wilting smile on her face.

"Bertha?" I said.

"You go ahead, dear. I need to locate my missal in this bag. I'll join you in a moment."

I stood, gathering my skirts when a hand was extended to me. "May I help you, Mrs. Pollard?" I looked down into the serious blue eyes of a blond man, dressed in a dapper gray pinstripe suit. He took off his hat, and held it in his other hand, where he also carried a silver fox-headed cane.

I placed my hand in his and stepped out of the carriage. We were exactly the same height. "Why, thank you, Mr.–"

"Cornelius Smart, but call me Shug. Everyone does. It's a pleasure to make your acquaintance, Mrs. Pollard." His accent was of Southern vintage, not Texan, but velvety, the consonants and vowels softened in a unique pattern.

An elderly lady in a blue cornflower print dress sidled up to him. "Now don't be shy with your laurels, he's *Doctor* Shug Smart!"

"Well, Eva, you weren't here to introduce me in style." He gave her a peck on her withered cheek.

"I haven't met the young lady myself," she said, raising her voice and looking pointedly at Bertha. "Welcome to the family, my dear. I'm Eva Pollard, Bertha's old-maid sister-in-law." She kissed me on the cheek, exuding the distinct odor of distilled spirits. "I'm so happy Bill found you. Now you come visit me anytime, y'hear!" She held my hand, and we both turned to Dr. Smart, still standing at attention.

"You're too young to be a doctor." I felt my cheeks burn, and tried to cover my embarrassment by saying, "I mean, back home the few doctors who have passed through have been old, and the curanderas, medicine women, are usually very old."

He laughed. "I'm older than you think. Thirty-two to be exact. I want to hear more about the curanderas of New Mexico. Folk medicine is an interest of mine."

Without giving me a chance to answer, he turned to Bertha, and winked. "Two beautiful Mrs. Pollards are almost too much for a man to bear in a single day."

Bertha smiled, despite herself. "You are an incorrigible flirt, Shug Smart. Now get over here and help *me* down." He went to her, a slight hitch in his stride, as if he were on uneven ground.

Eva noticed me watching him. "He was born with one leg shorter t'other," she whispered. "Never stopped him from doing nothing he set his mind to. Kept him out of the army, though."

A young Negro boy ran up to take the carriage away. The moment Bertha's foot touched the ground a group of people came over. Everyone talked at once. Dr. Smart made introductions, relieving my mother-in-law of that duty. Mexican or New Mexican, Catholic or Baptist didn't matter to Pollard's Corner, still a small town of 800, not counting slaves. The young wife of the sole surviving son of the town's original founder was a curiosity. Acceptance was assured, if only Bertha would lead the way. With the second ringing of the bell, I couldn't locate her, so Dr. Smart escorted me to our pew.

The minister welcomed me from the pulpit and I honestly enjoyed the proceedings. There was a comforting sense of community, and an optimism that we could do better if we tried harder. Even Pilar would've enjoyed the service. It was at these times, when I wanted to share a new experience, that I missed my sisters the most.

After the service, the ladies sold baked goods to raise funds for the school. Bertha worked at one of the tables, but didn't want my help. Eva and Dr. Smart stayed by my side throughout the afternoon. Everyone wanted the pattern for my dress. Fortunately, I'd brought it with me from Santa Fé. Eva directed her bright blue gaze at Bertha. "Why don't you invite these ladies over to make a copy of it? I'm sure Bertha wouldn't mind."

Dr. Smart spoke up, "She always wants an excuse for a party, don't you, Miz Pollard?"

"That's right, Shug Smart." She dimpled up for him, and said to all the ladies standing around me, "You all come over tomorrow, y'hear? I'm going to be my own best customer, and you'll get to try these dainties you see here!" She seemed genuinely enthusiastic, and I hoped things would go smoother now.

"My goodness, Shug, what is all the commotion about?" a throaty female voice said near me. "These ladies are clucking like hens at a hatching party." A young woman stood next to Dr. Smart. A pink satin bonnet sat slightly askew on her head and framed her peaches-and-cream complexion. The silk ties were undone and hung loosely along the front of her dress. Most hats had a curtain down the back which concealed the neck. But I could see her strawberry-blonde hair peeking out, appearing as if it might come undone at any moment. Even so, she was lovely, and I was surprised she took an interest in me. She examined me from head to foot.

"Polly Tarver! When did you get back in town?" Dr. Smart asked her. Women in the congregation whispered amongst themselves, not so discreetly glancing our way.

"Yesterday. I'm staying at the hotel. I can't bear to stay out at the farm by myself."

"Any word on Boyd?"

She shook her head slowly, still staring at me with a mix of curiosity and frank appraisal.

"Please forgive my rudeness, Mrs. Pollard," Shug said. "Mrs. Tarver is an old friend of the family just back from visiting her relations upriver. Polly, I'd like for you to meet Bill Pollard's new wife."

I extended my hand to her. She took it, peeking around and over my head. Her handshake was dry and noncommittal. "And where is that husband of yours, Mrs. Pollard?"

"On a cattle-buying trip," I said, feeling suddenly like a shy child. She returned her gaze to me, content to stare, but say nothing.

Dr. Smart kept up a steady stream of conversation. "Mrs. Pollard, Polly is practically a newlywed, too. Her husband Boyd is in Austin, serving as military attaché to the new President of the Republic, Anson Jones. We've been expecting him home for weeks."

"Please call me Alma. I still feel there's only one Mrs. Pollard." I glanced at my mother-in-law, who chatted with several ladies. "Maybe when Bill gets back things will change," I said. I felt my cheeks warm again, but Polly grinned.

"I know what you mean. Seems like the best part of being married so far was the honeymoon." I couldn't believe my ears, but she laughed.

"Don't be naughty, Polly," Dr. Smart said. "Alma here isn't used to our, or I should say, your, wild and wooly ways." He stage-whispered for my benefit, "I've known her since she was in pigtails. This is actually an improvement."

"Any wife of Bill Pollard's understands exactly what I mean, don't ya, sugah?" I felt my stomach quiver and knew there was more to her words than I understood, but she smiled at Dr. Smart. "And for your information, Shug Smart, I've never worn pigtails."

A passing group of young ladies caught her attention. She waved and yelled, "Hey, y'all, hold up there!" The women squealed hello, and Polly joined them without saying goodbye. I stared in their direction, and when I turned to Dr. Smart and Eva, they both studied me with concern.

Eva spoke up first. "Twenty years old, and as self-centered as a new-born. She's as brazen as she can be with all her daddy's money behind her. It still didn't get her Bill Pollard." She leaned toward me again, and another whiff of alcohol floated my way. "He traveled all the way to Santa Fé to get away from her and find you."

"She was after Bill?"

"Yes, ma'am, her family is the richest in these here parts. Her daddy built the school, gave money to the church, so they don't say nothing about Polly and her highfalutin' ways. Not wearing a bonnet half the time! Why if she weren't so rich, folks'd run her out of town." Eva finished with an angry harrumph and crossed her arms.

"Well, she's married now," Dr. Smart said. "I'm sure she's settled down."

A couple of ladies came over to discuss the party, and I was spared having to make a response. The rest of the afternoon flowed by in a haze of well-wishing, congratulations and 'see y'all tamahrahs.' Bertha and I didn't speak on the ride home, but she hummed a little tune under her breath, and seemed in high spirits.

I awoke at first light and heard the carriage drive away. I didn't remark on it at the time; I was too excited about the party. L.B. already had coffee brewing. "This sure smells good," I said, pouring myself a cup. I'd begun to love the rich, dark brew in the morning. "Where's Pinkie? I need her to help me move some furniture in the parlor back against the walls."

"She done went wit B.B. ta town." L.B. was quiet for a moment. "Leave the furniture be fa now. They be home soon, and we work it out then."

By eleven o'clock, they had not returned. I rearranged the furniture myself to keep from looking out the front door. The road leading to town stretched flat and barren of travelers. At one, a buckboard pulled up. Eva. She gave me a full hug, gracing me again with the odor of liquor overlain with vanilla. She stood back, still grasping the sides of my arms, whether to comfort me or steady herself, I'm not sure.

"Bertha warned them all off, dear." Eva slurred her speech, but her gaze was direct. "She's up to her usual tricks, like when she run off all my gentlemen callers. I used to live out here, took good care of my brother for years before he took up with her. He won't do nothing to stop her. He's as grateful as he can be that she let him on top of her. But don't you worry." She tapped her head. "Old Eva's learnt a thing or two over the years. I been waiting to give my sister-in-law back some of her own."

According to Eva, Bertha had gone around delivering the message I'd decided not to share my patterns.

"I knew she'd made it up, and a few of the ladies knew it too," Eva said. "Most are too cowardly to admit it. Others are more than ready to believe anything nasty about a person, especially a new one. The rest are too busy to care."

We sat in the kitchen, me drinking my afternoon tea, and Eva drinking coffee laced with corn liquor. "As an aid for my arthuritis," she said. I expressed no judgment, but she thought I needed convincing. "L.B., you heard Shug say I should drink it. Didn't he prescribe it?"

"Yes, ma'am. He say ta eat when you takes the medicine. I'll just fry up eggs ta go wit that. Yes, ma'am, corn liquor known ta cure most all what ails you, and if it don't, you's not likely to notice."

Eva invited me to stay at her house in town for the week, built for her by my father-in-law a few years after his marriage to Bertha. I packed up my patterns, and set off with her. Eva sipped from the bottle on the ride back into town, never taking her eye off the road. When she saw Bertha's buggy returning home, she snapped the whip at our horses. As we charged past, I caught Bertha's satisfied expression. Sitting next to her was Polly, her bonnet off, and her hair flying around her head.

The week passed in a flurry of small parties. Every day, Eva invited a group of five to six ladies over to copy my patterns. We also shopped for fabric so I could make a few more dresses for the coming winter. Shug Smart visited most afternoons, and sometimes stayed for supper. He was curious about the Sandoval herbals in our library in Santa Fé.

"Most were written as part of the diaries and recipe books of Sandoval wives," I said. "A few of my ancestors studied plants, classifying and collecting them." We strolled along the main street. "There's a diary full of recipes for various poisons, but Oratoria keeps it locked away." I laughed to myself.

"Come now, Alma, share the joke. Surely poisons are not funny?"

"No, but Oratoria's keeping it hidden made it more alluring. My sister and I tried to get our hands on it whenever we could." I had to crane my neck up to see most men, but with Shug all it took was a comfortable turn of my head.

"Your sister, let me guess, is younger, and it was your idea to sneak a peek at the forbidden book."

I shook my head. "Oh, no, definitely not me. Pilar is the brave one. It's always her idea when rules are broken." I laughed. "I tag along so she doesn't get into too much trouble."

"Tell me about the book of poisons."

"Oratoria hid it because it contained more than recipes for concocting poisons. The author murdered her husband, but not before the two of them played adulterous games, even falling in love with the same widow." He raised his eyebrows, and I blushed. "I'm sorry, you'll think I'm brazen. She wrote the diary in the language of love and betrayal, and it seemed as if she might be in love with the widow, or at least they'd been close friends."

"No need to apologize, ma'am. Widow ladies have caused more problems in small towns than I care to mention. No telling what folks'll do when they got time and money on their hands. How big is your library back home?" Shug stopped, and leaned on his cane.

"I never counted, but it fills a whole room. We also have a copy of a manuscript written in 1552 by an Indian doctor in his language, and translated into Latin by Juan Baldiano. It has drawings of about two hundred plants and their uses. Not sure how we got it."

"You read Latin?" We continued walking.

"Oh, yes, but not as well as Oratoria. She's studied it much more than I . . . oh, look." I stopped in front of the dry goods store. "I need some of that ribbon."

On the following Sunday, Eva, Shug and I attended services together, and most of the members welcomed me. My mother-in-law joined a group of other women, but Polly headed straight for me.

"Sugah, you come on home today. I need a girlfriend out there." She hooked her arm through mine, and led me away from the group. "Bertha drags me along on all her social calls. Have you seen that derringer of hers? She pulls it out every chance she gets to shoot at crows. She's about to drive me crazy. She only invited me out to cause trouble for you."

"How could you do that, Polly?"

"Well, honey, the whole town knew she was scheming for Bill to marry me."

She reminded me of Pilar. That alone made me ready to like her. "What did *you* want?"

"I always appreciated Bill, for reasons you can well understand." She appeared as cool as if she were telling me she preferred apples to oranges. "Thought I had him, too, but Bill had other plans. He swung by one night to tell me he was off to Santa Fé."

I was in torment. Clearly, this woman could have any man she wanted. She studied me again. Her face was perfectly symmetrical, an unbroken stream of curves and hollows, all put in exactly the right place.

She allowed a mischievous smile to sneak through. "He didn't want me. Or I should say, he didn't want to marry me. Told me he wanted a *true woman*. I think he meant a woman who would be true." She paused. "Bill told me something once. Said he wanted a woman with a soul. That's what Alma means, doesn't it? Soul?"

She'd given me the greatest gift. "Yes, it does."

"I'm going to be staying out at the ranch with y'all till Boyd gets home." Her manner was disarming, but I felt my stomach jitter, as if a live thing moved inside me. It was the warning quiver I'd always felt before the memories invaded my consciousness. I reminded myself that Bill had chosen me, and Polly was a married woman with obligations, the same as me. I had no thought of past lives. I was too busy living my own.

Polly and I became fast friends, and the joke was on Bertha. It was true we were different from each other, but we were also different from the other young women in town, and this drew us together. She had a bawdy sense of humor, and little modesty. Polly slept buck-naked, and was proud of it. We all learned to knock and wait a decent interval before barging in on her first thing in the morning. Unapologetic and straightforward, soon nothing she said surprised me.

One day we were driving back from picking up the mail in town. The road lay in an unbroken line straight to the horizon, corn on one side of the road, and cotton on the other. A strange configuration, not the same as in New Mexico, where the plots were much smaller. A few dozen Negroes bent over the cotton, stuffing the fluffy buds into burlap bags. They didn't raise their heads when we passed.

Polly broke the stillness with one of her outlandish questions. "When you're asleep, do you ever dream about making love?"

"No, but I've dreamt I was naked at church. No one seemed to notice, and I wasn't trying to cover myself up either. Do you dream about ... *it*?"

"Every night of my life, and in the daytime, too." She giggled. "I always ask women, see if there's anyone else on earth like me."

"Well, if it will help, the closest I've come to dreaming about doing *it* is when I dream of Bill, but nothing really happens. I mean, in the dream, we aren't doing anything, but I get this powerful feeling we might." I warmed to the exercise, breathless in the recitation. Polly listened intently, her lips parted, as if she were a doctor listening to me describe the symptoms of longing. "In the dream he's looking at me, and I want him to touch me, but he doesn't move. I feel it's about to happen, like I could make it happen. This wanting keeps growing till I can't stand it any longer. I'm almost there, it's almost about to happen. Then I wake up."

Polly laughed. "Slow down, girl. Take a few deep breaths. Come to think of it, I will, too." The dusty road stretched out ahead of us, and two crows hopped from corn hedge to cotton row, keeping time with us. "What do you do about it," she asked, "when you wake up?"

"Do? Well, I get up. I can't really go back to sleep."

She laughed.

"So, what do *you* do?" I asked.

"Well, that's the difference between me and most women. I don't have to *do* anything, because in *my* dreams I get touched everywhere I want. That's why I wake up so refreshed." Polly winked. "But you can bet if my dream didn't get to that point while I was asleep, I'd sure know what to do once I woke up." We laughed. She knowing, and I at the threshold of knowing . . . almost there.

Just like that the seed was planted, the sprout of permission broke ground and waved its happy green in the sunshine. In my next dream I was back on the roadside with Bill and I raised my skirt as I'd done then. This time, I parted my knees and he watched my hands slide down the inner slope of thigh, to hide myself, one hand over the other. His eyes pleaded for more. I moved my hands so he could see, covered myself again, one hand replacing the other, a game of hide and seek, the pressure of my hands increasing the tempo of the game.

I awoke to ecstasy, a pillow squeezed between my thighs. Radiating from my groin, exquisite spasms traveled outward and downward, causing my toes to curl, my foot to cramp, and me to jump up and stand on one foot, grinning like a ravished fool. I might have arrived at such rapture anyway. The Sandoval diaries said it could happen. But it is to Polly Tarver I am most grateful, for it was she, and not my husband, who taught me to command my own pleasure.

12

Dreamwife

"I curse you! If not you, then yours. You'll never know when—"

Pilar, *1845*
Santa Fé:

IN THE MONTHS after Monique left, I wrote to her about the changing seasons in Santa Fé, my new horse, my courtship with Geraldo, and my readings in mythology. I asked her countless questions about her life in New Orleans, and told her how lonely I was without her and Alma. A new year brought me only one letter from her:

Sister Isabelle met me at the port of this crowded steamy city. New Orleans is different from Santa Fé in every possible way, but I'm happy to be far from New Mexico, except I miss you, and wonder if we'll ever meet again. My life is now at the Angelique convent. The sisters try to do good in the world and pray to erase their mortal hungers from their souls. I try but I'll never be as good as they. We go out in the city to help the poor. New Orleans is full of strange people from all over the world and they stare at us, the men watch us, one man watches me. He wears a white suit in this dirty city. Sister Isabelle says we've allowed Satan to enter our souls and he has bidden us to think impure thoughts. I knew it was my fault. Sister Isabelle punishes herself and wants me to do the same. My friends here are Mary

*Catherine and Celeste. Their families live here. Mary Catherine doesn't
believe Sister Isabelle but she's never been raped. I think the man in the
white suit is the devil.*

I read the letter often, worried because it didn't sound like Monique.
I'd fold it away each time unsure of what it meant. She was recognizable
only in my dreams, even though they were thick and tangled with all
the messages of my waking life and the changes in my body.

Winter clung to us, but I dreamt the heat of summer, and the sizzle
of water on hot stone. In my dream, the yeasty smell of horse sweat
mingled with the moisture from my cleft pressed hard against the back
of the beast. I'd discovered that rapturous button riding bareback in the
moonlight, not the gallop but the slow march home, a rolling massage
of hot, wet muscles working beneath me.

Monique rode behind me the same as when we were girls. Caressed
by moonlight and lost among the stars in our own private ecstasy, she
put her arms around me and leaned her cheek against my back, her
hips tucked tightly against my buttocks. The horse beneath us, its heat
and motion, bumped us together, rolled our hips together as one. I
felt her pressing against me, hard nipples twin pinpricks on my back.
I turned to her. My spine curved along the horse's neck and my legs
covered hers. She was naked, her tawny skin golden in the moonlight.
I licked the dew from her lips and felt the sharp intake of her breath.
She arched her back, our nethermost lips touching, rocking on the
horse, on the hot beast—

I clung to my pillow, but a cold hand on my clammy forehead startled me from the land of my dreams. "Pilar, we will be late for Mass!
Get up, lazy bones. You're sweating." She sat on my bed and stared at
me. "Well?"

I sat up, an elbow supporting my head. "My dreams . . ." She nodded,
interested. Too interested. "Oratoria, this is not an opportune moment."

"Do you speak of time?" She didn't wait for an answer from me.
"Even without clocks, time exists in its own dimension. It governs our
lives."

"I think it's time I got married. The sooner, the better."

"Ancient memories and unrealized instincts can unwind in our dreams," Oratoria said. She felt my head one more time. "Trust your dreams."

We arrived as the last bells tolled for early mass at La Parroquia. Being late meant we avoided the sight and sound of Governor Armijo. He marched to church in full-dress uniform, along with his staff and whatever musicians he could rouse to the occasion. Trumpets and drums were his favorites, but occasionally he had to make do with a fiddle-player. He always bowed to me, nodded to Oratoria, and asked after my father.

The pews, which Oratoria had bought for the church, were full, but the one we always took, nearest to the altar, was sure to be left vacant. A young Franciscan priest began mass. Instead of marching to the front, Oratoria stopped at the last pew and stared at its occupants. Black-clad viejas, their rebozos covering their hair, swiveled their heads in our direction. Each crossed herself hurriedly and left her place until the bench was empty.

My sister surprised me. She usually avoided any show of the Sandoval power. She pursed her lips in the direction of the pew, the Santa Fé way of pointing. I sat, and as usual during mass, my mind drifted to daydreams—of horses, of Geraldo, of Monique. I didn't hear a word the priest said.

When he left the altar, I stood, anxious to leave, but Oratoria tugged me down. Everyone filed past, glancing sideways at us. I could hear them laughing and gossiping on the Church steps. The young priest came out of his vestibule and approached us.

"The time has come," Oratoria said.

"Don Geraldo has already visited me," he said.

Laughter erupted outside, and a youthful male voice said, "Para el gato viejo, ratón tierno." A tender mouse for the old cat. The priest blushed, and opened his mouth to speak, but Oratoria held her finger to her lips.

"El rico," a man spoke, his voice crackling with age, "so fortunate to marry a rich virgin, young enough to be trained!"

"He should teach that one who is boss," said the young man. "I've seen the way she handles a horse." More laughter.

Then a woman's voice, rich and velvety, in her prime. "The boss is the sleeping tiger between her legs. Don Geraldo rides after her like a dog chasing a bone." They laughed, the men and the women, young and old, and the young priest avoided my eyes.

Oratoria and I laughed on the walk home, dismissing the gossips. "Geraldo isn't so old," I said.

Her face revealed nothing of her own thoughts. "Love comes in many forms," she said.

"Ah, Oratoria as sibyl." I nudged her with my elbow. "Have you done more than read the diaries?"

"I'll never tell," she said, the slightest smile sneaking through.

"Ha! A joke. You're full of surprises today."

We walked elbows linked. Not until we reached our compound, and turned to shut the gate, did we see the straggling figure of a woman following us. Oratoria pushed me behind her.

The woman had uncombed hair and wore filthy clothes. She stopped twenty feet from us. A light breeze came up and she swayed as if it caressed her.

"You've taken everything," she said, almost pleading. She squared her feet and shoulders. "You weren't satisfied stealing my lover. You had Juan sent away, too. My blood milk fed him. He was mine."

I moved in front of Oratoria. "Juan raped Monique!" My sister pulled me back. "Who is she?" I hissed.

She didn't answer me directly, but said, "Go away, Consuelo. Geraldo has decided. If he finds out you have come here, it will go badly for you."

One side of Consuelo's mouth lifted in a lopsided smile. From the folds of her skirt, she took out a tiny doll with long black hair.

"A wedding present," she said. She kissed it and threw the doll at my feet. Its head was twisted completely around. "The demon's kiss is my gift to you, bought for the highest price from Satan himself. I curse you, Pilar Sandoval. With all the dark powers of Hell, I curse both you and yours."

Oratoria tried to push me behind the gate. "No," I said, not angry, but not about to miss this satanic performance.

The woman, her eyes fevered, her lips stretched in a manic smile, shrieked, "You will never know the day, you will never know the hour, when my curse will fall upon you and those you love!"

Oratoria reached across me for the bell that hung outside the gate, and gave it a hard pull. Several men came running. All armed. "Escort this woman back to town," she said.

"I curse you!" Consuelo pointed at me. The men grabbed her arms. She struggled and staggered forward, falling at my feet. Spittle clotted the corners of her mouth. "If not you, then yours. You'll never know—"

"Pilar, please, get behind the gate!"

I let Oratoria push me into the compound. She yelled at our men, "Get that madwoman away from here!" They surrounded her, trampling the doll. Oratoria shut and barred the gate. She stood there panting, staring into space, while Consuelo swore on the other side, vowing to consort with Satan, to do his bidding so disaster would rain into my life. The sounds grew faint.

"Spittle of a madwoman mixed with beer and given to an enemy bars them from your home," Oratoria said, quoting a moldering recipe book, and speaking more to herself than to me. "But what if the enemy and the madwoman are the same?"

"What do you mean? What was that all about? She knows Geraldo?" Oratoria stared at me, but said nothing more. "Ah, I see. She was his woman before me."

The same night, Geraldo arrived at our kitchen door, his sombrero in his hand. "Querida, I must speak with you."

I kissed him on the cheek. "You look guilty, Geraldo." I led him by the hand to the stable.

"Consuelo won't bother you again, Pilar."

"What was it like with her? You did what we do? Much, much more, I'm sure. Will it be the same or different with us? I think about what it'll be like when we're able to be naked together."

He blinked, his mouth slightly open. "I see I needn't have worried she frightened you."

"Me? I've beaten a rattlesnake with a stick. That was frightening, but exciting, too."

"The men said she screamed vile things."

"Ask Oratoria. She's more of a believer than me." He waited for me to say more, so I did. "I want to hear about the lovemaking. Is it the same with every woman?"

He ran his fingers through his hair. "I came here ready to get on my knees and beg forgiveness, not to discuss my relations with other women."

"All right, apologize."

He knelt before me. "No one will ever come between us. I love you more than I've ever loved any woman."

I knelt, too, and we kissed, but my mind still boiled with questions. "What—?"

"Please, querida, I don't think I can answer any questions tonight."

"Just one?" I held up a finger. "Where is she now?"

"My lawyer delivered silver to her, and she's left Santa Fé. She told him she was moving near Nambé pueblo. Now, please can we talk about a more pleasant subject?"

"Oratoria spoke with the priest today," I said. My lover kissed me again.

In the spring of 1845, though I was not yet sixteen, Geraldo and I married. There was standing room only in La Parroquia, and afterward the whole town gathered at the feast. Oratoria outdid herself and arranged for all the best cooks in Santa Fé to help her. A band of guitars, violins and trumpets played. We drank and danced and then ate and drank again. Even Oratoria danced, looking over her shoulder all the while. She hadn't forgotten Consuelo's threats, and had guards posted on the periphery.

The party raged on as if nothing was out of the ordinary. La gente clapped their hands and stamped their boots. Papá celebrated the loudest. The more everyone drank the more they all loved one another. All the old men wanted to dance with me. A wooden floor had been laid outside, but the hem of my wedding dress was soon soiled. I didn't care. After our honeymoon, I vowed to never wear another uncomfortable dress again.

Amidst the celebration was much talk about the annexation of Texas to the United States. Everyone felt sure the Americans would soon turn their attention to New Mexico and the lucrative trade on the Santa Fé Trail.

"I wish Alma was here," I said to Oratoria, first looking around to make sure Papá wasn't nearby. Laughter echoed around us. A drunken man and his wife crashed into a table, toppling it. Partygoers and servants rushed to help them up. They continued their dance as if nothing happened.

"Alma is well," Oratoria said, though we'd heard nothing from her. She tilted her head back and sniffed the spring air as if it carried a message from my sister. "The time is not right for her return. First the Americans must arrive."

The party wound down and the political discussions continued in earnest.

"Governor Armijo promised to protect us from the Americans," one viejo said.

"We should welcome the Americans," Geraldo said. "They'll protect us from the Navajo."

Some nodded, some shook their heads. I yawned. The men glanced at Geraldo, who took the hint and said goodnight to all. We left the party around midnight, and stayed in a small, sparsely furnished house off the plaza. We'd leave early in the morning for New Orleans. I'd received no reply from my last letter to Monique.

The wagons were loaded and waited outside town. But in the bedroom, my nightclothes had been laid out for me. "I don't think I can get out of this dress by myself."

Geraldo sat on the bed and undid the back of my gown. He helped me out of the rest of the female undergarments, so many of them I could barely breathe. "Arms up," he said, and slipped the nightdress over my head. Distant laughter and guitar-strumming echoed off the walls.

"The viejos joked about our wedding night," I said. "They thought I didn't understand."

Geraldo pulled me onto his lap, and nuzzled my neck. "Most young girls know nothing when they marry. They haven't had the benefit of the Sandoval diaries, or read all the myths."

"The mating with swans and bulls?" I raised his hand to my breast. "I've seen real horses do it, Geraldo, and cats. They want it and seem to like it when they get it."

He laid me on the bed. "Remember what we discussed? We won't—"

"Do *it* yet, yes, I know, but I still don't understand why."

"I don't think my first wife ever enjoyed our lovemaking. She did her duty and she wanted babies. I blame myself. I did better the second time and the third. This is what I have learned: it gets better for women as they grow older."

"Are you saying I have to wait until I have gray hair?"

His finger traced a line around my lips, down my chin to chest to cleft where he pressed his hand. I caught my breath, all focus there. "With more experience," he raised my nightdress, "with trust," he stroked me, "their confidence builds." He kept his eyes on mine. "Their eagerness grows until they become equal to the men who enter them."

I pulled his face to mine and kissed him. His tongue kept rhythm with his hand and was soon joined by the pulsing of my womb.

I awoke before dawn so excited I couldn't eat breakfast. I was about to begin my overland adventure. An armed garrison escorted us from the Santa Fé trail to Independence, Missouri. Geraldo quickly sold the buffalo robes and tongues, beaver pelts, and deerskins we'd carted across the desert and plains. After a brief stay in St.

Louis, we took a steamboat down the Mississippi River. Monique was constantly on my mind. We got to New Orleans in June, but she wasn't there.

She'd disappeared from the convent.

13

Homecoming

"I wish I could make childbirth easier for women."

Alma, *1845*
Pollard's Corner, Texas:

WEEKS PASSED WHILE we waited for our husbands to return. The sun had almost set one evening, and Polly, Bertha and I sat on the porch drinking lemonade. The dogs started baying. Off in the distance a pinprick moved closer, then separated into two men on horseback.

"Bill!"

I ran to meet him, the pack of dogs loping alongside, ears flopping and mouths agape in dog grins. They glanced slant-eyed up at me, eager for the chase. Bill jumped off his horse, and ran to meet me, planting a whiskered, tobacco and alcohol-scented kiss off-center of my lips. I sniffed again, my nose crinkling, at the sweet smell which underlay his usual horse sweat and leather scent. He looked away.

"Oooeee, Alma, you sure smell good. I must smell like a hog. Pop, go on ahead. Alma and me will walk, if she can stand to be next to me."

"All right, you two lovebirds. I'll see ya back upa t'house." Poppa Pollard's horse high-stepped around the hounds. He took another swig from a flask. "Just fortifying m'self."

He held the bottle toward Bill, who shook his head. "No, sirree, Pop. You got me in enough trouble already. You better get on home to Momma."

"No kinda trouble, son. Man's business." He slurred his words, leaning so far out of his saddle I thought he'd fall off. "Man's business, you hear me, son."

Bill shot a quick glance my way. "That's enough, Pop." He slapped the horse on the rump and it jolted forward, Poppa Pollard barely hanging on.

"What's he talking about?" I asked, but I really didn't want to know. I'd received my advance-warning signal—the stomach quiver. No longer an indicator of Sandoval mysteries about to descend upon me, it told me to scan only the surface of my life.

"He's drunker than a coon at a mash party." He stood back and examined me. "I sure did miss you, Alma. You filled out some."

"I can't get enough of L.B.'s biscuits and gravy, and Polly has taught me how to make sweet potato pie. I tried to teach her how to make tortillas, but she can't get the hang of it. L.B. caught on, but—"

"Whoa, slow down . . . Polly's *here*?" He stood stock-still, squinting toward the homestead where we could see Momma and Polly rising to greet Poppa.

I stepped out from under his arm. He had an open questioning expression, and leaned toward me. "Bill?" I struggled to find the right words. Finally, I blurted it out. "Did you ever make love to her?"

His features became guarded. I rushed on, the words spilling out, hoping to erase the tautness in his face, and get the soft Bill back again. "I mean, it's all right what happened in the past, because I didn't know the two of you, and now we're married, and Polly's married, and she's my friend."

"Momma brought her here, didn't she?"

"Your momma doesn't like me, Bill. She wanted me to tell her friends I was from France. She can't get over the Mexican part of New Mexico."

He threw back his head and howled. "Don't that beat all? From France! Well, I've got good news. The cattle buying and the cattle selling was a quick turnaround. Never done such business. Bunch of green-horns toddled in late to the auction, and bought the whole bunch off us. We've got the seed money for our own place come spring, and Pop will lend me the rest."

He swept me up in his arms, and kissed me again. His mouth tasted of tobacco and bourbon, and his whiskers brought tears to my eyes as they pressed into my chin, but I didn't care. "Come on, let's head on to the house." We walked hand-in-hand, him leading his horse. One of the stable hands ran up and took the reins from him, and Bill hugged me to his side. He gave me another whiskery smack on the lips. Before I knew it, we were climbing the steps of the porch.

Bertha stood, hands on her hips, glaring at Bill. He dutifully gave her a peck on the cheek. "Poppa's already passed out in the parlor," she said. "Couldn't even climb the stairs."

Bill ran his hand through his hair in an apologetic manner. "Well, Mom—"

"Say hello to Polly, son. She's staying here a while."

Polly stretched before rising, approaching Bill with a crooked smile. "Welcome home, sugah." He didn't move toward her, but she didn't seem to expect it. She stood on tiptoes and gave him a kiss on the cheek. She sniffed delicately, and glanced at me.

"Like father, like son?" She smiled conspiratorially at him. "You boys been up to no good." Polly graced me with her teasing smile. "I'd dip him in the horse trough before I'd let him in my bed, Alma. Well, I'm kinda tired. Think I'll turn in early tonight. I'll be thinking bout you two. See y'all in the morning."

I didn't let her embarrass me, but bold as can be reached for Bill.

"It would be good to get a hot bath," Bill said. "We were going to the barber's, and we got sidetracked."

Bertha's spectacles flashed red with the setting sun. "You went to Lulu's. There's no fool like an old fool, but you should have known bet-ter!" She switched her attention to me. "All men are the same!" She went inside, slamming the door behind her.

"Who's—?"

Bill touched his finger to my lips to silence me. "I'm bone-weary. Not up to much talking right this minute. Would you ask Pinkie to heat water? Then we can talk." He kissed me again.

My questions turned to smoke in the night air.

Bill was not in bed when I awoke early the next morning. I dressed in the semi-darkness, for the sun was just coming up. L.B. and Pinkie were in the kitchen, but the house was quiet. Pinkie arranged the tray she brought up to Bertha each morning.

L.B. set coffee in front of me. She didn't remove her hand from the cup until she had my attention. "The mare is foaling. Poppa Pollard and Bill out at the barn wit her. Polly out there, too." Her wrinkles were fathomless, but her eyes said everything.

A light tapping inside my stomach was not ignored this time. "I'll take my coffee out, and join them."

L.B. nodded. "Best wrap a shawl round ya."

In the barn, Polly leaned up against a post, observing the men in her detached way. The cold autumn air produced vapors from our exhalations. Steam rose from the sweating trio of Poppa Pollard, Bill, and laboring mare. It was a breech birth, a more difficult process with a horse than a cat. Bill had his shirt off and almost his entire arm inside her, attempting to turn the foal. Poppa Pollard held a blanket over her head so she couldn't see.

"Almost there," Bill gasped. "Think I've got it most of the way around. I'm going to ease on out girl." Blood and mucous covered his arm. "Come on girl, you can do it." Bill rubbed her down from forelock to rump. Another contraction. The mare grunted, farting with the effort. She ruffled her lips, and looked toward her backend as if she wondered what was happening. She laid her head on Poppa Pollard's lap, resting, waiting for the next push. We waited alongside her.

Poppa Pollard spat off to the side of the stall, and let out an exhausted breath. "We're going to have to cut her. I sure do hate to lose this mare." Bill kept on stroking her, crooning softly.

"I have an herb, cardo santo, that may help," I said. "We use it on goats and sheep."

"Sheep!" Poppa Pollard spat again, his lip curling.

"Go on and get it," Bill said. Poppa Pollard sat back on his heels, amazement creeping out of each pore in his body. "I've seen it work," Bill said, undaunted by his father's reaction.

"I'll help," Polly said, her voice deeper than usual.

As we left the barn, I could still hear Poppa Pollard grousing. "On *sheep*!" he said. "On those New Mex sheep. Never thought I'd see the day."

Polly shivered. "If I had to suffer like that horse in there, might as well put a bullet to my head," she said between clenched teeth. "I never want to have children. All that pain, all that sloppy mess! I could barely stand to watch it."

"My mother died giving birth to my sister," I said. "I wish I could make childbirth easier for women."

In the kitchen, I checked to see if the kettle was on the stove. "L.B., I'm going to need more hot water, and cool water, too." I ran upstairs to retrieve the herb, grabbing some bellota de sabina, as well.

The roots of the thistle plant, cardo santo, hastened childbirth. I wasn't sure if they would work on a horse, and measured carefully the amount to give her as I ground them with mortar and pestle. The bellota was juniper mistletoe, and used by women as an abortive, but it didn't always work. It helped sheep expel the afterbirth and cut down on the bleeding. We could give it to the mare when she had given birth.

Polly helped me carry the kettles to the barn. Bill had a funnel ready, and we poured six lukewarm cups down her throat. Tired and thirsty, she didn't object. We waited for half an hour before the contractions started again.

After the foal was born and wobbling around on its spindly legs, Bill grabbed me and swung me around. "Oooeee, girl, we got ourselves a stallion here!" He stopped, but the barn continued to whirl around me. I stumbled backward, felt myself fall. My view of the world turned upside-down.

I tried to focus on the hayloft and the rafters of the barn, and I swear to this day I saw a great barn owl at the highest point. It leaned over and blinked its huge eyes at me, regarding me with the same detached curiosity with which I observed it. I tried to remain conscious as darkness edged closer to that one bright pinpoint where it sat. Alerted to the eclipse of its world, it took flight.

In my dream, I heard the thunderous noise a large waterfall makes as it echoes off the rock walls of the cave it conceals. It was the clamor of my own blood coursing through my veins, pounding awareness into my brain. The riot of my blood quieted, and the whispers and shuffling in the room where I lay overrode it.

I awakened to candlelight on my bedside table. I saw it through half-closed eyes brimming with tears. The prism of water filtered the light into a million jagged patterns, each beautiful, each so unique, that I felt I might stay there forever. Cosseted by the deafening roar. Secreted away.

Someone held my hand.

"You're doing fine," Shug said. I reached for my midsection, which had grown slightly over the last several months. "So's your baby. Aren't you one for keeping secrets?"

"I wanted to wait until Bill was home to tell him first," I said, apologetic.

"You need to take it easy from now on. I want you eating lots of red meat and drinking plenty of milk. Are you drinking any special teas?"

"Camomile. Sometimes yerba buena."

"Those are fine. Let me know if you decide on anything else." He patted my hand. "I still want to study your arsenal of herbs. They shouldn't be kept around just for the farm animals."

I tried to sit up. "I didn't bring everything."

"Whoa, Alma, not now. You rest. I'm going to send Bill in. Bertha's pacing like a lioness in the hall, but I'm not letting her in." He winked at me. "You tell your husband. He's worried sick."

Shug got up, leaving the room charged with the scent of talcum and . . . and rainwater.

14
Of Nuns

"I'm not a lady, and I go where I please! Monique may be there."

Pilar, *1845*
New Orleans, Louisiana:

GERALDO AND I arrived in New Orleans and went to the Angélique convent in search of Monique. We met the Mother Superior, an ancient nun who told us of my friend's disappearance. "Such a pity you had to travel all this way," she said. Like a dried and cracked arroyo, her craggy face had deep lines, and was just as hard to read. A hunch in her shoulders and neck caused her to peer up at us.

"She had a friend, a novice named Mary Catherine?" I asked.

Something shifted in the Mother Superior's eyes. "Mary Catherine has died." She stood, revealing nothing except that she wanted us to leave.

"Sit down, Mother!" Geraldo's voice had a deep edge. She cocked her head, appraising him from this new angle. "Please," he stood and bowed, waving his left hand toward her chair. "S'il vous plaît. We have more questions, and we intend to remain until you answer them. Mademoiselle Jacquard is a childhood friend of my wife. Naturally, we want to do everything we can to find her." He laid a protective hand on my shoulder, and smiled coldly at the Mother Superior. "I assure you,

Mother, my acquaintance with New Orleans extends to the governor, and my family has ties with the Church, traversing Spain and France, leading straight to Rome. I will not let this rest." He nodded toward her chair again.

She sat, steepling her hands. "Well?"

"How did Mary Catherine die?" Geraldo asked.

"She fell . . . broke her neck. We grieve for her." The Mother Superior crossed herself.

"Did you bury her, or did her family? I understand she was from here."

Again the shift of the eyes. I'd seen the same expression on trapped animals. Her pupils tightened, receded, so that shiny rapier-points of black shot out. "We offered to bury her amongst our nuns. Although a novice, she showed great promise and it would have been an honor, but her family buried her in their own crypt."

I remembered the other nun Monique had mentioned. "Sister Isabelle? May we speak to her?"

The Mother Superior's hooded eyes opened wider, the lines in her fractured skin twitching. "What do you know of Sister Isabelle?"

A quiet knocking at the door stopped me from answering. A smooth-faced and portly nun entered. She smiled at us as she passed a note to the Mother. It was a relief to shift my attention away from the old nun, like turning your back on a parched, unyielding plain to rest your eyes on a moist and prodigious green meadow. When I focused again on the Mother, she'd regained her composure.

She made a short note and handed it to Geraldo. "This is the address of the Malone family. Mary Catherine's family. Sister Luke will show you out." She stood again.

Geraldo remained seated. "Sister Isabelle may know where Monique is."

"Impossible! She was quite ill, and . . . and she has returned to France to our motherhouse. She left before Mary Catherine's death and Monique's disappearance."

"One last question, Mother." Geraldo stood. "How soon after Mary Catherine's death did Monique depart?"

"Monique attended the funeral with the Sisters, but did not return with them."

Sister Luke waited at the open door for us, her smile replaced by a crease between her brows. She followed us out and remained solemn. We walked down the long, dark hall, lit from several four-paned windows set high in the stone wall above us. Thick wood held the glass, and the setting sun shining through the panes cast oblique shadow-crosses high on the opposite wall. They reminded me of the Inquisition stories in the Sandoval diaries. I stared up at the crosses, and imagined their vertical lengthening as the sun made its downward journey, the crossbeams shortening, until the shadow-crosses resembled daggers. I'd go crazy here and didn't blame Monique for running away.

We reached a small, round foyer with dark hallways connecting to it. Sibilant whispers from nuns praying in their cells swirled around us, reminding me of the restless spirits in which Oratoria believed. A large, heavily carved table sat before one wall, bare of any decoration. Above it hung a portrait of the heralded abbess who had founded this order. *L'ange de Deauville, Angélique Gravier*, read the plaque attached to the ornate, gilded frame. She smiled down at us, her expression demure. Huge gold rays like a living crown sprang from her head. She held a golden tray as if presenting it to the viewer. Upon it lay two round objects and an oblong pink one. I stepped closer, squinting in the semi-darkness.

"Her eyes and her tongue," said Sister Luke.

I jumped at the sound of her voice. She stood beside me smiling at the portrait, her former good humor restored. "Have you heard the story of our patron saint?"

I shook my head no. "A wealthy married man who admired her beautiful eyes and heavenly voice pursued her," Sister Luke said. "To maintain her chastity, Angélique gouged out her eyes and severed her tongue. She placed the bloody orbs and fleshy muscle on a platter and presented them to her pursuer. He renewed his faith on the spot and begged her forgiveness!" Sister Luke gazed with fierce pride at her saint. She turned to us, a determined lift to her dimpled chin.

"We have a proud tradition of sacrifice in our order. In New Orleans, we work not only with children, many of whom are of mixed race, but also with the sailors, prostitutes and others who inhabit this diseased swamp. We bring faith and education." Her voice rose, challenging us.

"We do much good here. We will not allow one rotten apple to spoil the whole barrel!"

"A rotten apple will not spoil all the others if it is removed soon enough," Geraldo said, almost whispering. "Some harm may come to those nearest it. That is nature's way. God's way. The good Mother is forever vigilant. She must protect the unblemished."

"The unblemished," Sister Luke repeated.

"Are you saying Monique did something bad?" I asked the two of them, angry at the thought.

"Not Monique," she said, unsmiling again. She pulled the heavy oaken door open. The muggy New Orleans afternoon, heavy with the smell of chicory, spice, and decay, washed over us.

"Thank you, Sister," I said, and clasped my hands together. "Please help me find Monique. She's my best friend."

With the door open only wide enough for her round face to appear, she whispered, "See Priscilla on Dauphine Street." She slammed the door shut.

I leaned against Geraldo as we walked along the wooden sidewalk, the banquette. "How are we going to find Monique now?" I asked.

"We'll walk in the direction of Dauphine Street. This Priscilla must be well known."

He held my hand in the crook of his arm and we headed into an area of the city crowded with multi-hued women and men going about their usual business. I heard a patois that was French, but sprinkled with English. Spanish grandees conducted their business along the way. Their Spanish sounded different from New Mexico. An occasional Missouri twang reminded me of the traders back home. Mingled with them were the Africans and the gens de couleur libre, the French-speaking free blacks from Saint-Domingue.

We stopped abruptly as a tall, handsome woman, colorfully dressed in a close-fitting skirt, came out of a shop carrying a bundle on her head. The bundle sat atop a red turban that covered her hair. She stopped to adjust her load with a slender but well-muscled arm. Her skin was pale, but not white, and tinged with yellow, which added yet another tint to her exotic appearance. "Très jolie," she said, smiling at me.

Until now, Monique and Geraldo were the only people who'd ever told me I was pretty.

"Pardon, mademoiselle?" Geraldo knew some French, but he was not fluent. She raised her eyebrows. "We are seeking someone. Priscilla, do you know Priscilla?"

She stiffened, intensifying her queenly demeanor. "What business you have with Prey-see-lah?" Her accent was a singsong calypso of the Caribbean. She frowned, not waiting for an answer, but jerked her head for us to follow her.

Her bare feet did not affect her stride. She rolled her hips, a feminine swagger much appreciated by the men who nodded at her as she passed. We followed her along several busy streets until she stopped. When we came abreast of her, she signaled with her chin to a line of identical houses straight ahead. "Her house the third one and Prey-see-lah waits within." She turned a glum face to us. "Caution, monsieur, she a tricky one!" Geraldo started to speak, but we heard a husky laugh behind us. A mature woman now stood in the front door of the third house.

"Adrienne, how you charming husband?" she asked our guide, and her laughter erupted again, this time louder. Our helpful companion hurried away, one hand on the bundle atop her head, her hips now stiff with fury.

The woman waved us over. "Come, come in, my lovely ones!" Standing with her hands on wide hips, she swept her green eyes over us. Her fair skin was wrinkled. Except for thick patches of white streaming away from both temples, her hair was jet black and wavy, worn piled high on her head. It was as if lightning bolts framed her face.

"Smell that?" She nodded toward the open door of her home. A spicy odor wafted out to us, a smell that overlay the entire neighborhood, and made my mouth water. "I been cooking the gumbo all morning. Priscilla know bout cooking the gumbo." She laughed again. "Come in, come in."

We followed her into a room that was a combination living and cooking area. It was clean and neat and furnished simply. Crocheted and knitted dolls were on every surface. Priscilla motioned for us to take two empty chairs across from a rocking chair. She sat, taking up a basket of yarn. She glanced at Geraldo, then shifted her attention to me. "Well, I see you two not need Priscilla's love magic. What you seek?"

"We came from the Angélique Convent. Sister Luke said you might help us find Monique Jacquard," I said, almost begging. "She's my friend."

"I see. I see," she said, and concentrated on winding the yarn into a ball.

"Where is Monique? Is she in any danger?" I asked again.

She stopped rocking and set her basket down. "If Monique want to be found, she will be found. Danger? I say to you—all women live with danger. That girl no different, she face it head-on." Priscilla leaned forward and took my right hand in hers, turning it palm upward. She drew her finger along several lines, then rolled the fingers closed and held my fist between her hands, closing her eyes.

"You are lucky, my girl," she said, finally opening her eyes. "You have much love in life, and waste no thought for sin." She smiled suggestively at Geraldo. "With that virtue in a wife, you are most lucky man!" She lapsed into her throaty laugh. "You want your palm read, monsieur?""

"No, madame. I am already an old man. I know what the future holds for me. How do you know Monique?"

Priscilla leaned back in her chair, rocking slowly. "Monique try to save my daughter, my beautiful daughter." She stared off into space. "I, too, am not young, monsieur. Eight children in the ground, all seem white. Celeste, she the whitest, go to Angélique school. The man see her. He want her. He take her to the Quadroon Ball to show her off, but he marry a rich, white Creole. He keep my girl till he tire of her. He cast her out." She flicked her wrist as if she were tossing trash away. "Celeste walk the streets, give herself to all." Priscilla held her palm up and spread her fingers for us to see. "Her line is short. She be in the ground soon, my beautiful, almost white Celeste. Monique try to save her, but Celeste save Monique. She go work a house."

"A house? You mean as a servant?" I asked, but Geraldo touched my arm, signaling me to be quiet.

"Where is the house?" he asked.

"On Carondelet. La Maison Carondelet. Only the most beautiful mulatto work there. Tell her I make gumbo—her favorite. She come eat with her old mama." She began winding the yarn again.

Geraldo stood and extended his hand to me, but I remained seated. "Why was that lady who brought us to you so upset?"

She smiled down at her work. "Adrienne? That high yella gal got a young husband, strong like an ox, bout as smart. He got no staying power. He on her and off her in a flash. Adrienne want a charm to fix him. I tell her send him on over." She looked slyly up at us. "Priscilla ain't no voodoo queen. The charms is harmless. People believe strong enough, they make they own changes." Her throaty laugh began again. "I see him. He look good to me, just need some teaching. I teach him good. He go home, practice on Adrienne what he learned. She real happy, wear a big smile on her pretty face. He come back for more lessons. Adrienne find out what my charm is! That the story of Miss Ungrateful!" This time we laughed with her.

We made our way back to the hotel. "Charms and magic seem to be everywhere," I said. "In Santa Fé. In New Orleans."

"People need to believe," Geraldo said.

"La gente believe the Sandovals have magical powers. They believe the same about Consuelo Benavides. She threw that doll at me. It's called a poppet here."

Geraldo said nothing, but his lips thinned to a tight line when he clenched his jaw.

"Do you believe?" I asked.

He stopped in the middle of the banquette. The foot traffic flowed around us, but all the sounds of the city faded as we focused on each other. "No, I don't believe, but I respect the beliefs of others. Power exists in belief."

"I don't believe, either, but Oratoria does. I guess Consuelo did, too, or she wouldn't have gone to the trouble of making that doll and twisting its neck." I laughed, but I laughed alone. Geraldo put his arm around my waist, his mood somber.

Our hotel was a grand affair copied from a French chateau, complete with sweeping staircase, chandeliers, many mirrors and lots of gilt. It was like living in one of the castles I'd read about. I didn't even mind wearing fancy clothes, except I couldn't move very much in them. We had a suite on the third floor, but when we reached the second floor landing, I hiked up my skirts and ran up the stairs. Once in my room, I laid out the dolls we had bought from Priscilla. Each doll had a different color of yarn-hair—red, yellow, black, brown, and wore a beautiful crocheted dress.

"All the dolls are white," I said.

"What did you say, Pilar?" Geraldo was in his dressing room, which separated his bedroom from mine. He felt married people should have privacy and a room to themselves. Our caresses had grown more intimate, but we still hadn't fully consummated the marriage.

I tried to imagine what I'd feel when he finally entered me. The only picture that came to mind was of a stallion thrusting into a mare. Not a fair comparison, but one I'd studied a great deal. I'd also pored over the anatomy books in the library. Oratoria had shown me diaries of ancient Sandoval women waxing either poetic or suicidal over their own deflowering. I needed Alma to advise me; I couldn't help thinking about her and Bill together.

"Pilar?" Geraldo stood in the doorway drying his face.

"I said, there are so many colors of people here in New Orleans, but all these dolls are white." He wore a black silk smoking jacket, which revealed a thick mat of curling gray hairs on his chest. The same hairs I found sticking to my breasts when I got up in the morning. A spasm in my nethers reminded me of the daily delight Geraldo gave to me. My body yearned for his.

"All in good time," was his constant refrain.

He smiled as if he could read my mind. "Would you like a bath before supper? I could arrange for us to take our meal here in your room?" Geraldo enjoyed watching me bathe, and we'd bought gardenia-scented bath salts at a parfumerie earlier.

"What about La Maison Carondelet? Aren't we going there tonight?"

He shook his head, laughing as if I were a child. "I will go late this evening to make inquiries. I'm afraid it's not a place for proper young ladies." He continued to laugh at his own private joke as he rolled a cigarillo.

"I'm not a lady, and I go where I please! Monique may be there."

"It is a house for whores, querida. Prostitutes."

I knew good girls stayed far away from such people and places. But I was now a married woman, and being a *good* girl had never been my goal in life.

"I'll dress as a boy. I'll go as your son." I lifted my chin, though I wasn't that sure of myself. Geraldo's surprised expression gave me courage.

Then he collapsed in a chair and laughed harder. "As my son? Yes, yes. I can see it now. We tuck your hair up in a cap. In trousers and waistcoat, you could pass for twelve or thirteen." He gave me a gleeful once-over. "I could say it was the way my family introduces their sons to manhood. The darlings of the Carondelet would love to get their hands on a young boy, an impressionable youth for them to put their stamp on. But the surprise would be theirs."

I tried to smile, to go along with the joke. "It wouldn't have to go that far, would it? I mean, couldn't we say I was only there to look?"

"They would never believe it. Shyness is their specialty." He pulled me onto his lap, still enjoying the joke, and ran his hand along my thigh. "You can dress as a boy for me anytime it pleases you."

I reached inside his jacket and tweaked his nipple, nibbled on his ear and whispered back, "Take me as myself—your wife! What will they do then?"

"They'll await instruction from me, to know my wishes." He was quiet for a time. "It's possible you could get more information regarding Monique's whereabouts than I. Such women hate being questioned." He thought for a moment. "It's unlikely they will touch you without invitation, but it could happen. If it does, say your husband doesn't desire it."

"Touch me? Touch me, how?"

"The same way a man touches a woman. Such women seek tenderness, and they often find it with each other." He stroked me gently on the cheek. "Come, let us dress for dinner and the notorious demoiselles of the Carondelet!"

15
Jezebel

"I was thinking of murder, mutilation and dessert."

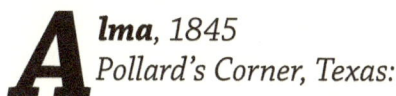

Alma, *1845*
Pollard's Corner, Texas:

WE WERE HAPPY that winter. Even Bertha seemed content, knitting for the baby, and retrieving a cradle from the attic. Bill was the gentlest of husbands, solicitous of my comfort and affectionate. But we no longer made love. Bill said Shug Smart had advised against it, delivering the message through Poppa Pollard for some reason. He said we shouldn't take any chances with my health, or the baby's. My fainting spell had put a scare into all of us, so I didn't question this decision.

Shug visited us often, bringing books for me to read. Lord Byron was my current enchantment. He questioned me about herbs and took notes, then stayed for supper. Polly continued to live with us, and was a light-hearted friend through the cold and damp winter. Talk of statehood had delayed her husband in Austin at the New Year. At the beginning of March, the American government voted for annexation of Texas. All bets were on that Texas would agree. I missed Oratoria and Pilar, but was still frightened enough of my father to delay contacting them. I hoped a grandchild might make a difference to him, especially if it were a son.

Polly was a good friend and I enjoyed having someone my age around, though I had my longest, most sincere conversations with Shug and L.B.

L.B. warned me against her. "Miz Alma, with friends like Polly you don't have much use fa enemies." She said I should throw a hissy-fit, the Southern belle's temper tantrum, and insist Polly leave. "Now you lis'en ta me . . . Polly the same as a mountain lion, all grow'd up. Is like she taken in with people, and learnt they way, but rub her in a wrong place at a wrong time, she scratch the living daylight outta you. Not think twice about it. She got the tracks for wild ways deep in her heart." L.B. set her wrinkles in a committed frown, nodding her head in rhythm to her pronouncements. "Polly make her own rules. She walk alone. She a Jezebel."

I shook my head. "You're too harsh on her, L.B. Polly *is* different, but I don't think she's as bad as you say. She's a married woman."

That alone set her apart from any hussy on the street. She'd taken a vow, made promises. Despite all I'd read in the Sandoval diaries about cheating husbands and wives, those tales no longer seemed real or relevant.

"And I trust my husband," I said. Bill loved me, of that I was absolutely sure. He wouldn't hurt me that way. "I'm used to having sisters around, and Polly's house is too far away for regular visits. It'll be all right. Don't worry so much," was my final argument. L.B. pressed her lips together and said no more.

I still rose early, but as I grew heavier the need to sleep overtook me in the early afternoon. One day I awoke from a nap in the parlor when the book I'd been reading slipped off my lap. I set it aside, first marking the place where I'd left off. I could hear L.B. and Pinkie upstairs, but no one else seemed to be around. Since the sun still peeked through bottom-heavy clouds, I decided to walk on the road toward town. I'd never walked in that direction. There wasn't much to see in the winter; only one small section of corn had been left standing. They had not harvested or mowed it down. I didn't understand why, but there it stood, as dry and huskery as it could be.

I'd walked about a quarter of a mile, and I was breathless and sweating. The air was still. I stopped and scanned the horizon, my hand shading my eyes. In the distance, charcoal streaks melted to earth from the sky, and lightning followed. I felt the rumbling thunder through my feet before I heard it.

Above the dried corn, two crows circled, dramatically cawing their distress. Below them, the tall stalks moved as if the circling birds stirred the air, causing a whirlpool. I heard laughter, and the crunch of stalks being broken. Bill and Polly stepped out of that dried Eden, holding hands, covered with leaf litter. They kissed, and turned toward the road where I stood.

The crows sang their delight, and descended back into their withered nest. Bill came to me. "Alma," he said. "Alma."

He said other things, but I don't remember them. What I recall is the stark reality of the moment . . . hopes and fears, desires and plans, all leading to this fallow field. Raindrops pelted us and mixed with our tears.

I finally listened to what his eyes had been telling me all these past months. They revealed the depth of his soul, and it did not match mine. I looked up at him, and felt small, growing tinier by the minute. The distance between us seemed insurmountable. The morose sky framed his face, and I saw his ordinary frailty.

I glanced at the corn patch again, but Polly was gone. I walked away.

"Where are you going?" Bill called after me.

"Home," I said. "To my sisters."

I have no memory of the walk back. Thunder seemed to shake the house, and I must of screamed because L.B. and Bertha came running.

"Is it your time?" Bertha asked.

"It's *your* time, Bertha," I said, steeling myself by leaning against L.B. "You can have your son and Polly, too. I'm going back—"

Another clap of thunder cracked over our heads and the vibrations entered my womb. I felt a gush of water run down my legs.

"Get her into bed," Bertha said. "I'll send for Shug."

L.B. tucked me into bed, and left to make tea. I closed my eyes for a moment, and when I opened them, Polly stood beside the bed.

"It didn't mean anything," she said. Her voice echoed off the walls, sounding hollow. "I don't want him any other way, and he wouldn't have me otherwise. It's the way I am. He's been going to Lulu's regular anyway. You should be angry at Bertha. She's the one who lied about you and Bill not having relations. Shug never said a word about it."

I knew returning to Santa Fé would be difficult; Bill and his mother would move heaven and earth to stop me now that a grandchild was involved. Even if I managed to get home with babe in arms, I might not be welcomed. But I could do one thing, and I intended to do it immediately.

"Get out!"

Polly stood where she was, uncomprehending. She always got her way, after all. My body felt bruised and battered, every movement sluggish, as if I were mired in mud, but I got out of bed and took Polly's hand. She flinched as if she expected me to scratch her eyes out. I had only enough strength to lead her outside my room. Softly, I shut the door on the faltering perfection of her face. Through a light sleep, I heard the clatter of horse and buggy as it carted her out of my life.

Willy was born the next day, March 14, 1845. My world shifted to him at its center, but once Pollard's Corner finished congratulating Bill, their talk turned to annexation and the German immigrants who had practically taken over central Texas. The home wars continued at the Pollard Ranch. Bertha was outraged when I rejected a wet nurse. *My milk for my baby,* I insisted.

Bill supported my decision. "Alma knows what's best for him," he told her, his voice deep, ready for battle. He wanted my approval. And forgiveness. I avoided any contact, and asked him to sleep in another room.

The sun slanted through my bedroom window each morning, following a pie-shaped arc. Willy and I tagged along in my rocking chair, he alternately nursing and sleeping, me purring in my mind like my childhood pet, that happy mother-cat Concha. This was the time when I missed my family the most. Not only did I want to show off my baby to Oratoria and Pilar, I also wanted him to grow up knowing them. My father's reaction was harder to envision, still making me uneasy. I was frightened of him, and not sure he would accept me or my child, especially if I returned home without a husband.

Bertha adored her grandson, caring for him whenever I'd let her. "How could you even think of leaving this precious bundle behind?" She smiled at Willy while she bathed him. I was too stunned to reply. It wasn't me she'd try to keep in Pollard's Corner, but my son. "A woman's lot is never easy," she said, "but children make it worthwhile." Clearly, she considered my place was at my husband's side, no matter what.

Bill and I treaded shyly around each other, never speaking of that stormy day of discovery again. We came together in joy when our child, now three months old, lay between us, his fist curling tightly around Bill's finger. We laughed at his baby strength, our eyes meeting. Bill took my hand, and kissed the fingertips. My traitorous thighs clenched and my breasts tingled, the urge to suckle brought on by Willy's cry, now mysteriously confused with desire: their job never done, it seemed.

My body had sent me a clear signal it was eager for pleasure. We entered our marital bed that night hungry for release. Afterward, Bill curled fetus-like next to me, depleted. I was naked and spread-eagled, the damp sheets kicked aside. Sweating and satisfied, milk tears rolled down my sides.

We went on as before, at least as far as everyone else was concerned. Even Bill seemed content, but I was in deep mourning for the loss of my illusions. I'd learned Bill's limitations; I was also coming to terms with my own.

Love took a curious turn inside me, twisting anguish and anger with lust. I was a Sandoval, after all, and the old blood spilled its secrets into my soul again. Instead of haunting me, the endless despair of my ancestors comforted me: I was not alone.

I kept my eyes open when we coupled, watching him, watching myself. It made me feel less tiny, more in control. I touched myself as he entered me, daring him to pull my hand away. My narcissism fired his passion, and I didn't deny him.

With each passing day, the call of the Sandoval blood grew stronger, telling me I did not belong in Texas. Poppa Pollard and Bill would return home drunk, swaggering, demanding supper and the attentions of their women. Bertha would fume and stomp up the stairs, locking the door to her bedroom.

But I would smile, recalling the recipe for Providencia Sandoval's *Pious Pie* (the poisoned version). On another day, Bertha might complain loudly that Willy suffered colic because of my Mexican mothering, and I would remember Ignacia Sandoval's instructions for delectable empanadas made of minced mother-in-law's tongue (said to induce peace and harmony in your household), or the gonads of your cheating husband (a savory dish to add spice to your lovemaking). Add a little cinnamon and sugar, a few raisins, perhaps—maybe even some brandy—hum a happy song and life goes on.

More than once I found Bill studying me as I smiled to myself, but he never voiced a question. "Penny for your thoughts," he might have said.

"I was thinking of murder, mutilation and dessert," I could have answered, a return to honesty, at last. But, I never volunteered a thought, feeling, or an opinion.

On the outside, I remained the good, placid Alma.

16

The Demimonde

"Are you saying Monique is a prostitute?"

Pilar,*1845*
New Orleans, Louisiana:

GERALDO HIRED A fancy carriage cushioned in velvet to take us to the Carondelet. I felt like a queen going to a ball. He chose a gown of red Chinois silk for me. "If we're going to shock the good citizens of New Orleans, let's do it in grand fashion," he said. I wore my hair parted in the middle and drawn back into a twist at the nape of my neck. It made me seem older.

La Maison Carondelet was an elegant mansion on a street of old and decaying grand homes, many of which were said to be haunted. The former owner had been notorious for torturing slaves, and many of them had died "accidentally" under her care. After her death, groans and screams were heard from the building, though no one had lived in it for more than fifty years. An enterprising Parisian madame bought and refurbished it, and cries of pleasure now replaced the anguished moans.

A stony-faced Negro butler led us to a parlor, which had too much red velvet and brocade for my taste. A curving staircase led to the second floor, and mirrors reflecting the candlelight were hung in multiples on each wall. Women, seated together in small groups, laughed and played cards; a few nodded and smiled. Several men stood at a bar where they drank and looked the women over. The air was thick with perfume and cigars. A few notes of music from another room didn't lighten the mood, but sounded ghostly. The place was set up for fun and relaxation, but it felt dangerous to me, as if everyone's future, not only Monique's, but mine and Geraldo's, and all the young women here, depended on what happened tonight. I poked Geraldo with my elbow; a portrait of a naked woman reclining on red pillows hung over the mantelpiece.

"This picture is better than the one at the Angelique," I said.

"They both show a woman—"

"Offering parts of herself," I finished for him.

"Pardon, monsieur, would you care for an apéritif?" Another black butler, younger, but with the same blank expression, held a tray of champagne. "Compliments of Monsieur Delmaire who admires your taste in women," he said. "He invites you and the mademoiselle to join his party. He is seated by the doors to the balcony."

Two young women sat on either side of a grizzled, ruddy-skinned old man hunched over a cane with a silver knob atop it. One had her hand on his thigh and the other passed him a glass of brandy, which he raised in our direction.

Geraldo offered a glass to me and took one himself, returning the salute to the trio by the doors. "My *wife* and I would be pleased to join him for a drink later." Geraldo placed a silver coin on the tray. "Is Mademoiselle Celeste in this evening?"

The butler palmed the coin and put it in his pocket without so much as a blink. "I will see if the lady is in, Monsieur." He bowed slightly, heading in the direction of Monsieur Delmaire who whispered to one of his consorts. The other one moved her hand higher on his thigh and smiled lopsidedly at her companions.

A burst of music and laughter drew our attention to an anteroom whose doors were flung open by a plump gray-haired woman. Men and women were seated around gambling tables in there.

"Ah, this must be the chatelaine of the Carondelet," Geraldo said. She stopped to chat with various groups, always leaving them laughing. The young butler whispered in her ear. She grinned as she walked over to us, but in her expression I saw the same calculations men make with horseflesh.

"Welcome to my home! I am Madame de Valery."

Geraldo bowed, and took a step away to speak privately. Couples climbed the stairs together, while others came down. The returning couples parted, the men going into the gambling room. Despite their rouge, the women appeared not much older than me. They acted bored with the other lone women until a man approached, then they became lively and flirtatious. I turned to Geraldo and Madame de Valery as she accepted a small pouch of silver from him. I felt a chill when she smiled at me. Geraldo had told me she'd think we were buying Celeste's services for both of us.

"Celeste is in the room at the end of the hall upstairs," Geraldo said, when he rejoined me.

"The door is unlocked," a soft voice said from inside the room. A pale and thin young woman wearing a cream-colored velvet gown, cut quite low in the front, sat by the fire reading. As we entered, she marked her place in the book with an envelope and set it aside. Celeste stood slowly as if to steady herself, but came forward at a deliberate pace, her hand extended to shake in the American style. "Welcome. The champagne has arrived," she said. "I hope you don't mind, but I've already started. May I offer you a glass, monsieur . . . madame?" She spoke in slow, lengthened tones, and inclined her head first to Geraldo, then to me.

Her eyes were the same green as her mother's, and black hair fell to her shoulders, held back by a satin ribbon. Her only other adornments were long filigree earrings set in green gemstones.

"I see you admire my baubles." She flicked her hair back, causing the earrings to sway and catch the firelight. "Emeralds from an appreciative lover. I gave him the golden honey of my love, and he gave me the heirlooms meant for a future wife." She laughed, bitter and false as she poured our champagne. Handing each of us a glass, she returned her provocative gaze to me. "We shall become fast friends, you and I. Have you heard the motto of our house? *It shall be our little secret.*"

"We didn't come here for you," I said, anxious to get answers. "We're looking for Monique Jacquard?"

Celeste drained her glass before answering. "I'm not sure I know a Monique, and if I did, why should I tell *you* anything about her?"

I held out my hands, pleading. "Your mother sent us."

She arched an eyebrow, but gestured for us to sit.

"I'd like to come right to the point," Geraldo said. "Of course, we will pay you for your time."

"By all means, come right to the point. All the men I entertain come right to the point. Why should you be any different?"

"First, I think introductions are in order. I am Geraldo Quintana. This is my wife, Pilar Sandoval."

"Pilar? From Santa Fé?" She set her glass on the table next to her. "Monique said you would come for her, but I didn't believe her."

"Where is she?"

"You're exactly as she described, lean and dark . . . and impatient."

"Where–"

"Monique is not here. She's no longer in New Orleans," Celeste said. "She's traveling the capitals of Europe with the best chicken-man a girl could have." She leered at Geraldo and laughed. "Unless you've already got him."

I stood, upsetting my champagne. "Are you saying Monique is a *prostitute?*"

"You make it sound very dirty," Celeste said, the slightest curl in her lips, not a smile but a sneer. "What choices did she have? Marriage, the nunnery or this." She waved her hand, including me in her description. "Captive. We are all captives, the good sisters and the good whores."

"She's gone," I said to the room, trying to make sense of it all. Geraldo tugged my hand, and I sat again.

Celeste continued as if I hadn't spoken. "You can give your heart to God or give your heart to a man, but it's all slavery. At His will. Give your body and keep your soul is what I say. But I wasn't the first to say it. Isabelle, the whore of Christ, said it first!" She crossed her arms, breathing hard, furious.

"Do you mean Sister Isabelle? Monique mentioned her and Mary Catherine in her letter. We saw the Mother Superior today, and she said–"

"That Mary Catherine *accidentally* died and Isabelle has gone home to France?" Celeste scowled. "She's a liar! Mary Catherine was murdered and Isabelle is at the convent, locked up–"

"What's this have to do with Monique?" I asked, my voice calm though I felt an urge to smash champagne glasses.

"It's because of Isabelle that Monique had to flee."

"Monique said she was strict, disciplined, that she prayed a lot."

Again the sneer. "One night I saw Isabelle in the alleyways near the sailor's pubs, and she wasn't servicing their souls. She'd taken an orphan girl from the school with her."

She paused and gulped down another mouthful of champagne. "The next day I heard she had been up most of the night punishing herself, and the alms box at the Church had been filled. A large donation appeared anonymously once a month." Celeste studied me for a moment. "You don't believe me, do you? Neither did Monique, until–"

"I'm not sure what to believe. She came here to escape danger," I said.

"Monique left two letters for you," Celeste said. "You may not believe me, but you'll believe her. She wrote it all down exactly as I said."

She didn't move, only stared at Geraldo.

"As I promised, we'll pay you for any help you can give us," he said.

She took the envelope from inside the book we'd seen earlier, and a much thicker missive from a drawer. One envelope was light, almost weightless, but the other was heavy and sealed with wax. I held the letters, trying to focus on the words written on the outside. *My Pilar,* they said. Meant for me, written in a hand I knew well, but all I could do was stare at them.

"Open them, querida," Geraldo said.

I ran my finger over the bumpy wax impression on the larger package, a bird in flight. Monique had sealed it because it was meant for me to read in private. The other was not. I read it to myself first:

You have traveled far to find me. I've held back from you too long–all my fears, all my love for you–but the truth is in these pages. I must hurry now. He's waiting for me.
    Yours,
    Monique

I held the heavier package in two hands caressing the ends with my thumbs. "She started a diary," I said to Geraldo. I looked up at Celeste. "But, Monique is with this man . . . this chicken-man?"

"I can see you have no idea what the term refers to." Celeste took a deep breath and in her slow, weary drawl explained. "A man who prefers young girls is a chicken-man. I guess most men qualify for that title." She smiled at Geraldo again. My neck and cheeks felt hot, not from embarrassment, but from anger.

"I've heard enough," I said, and stood to leave.

Geraldo remained seated. "Which ship did they take?" he asked her.

"They sailed on the *Prytania* for Paris last week. You'll want to know *his* name—Louis Hector. He's Belgian, a harmless, pudgy old man, who will indulge her every whim as long she does the same with him. He just wants to touch." Celeste yawned, covering her mouth. "So sorry, I'm exhausted. Where was I? Oh yes, Hector is well known in our little circle of sisters here. He used to follow the novices and students from Angélique, and he'd already seen Monique. Once he knew she was here, he pursued her with great vigor. He thinks she's a virgin, and he'll want to keep her that way, playing children's games of touch and look and perhaps, taste." She gave Geraldo the same seductive smile, as if he were another Hector, another chicken-man, as if she knew we had not fully consummated our marriage. I hated her at that moment, and New Orleans, and Geraldo, too.

"Will they marry?" I asked.

"Ha, ha!" Her laugh was a dry challenge. "It's possible, but right now, she's traveling as his niece. He bought her all these pretty schoolgirl outfits. He won't want her to appear womanly. A wife falls into that category. Monique is an actress. She's grateful to play the part of a spoiled child for the time being. Don't we all, given the chance?"

Geraldo left a great deal of money on Celeste's dresser, and we said goodbye. In the hallway, a butler carried a silver tray covered with a towel. He knocked on a door.

One of the young women who'd been sitting with Monsieur Delmaire opened the door. She winked at us as she took the tray. The door opened a bit wider so we could see the gentleman himself. Hunched over in a chair as he had been previously, still holding his silver-knobbed cane—but now completely naked! His feet were in a bowl of steaming water, and the other young woman sat on the floor bathing them. She was naked, too.

"Ah, the hot water bottle," he said in his old man's gravelly voice to the woman holding the tray. "Excellent!" He saw us, raised his cane in salute, and the door closed.

"The party never ends here, does it," I said, angry, those young girls with that miserable old man upsetting me. "He thinks you're a chicken man and I'm your whore."

Geraldo put his hands on my shoulders. I stared up at him, defiant.

"He knows you're my wife because I announced it. Pilar, we are like Monique and her *uncle* only in terms of age. I love you with all my heart and soul."

And I loved him in return.

I leaned into him and he guided me out of La Maison Carondelet. On the ride back to the hotel, I clutched Monique's diary to my chest and thought about what a lucky imposter I was. I'd said I wouldn't marry, but never had to think it through how I could possibly avoid it. It was each woman's fate if she had the opportunity, and if she didn't the poorhouse or the whorehouse awaited her. Celeste was correct on that account.

Geraldo, my chicken man, had saved me from all that.

I ran my finger over the wax seal again. Monique had not been so lucky.

17

La Soltera

"She wants you to marry her. Her revenge almost complete."

Oratoria, *1845*
Santa Fé:

I LIVED ALONE in the hacienda for months on end. Alma in Texas. Pilar in New Orleans. Estevan wherever he went when he did not return for weeks. 1845 wore on, and I found the life of a soltera, an old maid, suited me. My work—my real work—went on without them. I could pore over the manuscripts by candlelight all night and greet the dawn unworried about meeting their needs in the day. My goal: the history of the Sandovals in one volume, meant to reveal the secrets of the old blood to future generations.

Without my family, I could leave the diaries open on my desk with no fear my sisters would read the dark passages, and spoil the romance of their young lives. For weeks on end I studied Providencia Sandoval's diary, the journal of a murderess handed to me in innocence by Teresa, who sought the way to keep her husband's interest.

Written 1563-1578, starting when she was a young bride of eighteen, Providencia's journal is a sordid compilation of detailed recipes to enhance a sexual appetite that knew no bounds, except when it came to murder. Only then did she rein herself in, show a preference, and limit herself to poison.

"*At first, his caress was soft as an errant breeze on a hot day, pleasant but never enough,*" Providencia wrote of her first husband, her first love, in 1563. "*I knew fire was beneath his gentle embrace, but how to release it, let it run free, consume us?*" She sought the usual herbal remedies: damiana, raiz del macho, marijuana, but his feathery touch persisted, the gentle probing, his culminating spasm more a gulp than a gasp.

Like many Sandoval heirs who have turned to her yellowed diary for guidance, Providencia sought advice from her predecessors. Tired of their ambiguous references on the subject of el amor, she studied the chart showing the various branches of the family to see if she had missed anyone. Each marriage, and its issue, if any, was noted. Each person, male and female, had their full name written out referencing their mother, father and region of birth in Spain. Thus, each person had at least three names, often four, and usually more.

Except for one.

Hidalgo Sandoval, born in 1450, married Francisca Gomez de Moya. They had two daughters who died without issue. The effective end of their line. Except another branch led from Hidalgo's name concurrent with that of Francisca. Next to it was the letter C. Thirteen lines led from that initial, but contained no names. A mystery. One perfectly suited to the charms of Providencia, who was her father's favorite child. She had only to get him to reveal the story of Hidalgo Sandoval. The description in her diary was detailed and vivid:

I sat on my father's lap and kissed him, no longer the newlywed, but still the most beloved daughter in the household. I asked him about the family chart. He was gratified I took an interest in our history. I stroked his hair and tickled him. I asked him about Hidalgo.

"He was my father's cousin, and a notable man with a position of great responsibility. He was a Grand Inquisitor," my father said, and winced. He adjusted the way I sat on his lap so we could both be comfortable, the same as he had done when I was a young girl. I began to rock slightly in his arms, the same as I had once done, moving my buttocks almost imperceptibly.

"He left no heirs?" I wrapped an arm around Father's neck, and tickled his earlobe. I nested my head into the hollow of my shoulder, and walked the fingers of my other hand up the inside of his arm.

His breathing changed. "No . . . yes." He was not concentrating. I stopped rocking and looked at him. His face was flushed. "Hidalgo left no legitimate heirs." Father pulled my head down again, giving my hips a little nudge to start them rocking again. "He had taken up with Catalina Nuñez de Ribera. Her mother was a midwife in the Jewish district."

"She was a Jewess?" I tried to raise my head, but Father held me cradled like a baby. My hips no longer moved of their own accord. He moved them for me . . . and for himself.

"The mother peddled trinkets and charms to ward off the plague. Hidalgo tried her for witchcraft." Father's breath came in trembling gasps, but he continued. "Of course, she was found guilty."

I moved my hand inside his coat, and tapped his right nipple in time to my words. "And Ca-ta-li-na?"

"He took her as mistress. She bewitched him, took advantage of him, and kept him at her side even when his own daughters were dying."

My lips at his ear. "Where is her diary? I must have it." I pinched his nipple—hard.

"There, it is there." He pointed to his desk. I stiffened, stopped moving. "The key . . . in my waistcoat," he said, nudging my hips again. Slipping two fingers into the tiny pocket, I removed a silver key, stuck my tongue into Father's hairy ear–a simple reward–and went to the desk for the diary.

I glanced at the first few pages, shut it, and held it close to my heart. "This book will teach me everything about love."

Father sat in his chair, sweaty and disappointed. He shrugged. You would have figured it all out sooner or later." He smiled, and patted his lap. "Sooner?"

Catalina's diary sits in our library now, dusty and unread, except by me. It is probably the best-kept secret in a family ripe with ill-kept secrets. Her single-minded chronicle is not one of fatuous longing, or the usual debauchery. It does not contain one single recipe. Except for the bloody beginning where she matter-of-factly describes her mother's public disemboweling, and her own subsequent rape at the hands of the Grand Inquisitor himself, Hidalgo Sandoval, it is mainly an account of her subversive activities.

Spaniards needed a *limpieza de sangre*, the legal document showing the clean blood of four generations of Catholic ancestry, for key posts in the empire, as well as for emigration. Doña Catalina became a procuress of counterfeit limpiezas, first for her own children by Hidalgo, and then for countless other Jews. She operated right under the Inquisitor's nose, and he was none the wiser. Perhaps, she did bewitch him.

The first ingredient in Catalina's arsenal was desire. Hidalgo's desire for her. Clearly, except for this, she was powerless in that world. A man's desire fades, and women have sought to hold it for centuries. It meant her own survival, and that of her brothers and sisters, of her own children when they arrived, and finally, of her people. Merely giving in to his desire would not work, so she did the only thing she could do.

Catalina alternated powerful opposing forces: cold and hot. Attraction and indifference. In the beginning, she had let him take her, and lay there like a dead fish, her head turned away, staring off into space. Out of boredom, she began to stare at him above her as he pounded at her door, so to speak. She saw softness in his eyes, vulnerability, a blurring at the edges of his judgment, almost as if he had entered another realm. She wrote it was the same open and accepting bearing one can see in depictions of Catholic saints and martyrs, as if they would do anything to remain right where they are, caught in God's embrace.

Catalina floated in the pleasure reflected in his expression, and did a simple thing: she arched her neck. She had not planned on doing it. Her hips had long ago responded of their own accord, a duet of rhythmic movement being easier on her than a solo buffeting. But, the neck, so subtle a gesture, presenting one's jugular, implied surrender to a carnal urge he had aroused in her. Hidalgo groaned, and kissed her neck. His kisses flowed down to her breast, and still he plunged into her, suckling and stroking. In her diary, Catalina described the dual sensation, the pleasure she felt, and her dismay at it. She did not want this . . . this rapture, but it was hers, nonetheless. She did not want to be a martyr to it. She would not be passive.

He had frequently sought her mouth. She always twisted away, but now she licked her lips and pulled his head to hers, sucking his tongue into her mouth. Catalina wrapped her legs around him, and rotated so that he was under her. He had not bothered removing her clothes, merely lifted her skirt and entered, much as he did with his wife, who had never complained. Catalina removed her clothes now. She stroked her breasts as she rode him; she moved his hands there.

She paid attention to his reactions beneath her, slowing her movements when she felt him nearing his peak, sometimes removing him completely from inside her, and holding him while they kissed. He told her she was beautiful, yes, and that he would take care of her forever. He said he had never seen such passion in a woman, especially in one he knew to have been a virgin, had seen the blood himself. He was surprised at how much her passion added to their sinful act of fornication. He said he would have to confess.

Instead, the next day, he came to her and begged *her* forgiveness. Not for the murder of her mother, but for unleashing the sin of Lilith in her. She refused him. He knelt before her, burying his face in her skirts. The touch, the smell of her, proved too much, and the two repeated their carnal act of the day before, with a few added flourishes. He returned later in the day, and she rebuffed him. He returned the next morning, bearing gifts for her brothers and sisters, and Catalina declined again, but promised to spend time with him in the evening. Thus, it went. For the next twenty-five years, it was yes, and then no, and perhaps yes, again, all with intermittent variance in the heat and creativity of the moment.

I came away from Catalina's diary with a profound respect for this resourceful woman who had not become a victim, a sexual slave, but used sexual passion as a lifeline for herself and for her people. Providencia read her diary for the lurid details, impatient to try the stratagems on her young husband.

Providencia baited and released him, teased and withdrew, brought them both over the top of an ecstasy that grew too large for two. They bedded others, both men and women, together and separately. The sheer diversity of their sexual experiences diminished, rather than amplified, the joy of their lovemaking.

Providencia grew bored, and this time she was not pretending in order to heighten their congress. Her husband sought solace elsewhere. This had been a satisfactory arrangement while their mutual passion lived hot and deep in their skins, but once hers cooled, Providencia could not accept that his ardor had revived outside the circle of her arms.

So she killed him. Poisoned him with ground castor beans, sprinkled on his beef, and baked into his favorite fruit pies. Providencia murdered him in the same way she had catapulted his desire for her onto a higher plane. A little bit at a time.

He would feel ill, and she would nurse him back to health. He swooned in her arms as he had once done in ecstasy. His eyes would open and find only hers. He weakened daily, confined to their chambers. She fed him, bathed him, stroked his member into life in the early days of his decline, and climbed atop him. His fevered touch, his delirium, inspired her further. She spoke to him as he lay dying, of her love for him, her passion, her wish to keep him with her always. Her lips were close to his. His last breath had the taste of her words in it.

So it was with her next two husbands, and innumerable lovers between. Providencia created a lover's lair from which few could escape. Along with her diary, she left a necklace of castor beans for future Sandoval wives. It's safely locked away in the secret drawer in my desk.

I removed her journal from the library, and kept it locked away, as well. I allowed my sisters access to all the other books but these. Reading them left me with no desire for marriage. I had the love of my sisters, and I *knew* they would return. The old blood flowing in their veins would demand it.

In her search for a magical solution to keep Estevan at home his wife and my teacher, Teresa, had pulled Providencia's diary from the shelf in the library. Better Teresa had found happiness in her solitude. As I have.

I walked to Church alone every Sunday. La gente stepped aside or crossed to the other side of the street when they saw me coming. A few remembered I was not a true Sandoval daughter and whispered that I should not be living alone with a widowed man, especially one such as

Estevan. A few paused and nodded out of respect and gratitude. Sandoval gold had come to their aid in the past, and they might require it in the future. I took our pew at the front of the Church, and knelt, silently praying, my eyes closed.

I smelled him before I felt him near me. Estevan. He'd attended Mass sporadically in the past, but for the second Sunday in a row, he'd removed his sombrero and slid silently in beside me. He sweated alcohol, and I wondered why he didn't go up in flames when he lit his cigarillo after services. Worse, he insisted on returning home with me.

"Why do you walk, Oratoria?" Even his horse, who trailed behind us, head down, appeared hungover. "We have three buggies in the barn."

"Two. Alma and Bill took the third." I stopped. "Why do you insist on accompanying me? Get on your horse and ride."

"Don't be stubborn. You are a woman alone."

"I've been a woman alone for thirty-three years. It didn't concern you before."

"Pilar and you were not alone." He still refused to say Alma's name. "Oratoria?" He wiped the sweat from his forehead. "We are both alone."

His meaning was clear. "You are my father—"

"I am not—"

I held up my hand. "The only father I remember. I can't forget that."

He nodded, his shoulders hunched like an old man. Estevan's eyes were bloodshot and yellowed, and the veins on his nose and cheeks made him look permanently sunburned.

"I am . . . I have . . ." He swatted his pants leg with his sombrero. "I have been spending time up near Nambé. I met a woman there. A bad woman."

My scalp tingled at the base of my skull. "You specialize in bad women, Estevan. They suit you."

"Consuelo Benavides." He began to weep.

"You consort with the woman who cursed your daughter?"

He fell to his knees, his hands covering his big, ugly face. His tears cut through the oily grime on his skin. "I barely got away. She's done something to me. It's in the drink, the food, and the air around her. The pull is strong." He grabbed my skirts. "Her sex is like no other woman. I've never felt so alive. But now I can't eat, can't sleep. I drink what she gives me. It begins the passion again, until I am nothing, and still she wants more." He peered over his shoulder, and whispered, "I dream of a lizard on my back, its serpent tongue wrapping around my throat, choking me—"

"She wants you to marry her," I said, not a question, but a conclusion. "Consuelo, the doña at last. Her revenge complete when she has her hands on the Sandoval fortune."

He nodded, his eyes wide and almost innocent. "I would give her everything, and then I would be sure to—"

"Die," I said. I didn't have the heart to tell him he would soon die, anyway. I could see it in his eyes, and in his swollen, trembling hands. Whether from some vile nostrum of Consuelo's, or from his self-indulgent life, I did not know. I was sure of only one thing. I would have to marry him. Immediately.

My soltera life was over.

18
History Lessons

"I don't want slaves on our property, Bill."

Alma, *1845*
Pollard's Corner, Texas:

THE HEAVY RAINS of early summer were long past when one Sunday evening we sat down to supper. The Reverend Paul Slocum and his wife, Ida, were there, and Aunt Eva, as I'd come to call her, and Shug Smart. The discussion turned to politics. Since the United States had annexed Texas, all that remained was approval by a majority of Texan voters for it to become the twenty-eighth state in the union.

"Well, that won't be the end of it," Reverend Slocum boomed, forgetting he was not in the pulpit.

"Dear!" Ida gestured, her palm down for him to lower his voice.

He shot her a sharp glance. "All the same, the Mexicans aren't gonna sit back and let us set the boundaries," he continued in a softer, but still urgent voice. "The Gomez brothers visited their sister the other day, and I heard 'em talking." He touched the side of his nose in a sly manner. "I never let on I understand that Mex talk. That way, I know what plans they're hatching." He nodded and smiled with satisfaction. "They want her back in Mexico. They're worried there's gonna be a war."

126

"A *Mexican* woman lives in Pollard's Corner?" I asked, incredulous. I'd been here for a year, and not heard a single word of Spanish.

"The Gomez family has lived here for some time, dear," Ida said. "They were here when we arrived fifteen years ago, weren't they, Paul?" Reverend Slocum inclined his head in agreement, more a twitch than a nod, and focused on his meal. "Inesita Gomez married Gustav Beider, the baker. They've got two girls and two boys, all blonds but one. She stays home most of the time, especially since the troubles. Most of her family went back to Mexico after they lost their property. When the Catholic Church closed, there was talk of Beider moving out lock-stock-and-barrel, but he never was a Catholic."

"There was a Catholic Church? *Here?*"

They looked at one another, back to me, and finally to the Reverend Slocum. Not eager to abandon his meal, he sighed, but laid down his fork and knife. He peered down the barrel of his veined nose, and spoke slowly, as if to a child. "Miz Pollard, history shows two Papist countries ruled these here parts–first Spain, and then Mexico."

"Yes, sir. I'm aware of that," I said, clipping my tones. "Pollard's Corner was part of the Mexican state of *Coahuila Y Tejas.*"

He forced a chuckle, his cheeks gleaming with superficial magnanimity. "Well, of course, you remember your *Mexican* history. But did you know the Mexes insisted everyone had to be a Catholic?" He didn't wait for an answer. "Thought not. Didn't make 'em too poplah. When Sam Houston's troops defeated 'em in '36, and the Republic of Texas got started, just about all the Mexes hereabouts took off. Weren't enough Catholics to fill the Church, so we took it over. Serves 'em right, in my opinion." The clinking of silverware, the gurgle of water swallowed by unwilling throats, and the guilty rustle of clothing resounded in the oppressive aftermath of my history lesson.

I smiled . . . and cut my steak into tiny pieces. A cavalcade of bloody conquistadores marched behind my eyes, forcing naked Indians to bow before a golden crucifix. History repeats itself. Oratoria had drummed that lesson into my head. I wondered what the new order would be in the coming decades. I imagined Reverend Slocum naked, his pink-sausage body supine before brown-visaged nuns who flayed him with their rosaries.

"Alma?" Eva patted me on the hand, jerking me back to the danger of the commonplace. "I say, Alma, you're a thousand miles away."

"I was dreaming about our new home," I lied. "The ground should be dry enough to start soon?" I stared at Bill.

Before he could answer, Poppa Pollard cleared his throat, and set his silver down deliberately. "I reckon this is as good a time as any to make our 'nouncement." He glanced at Bertha. She smiled, and the candlelight glinted off her teeth. "Me and Momma know you two been drawing up plans, and dreaming bout what you might build, and we wancha to get started right." Bertha nodded encouragement, and he squirmed in his seat, barely able to contain his excitement. "So we cut out a string of five niggers to help build it. You'll have your place up in no time!" He sat back, happy as he could be.

Everyone smiled their eye-winking approval. All except for Shug Smart who sat regarding me with concern.

"Alma, honey, don't think we left you out," Bertha crooned. "I'm gonna send Pinkie over to help, now that I finally got that lazy girl trained!" She tittered. "I'll have to start over with some little thing happy to get outta picking cotton. Hope the next one is smarter than the last!" She shook her finger at me, and looked around the table. "Now, don't let Pinkie fall back into her old ways! I swear, I think Alma'd just as soon jump up and do the cooking, and have the niggers lounge around all day picking their teeth." More laughter at the table.

Heat rose up my bodice, making my dress stick to my back. I stared at my hands until their trembling stopped. Then, I raised my chin and spoke to Shug's kind eyes. "I wouldn't dream of taking Pinkie away from this happy home, unless she chose to come." I stood without scooting my chair back, and it fell over in an unfeminine crash. I turned to my husband. His mouth was open in that boyish way I'd once thought showed his innocence.

"I don't want slaves on our property, Bill," I said. "It's wrong."

He came around to my side of the table, and took my hand. "Alma, can I have a word with you?"

We left the room to the growls of the men undercut by the sibilant whispers of the women. "No good'll ever come of it!" the men said.

Bill was implacable, reminding me of our conversation on the road to Pollard's Corner. I'd made desperate promises then, promises not to question, to go along in order to get along, and he flung them at me now. When I remembered happier times with him, in Santa Fé, my view was dim, like a faded print of a far-flung land where the distant figures of a young man and woman seemed on the precipice of love. The memory of a feeling remained, but not the feeling itself.

In this battle, love didn't matter, nor did logic. Bill began the construction of our new home with the help of slave labor. People crossed the street when they saw me coming, not out of fear and superstition as they had in Santa Fé, but out of distaste for my opinions on their way of life. I developed a reputation for being an uppity female from the recalcitrant town of Santa Fé, an area the Texans coveted. It was bad enough I was foreign, that I insisted on calling myself a *New* Mexican, when the old Mexicans were trouble enough. But when word got around about my objections to using slave labor, thanks to the voluble offices of the most Reverend and Mrs. Slocum, I became even more suspect.

L.B. advised me to lie low for a while—let it all blow over—but the old blood would not let me rest. While sewing or tending the garden, my lips moved of their own volition, repeating the endless litany of Sandoval joy and misery. I'd catch myself, bite down hard on my lip, and try to rein in my memories. Still, the stories found their way into my sleep.

"El veneno! Be careful," I screamed.

"Alma, honey, wake up! It's just a dream, sweetheart," Bill said, rocking me in his arms. I wept, and was wet with sweat. "El veneno, that's poison, isn't it?" Guilty, I could only blink my response. He smiled as if I'd made a joke, instead of revealing the treachery of my kind.

I covered my lips with my fingertips, knowing I was about to reveal all, but I couldn't stop myself. The words tumbled out, "My ancestor Providencia Sandoval murdered three husbands by baking poisoned pies. Three different recipes for three different husbands." There! Now he knew.

"Her flaky crusts were famous," I added, because it was true.

"You was thinking bout baking some pies, sugar?" He tossed back his head laughing. I found myself giggling along with him. I forgot my fears as he kissed them away.

"Sounded like you was warning me, honey," Bill whispered before sleep.

Bill suggested I spend a few weeks in town with Eva. I drove with Pinkie, teaching her how to handle the horse and buggy. Willy slept most of the way in his basket, but when he awakened, I put Pinkie in charge of the buggy, and nursed him. At five months he sucked hard, staring at me, his hand playing with the ribbons of my bonnet. He'd grow distracted by the ribbons fluttering in the wind, release the nipple with a resounding smack, turn back and suck vigorously again.

Tethered, we dreamt in each other's depths, and I started the long recitation of the family history, aloud this time, mellifluous Spanish flowing off my tongue like a well-rehearsed fairytale. Willy let the nipple go, content to let it graze his cheek, and listened, his eyes moving to my lips, my teeth, and my tongue.

"Beatriz Sandoval married for love five husbands: each lost to war, or adventure in the new world, and in the last case, the collapse of a ladder as her husband, a scholar, reached for a scroll in the top-most shelf of their library. Beatriz never had a problem finding a husband. With each marriage, she gave birth to at least one child, usually two. All her children were males, and each new spouse felt assured of the birth of a son. But with her last husband, the pasty-faced historian with delicate hands, she gave birth to a feisty daughter.

"Because her daughter was larger than any of her sons at birth, Beatriz named her Imelda, after a saint who had been a powerful fighter. Imelda needed to be strong to contend with seven older brothers. Beatriz married no more, devoting herself to her youngest child. She did not waste her dedication; Imelda's life was rife with adventure."

I stopped, and for the first time wondered how much I should reveal. Nothing had been hidden from me, but the memories had haunted me, rather than helped me. "Imelda never married, but she hinted at lovers," I said, thinking that was enough information for now. Willy laughed and waved his arms. "You'll enjoy her diary when you're older, but for now I'll tell you about Sancho, one of the best fathers in the Sandoval line. He never married, either." On it went, the words of our bloodline, the never-ending story of the foolish inconsistencies and faded wisdom of the Sandovals.

While in town, I visited Inesita Gomez Beider. She and her family lived above their bakery, but I'd never seen her. I climbed the stairs at the back of their store with Willy on my hip. A smiling woman opened the door, her round, brown cheeks dimpling deeply on either side. She wore a simple calico shirtwaist, and her hair braided and wrapped around her head like a crown.

A young boy stood behind her, his hair so blond it was almost white. She and her son didn't look as though the same blood ran through them.

"Pete favors his father's people," she said, acknowledging my unspoken thought. Her English was perfect, the accent pure Texan.

Their house was not the simple abode I'd imagined. Heavy, dark furniture covered in lace doilies lined the walls. She set up a kind of crib for Willy in the corner, but low to the ground, almost at floor-level. "We call it the corral. Gustav cut off the legs. My last two are only ten months apart." She blushed. "And the second to the oldest was four when Pete was born. I needed to have a way of holding them in one place."

I put Willy into it, and handed him his doll, but he focused on Pete. "He hasn't been around many children."

I followed her into the small, warm kitchen, where she served us coffee. "¿Quieres hablar español?" I asked. "Do you want to speak Spanish? I've missed hearing it."

She shook her head, but said nothing more.

"Have you lived in Pollard's Corner long?" I asked.

"I was born here." She set her cup down and stared calmly at me, as if expecting more questions. Her eyes had an upward tilt to them, but her eyelashes pointed down. An unrevealing slant, and like Oratoria's, impossible to read.

"But your family has returned to Mexico?" I loosened the top button of my collar, it was getting warmer.

"The heat rises from the bakery. Good in the winter, not so good in July." She sipped her coffee. Silent.

"How old are your children, Mrs. Beider?"

"My oldest, Henry, is twenty-two. Mary is thirteen. Alice is nine and Peter is eight. I lost several children between Henry and Mary, mostly to miscarriage. Yellow fever carried off one." Instinctively, I listened to the boys. Pete loudly dramatized his play with lead soldiers, and Willy's happy gurgles told me he enjoyed his role as audience. "I'm so sorry. Is yellow fever much of a problem around here?"

"Can be anywhere along the river. Some years are worse than others." She sat with her hands folded in her lap, staring at me again.

I felt a tingle on my scalp, as if a trickle of icy water meandered through the forest of my hair. This meeting wasn't going as I'd hoped. "Well, thank you, Mrs. Beider, for having me and Willy over. Would you and Mr. Beider care to join us for supper tomorrow night at my aunt's house? You must know her?" I stood to go, but she remained sitting.

"Mrs. Pollard, you do me a great honor, but it would be better if we didn't meet again. I can see that your Spanish blood runs strong in your veins. The temptation to speak Spanish would be too strong for both of us." She gestured for me to take a seat again, which I did. "Yes, I speak Spanish. I'm the only one who does except for my firstborn, Henry, which I taught him. I also taught him to be proud of his heritage. All of it—the European, the Mexican, the Texan." She stared morosely at her cup.

I loosened another button of my collar, noticing that Inesita remained unperturbed by the heat. The muffled sounds of customers entering and leaving the bakery floated upward.

"He's the only one who looks like me," she continued. "A dark, handsome boy." Her lips and chin trembled, but she kept her voice steady. "In 1836, after the Alamo, a group of men rousted out my people. The men and the boys. People who'd known them all their lives beat my brothers and my son almost to death. He was thirteen."

She got up and removed the cups and saucers, setting them in a pail of water.

"Where is he now?"

132

"In Mexico with my family. He recovered. At least on the outside, but now he's filled with hate for Texans. My brothers were older, and their fear is greater than their hatred." A breeze wafted through the curtains, providing some relief. "My family is divided, but my life is here with my husband." She twisted her hands together. "Please forgive me, but I must warn you. I can speak plainly?" Inesita bit her lower lip.

I took her worried hands into mine. "Of course, speak plainly, Inesita, if I'm never to see you again."

She lowered her voice and leaned close to me. "People say you're a nigger-lover." I snapped my head back as if I'd smelled something acrid and spoiled, but she pulled me toward her again. "That's how they think! You must wear the Pollard name with pride, for the sake of your child. It's your strength during the times to come. You must not speak Spanish. You must hide your rosary and your santos!"

The divide between Inesita and me was greater than our common language could bridge. I'd not bothered bringing a rosary with me to Texas, and as for statues of saints, they'd long ago vanished from the niches in the Sandoval homestead.

"But, why?"

"Don't you see?" Her voice cracked. She seemed on the verge of hysteria. "If they see us together, if we keep the old ways, they'll think we're spies!"

She frightened me, and I wanted to get away from her. I went to the door and peeked into the other room to check on the boys. Pete lay stretched out on his side next to the corral, still playing with his soldiers. Willy slept on his stomach, one hand stretched through the bars of the corral. It rested on the cloud of Pete's hair.

Reluctantly, I turned back to Inesita. "Spies for whom? For what?"

"For Mexico. There's going to be a war!"

I wrote three letters that night: to my father begging his forgiveness and warning him about the possibility of war; to Oratoria telling her of my wish to return home, of my meeting with Inesita, and of the return of the memories; and to Pilar about my herbs aiding the laboring mare.

I told all of them about Willy, and a bit about my in-laws and Pollard's Corner. I urged them to write when possible. I knew it would take months for my letters to reach them. There was no regular post to Santa Fé, only wagon trains and individuals who agreed to carry mail. I said very little about my husband, except that he was building a house for us on Pollard property.

I remained at Eva's throughout the summer, but didn't see Inesita again. Pete, and sometimes his sister Alice, ran errands for me. They'd tickle Willy and make him squeal. Bill alternated staying at his childhood home, and with me. He'd chosen a tract of his father's land closer into town to please me. I was happy to be away from Bertha, and being close to the town made me feel less isolated. I resigned myself to having slaves, but got Bill to promise he wouldn't separate families. He designed decent quarters for them, too, against his father's loud complaints.

By December 1845, when Texas became a State, we'd settled in. Pinkie joined us, eager to leave Bertha's home. At the start of the new year, Willy crawled on the floor, and pulled himself up on the furniture. I still nursed, but people asked when the next one would come along. Bill and his father planned to put in more cotton, Bertha mistreated a new young Negro servant girl under the claim of training her, I ordered herbs and flowers from a seed catalogue, and President Polk authorized troops to advance to the Rio Grande to force Mexico to give up more land.

The Mexican War started in earnest in the spring of 1846, when their troops shed American blood at Palo Alto, north of Brownsville. The Texas Rangers sounded a call-to-arms, and Bill was one of the first to sign up, joining the Texas Mounted Riflemen under Colonel Hays. I didn't want him to leave, but I didn't try to stop him, either. My friendships with Shug and Eva and L.B. sustained me. Only in the marriage bed did Bill and I meet as partners.

We lay side-by-side the night before he left, having completed our carnal goodbye. Bill slept, while I pondered the mysteries of desire that allowed us to ignore the shrinking common ground of our life together, and leap to the sure ground of physical ecstasy.

"Will you be here when I get back?" he asked me that night.

I kissed him hard, the well-practiced frenzy starting anew, requiring no further answer from me than a compliant passion. Only when I clung to him, pulling him more deeply inside, wanting him to fill me, could I feel the spark of our old love. Only when I was most vulnerable could I persuade myself we were the same now as then.

19
Friends and Lovers

*They bound my hands and mouth and carried
me to an isolated basement room . . .*

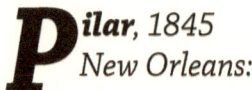**ilar**, *1845*
New Orleans:

WE DIDN'T SPEAK on the ride back to the hotel. My heart, pressed against Monique's diary, pounded in counterpoint to the clip-clop of the horse's hooves. When we reached our suite, Geraldo kissed me goodnight and left me alone. Shuffling noises from his room told me he was awake. I gazed at my friend's journal as if it were a memorial, thinking this was all I might ever have of her. I sat in the wing-backed chair next to the fireplace and stroked the waxen bird-in-flight again before breaking the seal:

Pilar,
    You've never gone back on your word to me, so I knew you would come for me. I know you so well, I'm sure you're thinking dire thoughts, that we shall never see each other again. Stop it! We're still so young. I'm still young! This realization means so much to me. Is it possible I'm still the me you knew?
    I'm writing this to make sure the best part of me, the person you knew, remains alive. This diary is so you'll understand how I've changed and what

changed me. Hiding from life in a convent didn't work, but my experience there made me stronger. A precious friend died trying to save me and you're the only one from my past I can tell about it. The story begins with Sister Isabelle, but it ends with Mary Catherine.

Celeste helped me, too. She and Mary Catherine are—were—my best friends in New Orleans, the heavenly angel and the fallen angel. Celeste mocked Sister Isabelle, but Mary Catherine said Celeste was confused. She denied the evil in the Sister until it was too late.

Something was working inside of Sister Isabelle, working its way out of her. I see that now. Late at night, she'd rip the most confused, the most wounded and vulnerable of us out of our beds and accuse us of doing things with our bodies none of us understood. We were whipped dogs, slouching around with guilty expressions even though we tried so hard to please her.

Each day, I came under her spell more. Celeste left the school and was kept by her lover for a time. He abandoned her, and she took to the streets. It seemed as if she wanted to punish herself. That urge is in me, too, but all I did to help her was to pray. One night she saw Sister Isabelle down by the wharves. She'd taken one of the orphans from the school with her, an eight-year-old whose mother had abandoned her in a brothel. At first I didn't believe Celeste, but the times she saw her there—with men—were also the times Sister Isabelle used the whip on herself. The sound of that lash, and her moans and prayers, echoed through our dormitory. Mary Catherine and I prayed and fasted, and offered our wasting bodies as a sacrifice to God to save the Sister's tormented soul.

One night, the same little girl Celeste had seen with Sister Isabelle awakened me. We were to go into the city to meet the Sister, to seek redemption at her side and prostrate ourselves before God and man. Before leaving to join them, I went to Mary Catherine and asked for her prayers. My friend begged me not to go, but I felt I must obey. I can't explain the compulsion, Pilar, but sorting out the good from the evil in this world was not possible for me at that moment.

I followed the girl to the tavern area near the wharves. A group of men stood in a circle laughing and passing a bottle. She walked around them without fear and picked up Sister Isabelle's habit, which had been cast aside. It amuses me now, but my first thought was not about what the Sister was doing, but surprise that she was not bald, her hair not shorn. Long, curly brown locks bounced around her head. She kneeled in the dirt. A pock-marked beggar, his pants at his ankles, stood in front of her. Her hands and mouth were full of him.

A few seconds had passed. I didn't see the man who grabbed me from behind. I screamed, but no one helped me, except for one person. Mary Catherine! My friend had followed me. My shock at seeing her, kicking and tearing at the man's hair, froze my terror for a brief moment.

He flung her aside. Her head hit the tavern wall with a crack like a tree limb splitting in winter. She made no sound, not even the merest sigh. My attacker dropped me and ran off, as did all the other men. I crawled over to Mary Catherine. She lay there, her limbs at odd angles, and her eyes blank. I shook her and called her name. Blood gushed from her head, encircling it like a dark halo.

"We must leave," was all Sister Isabelle said. The orphan girl took my hand and the next thing I knew, we were back at the convent. I sat outside the Mother Superior's office and heard Sister Isabelle say Mary Catherine and I had run off in the night and she'd followed us. I screamed no no no. They bound my hands and mouth and carried me to an isolated basement room where I was tied to the bed.

That first night, I wanted to die, too. It seemed I did not sleep, but I must have for in my dreams I heard wailing and cursing and laughter. A woman called on Satan to destroy the convent and all the whores inside.

When I opened my eyes the next morning, the Mother Superior was at my bedside. She'd brought soup and fed it to me herself while explaining what I must say in order to leave. Not return to the dormitory, but leave Angélique and New Orleans forever. Things had to be kept quiet, for Mary Catherine's family is quite prominent. Her plan was to return me to Santa Fé. At least, that's what she said, but she projected more malice than Sister Isabelle ever did. The Mother Superior wanted my silence and at any price. I felt sure she preferred me dead, and that old stubbornness you always teased me about took root. I'd be damned if I'd die because she wanted it!

On my second night of bondage I heard the click of the lock to my door, which was unusual this late. I feared an assassin was near, but a waft of perfume announced a different visitor. Celeste hurriedly cut my ties and slipped my feet into shoes.

"How—"

She held her finger to her lips and looked over her shoulder. A figure shrouded in black held the large ring of keys usually hanging from a nail in the Mother Superior's office. I couldn't make out who it was. Celeste threw a cloak over me, and we turned to leave: the person at the door was gone. We scurried away, trying to make no noise, but the stone walls amplified every sound. I heard a door slam, followed by more laughter.

I've hidden here, at La Carondelet, for over a week, and I've met a different sort of Mother Superior—Madame de Valery. Sister Isabelle had the wrong vocation, and without the excuse of sin she might have been a more successful whore than Madame. We laugh a great deal here, but I laughed the hardest when I learned it was the Sister who unlocked the door to my prison. Celeste went to her and begged for help.

Celeste works the house, which is safer than walking the streets. So far they've put no pressure on me to do the same. Madame never forces anyone. She says, "This work demands a high-caliber lady. You are either a natural, or you are born to be a great actress. I prefer the great actresses, for the naturals fall in love too frequently."

I think I might fall into the actress category, and that's fine with me because, sadly, Celeste is a natural. She suffers for love.

News filters in from the convent. Sister Isabelle is the one locked up now. She curses and begs—prays to be raped—to be punished. I wanted to tell the Malones what really happened, but Madame discouraged it. I think she's right. Who would you rather believe: the good sisters of Angélique who claimed Mary Catherine had slipped on a wet floor, or my version of defilement in the name of God?

I'm a problem as long as I remain in the city.

A man visits me. He demands nothing from me. So far. There are no real comparisons between your Geraldo and my Hector, but I understand now what it is to be admired for your innocence. No, that's not right. I'm not innocent and you don't want to be, not really. But, a small part of me longs for it. And I'm an actress, so I can play that part. He wants to travel with me in Europe.

Madame says Hector is tremendously wealthy, and she's shown me how to come out ahead of the game. We've even drawn up a contract so that my *safety is assured, but Madame has cautioned me this arrangement has an end. Hector will tire of me, and I must be prepared to take a next step.*

What will that be? I have no idea, but I'm excited to find out. I'm thrilled to be alive and to feel in control. I think this is what you feel when you ride under the moon.

You, and Santa Fé, are part of my future, Pilar, and I promise to return to you. I'll grow up, and so will you, and I hope we will grow old together.

All my love,
Monique

I reread the letter until I had no tears left. Monique's plans seemed dangerous and risky to me, and I hoped she had learned that sense of control she boasted about. As for my riding, no one but Geraldo, and maybe Oratoria, understood I wasn't in control during my midnight rides. Nor was the horse. We were one, united with the same goal–to run until we were spent.

The fire dimmed, but the noises continued next door. I wasn't sleepy, so I knocked on Geraldo's door.

He opened it immediately. "Querida?"

"I'm fine. Done crying. Monique is set on her path, Geraldo. I have to trust her." I pressed myself into his warm chest. "Ahh," I said. "This is what I need."

He rocked me in his arms for a long time, then whispered, "I have a surprise. Close your eyes."

He led me into his room. "Now, look!"

Right in front of the fire was the largest bathtub I had ever seen—it was two bathtubs joined in the middle.

"His and Hers: The Honeymooner's Delight," Geraldo explained, thrilled about this new extravagance. "I saw one of these in a catalogue. When the hotel said they had one, I couldn't resist."

I wanted no sad thoughts, so I imitated the suggestive smile of the girls at the Carondelet, a half-smile, a lowering of the eyelashes and rolling of one shoulder. Geraldo didn't react.

"Let's add the bath salts," he said, and poured small amounts into the steaming water on each side. The scent of gardenias filled the room. "I'll undress in your room while you get into the tub."

I tried the seductive gesture again. "Please stay."

"If you like, my dear. Is your shoulder bothering you?" He was concerned, always polite, and . . . and a bit controlling. *Tonight is the night,* I thought, determined to make it happen. Monique was right, I didn't want to be innocent.

"Nothing a hot bath with you won't cure," I said. "Sit, Geraldo. Relax. Have a smoke."

He sat in a chair and took out the makings for a cigarillo as I undressed. With each confining piece that fell away, I felt more free and unfettered, more the real me, the genuine Pilar who might fail as coquette but who rode stallions bareback, knew the entire Greek and Roman pantheon, and who swam naked in the river. When the last piece of clothing was off, I stood before Geraldo, loosening my hair and pinning it higher on my head. He wasn't smoking. His hands were frozen in the act of rolling his cigarillo.

"Pilar, you're beautiful."

Standing above him, I felt powerful, and *large* in a mythic way. "Now you," I said, a silky command that brought him to his feet. "I'll help you."

I unbuttoned his shirt, burying my fingers in the tangle of silver on his chest. My hands slid up to his shoulders, leaning into him to take hold of the shirt and slip it off his still-muscular arms. My nipples grazed the surface of his skin. The shirt dropped to the floor. I kissed him as he'd taught me. He pulled me close. I stepped back. His hands dropped to his sides. I kissed him again, this time unbuttoning his pants. He poked out through his underwear.

"I've never had a good look at one of these," I said.

"Querida, tonight you'll get more than an eyeful."

We entered the tubs from opposite ends, a sloping back on each side so we could semi-recline and see each other. We couldn't touch, unless we leaned forward and held hands.

"Too bad this isn't one big tub instead of two tubs joined," I said.

"A very good idea. Metal is hard to get in New Mexico, but perhaps we could have one made in St. Louis, and shipped to Santa Fé."

We talked, relaxed and playful, not wanting to focus on serious subjects, until the water cooled. Geraldo got out first, drying himself briskly. I started to rise. "Wait. I'll warm a towel for you," he said.

He held a large towel before the fire. I stepped out of the tub and he wrapped it around me, from front to back, so my arms were pinned at my sides. His kisses found their way down my neck and back to my mouth again. "I adore you," he whispered.

"I want to be everything to you, Geraldo."

He loosened the towel and dried my back and arms, bending to kiss the inside of my elbow and crossing to my chest, circling each nipple with his tongue. Kneeling, he rubbed my legs with the towel, rising to kiss my belly. "Open your legs a little," he said.

He drew the towel between my legs, kissing my thighs and the bristling hair on those other lips, those needy lips, his fingers stroking, finding their way inside, making a path his tongue followed. My knees buckled, unable to bear the piercing pleasure, and he carried me to bed.

I lay limp except for the occasional delicious shudders that ran through my body, watching Geraldo on his knees between my legs. He tied a membranous sheath onto himself. Before I had a chance to wonder about the feeling I was finally about to experience, he'd glided inside me, my warm slope made ready, open. Soon, our bodies were sticky with the dew of the New Orleans' night, and the sweat of our pleasure.

I was going to be good at this!

"Did it hurt very much, querida?"

"It didn't hurt at all, Geraldo. Maybe I wasn't born a virgin, after all. We can try again, and maybe it will start to hurt."

He laughed weakly. "I don't want it to hurt. Nothing should hurt you, my love. It's getting light outside. Let's rest a bit and then I'll let you ride me like your stallion!"

We stayed a month in New Orleans, shopping and eating and making love. We had a daguerreotype made, the only one I own of me in a dress. I'm young and uncomfortable in all my finery, but Geraldo is smiling, his fine dimples and sparkling eyes staring into the camera box.

I concentrated all the energy I might have expended in Monique's direction toward my husband. Her long absence from my life froze her in time for me, and when I thought of her she was still a skinny girl triumphant on the rope swing. Her rare appearance in my dreams was the opposite, for she appeared full-blown and womanly, her hair a tangle of blond curls as we raced horses in the moonlight.

These dreams were tantalizing, but didn't worry me. They were innocent compared to the desires recorded in the Sandoval journals. My study of mythology had long ago taught me to trust my dreams, as I trusted myself. I felt Monique's presence in them, and seeing her as a woman comforted me. I knew she was safe.

We saw Priscilla often, and occasionally Celeste. I arranged for Priscilla's dolls to be sent to Santa Fé in the trade pipeline Geraldo had established. She also helped me find a source for sea sponges, a time-honored birth control device Oratoria had never seen, but had read about. These would be of interest to Alma, as well, when she finally came home.

After the initial fascination with New Orleans, I grew tired of the heavy air and longed for the comforting ring of mountains encircling Santa Fé like a vow. I wanted the play of light and shadow, and the subtleties of color, which only a mountain desert could produce. Instead of the thick and sluggish drip of New Orleans' rain, which never seemed to wash the city clean, I needed the drama of black starry night, and the passion play of electrical storms, charging even the air we breathed with its energy.

I missed Oratoria. I missed my horses. I'd grown up, and I was eager for my new life in Santa Fé.

20

A Woman Doctor

*"... that feeling ... that knowing you
wanted someone right away."*

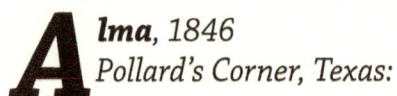**lma**, *1846*
Pollard's Corner, Texas:

WITH BILL GONE, the Pollards invited me to move back to the ranch,
but I preferred to live in town with Eva. Bill sent word that General
Kearny had marched into New Mexico and occupied Santa Fé. He
assured me they would treat the citizenry well, but anticipating my
first reaction, he warned me not to attempt to write to Pilar or Oratoria.
An intercepted letter could be construed as helping the enemy. They
might hound my sisters as spies, and label the Pollards traitors. I'd
already written, but either they hadn't received the letter or their reply
was already in the hands of the enemy.

Which enemy? I wondered.

I felt sure the people of New Mexico could handle these new con-
querors as they had all the others. They'd insinuate their ways pain-
lessly into the gringo mentality, and enchant them, until the conquer-
ing heroes would think an adobe the best building material ever, chile
colorado the perfect cuisine for high altitudes, and the bailes with pretty
señoritas the height of culture.

The Mexican War continued, and Texas sent recuperating soldiers to Pollard's Corner. We put them in private homes, under the care of Shug Smart. Several women in the ladies' auxiliary volunteered their time as nurses. Over supper one night at Eva's, Shug asked me to help out, explaining between bites of cornbread he didn't want me to nurse soldiers. "If the war lasts much longer, I'm going to need help with my everyday practice. The births, sore throats, sprains and broken bones of the good citizens of Pollard's Corner need attention, too. I'll train you, Alma. I think you would make an excellent doctor."

"Doctor!" Eva and I exclaimed at the same time.

Willy had been busy gnawing on a corncob in his high chair, but echoed our enthusiasm. "Doc, doc, doc," he shouted.

"See, even your son is smart enough to know doctor material when he sees it," Shug said.

"Imagine . . . a woman doctor," Eva said, and gulped down her *medicine*. "Well, why the hell not? The men in these here parts have all taken off to play soldier, and left the women to tend the farms and children both." She hiccuped, bleary-eyed. "I've seen you tending to those negra children back at the ranch when the influenza was laying folks low. Healed 'em all!"

I went over to help her up. "I did what Shug said to do." I took the glass from her hand, and set it on the table. "You barely touched your food, Eva. You're not supposed to take the medicine on an empty stomach." Eva teetered toward me, and said in her most feeble voice, "I've been feeling a might poorly of late. Thought an extra dose might do me some good. If you'd help me to my room, dear, I'd surely appreciate it." I put her to bed, pulled the coverlet up under her chin, and kissed her on the forehead like a child. In the dining room, I found Shug trying to wipe my son's mouth and hands.

Willy didn't make it easy for him, turning his head this way and that. We three adjourned to the parlor, and the two of them rolled around on the rug in mock combat, until Pinkie arrived to get Willy ready for bed. Shug lay on the rug smiling, his hair mussed and his suit in disarray. I drank my tea, comfortable in the silence, and studied my friend's profile. Shug was handsome; a childhood prettiness had probably been there once, smoothed over now by intelligence and humor.

145

"I always wanted children," he said.

"Get yourself a wife, Shug. What have you been waiting for?" I assumed a jaunty tone to cover my uneasiness. I had heard a rumor Shug's disability might involve more than his leg.

"I had a wife. She died of cholera in 1834. We'd been married a short time."

Without thinking, I dropped to my knees at his side. "I'm so sorry. I had no idea." He turned to me, his expression soft, open. "You were very young," I said. "Was there never anyone else in all that time?" He still appeared young; careworn lines accentuated his best features—sincere, yet mischievous blue eyes, a generous mouth.

"I've poured myself into my work since then." He sat up and took my hand in his. "My family expected me to follow in my father's footsteps, and take over his medical practice, but I wasn't a good student. I'd developed a devil-may-care-attitude to compensate for my short leg, and took far too many risks—flirted outrageously, hung out with lowlifes and loose women, spent as much of my father's money as he would allow." He laughed, still holding my hand. The two of us sat on the floor like picnickers.

I felt close to him, relaxed. "Lowlifes and loose women? Are we still talking about you, Shug? You're so responsible, so caring."

"Lydia brought it all out. I walked into my father's office one afternoon, prepared to ask him for an advance on my allowance, and she was there." He stared into space, as if seeing her again.

"Was she beautiful?"

"She was to me. It's hard to explain her effect on me without making her sound sordid, or like Polly." He snickered, acknowledging my confidences in him. Only he and L.B. knew about Bill's infidelity. "Lydia was older than me by eight years. She'd been married to a doctor, and widowed. She invited me to her home for dinner one night. She'd worked it all out, and planned to seduce me." He laughed, throwing back his head. "My interest in medicine took a turn for the better, much to my father's satisfaction. I spent every waking moment, when I wasn't in Lydia's arms, learning to become the best physician that I could."

"She would be proud, Shug." I looked at our entwined fingers. "You never had that feeling again, that *knowing* you wanted someone right away?" The question sprang to my lips before I'd given it much thought. But I wasn't being honest, for I'd always wanted to know.

We gazed at each other for a long time, longer than necessary to answer the question, for so long that the answer saturated the silence between us. The heated sap in a log exploded, the loud pop from the fireplace startling both of us. Shug stood, still holding my hand. I smiled up at him, uncertain.

"So what's your answer? Are you going to help me in my practice?" He gave me a slight tug, helping me to my feet.

My foot caught in my petticoat, and I pulled him off-balance. We grabbed each other's shoulders to steady ourselves. He stood so near to me I could feel the heat from his body. My heart pounded in my ears, and I was sure he could hear it. I avoided his eyes.

"Alma?" he said, his voice tight.

I stepped back. "Of course I will. When do you want me?" His cane leaned against the sofa. I handed it to him, standing shyly at arms-length. He stared at me with a bemused expression, and I blushed. "Shug, when should I start?"

His face assumed its usual impish contours. "The sooner we get started, the better. A new year is upon us."

21
Señora Sandoval

I pulled Oratoria aside. "Exorcism? Marriage to Papá?"

Pilar, *1845-46*
Santa Fé:

WE TOOK A steamboat up the Mississippi River from New Orleans to St. Louis, and picked up the trade goods Geraldo had ordered. A switch to the Missouri River got us to Independence for the overland part of our journey. Our caravan was huge; sixty-five wagons moved slowly on the Santa Fé trail, headed west, heavy with goods for our personal use and for trade in Santa Fé. We were getting a late start, but Geraldo was confident that good weather holding and no problems from Indians, we could expect to arrive in Santa Fé in October.

On the trail, one week flowed into the other until the morning I awoke before first light. A shimmering spray of stars curled around moonlit clouds. Their winking pattern reminded me of my nights alone back home when I rode my father's stallion. I stretched my arms overhead and yawned, sucking in air drenched in dew and star beams. It smelled and tasted light and fruity. I smacked my lips, and breathed deeply again. The merest pink, the color of a newborn's fingertip, flowed onto the horizon.

New Mexico! We must have crossed into the territory of home yes-terday, and no one had bothered mentioning it. Soon, I'd enter the Quintana hacienda as wife, but first we'd stop at my home, no longer my home, to see Oratoria, my horses, and Papá. I frowned at the stars. I hadn't thought of Papá in months, not since the day at the paddocks when Geraldo had negotiated—no, demanded—that I ride using a normal saddle. Now, I couldn't shake him from my mind. I sat up and looked at my husband sleeping next to me in the featherbed that was set up for us each night when we camped. No bride had ever traveled in such comfort, though I insisted on sleeping in the open air rather than in a wagon. A screen surrounded our bed to give us privacy, but I could hear the early morning grunts and grumbles of our men.

I felt uneasy. Something was wrong at home. With Papá. Oratoria and Papá. Papá and Oratoria. I shook Geraldo awake. "How close are we to home?"

"Today." He smiled, drawing me down next to him. "I knew if I told you yesterday, you'd never sleep."

I kissed his grizzled cheek, and sat up, my knees folded under me. "Something is . . . I don't know how to explain it. I've never felt this before." I pressed my fingertips into the area below my breastbone and remembered Alma explaining about her stomach quiver.

Geraldo sat up, his smile gone. "Are you ill?"

"I feel . . . strange. We need to get home."

"Ah, the Sandoval intuition."

"Alma has the memories, not me."

He gave me a skeptical look and reached to the side of the bed for his boots, turning them upside down and pounding them against each other to shake out any critters that may have moved in during the night.

"¡Compadres!" he called to the sleeping men around us–cowboys, teamsters, cooks, hunters, and adventurers. "¡Vámonos! Let's go."

I raced ahead of the caravan, astride the mare Geraldo had bought for me in New Orleans. My father's men, on guard in the torreón and posted along the way, would spot us from miles away and alert Oratoria.

The gate stood open. No one met me in the yard.

Oratoria was not in the kitchen. I sniffed the air, hoping for the comforting smell of her cooking. A fire was lit, but nothing bubbled over it. She was not in her room. I headed for my father's room on the other side of the house. The door was open, and Oratoria sat on his bed, her back to the door. She held my father's hand.

"He waited for you," she said, without turning. "Estevan, your beautiful daughter has come home. Her cheeks bloom with health. Marriage suits her."

"Alma," he said, his voice faint.

"Papá?" I took my sister's place on the bed and squeezed his hand. It was wrapped with bandages, put there to contain weeping sores, which also covered his face and neck. "It's me, Pi— "

A soft touch on my shoulder. Oratoria. She shook her head.

"Yes, Papá," I said. He wanted Alma, which must mean he was ready to forgive her.

"Where is your Texan, my naughty girl?" A viscous sheen made his eyes milky. He could not see us, but still looked over my shoulder to my sister. "Oratoria?"

"I'm here."

He took a deep, fluid-filled breath, and turned his head to me. His expression shifted, and he said, "Pilar, you are the only Sandoval woman to reek of horse sweat." He gazed beyond me again, to Oratoria. "I'd like you to meet my new wife."

I saw the gold band on Oratoria's left hand. Papá laughed, a fevered chuckle that soon turned into gagging. She lifted a washcloth from a basin and held it to his lips. Spots of blood dotted the cloth when she took it away. "The other one thought she'd won," he said. "You Sandoval sisters . . ." He fell asleep before finishing.

Before I could ask any questions, Father Jacquard arrived. Papá awakened and the Padre performed the holy rites, anointing him with oil, and listening to his whispered confession. He held the crucifix to Papá's lips. Papá clutched the Padre's hand, his eyes wet with fear. His breathing gurgled to a halt.

I turned to Oratoria for words of comfort, but she stared past me to our father—her husband. Her lips parted and I heard her suck in air. That's all. But it was enough. I followed her stare, and jumped away from the bed. Papá's body shriveled in front of us, caved in and collapsed upon itself.

A stink filled the room, and we held handkerchiefs to our noses. Oratoria opened windows and burned sage throughout the house. She asked Father Jacquard to perform an exorcism. Without even raising his eyebrows, he set about casting holy water and reciting the sacred text.

I pulled Oratoria aside. "Exorcism? Marriage to Papá?"

Oratoria looked haggard and exhausted. She was thinner than I'd ever seen her. "There is no time. Help me with the shroud. We must burn him immediately."

I held her shoulders. "We're not burying him in the family cemetery?"

She stopped moving for an instant, and leaned into me, hugging me tightly. "Consuelo. It was Consuelo," she whispered into my ear. "She wanted to marry him, and he would have done it, too. He came to me to save him, and to save everything for his daughters. Now, help me."

Geraldo and our caravan arrived in early evening. Two men followed him into the kitchen, each carrying a hefty leather chest. They found Oratoria and I sitting in the kitchen, staring silently at our teacups. "Presents for the eldest sister," Geraldo said. "Books and herbs and seeds for the most magnificent garden Santa Fé has ever seen." He kissed me on the cheek, and did the same to Oratoria. "We followed the smoke rising from here for miles. I worried the hacienda was on fire." He waited. "We saw the smoldering ruin of a bonfire outside the compound."

"Papá is dead, Geraldo. Not five hours ago. I arrived in time to say goodbye." The two cowboys looked at each other and headed for the door. "That was his funeral pyre you saw." The men sped out of the kitchen to tell the camp about the ominous stream of smoke adding its hue to the sunset. The group had been ready to celebrate a successful crossing, but the prairie would be silent tonight.

Geraldo embraced me and Oratoria. She managed a brief smile, rose heavily and went to her desk where she flipped open the lid on a wooden chest sitting next to it. Coins and jewels sparkled inside.

"There are more in a locked room off the basement. The plunder from the golden cities of Cíbola is in our own basement." She returned to the table carrying several ledger books and parchment rolls tied with string. "These are the ledgers detailing our various business interests. These rolls are our treasure maps. In matters of capital, we are now the mistresses of our own fate. I think you might have talent in this arena, Pilar."

"Shouldn't it all go to his widow?"

Oratoria removed the golden band from her finger and dropped it into the wooden chest. She rummaged through pearls, and gleaming coins, and brought out a silver goblet. Grabbing a bottle of brandy she poured it into our teacups, and filled the goblet for Geraldo. She raised her teacup. "A marriage in name only. I remain a Sandoval virgin until the end, a virtue of choice." She drank deeply. Wiped her mouth with the back of her hand. We didn't move. "Drink," she said, startling us. We raised our vessels to her and drank.

Geraldo cleared his throat to speak. "Oratoria, you are—"

"Our strength," I said, and reached for her hand, grabbing Geraldo's at the same time. He held out his hand for hers, brown and tiny when she laid it inside his, the hand of a scholar, a sister, and the only mother I'd ever known.

A teacup of brandy for Oratoria was surprising, but her second one was astonishing. "I've had difficulty sleeping. So much work." She sat and gestured to her desk, usually well ordered, but now diaries were stacked six-deep. "I didn't want to underestimate Consuelo."

Geraldo slammed his goblet down. "Consuelo!"

Oratoria pursed her lips in my direction, my cue to explain what I knew. She poured more brandy into her cup.

"Papá was with her," I said, "in Nambé. Oratoria says Consuelo bewitched him." I cleared my throat and raised my eyebrows. Geraldo knew I hated all that witch nonsense. "He married Oratoria to escape her . . . her—"

"Her hex. Her demon's venom," Oratoria said. "The poison was already in him, rotting him from the inside out." She stared into her drink. "They've burned several witches from Nambé pueblo in their own homes. Not Consuelo. Yet." She looked at Geraldo.

Geraldo's face flushed dark and I knew it was from more than the heat of the liquor. I wondered if it was because Consuelo had interfered with my family again or because she'd tampered with witchcraft.

I stood. "Those people—those believers—will kill anyone who is intelligent, old, beautiful or different in any way. You've said so yourself. My father was un borracho espectacular. A spectacular drunk. He'd believe anything, but you . . . and you." My sister pushed the brandy away.

"One house burned to ashes in Nambé," Oratoria said, in a monotone. Her eyelids drooped with exhaustion. "But in the adobe walls they heard noises, something trying to scratch its way out. La gente broke the mud bricks and found dolls that danced about when they, too, were burned. That power, that knowledge, is ancient." She looked again at her diary-laden desk. "Many Sandovals have sought dominion over its source. It robs your soul of innocence to pursue it." All was quiet. Oratoria pushed herself up from the table. "Consuelo will never stop."

Over the next few days, Geraldo studied the ledgers, running his finger down columns of numbers. "Estevan kept good books until the last year. The Sandovals own much of the land around the plaza, and the merchants pay rent. You own ranches running sheep, and even cattle, and mines in Mexico. Let's study those maps." He unfurled them, each a detailed drawing of the hacienda, the outbuildings, and the surrounding land. Geraldo shook his head, chuckling. "The old scoundrel, there's gold and silver buried everywhere." He leaned back in his chair, and rubbed his chin. "Santa Fé needs a bank with a strong safe."

"Where do you keep your money?" I asked.

"Bank of Missouri. And buried." We laughed. He pulled me onto his lap. "You have much to learn about running a ranch and defending your land. I won't be around to protect you forever."

I pulled away from him. "Don't–"

"It won't be tonight, and most likely not tomorrow, but I'm already an old man." He pulled my hands from around his neck and kissed them. "No widow in New Mexico will be more informed, more capable of handling the changes that are about to come than you, Pilar. More Anglos arrive each day. Soon, they will take over. Their laws are different. Your English will serve you well in the days to come."

"Are you worried about Texas becoming a state?"

"It's sure to happen and Texas wants New Mexico. Will the Americans keep Texas from our doorstep, or will the Texans encourage the Americans to conquer us?" He was quiet, and then he said, "Either way, they will come and they will hammer at your door to marry you—"

I put two fingers over his lips. A flash of light cut through the darkening room, followed by a grumble of thunder. "I want you inside me during the storm," I said. Geraldo ran his hand under my skirt. I stopped its progress up my thigh. "Remember when we spoke of me dressing as a man—"

"A boy!"

"I have a few things, a pair of knickerbockers—"

Geraldo laughed. "Knickerbockers! You want me to undress you in order to dress you as a boyish dandy? You learned more than I had imagined at the Maison Carondelet."

"Perhaps I could teach you a few things," I said, and stood. Geraldo followed me to our bedroom, ever the eager student.

That winter Geraldo's prediction came true when the U.S. signed Texas into statehood.

"If we become part of Texas, Alma coming home will be no problem," I said to Oratoria.

"Now that Estevan is dead, now that he has made his peace with her, there is no reason Alma cannot return," Oratoria said. She took a breath as if to say more, but hesitated.

"Why hasn't she written?" I asked.

Oratoria stared off into space as if she were listening to a silent messenger. "Perhaps her letters are strewn across the prairie. She'll be home soon. Have patience."

In all the rush of my return, and my father's death, I'd barely thought of Monique and Stinky. I wrote to him, unsure whether they would allow a priest-in-the-making to answer. His mentor, Padre Martinez, had started the first newspaper in our area—*El crepúsculo de la libertad*. The dawn of liberty. La gente said he was a scholar. It was also rumored he had a wife and children and that he would fight to keep New Mexicans in control of their country.

Oratoria helped me set up my household at Geraldo's. But he often found me at my sister's working quietly in the kitchen, she at her desk with the Sandoval diaries, and me at the main table with the ledgers and receipts. I found I had a talent for numbers *and* for horse-trading. Geraldo's contacts in horse breeding were international so I handled his correspondence. Our business interests were so diverse I needed more space. A corner of the Sandoval library became mine.

Parts of my old life stayed the same: I rode on the night of the new moon, and came home at dawn to my childhood home where I settled into my paperwork. Later in the morning, I'd hear Geraldo and Oratoria laughing. He always spoke to her on his way to me. His spurs clinked across the patio to the library, and I'd meet him at the door.

He began the same way each time. "I missed you this morning. You rode last night?"

I nodded. He sighed. Geraldo didn't want me riding in the dark alone, but he never asked me to stop. "Then you came here," he said. I led him to a chair, and pushed him into it, snuggling onto his lap.

"Can't we live here, Geraldo? It would be so much easier."

He held me for a long time without answering, running his hand absent-mindedly along the leather pantalones I'd begun to wear when I rode or worked around the ranch.

"We could breakfast together after your rides," he said. From that day forward, Geraldo and I lived at the Sandoval hacienda.

Before the heavy snows arrived, we remodeled a section of the house to accommodate our modern tastes. Geraldo had shipped a double bathtub from the East, and now he added clay drains underneath the house to cart the wastewater away. We did the same for Alma's bath.

Oratoria didn't want her room disturbed.

I created my own treasure map for the trove of jewels in our basement, burying selected pieces underneath the new construction. Oratoria helped identify certain items based on descriptions in the diaries.

An emerald brooch, meant to be buried alongside a young daughter, but snatched by the child's father at the last minute to pay off his gambling debts. He died mysteriously the same night, clutching the brooch to his heart.

A garnet-encrusted tobacco flask had been a gift to a talented lover by a neglected Sandoval wife. Her husband discovered the two together and stabbed the young man. Out of spite, she took a different lover every day.

An opal, larger than any I'd ever seen, its fire unquenchable through the centuries, was a gift to a much-loved Sandoval wife from her satisfied husband. I attached a note to each cache of gems and coins:

Green the bud of youth: Esmeralda Sandoval, 1513, dead at age eleven.
Red the blush of passion: Josephita Sandoval, 1749, her lust overlain by revenge.
All colors whirl hot in the opaline heart of a dragon: Maximo Sandoval, 1601, loved his wife.
Emblems of love and greed and hate
These gems color the Sandoval fate.

Pilar María Sandoval, 1846

I showed the jewels and my note to Geraldo before wrapping them in velvet, and putting them in a small wooden box. "Keep the opal," he said. "It was given with love from a happy man to his wife. No taint."

"I'd never wear it. It'd get in the way of my work."

"I saw you mending fences yesterday."

I stopped my wrapping. My husband gave me a complete once over, from boots to pantalones to my blue work shirt and leather vest.

"Let me see your hands."

I held them out for him, and he traced the calluses and blisters blooming there. I pulled back, embarrassed despite my intention to go on working as I pleased.

"They say a man desires a woman's soft touch. I guess I don't have one anymore with these hands."

"Who says?"

"The diaries."

"You consult them about love? You're full of surprises, Pilar. I desire your touch no matter what vile work you do."

"And the men's clothes?"

"I suppose they're practical, but they make people uneasy. There's talk, and not just about your clothing."

"I don't care what they say about me."

"It's not only about you. Many blame Oratoria for Estevan's death. They say she murdered him."

"What!" I stood, ready to fight the town. "What about Consuelo?"

"Estevan marrying Oratoria surprised everyone. His death a week later made la gente suspicious. It upset the usual order, which is already in danger if the Americans come. They say Oratoria is now rich enough to be safe from the Anglo devils. To make matters worse, Estevan called in loans and grabbed up land when the borrowers failed to pay."

"Yet they sympathize with Papá?"

"Not sympathize. They resent all the Sandovals, but Estevan is not here. The focus has shifted."

"We'll give the land back," I said. "Extend the loans."

"It gets more complicated. Estevan sold the property. To Americans. I can find no trace of the money he received."

"Oh, no. What was he thinking?"

"He wasn't thinking. That's the problem."

"Consuelo?"

Geraldo blew out a bellyful of air, resigned to telling me more. "No one has seen her. No one in Nambé will admit they know her. They're frightened."

"You went there?" Curiosity replaced my anger. "Is it the same as Santa Fé?"

"It was as if a plague had visited them. I left money, and a draft to be drawn on a bank back east thinking she would have to go there to get it. I got this letter from an attorney yesterday."

Don Geraldo Quintana,

Sra. Consuelo Benavides has retained my services to return monies and bank draft. Sr. Estevan Sandoval saw to her welfare before his death.

Sincerely yours,
J. Peters Bleakman. Esq.

"Papá gave Consuelo the money from the sales," I said. Geraldo nodded. "Why does she want you to know?"

He shook his head slowly. "It doesn't bode well, but it's useless to point fingers at Consuelo. It's our word against hers, and she's one of the people. Perhaps she will be content and make a new life for herself. If I'd understood she could be this troublesome, I would never—"

I put my finger against his lips to stop him. "I don't begrudge you your past. Now is all that matters to me."

He inspected me again. "A young man, with your hair tucked up, nothing more than a young man on the brink of life. It will upset the people, but whatever happens in the future, you'll be safer as a pretty boy than as a beautiful woman alone."

"Geraldo, please stop."

"I have a present for you," he said. "Not jewels." He reached behind the chair for a large box. "For the most unique woman in all of Sandoval and Quintana history." Inside were gloves of soft leather. Underneath those were canvas pants with a blue stripe traveling down the leg, and a multi-hued sash to tie around my waist. On the bottom lay a finely tooled leather holster with a Colt 5-shooter inside it.

"Learn how to use it." He reached inside his boot and removed a tiny pistol. "And this. It only fires one shot, but one shot may be all you need."

I ran my finger along its silver inlays and mother-of-pearl grips, and traced the engraving of a centaur on its side. "It's beautiful. Centaurs were shape shifters. Wizards. Born of the mare-headed Demeter, they castrated her priests. They wore female dress—"

"Ah, yes," Geraldo said. "Perfect for my own little Sandoval shape shifter."

Spring came late to Santa Fé in 1846, but the first traders traveled across the trail with news that war between the States and Mexico had begun. "It's all up for grabs now," Geraldo said. "Be prepared for anything."

In the summer, we got word General Kearny and his Army of the West were coming to claim New Mexico. Americans had been visible on the streets of Santa Fé for some time, usually as the result of their trading ventures. Many New Mexicans, including Governor Armijo, had become involved in the trade. Both my father and Geraldo rode the trail often. A few men traveled with their wives, usually Indian or Mexican women, but I'd never seen an Anglo woman cross the trail. The plaza was packed with men—American, New Mexican, Spanish, and a few French. For the most part, I passed as one of them.

Everyone spoke of the crisis. Time passed. The color of the trees that graced the sides of the Sangre de Cristos had begun to change when I heard two Americans at the plaza chanting this ditty:

Oh, what a joy to fight the dons,
And wallop fat Armijo!
So clear the way to Santa Fé!
With that we all agree, O!

They chuckled, spat off to the side, and then noticed me watching them. "Yo que tú. If I were you—" one began, stopping mid-sentence to tip his hat at two señoritas walking past. The Americans moved on, and left me to my own thoughts.

The Missouri traders were all for the Americans taking over. They wanted it done peacefully so as not to disturb business along the trail. They also wanted to get rid of Armijo, and the high levy he put on each wagonload of goods. Many, including Geraldo, suspected the receipts of the tax went into Armijo's pockets. He had made himself unpopular with the locals by taking land from the public domain and giving it to his friends, many of whom were Americans involved in the Santa Fé trade.

The Vicar General, Father Juan Felipe Ortiz, warned the people the soldiers would not only steal the land from under us, but rape the women and desecrate our churches. Many closed their homes and fled to the mountains, others remained behind to fight, and sent their women to hide. The roads leading into and out of the city were packed with people who fled and others who rushed to the safety they felt the town provided. Some wondered if we shouldn't tear down the churches to prevent them from being used as barracks for the soldiers.

Armijo said he'd defend Santa Fé, but we discovered later he had liquidated his businesses. He rounded up local volunteers to form a militia, and with his squadron of Veracruz dragoons headed out of the city to meet the Army of the West. His militia had set up a stronghold at Apache Canyon. But Armijo kept on going . . . all the way to Mexico.

I stood beside Geraldo in the plaza when General Kearny and his army of more than sixteen hundred men entered Santa Fé in August 1846. Hundreds of supply wagons, more than I thought possible, followed the army–1500 oxen, 3600 mules, and 450 horses pulled them. A caravan of eighty merchant wagons traveled with them, ready to set up shop when the city changed hands.

"It's an entire country!" I said. A few men nodded their agreement.

"An invasion," Geraldo said. "A military occupation. They're placing a cannon on the hill overlooking the city."

Acting governor Juan Bautista Vigil y Alarid surrendered the city. Not a shot was fired. When the Mexican tricolor was lowered, women sobbed and soldiers cheered.

The United States had conquered its first foreign capital.

22

The First White Woman

"Let me have the damn crow feather! I'm not afraid of witches."

**ilar,** *1846*
Santa Fé:

"SOME OF YOUR priests have told you that we would ill-treat your women and brand them on the cheek, as you do your mules on the hip. It is all false," General Kearny said to the crowd of New Mexicans and foreigners filling the plaza.

"Hear, hear," the Americans cheered.

"He cuts a striking figure under the star-spangled banner," said a female voice behind me. I turned and saw an American woman, about my own age. She spoke to another woman, her servant by the style of her dress. "Our countrymen will remember this day forever."

"Mine, too," I said. She searched for who had spoken among the assembled men surrounding me. An officer standing next to her eyed my holster and stepped between us.

"Just a boy, ma'am," he said to her.

Over the next few days, Kearny worked alongside lawyers he'd brought with him to draft a set of laws to govern the American territory of New Mexico. "The code is workable," Geraldo said later. He rubbed his jaw, speaking as much to himself as to me. "But the lawyers are out for themselves."

My business and political lessons never seemed to end. Geraldo rushed to fill me with a lifetime of what he had learned. "Hire several lawyers, pay them well, and have them check each other's work. Are you listening Pilar?" Satisfied he had my attention, he continued, "Honesty is hard-won in rough country. In the short run, the clever and dishonest will run the territory of New Mexico. Make sure both sides work for you."

"Stinky said practically the same thing in his letter," I said. My friend, still in Taos, had written and asked about Kearny. "He wrote that Padre Martinez said the American government in New Mexico is like a burro that only lawyers will ride."

Geraldo shook his head and chuckled. "What else did Stinky say?"

"He asked if I'd heard from Monique, and promised to write more often. He wasn't sure if he'd stay in Taos. Oh, and he wanted me to write if anything *unusual* happened. I'm not sure what he meant."

"He means the Americans," Geraldo said. "Be careful what you say. Many are unhappy with the new laws."

"The only news is the Fort going up on the hill, and Kearny is leaving for California. Stinky must know that Bent's been appointed governor, since Bent's family is in Taos. Oh, and there's an Anglo woman here. She's the first white woman to cross the trail into Santa Fé. I saw her at the plaza."

"She isn't the first. You're too young to remember, but an Anglo couple ran a hotel here for a few years. The life was too rough for them and they left. But you should meet this new woman. She'll be at the fandango tomorrow night. Shall we attend?"

I didn't want to wear a gown to the dance. Instead, I chose a new outfit made from the whitest and softest deerskins. My pantalones had silver filigree buttons down the sides, each surrounded by an embroidered rose vine. Rosa, the dressmaker who embroidered the hides, was new to Santa Fé, but she had a good reputation, and got the best tanners to help her. The pants flared gradually outward from the knee, covering the tops of my boots, which were new, too, with red roses on the sides. A matching short vest and white silk shirt felt cool against my skin. The collar was high, and I'd rummaged through our treasure trove for a brooch of rubies set in ebony. I tied a red sash around my waist, and pulled my hair into the same fashionable knot at the nape of my neck I'd worn in New Orleans.

"My beautiful rose-red springs from newly fallen snow," Geraldo said before we set off the next night. He twirled his forefinger for me to turn around. "Your own design? What, and no pistols?"

"Do you think I'll need them?" I practiced daily and could shoot straight.

Geraldo smiled, and I knew he was teasing. He held his elbow out for me. "Off we go to meet the Americans."

The officers gave the ball in honor of the traders. They'd taken over one of the larger saloons to accommodate the crowd they expected. It was an ordinary fandango except American flags hung from the walls, and both the men and women were dressed up more than usual. The women wore silks and lace mantillas, ruffles and flounces, their necks and shoulders exposed. Two violinists and a guitar played somewhere in the crowd of New Mexicans and Americans. The usual cloud of smoke hung above them all. People nodded at Geraldo, and bowed to me. They tried not to stare at my clothing. A few viejitas who sat along the walls frowned in my direction and whispered behind their fans.

A high-pitched titter drew my attention to a group of laughing officers. "Oh, please stop, Major Swords, if I laugh any harder I may faint," said the American woman from inside the circle. I peeked through a gap at her.

"Have you noticed the women smoking?" Major Swords asked her. He bowed low and offered her a cigarrillo. "Pleese, madama, smoke eet, feel jour lungs weeth it, make thee lovely smoke around jour head, like all thee other preety señoritas." The group laughed louder.

She covered her mouth with her small, white hand, and laughed along with them. I backed away from the group, and bumped into Geraldo, who'd been standing behind me the whole time. He held me firmly.

"Excuse me, sir," he said. The music stopped at that moment, so his voice carried across the room. The Americans turned, at full attention. The viejitas peered around their fans. "I'd like to present my wife, Pilar Sandoval de Quintana." The men bowed, and a Colonel Warner introduced me to Susan Shelby Magoffin, who shook my hand. Her eyes passed quickly over my clothing. She wore blue silk, edged with lace at the sleeves and neck.

"Are you enjoying your stay in Santa Fé, Mrs. Magoffin?" I asked.

"Oh, lovely, you speak English! I've learned some Spanish, but I'm afraid it's poor. Won't you have a seat?" She patted the bench next to her. "Feel free to smoke, doña Pilar. I won't mind in the least."

"Not all New Mexican women smoke," I said, but looked directly at Major Swords.

"Oh? I didn't know. Hardly any women in the States, I mean women of a certain class don't smoke, they wouldn't think of it, especially in mixed company." She glanced at the men standing at attention above us, and shooed them away with her lace-trimmed handkerchief. "You gentlemen run along now."

Geraldo winked and walked off. La Tules Barcelo grabbed his arm, laughing loudly, and dragged him over to another group of American soldiers.

Mrs. Magoffin spread her fan, and leaned into me to whisper behind it. "Is that La Tules? Is it true what they say about her? That she deals monte in a saloon . . . where there are loose women?" Her last words were choked out.

"La Tules *owns* the saloon," I said, feeling testy. "I think you'll find New Mexican women don't have the same rules as American women, and I hope that never changes." I took a deep breath, wishing I'd never come to this ball.

"I see we've offended you. May I call you Pilar? Please call me Susan." She reached for my hand. "I'm so sorry you witnessed that little comedy of Major Swords. Criticizing the natives was rude and unfeeling of us."

I'd never been called a native before, and raised my eyebrows, but she went on, unaware. "Your ways are different from ours. Both sides need to change, especially now that you are to become an American. I do so want to be friends. Why already I can see we have much in common. I'm eighteen and married to a man twenty-seven years my senior. My parents considered me too young and inexperienced when I fell in love with my tall Kentuckian." She paused and stared wistfully across the room at a big-boned man fitting her description. "*Mi alma,* my soul." She pressed her handkerchief to her heart and sighed. "But I talk too much. Did your parents have the same objections to your marriage?"

"My father arranged my marriage. But I fell in love with Geraldo and we married last year before my sixteenth birthday."

"Why, you were even younger than me!" A group of soldiers came over, and Susan made introductions. One man, Captain Elder, stared intently at me.

"I say, señora Quintana, are you the fine horsewoman I've heard about?" He was young and fair, and had a bright-red sunburned nose.

"I love horses," Susan said before I could answer. "Shall we plan for a ride tomorrow, Pilar. Would you care to accompany us, Captain Elder?

He bowed slightly. "My pleasure. It'll give me a chance to look at the land hereabouts. No reason the lawyers should be the only ones grabbing it up." He cleared his throat. "I hear you raise some fine horses. My sisters ride astraddle, too, all ten of 'em."

"Well, I hope you two won't mind if I ride sidesaddle," Susan said.

"You may ride, or say, or do anything that pleases you," I said. "I always do."

Susan gave my clothes a quick glance again. "You were the boy who spoke English in the plaza! I knew I'd seen you before. What a surprise that was, and what a lovely boy you make." She nudged me with her elbow, giggling, and I couldn't help smiling. "Is your clothing an accommodation to riding?" Captain Elder leaned in to hear my reply.

"It started that way, but now I wear pantalones all the time. They're comfortable and practical."

"May I?" She rubbed the leather between her fingertips. "So soft. How do they get the skins so white?"

"Tanners use brains and urine," Captain Elder replied for me. "Beg your pardon, ma'am," he glanced at me, and continued, "they save it up, and soak the skins in it. It takes a lot of patience and skill to get it unblemished. I'd like to have some skins done up for my sisters, if you'd care to share the tanner's name. They'd take to the design of your outfit, too, but the town folk back home would be put out about it."

"I'd be happy to give you my seamstress' name, but I don't know the tanner she used. As you can see . . ." I pointed with my lips to the viejitas across the room, still whispering and casting hard faces my way, "the town folk aren't happy about my appearance. Anything new upsets them." He looked over his shoulder, and the old ladies dropped their fans and smiled at him. "Either that, or they're jealous Susan and I are getting this soldierly attention."

Susan sighed. "Yes, dealing with all these gentlemen *is* very trying." We laughed again, but this time a bevy of uniformed men joined us. I caught Geraldo's eye across the room, and he came right to me.

We danced together for the first time since returning from New Orleans. "You're enjoying yourself, querida?"

I nodded. "Susan and I are planning to ride tomorrow. Captain Elder may join us. He says lawyers are buying up land all around Santa Fé."

"Not always buying. The land grab has begun."

The itching started on our ride home from the ball. I ran into the house and stripped my clothing off. Huge welts ran in vertical stripes down my legs and the inside of my arms.

"Don't scratch them," Oratoria said. "A warm bath and an aloe vera salve will sooth these." She picked up my outfit and sniffed, tucking it under her arm when she left the room.

My outing with Susan was put off since I stayed in bed all the next day, my arms and legs splayed out on pillows. Even the slightest touch of fabric made me want to scratch. Oratoria made a poultice of the flowers of toloache, soaked them with tobacco leaves and rolled them in lard.

"Sit up," she said. She smoothed the ointment on the backs of my legs. "Drink this." She handed me a teacup.

I sniffed the warm brew warily. "Whiskey?"

"And the root of oshá." She was tying other roots onto my bedstead.

"What are those for?"

"Brujas. I burned your new outfit this morning."

"What?" I choked on the tea. She waited until I stopped coughing to explain.

"I found this inside one boot, under the leather cushioning the inside." She held up a single crow feather, glossy black and no longer than the spread of my thumb and forefinger. I reached for it, but she pulled her hand back.

"Did you burn my boots, too? Let me have the damn crow feather! I'm not afraid of witches." I moved toward her, naked and gleaming with lard. "I'll hold you down and rub bear grease on you, Oratoria."

For once, my sister seemed surprised. She handed the feather to me. I stuck it behind my ear, and got back in bed.

"Your heedless attitude toward what you do not understand may be your damnation, Pilar," she said. "Call me if it feels like your ear is about to fall off."

"Ha! You made a joke, Oratoria. Did you have any of this whiskey anti-witch formula?"

She didn't even smile. "I plan to visit Rosa and find out who cured the skins," she said.

The redness and swelling faded by the next day, and the itching was tolerable, so I sent a message ahead to Susan I'd be in town. Oratoria and I arrived in the carriage to find Susan had other guests. Captain Elder and señora Juliana Alarid, the oldest and richest woman in Santa Fé sat in her parlor. When visiting, doña Juliana always brought a servant who sat at her feet. The captain bowed to Oratoria and Susan shook her hand. Señora Alarid nodded, but did not smile, or at least I didn't notice her wrinkles move.

I explained about my rash. "Oratoria thinks it might be something used to treat the hides, so we're going to visit the dressmaker."

"Perhaps we could come along," Susan said. "Captain Elder wants to meet her, and I could use a little exercise and fresh air. Would you care to join us, doña Juliana?"

"Is this Rosa you will visit?" doña Juliana asked. "An excellent dress-maker, and always pleasant. I am sure her work is not the cause of your ailment. Let me see."

"It's almost gone," I said. "Oratoria made me drink a tea of oshá."

"You suspect mal de ojo?" Doña Juliana leaned on her cane and glared at Oratoria. "The evil eye did not come from Rosa. She is a good woman." Susan and Captain Elder glanced at each other, but said nothing.

"We shall see," Oratoria said.

Rosa met us at the door of her two-room adobe, laughing as usual, and happy to have so much business at once. "Doña Pilar, doña Ora-toria, doña Juliana, welcome! I have new fabrics, new silks and even satin." She was tiny and plump and usually barefoot. Rosa knew her craft and bargained hard with the traders who brought her supplies from the East.

Susan and doña Juliana scrutinized the merchandise, while Cap-tain Elder and I stood near the door, where a cool breeze blew. Doña Juliana's servant sat on the ground outside. Behind us, Oratoria cor-nered Rosa. I tried not to listen, but whispers draw attention to them-selves. Words and phrases floated our way: *Nambé, only the finest.* The whispering grew sibilant and fierce, and now Susan and doña Juliana also listened. More words, louder this time: *the Sandoval business, a hardworking woman, never a problem before. Consuelo.*

Oratoria's back was to us, but the color rose and faded on Rosa's face—anger, then fear, and anger again. She wrung her hands and tried to smile.

"Rosa," I called out, interrupting the flow of accusations and denials. "Your work was well-received at the American fandango, and Captain Elder here," I nodded toward him, "wants to order the same skins for his sisters." Oratoria turned, poker-faced, her hands folded across her stomach. She said nothing.

Rosa pulled her lips wide in a semblance of a smile. "Of course, Captain Elder. The tanner who prepared those white skins . . . is not here." She glanced at Oratoria. "I'll find someone else to do the work, even if I have to do it myself." She pressed her lips together. "How much time do you have?"

"I'm posted here for at least another three months." He went over to her to finish negotiations.

Oratoria rubbed satin between thumb and forefinger. "This is lovely, Pilar, but I don't suppose you'll ever wear satin again."

"No, I don't suppose I will. How about you, Susan?"

"Oh, yes. Someday, I hope. But not while we travel. We'll soon be heading for Chihuahua."

Captain Elder rejoined us. "And from Chihuahua back to Kentucky?"

"Yes, with a stop or two along the way. Perhaps New Orleans."

"I honeymooned in New Orleans," I said. Susan clapped her hands and bombarded me with questions, as new whispering broke the flow of our conversation, this time from Rosa and doña Juliana. Again I caught disjointed words and phrases: *married the father, stealing land from the people, mal de ojo. The Sandoval witches.*

Rosa may have been angry, but she accepted the silver Oratoria gave her for several bolts of muslin and calico, and she was happy to receive a deposit from Captain Elder for the skins he ordered. I looked back at Rosa as we left the shop. My good-natured dressmaker spat in our direction.

Captain Elder saw us to Susan's lodging, and took his leave, as did Susan. We offered doña Juliana a ride to her home. "I prefer to walk," she said. Doña Juliana planted her cane firmly in the ground, and scowled first at Oratoria and then at me.

"I will not waste my breath with this one," she said, inclining her head toward my sister, "but you have plain horse sense, Pilar, even if you do not always show it with the clothes you wear, and your incessant riding of horses. At night! Under the moon!" Oratoria moved restlessly beside me. I knew she was giving me an I-told-you-so face. "You think no one knows? Everyone knows. Your dealings with the American lawyers are well known, as well."

"We work with—"

Doña Juliana went on as if I had not spoken. "The old families must set an example. You think what we have cannot be taken away? The people have risen against the rich before. You think witches are only amongst the poor?" She swayed with the vehemence of her words. Her servant, crouched at her feet, wrapped his hands around her cane to steady it. She ignored him.

She spoke to Oratoria. "If evil is afoot, la gente will seek those who have gained the most. Do not make accusations you cannot prove. Do not use the word bruja carelessly." Doña Juliana walked away, her servant scuttling ahead to clear the path of stones and droppings.

"What did you say to Rosa?" I asked.

"I told her that not only would she lose our business, but the business of many others, if she continued to employ the services of Consuelo Benavides."

"Consuelo! Ah, yes, I understand now. She did the tanning." I smiled. "You must admit, she has a talent."

"Rosa didn't believe me about the crow feather. She thinks Consuelo is a poor, hardworking woman, the same as herself. She didn't know about Geraldo and Consuelo. She finds it hard to believe he would leave Consuelo, in the full bloom of womanhood, for a skinny child like you, unless spells and charms were used."

I laughed. "She thinks I bewitched him?"

Oratoria didn't laugh, her silence my answer.

Susan left Santa Fé in early October, sending a short farewell note apologizing for the American soldiers. Whiskey shops had sprung up overnight and the soldiers partied nonstop. They blew their trumpets drunkenly around the plaza, and practiced Indian war whoops at all hours of the day and night. Geraldo begged me to stay close to home, and Oratoria promised to follow me everywhere. I could take care of myself, but I wouldn't risk endangering my sister. After that day at Rosa's, Susan and I never managed to get together again. Her husband became ill, and then a bad cold settled in Geraldo's chest.

The husband is the whole world to women, she wrote, *and I will follow mine to the ends of the earth.* She was even more romantic than Alma, but those lines repeated in my brain as I brought a hot water bottle to my husband in his sick bed. Shadows and bags hung under his eyes as if he'd gone without sleep for days. He stared at his folded hands, preoccupied. His hair, completely white now, fell forward, but I could see his frown.

I wrapped the hot water bottle in a blanket and slipped it under the bedcovers near his feet. "This is going to feel good," I said.

"Pilar." He held out his hand for mine. A lightning strike of heat traveled through our flesh. It was all I could do not to jump on Geraldo and bear hug him. He used to encourage me to do this, but I'd felt him wince since he'd been ill. He tried not to show it, but it was there. I sat next to him and pushed his hair away from his eyes. Geraldo's frown softened. His love for me melted away whatever had made him sad before.

He kissed my fingertips. "I'll be well soon."

I closed the space between us and kissed him. He turned his head aside, and coughed.

"I want to be sick with you," I said.

"You have never had a sick day in your life. You are as strong as a horse." He coughed again. "Which reminds me, tonight is a full moon. Promise me you will stay home. Please do not ride tonight." He'd never asked this of me before.

I stayed home, but I didn't stay inside. The full moon in October, the witches' moon Oratoria reminded me, was too bright. A pallet laid on the ground outside the kitchen door gave me unwelcome comfort, and a different physical sensation from riding a pounding horse. In the moonlight, I gave myself to the horse, to its rhythms, felt its heartbeat. Its breath became mine.

But on the ground, I felt the rumble of an approaching coach before I heard it. I figured travelers on this cold night—the snows were late but the smell of it hung in the air—would pass us by.

The sound grew louder as it came closer to our compound. I sat up, and was about to call Geraldo when Oratoria appeared at the door, her rebozo pulled tightly around her, her hair loose from its braid. My husband was right behind her holding a shotgun.

Oratoria said, "She will be hungry."

"She?" I said. Oratoria didn't answer, but busied herself in the kitchen. The bell outside the gate rang twice, and Pedro scurried over to it.

"We'll soon find out what Oratoria already knows," Geraldo said.

"¿Quién es?" Pedro called out.

"Padre Lopez," answered a deep, yet unmistakable voice.

"Stinky!" I yelled. He wore the long black robes of a full-fledged priest. I gave him a hug, or tried to; he was taller than me by a foot, and wider by at least three times that. "Are you really a priest?" I peeked around him at the coach, and saw movement inside. "Is someone with you?"

The door opened, and out stepped Monique.

23

Sons and Lovers

"If Bill died, I wouldn't remarry. I'd go home. To Santa Fé"

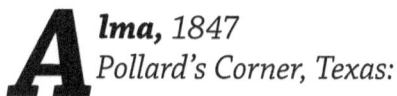**lma,** *1847*
Pollard's Corner, Texas:

MY WORK WITH Shug began easily enough early in 1847: influenza, sprains and broken bones, along with the usual childhood illnesses: measles, chicken pox and the occasional mumps. Superstition and hazard surrounded births. Unlike some doctors in Texas, Shug ministered to the slaves, and they called him in for difficult deliveries. Often, the families of the laboring mother would place an axe beneath her bed to "cut the pain." Also, unlike many doctors, he insisted on absolute order and cleanliness surrounding a birth.

Those were heady days, the rush of time unfelt, marked by the steady growth of my son. By the age of two, he was clearly going to be big, and like his father, he knew no fear. Willy's blond hair darkened and his fair skin took on color well. Overall, except for his brown eyes, he resembled his father, a father he hadn't seen in over a year.

My apprenticeship to Shug meant so much to me. Without it I would not have had enough to occupy my mind, and my bitterness toward Bill would have darkened further. Shug showed me a way out of myself. Not since the early days of my courtship with Bill had I awakened eager for a new day. Work, friendship and conversation, the care of my child: in such ways did more time pass away.

We walked home together when Shug nooned with us. Willy would run on fat little legs, and fling himself at Shug, who would sweep him up and carry him into the house on his shoulders, the ride slow and bumpy because of Shug's limp. On one such day, we returned to an empty yard and a quiet house: Bertha had come to visit. Eva had walked into town earlier to pick up the mail, so Bertha made herself comfortable. Children were to be seen and not heard, in her opinion, and since he'd turned two Willy had not stopped talking. He'd been banished to the nursery, but he heard us arrive.

He screamed, "Shug! I want Shug!"

I went to the foot of the stairs and called, "Bring him down, Pinkie."

"You're spoiling him, dear," was Bertha's opening salvo, "it's never too early to teach a child manners. How nice to see you, Shug. You never come around unless it's to treat the niggers."

"Well, Bertha Mae, your good health puts the rest of Pollard's Corner to shame. Nothing to stop you from coming into town now and then to visit." He kissed her on the cheek.

Pinkie came in carrying Willy on her hip. He squirmed out of her arms and ran to Shug, who sat and pulled him onto his lap. I knelt next to Shug's chair. "Don't I get a hug and a kiss?" Willy leaned into my arms, squeezing my neck and burrowing his nose into my cheek by way of a kiss.

"What a happy family portrait the three of you make," Bertha said. She glared at me. "If my only living son dies at war, you can go on with your life as if he never existed."

"That's outrageous!" Shug said.

"Oh, is it? The whole town is talking about you trying to take my son's place!"

"Is this why you're here today? To tell me the latest gossip?"

She gripped the arms of her chair, then stood, gathering stature with her fury. "Bill's missing. Near Veracruz. One of Hay's men came out our way. Looking for you." Her disgust was evident in the crisp way she collected her things. She stopped at the open door, her back to us, and stared at the passersby as she pulled on her gloves.

I handed Willy to Shug. I knew she wasn't finished. "I'll walk you to your buggy."

Bertha said nothing until seated in her carriage. Her eyes bored into me from her aerie, as if she were a mother eagle, sharp-eyed and hunting without mercy, and I her meek prey. "Would you marry him if Bill didn't come back?"

"I expect Bill to come back. I wrote him that I was working with Shug." She waited for me to ask for the information. "What did the ranger say?"

"Bill's in a special force doing very dangerous work. The Mexes call them Los Diablos Tejanos," she said in her *that's my boy* voice, "I guess you know what it means."

"The Texan devils." An involuntary shiver ran through me. Hays' rangers were gaining notoriety for their fierce fighting and lack of military discipline; his *irregulars* carried out an independent war of sabotage and harassment. The Rangers were well mounted, and had an ample assortment of weapons, while many Mexicans were ill-equipped peasants from isolated villages trying to protect their women and children. I was sorry to hear Bill was a part of it.

"Is that all?" I asked, weary of the whole exchange.

"You and Shug are close, it's plain to see. Willy already thinks of him as his father." She barely suppressed a smile, almost a leer, reminding me of Poppa Pollard when he'd been drinking.

"I'm a married woman, Bertha. I've not forgotten that."

"You're talking duty, not love. I'm not sure duty is enough for Bill."

"You mean like it's been for Poppa?" My aim was sure. She recoiled with the impact. Satisfied, I took a deep breath, willing myself to speak calmly: "If Bill died, I wouldn't remarry. I'd go home. To Santa Fé."

Her skin turned florid, except around the lips, which had lost color. "It'll be a cold day in hell before I let you take away *my* grandson!" With that, she snapped the reins, and took off down the main road. Her exit caused quite a commotion, stirred up the dust and made lackadaisical walkers leap out of the way.

Shug handed Willy over to Pinkie when I came back inside. "I'll come up and say goodbye before I leave, Willy-boy," he told him. "Now you be good while I talk to your mama." We were quiet for a moment, each lost in our own thoughts. "We need to talk about this," Shug said. "I think Bertha's exaggerating, but perhaps we shouldn't—"

"We work together. You think I care what these people think?" Like Bertha, my fury did not require an answer. "I don't want to stop. I'm learning so much!"

His expression softened. "Is that all it is to you?"

"Of course not. You're my best friend. Willy adores you, and I . . . I . . ." *Love you,* was what sprung to my mind, but I wouldn't allow my lips to say it. I sank into a chair, my head bowed in shame.

He said it for me. "I love you, Alma. More with each passing day." He came and knelt beside me. "Look at me, please." He cupped my chin and kissed me.

Not the kiss of a stranger, nor that of first love, but a kiss full of the comforts of friendship and shared ideals. Not the kiss of a lover, but that's what my lips craved. Our kiss grew deeper. My hand rose of its own accord to pull him to me, his tongue sought mine, and I was lost. Craven and lost amongst the leering faces of the Sandoval wretches.

A jostling at the door. Shug sprang back from me with all the lithe-ness of the guilty, a mischievous smile covering his discomfort, as if he were a cherub discovered spying on bathing nymphs. I remained sitting, in the grip of my desires. I didn't want Bertha to be right, and worse, I didn't want to feel any sympathy for Polly and Bill's weakness.

Eva walked in holding several packages. "Well, don't just stand there, Shug Smart. Lend a hand to an old lady." Shug limped over to her, and took the parcels without a word.

"I saw Bertha hightailing it out of town. What do you suppose got into her?"

I told her what Bertha had said, and asked if she'd heard gossip about Shug and me.

"Some," she said. "Folks always ready to think the worst." She examined me and Shug as if she'd just met us. "Wouldn't hurt to slow down. Stick to the birthings and such. At least till Bill gets home. Time's on your side."

Shug and I let time ride over us. Spring transformed into fall by the turning of a leaf. My help was limited to births, so we saw less of each other, but when we worked together the air filled with more than the central event. Each gesture, look and word was fraught with deeper meaning. He still came for supper occasionally, but always under Eva's watchful eye. Bertha visited, but she had little to say to me, and focused all her attention on Willy.

We didn't hear from Bill again, although rangers from his *special* battalion came through with various tales, each more heroic than the last: one said Bill had recovered from cholera, another that he'd been captured and tortured but managed to escape, and yet another that he'd been wounded, recovered and reassigned. I tried to think of the old Bill, the one from our Santa Fé days. The horror stories of ranger atrocities against the citizens of Mexico continued to filter through. Pollard's Corner took them in stride, were proud of their boys. I wished with my whole being Bill was not a part of it.

Late in 1847, I got a message from Inesita. I went to her home on the same day. A faded version of the woman I had met a few months earlier opened the door.

"Inesita! Are you ill?" I felt her forehead, which was cool to the touch. She attempted a smile, this time leading me into the parlor. She'd covered all the mirrors with black cloth. "It's my son, Henry. He's dead. Captured. Killed." Her expression revealed no anger, only bottomless sadness.

He had joined in the fighting on the side of Mexico. The Mexican government knew of the prejudice against immigrants recently arrived in America, and warned them the United States didn't just want land, they intended to destroy Catholicism. John Riley, a deserter from the Fifth United States Infantry, organized American deserters and other foreigners to form the San Patricio Battalion. Henry was an ideal candidate, speaking Spanish and English fluently, and full of hatred for Texas. American forces approached Mexico City, and the San Patricios fought from a fort and convent at Churubusco where they ran out of ammunition. They were captured, tried as deserters, and sentenced to be hanged.

"They let Henry write a letter before he died." She laid her hand on mine. "He saw your husband there. Bill Pollard spoke up for him."

"Bill! Are you sure? I haven't heard from him since the end of last year." I wanted to ask more, but she squeezed my hand, her sadness deepening.

"He was there, Alma. He's known Henry his whole life. My son said he didn't recognize him at first. Bill was ill, his arm in bandages. He saw Henry, and dragged himself out of his sickbed to explain about him, how young he is. Was. About the beatings." She stared at our hands, still resting on the table together.

"Bill did that?" I was so pleased, so proud of him. "What happened? They wouldn't listen?"

"Oh, yes. They listened. They pardoned several men, but Henry asked to be hanged." I gasped, but she continued. "They sent along his letter. On the bottom, someone has written a note." She removed a folded letter from her pocket, shuffled the pages, and handed it to me, pointing to the last passage:

Dear Mrs. Beider,

Your son died quick. I do not think he suffered. May his soul rest in peace. Bill Pollard was not so lucky and died of the gangrene. He was a good ranger: fearless, a true shot, and loyal friend. Appreciate you letting his Mrs. know.

Yours,
Abe Stuart

I read those six short lines over and over. The facts would not penetrate. After hearing so many stories of Bill's near-escapes in a dreadful war, I felt sure we'd soon hear he had escaped death again.

A decisive victory in the war occurred when Americans occupied Mexico City, but it wasn't until the following year, in 1848, that they signed the Treaty of Guadalupe Hidalgo, ending the Mexican War. The United States got all the land they wanted, including New Mexico.

We got official notification Bill had died.

My grief had taken place long ago when I buried my illusions of Bill, my love overwhelmed by disappointment. Our time together was brief, and dominated by others: my father's plans for me, his parents' demands on him, history's urgent need for adventurous youth, and Bill's own headlong rush to glory. He didn't deserve to die, but he chose a path where killing would be his primary objective.

I put on my bereavement each day with the widow's weeds tradition required, but my heart did not match those solemn colors. Life was all around me, in Willy's astounding growth, and in my work with Shug.

In my growing love and respect for Shug.

24

The Prodigal Daughter

"She doesn't want any men."

**ilar,** *1846*
Santa Fé:

STINKY MOVED ASIDE, the door to the carriage opened, and Monique stepped down.

Nothing else existed, no sound, no person, not the slightest breeze. I felt light, without body. She held her arms wide: I was inside them, with no memory of having taken a step.

"Monique," was all I could say. She hugged me and began to cry. "Don't. You're here, we're together again."

She kissed me on both cheeks and on the lips. Stinky and Geraldo watched us, grinning shyly. Geraldo still held the shotgun.

"Don Geraldo," Monique said, her voice pitched lower than I remembered. "I come in peace."

"Welcome home." He kissed her on the cheek, and turned to Stinky. "Should I kneel and kiss your ring, Padre, or shake your hand, or pound your back like a compadre?"

"Kiss his ring? That'll be the day!" I said. "Let's go inside and see what Oratoria is up to."

Monique tried to hug my sister. "I've dreamt of you, and this kitchen, almost as much as I've dreamt of Pilar. It's home to me."

Oratoria waved a dishcloth at her. "Go on now. Breakfast will be waiting." She focused on cooking. I shrugged, and led Monique to Alma's room.

"It's beautiful," Monique said. The room was lit from the glow of the fireplace. Oratoria had seen to everything.

"Look at this," I said, showing her the bath. "You can heat the water right here, and it goes out in special drains under the house and waters the pasture. I had the swans painted special on the tub. Do you think Alma will like it?"

"She'll love this room. Who wouldn't?"

"Oratoria!" we said in unison, laughing.

She still held my hand. "Is Alma happy in Texas?"

"We haven't heard from her. Not one letter has made it through, but Oratoria says she's well, and will come back to Santa Fé."

Monique pursed her lips. "Yes, we all come back."

"No word from Alma. No word from you. Where have you been?"

"To Europe and beyond. I've even been to India," she said. She smiled, but her eyes did not. "My heart has always been here, Pilar. In Santa Fé. You must know that."

A knock at the door. "Come in," Monique said, in a soft, yet commanding way. Pedro entered carrying her trunk, followed by two helpers hoisting wooden boxes. "Set them over there. ¿Cómo estás, Pedro? ¿Y su familia?"

His smile revealed a new gold tooth. "Muy bien, señorita, gracias a Dios." He turned to his companions. "Let's go, watch your feet."

We stood hand-in-hand. Monique sniffed the air. The room smelled of cedar, the outdoors and rough men. "I'll open a window," I said.

She held my hand tighter. "No, I like it. Well, maybe not so much Pedro and his men." She raised my hand to her cheek. "Your hand is more calloused than I remember." Ashamed, I tried to pull away. She looked at my clothes, and I suddenly felt itchy and uncomfortable. She let me go, and ran a fingertip along my shoulder and down my arm. "In the entire world, there is no one like you, Pilar. You've become what you were meant to be, and I've become ... well, probably the same thing for a half-breed, but at a higher level." She laughed, and then her voice dropped, "Don't you dare feel sorry for me." She opened her trunks. "If you were the same as other women, I'd show off my dresses, and we'd giggle and you'd beg to borrow some of them. But that's not going to happen, is it?" She sat on the bed, and patted the mattress for me to join her.

"They're fine for you." I sat next to her.

She pulled the pins from her hair. "I want my hair the same as yours–loose." It fell in locks to her shoulders, each curling in a heavy question mark. I lifted one and twirled the curl around my finger. I'd forgotten how rich and exotic her café con leche skin appeared with blond hair. "Tell me about being married," she said.

"I work the horses, breaking them, breeding and trading. I clean and repair their equipment. I've mended fences. I'll do anything if it's outdoors, but I also keep the books on Sandoval businesses around the plaza, collect rents and such. Geraldo wants me to understand every-thing. He doesn't want me to be a helpless widow." I frowned, thinking of Geraldo's endless planning for his death.

"You love him," Monique said, not a question. She removed her jewelry, tossing it into the middle of the bed.

"With all my heart. He's my best friend since you went away."

"But, no children?"

"He's afraid for me. He lost three wives to childbirth. When I have more time, we'll have children, but for now we use sea sponges we found in New Orleans and he has these sheaths, and there are alternatives to—"

"I'm familiar with the alternatives *and* the preventatives. But, you *like* what you do with him?"

I nodded. "Are you going to help your father at the mission? Have you spoken to him yet?"

She bit her bottom lip. "No and no. I have some ideas for a busi-ness, and money to start it, but I still haven't figured out how to tell him. That's why I came here first." Monique opened a trunk and rummaged among the ruffles there, removing a simple blouse and skirt. She stood in front of me, looking down at my upturned face. Her light brown eyes had flecks of gold in them. She took off a tailored jacket, the blouse under it, and turned her back on me. "Unlace, please. I can't wait to get out of this corset."

Her bare arms on hips reflected creamy curve upon creamy curve in a compact frame, much the same as the portrait of the naked woman at the Carondelet. Even her elbows were delicately dimpled with perfectly etched spheres. She threw the corset aside and pulled off the camisole under it. Angry creases from the corset streaked her back and waist.

"Scratch my back, Pilar," she said, and I did. "Oh, it feels *sooo* good." She turned again and I was face-to-face with her rosy pink nipples. Festive and lush, I understood for the first time why artists paint them. I caught my breath over the realization, but I wasn't embarrassed. Not in the least, and neither was Monique. "They've grown since our swimming days," she said. She slipped a fresh camisole on, and a loose blouse over it. "Do you still swim?"

"Not since, hmm, not since—"

"Oh," she said on a down note, but finished on an up note, "I never think about it. Never." She stepped into her skirt. "These shoes aren't right. I'll get some moccasins from Mother when I see her." Her voice trailed off, and she lapsed into thought again. "You went to New Orleans searching for me?"

"We honeymooned there. We had a daguerreotype made. We shopped and bought herbs, and scent, art, and horses." I pointed to an oil painting of a turbaned Negro woman dressed in a hodgepodge of colorful fabric. "We met the Mother Superior, and Madame Valery, and—"

"Ha! Geraldo took you to the Carondelet?" She laughed. "Well, you know what a brothel is then, don't you?"

"That's the business you're thinking about, isn't it?" I rushed on, not waiting for a reply. "You don't have to do that work anymore. You can live here with me and Geraldo and Oratoria and Alma, when she comes back."

"I plan to deal monte, and have a few girls around. I wouldn't have to do the "work." That's my—"

I stood. "What if they wanted you?"

"It's what I know."

183

"But you don't like it. Why do it? Don't do anything you don't enjoy." Monique blinked, disbelieving. I was the same. She wasn't. "What about your father?"

"He has no problem with gambling, but he'll want me at home, or married off—"

"You always wanted to marry." This seemed a good solution, and so easy. Monique always dreamed of us living near each other. I'd give her the land.

"And *you* never wanted to marry." She laughed, weak in the knees, collapsing on the bed. "Look at us now. Did Celeste tell you about Hector? Well, he lasted less than a year. I moved on. To another man, and then another, yet another, and even to a married couple, a wealthy middle-aged English couple. *That* experience was enlightening. And comforting. At least with the wife." She laughed again, but seemed miserable. "She brought me to joy. I think you know what I mean, and that's why I'll never marry." She stood, arms crossed defiantly. "We've never kept secrets."

"I don't care what you've done," I said. "I saw the women at the Carondelet. They laughed a lot, but they didn't seem happy." Monique bit her bottom lip. "I have an idea."

"Maybe that's what I counted on in coming here." She sat next to me. "Tell me."

"On my first ride with Geraldo, he told me my father had offered me as a replacement bride for Alma. He promised he would never expect me to be anything other than what I am. I couldn't believe my good luck. In New Orleans, I wondered what would happen to all the girls at the Carondelet. Geraldo said some would marry, that many a founding family counted a former harlot among its matriarchs. He said it happened on every frontier."

Monique raised her eyebrows. "Santa Fé is a frontier! Two girls will be here soon."

"Would they be willing to leave the business for marriage?"

"Most will. There's always a stubborn one in the group."

"I know the type well," I said.

She tried to laugh, but stopped when I didn't join her. "They'd jump at the chance to change their lives." She tapped her chin. "A hotel.

Plenty of travelers on the trail would pay a premium for a well-kept, fashionable boardinghouse with . . . maids."

"Your father might go along with it. You'd be helping wayward girls. It's missionary work."

"Yes, a respectable boardinghouse for tired travelers, explorers and merchants. A place to rest their weary backs." She crossed her palms over my left breast. "I see my future in your eyes, Pilar, and in your heart."

"In all our hearts. Geraldo will help you."

"Yes. Your husband. I'll have to get used to saying those words, but it seems strange."

"But, we're not girls anymore, and . . . and someday you'll find love. I know you will."

"You almost make me believe it, too." She kissed me on both cheeks again, and on the lips, barely touching. She stayed there for a heartbeat, and stole my breath away.

The next day was cold and clear, with snow on the ground and a bright sun overhead—a perfect New Mexican winter's day for a ride alongside old friends. The crunch of horse hooves on snow punctuated the icy stillness around us, and frosty little clouds accented our laughter. At midday, a wind blew down the Sangre de Cristos, and we headed back, hunching our shoulders and turning our collars up. By 3:00 p.m. it was getting dark. We each retired to our rooms for a short rest before supper.

Geraldo read by candlelight in our bed. Without my asking, he set his book aside to help me take off my boots. I flopped down in a chair and held my leg out, and he straddled it backwards, holding the boot tight. "Pull," he said. He dropped the boot and straddled my other leg. This time I placed my foot against his rear and kneaded his butt with my toes. That made him turn. I flicked my eyebrows up-and-down suggestively. He yanked the boot off and before he had finished turning toward me, I was in his arms, kissing him with all my might and tugging at his belt.

I walked him backwards until he fell onto the bed, his legs hanging over the side. He let me undress him. I dropped my pants and mounted him, one leg still on the floor and a knee on the bed. He stroked me in rhythm to my movements until my breath came in gasps and my standing leg quivered. He watched me the whole time, patient until he saw I couldn't wait. He rolled me on my back, pushed into me, bucking me harder than the most stubborn horse, pounding me, riding me into the wilderness.

"You had a good ride, querida?" Geraldo said, his voice muffled because his mouth was smashed into the bed where he'd collapsed afterward. "Today, I mean. With the Padre and Monique?"

"A good ride," I said. "It turned cold."

He rolled onto his back. "And you needed warming up, my lusty one. Now, tell me about—" He began to cough and sat up. I poured him a cup of water, and wrapped a blanket around him.

"I'll make you some tea," I said, and reached for my pants.

"No, I'm fine." He grabbed my hand. "I'll sit in the chair by the fire." He pulled me onto his lap. "We'll wrap the blanket around us. I want to hear about Monique and the Padre."

"Stinky is the same, better, more sure of himself. As much as I hate to bow and cross myself around him, I have to admit the priesthood suits him. But Monique has changed."

"She is very beautiful," he said.

"She is, isn't she?" I checked him for signs of desire. His gaze was soft and calm. "She doesn't want any men," I said.

"She's done with all that?"

"It was work for her." I laid my head on his shoulder. "An English couple hired her. Monique was for both of them."

"With enough money you can buy anything." We were quiet for a bit. "Did they treat her well?"

"I think so. She was fond of the wife."

"Monique was candid with you."

"She says she'll never marry, Geraldo. That makes me so sad. How can she live without love?"

He kissed my forehead. "She has love, querida. She has you."

25

At the Plaza

*"A father dies, a husband, too, and the widows,
sisters all, dance under the witches' moon."*

Oratoria, *1846-48*
Santa Fé:

HER MOONLIT RETURN was inevitable, and she dressed for the occasion. Monique's traveling suit was made of an alien bluish-purple silk, so luminescent it caught the moonbeams and radiated their light out at us. This was the color of dreams. Her hair was blonder than when she left Santa Fé, piled high on her head, with wispy strands curling around her forehead and cheeks. She embraced Pilar and kissed her on the mouth. I touched my lips, and went into the kitchen.

"Welcome home," I heard Geraldo say. I'm sure he kissed her on the cheek. Stinky mumbled something indistinct. There was laughter, the sonorous ha ha ha of the men, and a girlish titter from Pilar and Monique that I hadn't heard in years, followed by Geraldo's hacking cough, which hadn't left him.

Pilar led Stinky and Monique into the kitchen where I'd had time to recover. They surrounded me, trying to hug and kiss me, but I'd grown used to my solitary state and waved them away.

"I think Monique would be comfortable in Alma's room." I studied the two of them standing next to each other. Monique was still petite, a good inch shorter than my sister. Pilar, the ranch hand dressed in rough clothes, grown into a wealthy young woman, and Monique, the half-breed outcast, grown into a beautiful . . . what? Still an outcast, and one, I feared, Pilar would protect till her dying day. She led Monique by the hand to Alma's room.

Over breakfast the next day, Stinky had much to say: "I've been assigned to Santa Fé, arrived three days ago—"

"Three days," I said. "And no visit? What have you been doing, Sti . . . I apologize, Padre—"

"Among friends, that old name of mine sounds good, and Pilar will use it every chance she gets." He appeared pleased and wary at the same time.

"Even Pilar can change," I said.

"I meant to come here, but there's been so much to do, readying my parish, meeting la gente. With all the soldiers and wagon trains arriving, I halfway expected to see you in town, but who should I see instead? Monique Jacquard! Standing beside her coach and flirting with the soldiers."

Geraldo and I exchanged a glance.

Stinky acknowledged our thoughts with a nod. "I didn't get any details about her life on our ride out here. She got me talking about myself, and about the Americans, about their ways." His round face turned anxious. "Santa Fé has changed, and not for the better. I've heard rumors about a rebel plan to kick out the Americans."

Geraldo nodded. "Just talk. Anyone foolish enough to try would be outnumbered."

"Not if the Pueblos join in," Stinky said.

Geraldo cleared his throat, and spat into a handkerchief. "Is this a warning or an invitation?"

"Padre Martinez didn't send me, if that's what you're asking. He wants New Mexicans in charge of New Mexico, but he'll work with the

Americans. Lot of angry talk. General Kearny is leaving for California. People say it's a good time to strike." He took a deep breath. "Monique was the sign I should come here."

"You did right" Geraldo said. "I've heard the talk, too, but I doubt anything will happen."

Geraldo underestimated the people. And their shame. Many were embarrassed by our former governor's cowardice at Apache Pass. They loved New Mexico, and saw themselves swept aside by the Americans. They didn't want to give up control over the territory their families had worked for generations; they didn't want to give up without a fight. Many refused to take the oath of allegiance to the United States. They planned to hide in the church, then seize the cannon in the plaza, and attack the Governor's Palace across the street. The signal would be the church bell at midnight.

Throughout the northern villages and towns of New Mexico la gente whispered their secret, and waited for the uprising in Santa Fé to join the rebellion. Word leaked out—the gossips said La Tules went to the military. General Price rounded up many of our leading citizens on December 21.

"They've got don Geraldo!" Stinky said, breathless and red in the face from racing to our hacienda to warn us.

Geraldo hadn't joined Armijo when they defeated the Texan Santa Fé Expedition, nor had he answered the call to arms when the Americans entered Santa Fé. He'd studied the known map of North America, and he saw the future: it included all the territory in the West as part of the American nation. He'd signed the Oath of Allegiance, but they arrested him, nonetheless. He was on his way into town when a small contingent of soldiers surrounded him, and escorted him into the city. They didn't allow him to speak to his lawyers or send a message home to his wife.

"Stay here with Oratoria," Pilar told Stinky. "Our men are on guard." She fastened her holster onto her hips, removing the revolvers in turn to check they were loaded. Monique entered the room, dressed again in her traveling costume, but this time with a bonnet perched on her head. "Where do you think you're going?" Pilar asked.

"With you," Monique said. "This could take time and we may need to stay in town. I'm a bit more . . . well, let's just say, I know how to handle soldiers." She glanced at the guns peeking out from beneath Pilar's serape. "The last thing we need is a shoot out."

"Monique is right," I said, and turned to Stinky. "Father, please give them your blessing."

Stinky pressed a rosary into Monique's hands, and she knelt before him. "Bless me, Father," she said. He made the sign of the cross over her head. Pilar stared in disbelief at her friend.

"Pilar, now you," I said. She didn't move.

"Kneel," Monique said. Pilar's leather boots and holster creaked as she lowered herself to the floor. She bowed her head, but peered up at Stinky, so it seemed as if an invisible hand forced her head down.

"May God be with you and protect you," Stinky said.

Pilar stood, and helped Monique up. "Thank you, Father . . . um, Father—"

Stinky looked heavenward, impatient. "Stinky! Father Stinky. Go ahead and say it. I give you permission this once."

"The fun goes right out of it when you put it like that," she said.

Monique's coach pulled up, and we posted three men with shotguns to it. Pilar rode ahead of the team. She went straight to Geraldo's lawyers. Monique paid a visit to La Tules.

That day and the night following passed slowly. The gate to our compound was kept shut and bolted. Geraldo had already prepared the men to defend our homestead, and I joined them in the torreón several times to scan the snow-covered desert. Nothing. Another day. Mist covered the sun, making it a blurred orange in a landscape of gray. It finally gave up and sank into the horizon taking its winter veil with it. The stars appeared, but I could find no solace in their spasmodic gleam, cold and heartless above me. The snow reflected the light of the moon, bluish and ghostly. Nothing moved in the desert.

I lit no candles that night. I read no diaries. Perhaps I slept in my chair by the kitchen hearth. I awoke, my decision made.

Leaning out the kitchen door, I yelled for Pedro, "I'm going into town."

He removed his sombrero and nodded. "I will prepare the men," he said.

"The most loyal," I said, and hesitated. "Young Montoya—we send food to his mother every winter, and Ortega, the handsome. Pilar paid the dowry for his wife when her father wanted to marry her off to old Santiago. And—"

"And me, señora. I would not be alive today if it were not for the Sandovals."

It was my turn to nod, and to take the measure of this man who was always there to do my bidding. "Pedro, you are too stubborn to die, but we need you here. You are the only one, other than me, who knows where everything is. You choose the other men. Arm them well."

I gathered food and medicinal herbs from a storeroom off the kitchen, tucking it into baskets alongside cloth for bandages. Beneath each bundle, I secreted a loaded pistol. No telling what we would find at the plaza.

The double-seated buckboard was loaded, and I climbed in next to Salvador Lara, a pious man who added extra prayers to whatever penance the priest assigned. Renegade Navajos wiped out his family, except for the youngest child, a newborn. Salvador, with an arrow sticking out of his back, had laid his dead wife atop the child, and himself atop her. He held that position until the Navajos departed. The child remained so still he feared it had suffocated. When he moved his wife's body aside, the infant stared at her father, but she didn't cry. Salvador cradled his daughter in his arms on his walk to Santa Fé. One of our wagons returning from a trading trip to Mexico picked him up. I found a wet nurse for little Delfina and she had supped on our goat's milk, as well. Pilar taught her to read, and Salvador knew we guaranteed a dowry for his daughter when she was ready to be married. He would not tolerate any threats in town.

I hugged my blanket around me and said, "Go."

A crowd of women milled around in front of the jail. From the buckboard I could see Geraldo's bare head, flashing silver in the sunlight. Monique and Pilar stood next to him. "Los ricos sin vergüenza," a woman yelled at them. The rich without shame. "Putas, whores," others called. The slings of bitter, helpless women, easily ignored, until they flung the most dangerous barb. "Bruja," someone shouted, and the pack closed in, chanting bruja bruja bruja.

I stood, letting the blankets fall away.

A single female voice rose above the others, quieting the crowd:

"A father dies, a husband, too, and the widows, sisters all, dance under the witches' moon."

I knew the voice, but a name did not come to me. The other women took up the dirge, repeating it. It grew louder with each recitation.

Our men on horseback stayed close. "Is that your mother?" Salvador asked Montoya, his chin and lips pointing to the fringe of the group.

Montoya's jaw tightened. He rode forward slowly. ¡Híjole, mamá! ¿Qué haces por aquí?"

Señora Montoya ran to her son, and kissed his boot in the stirrup. "Ay, son, I thought they had arrested you, too." Many of our other men called out to their wives, sisters, and novias. The chanting slowed. Only a few stubborn voices on the far side of the group continued. "These women are waiting for their men," señora Montoya said. "The Americans have taken their sons, their husbands and brothers. They have released only don Geraldo."

She frowned at me. Her son stared at his mother, a mixture of sternness and affection in his expression. She released his boot and approached our buckboard. "Doña Oratoria," was all she managed to say before the other voice, the one like a bad dream at the edge of memory, rose again among the throng.

"Is that the other witch?" she yelled. The crowd parted to reveal an almost unrecognizable Rosa, our dressmaker. Her back curved as if she were very old, when I knew her to be my age. Consuelo stood next to her, their bodies touching. She stood straight and tall, her beauty undiminished by time and tribulation. Her demeanor was far different from the madwoman who had screamed profanities outside our gate.

Consuelo's lips moved, but Rosa spoke, "She is the daughter, the wife, the widow."

Rosa spit out each word as if it was poison, and swept her hand down her body. Her knuckles were swollen and the fingers crisscrossed stiffly over one another. "I've been this way since your last visit, doña Sandoval." A collective sigh rose from the women. A few muttered pobrecita, but no one moved.

"I gave you nothing to eat or drink. Took nothing with me, but I see you have a caretaker. One with whom you sup?" More murmurs from the crowd, a few nods, others shook their heads, all the while clutching their rebozos.

Consuelo did not look my way. She focused on Geraldo. Pilar and Monique stood on either side of him. He wrapped a protective arm around each of them. I could see La Tules peeking out from a window in the jail. Many women pointed to her. "The whore!" they said. "Fuck her and her friends."

I got off the wagon. "The Sandovals stand ready to help you, Rosa. I have medicines with me."

"I'll take nothing from the devil's hands. Witch! You think your blood is sacred, don't you?" Rosa yelled, her voice cracking. "You came from Mexico the same as the rest of us. Not from Spain. Eres una salvaje negra." She raised her club of a hand again, gesturing in my direction. "She's rich now, and I know how she got that way."

"Thief!" a woman yelled from somewhere deep in the mob. "You're in league with the Americans!" Other women shouted their agreement, and the bevy of female voices grew shrill, like the chatter of birds before a storm. The ring of women tightened around Geraldo. I could no longer see him or Pilar.

I heard the click of our men's pistols, a metallic command that silenced the women. "The Sandovals will do everything we can to help get your men," I said. "Now, stand aside. I'm taking my family home."

Montoya grabbed the reins of our lead horse, and led the wagon into the crowd, which parted grudgingly, amidst the sibilant return of whispers and prayers. I walked on the other side; Ortega behind me. We stopped at the doorstep to the jail. Monique was frightened, but defiant, and Geraldo helped her, and then me, onto the buckboard. His hand was wrapped in dirty bandages, and fresh blood was visible.

"It's nothing. An overzealous soldier." He turned to Pilar, who nodded to a few women in the crowd, unflustered. "Get in," he said.

"They corralled my horse down the street," Pilar said. "I'll be right back."

Geraldo spoke firmly. "No, Pilar. Get in the wagon." He put his hand on her shoulder.

"I'm not leaving without my horse!"

Before he could respond, a woman broke through the throng. She reached up to Ortega, still atop his horse, and shouted, "You've come for me!" The whispering lips of the spectators were silenced by this new drama. "I knew you'd come back. You would never have left me if *she* hadn't interfered." The woman glared at my sister, who blinked at her, as surprised as the rest of us.

"Who is this woman?" I asked Ortega.

"I knew her before I got married," he said. "Before doña Pilar paid the dowry for my wife."

"Before Sandoval money bought you off!" the woman said, still focused on Pilar. Her rebozo fell away and revealed the pistol in her hand. "Blood drips from your money," she said to Pilar. "Can't you see it?" She looked at the weapon in her hand. "Yes," she said, as if speaking to an unknown advisor.

I looked at Consuelo. Her lips moved without sound.

The woman lifted her tear-strewn face to Ortega. "You'll be released."

Ortega reached for his gun, prepared to defend himself, but the woman pointed the weapon at Pilar.

Geraldo whirled in front of my sister, as if to embrace her, his back to the woman. The impact of the bullet pushed him into Pilar, knocking her against the buckboard. The startled horses jerked the wagon forward. I feared the wheel would crush them, but Pilar fell into the muddy street with Geraldo, his arms wrapped tightly around her.

I jumped from the wagon, barely aware I had screamed *no,* a word that kept repeating in my ear, until I found its source. Consuelo. Fighting the grasp of our men to get to Geraldo, her repeated *no* a wail of disbelief, of misspent love and loss.

194

We pulled Geraldo off Pilar. She was bloody. I searched her body for a wound, but she fought me off and knelt over her husband, trying to kiss him back to life.

Consuelo had not found the proper target.

I heard doors open and shut, the sound of the women departing, except the one or two who surrounded Consuelo, now doubled-over with grief, a mirror image of Rosa, her pawn.

We lifted Geraldo onto the back of the wagon, and Pilar tucked a blanket around him, not admitting he was past feeling the cold. She lay next to him, cradling his head in her arm. "My love," she kept repeating, as if it were a magical incantation. Monique sat quietly by their side.

La Tules climbed into Monique's carriage and took off in the opposite direction. Several men, Americans, stood together surveying the scene. One of them approached Consuelo. He offered his arm to her, and they left. A few women guided Rosa away. La gente had scattered, but now the Americans grouped together, discussing what to do about the murderess. They wouldn't deal with accusations of brujéria, witchcraft, the way the Spanish courts had done, but they knew a jealous woman when they saw one.

The men carried Geraldo into the kitchen, and laid him on the table. Stinky rushed to his side and began last rites, but Pilar pushed him away.

"No! He belongs in our room," she said. Tears slid down her cheeks, but she did not sob, nor wail, nor berate god as women usually do. The men hesitated, shocked at her behavior toward the priest, but when Stinky nodded, they relaxed.

They set up a table in Pilar's room, laid Geraldo on it, and hurried out the door. Caring for the dead was women's work. I stayed with my sister. We removed his clothes and wiped the blood away from his back. The bullet had not exited. He held it tight inside his body, protecting my sister to the last.

Pilar ran a wet cloth through the nest of silver hair gracing Geraldo's chest. She followed the triangular outline of hair down to the point leading to his navel, and farther still to his fleshy part, resting innocently in that other nest of gray. She lifted it carefully, and cleansed there, as well. Monique waited by the door. She watched, lips parted, as if she were witnessing an unearthly secret ceremony.

Pilar wrung out the cloth in clear water and washed every part of her husband: between his toes, inside his ears, underneath his fingernails. She pressed his hand into her breast.

"Touch me again," she said. Pilar caressed his cheek, whispered in his ear, and kissed his lips. Her tears glistened on his face, almost as if he had shed them.

Stinky approached her. "May I give him the last rites?" he said, touching her lightly on the shoulder. "It's my duty, Pilar."

She looked from him to Geraldo. "Everything's been done. I've blessed him with my body a thousand times and he's done the same to me. She looked up at her old friend. "What can your priestly kiss add to that benediction?"

"Please—"

"No! No one touches him but me."

They stared at each other. Hard. "I'll show you what to do," Stinky said.

I left when they began the ancient rite of passing for Catholics. "I need coffee," I said to Monique who still stood at the door. "And perhaps something stronger."

In the kitchen, I set out cups and a bottle of brandy. "Will you do the honors?"

A corner of Monique's mouth lifted in a half-smile. "You're full of surprises, Oratoria." She filled the cups halfway and I added coffee. We stirred, each focusing on the meditative swirls.

I said, "La Tules has your carriage."

"She also has the ear of the military, as any good saloon keeper would. I gave her the carriage hoping she'd convince them to let Geraldo go. I made it easy for her to do the right thing."

"She will appreciate the smooth ride."

"Yes," Monique said. "She's had a few too many bumpy rides in her life. Her words, not mine."

"The lawyers were not helpful?"

"Pilar brought them to the jail, but La Tules had already worked her magic."

I raised my cup for a toast, but this was not a celebration and I was unable to keep the bitterness out of my voice. "To La Tules and the Americans, partners in the new New Mexico." We drank. I poured more brandy.

Monique raised her cup. "To the alchemy of whores and witches." She drank again. I did not. "Who was that dark woman?" she asked. "The one who stared at Geraldo so hard."

"Consuelo Benavides."

"She seemed to control the crippled woman."

"You saw? Consuelo wanted to marry Geraldo, but he chose my sister. She cursed Pilar and the Sandovals into future generations. She called upon demons in the netherworld to help her." I sipped my brandy. It burned its way to my stomach adding more fire to my anger and fear. "Pilar doesn't believe, but the danger is real. What matters is what la gente believe. Their fear is high because of the Americans. Add superstition and jealousy to this fear and they'll lash out. If they can't rid themselves of the Americans, they'll strike at a closer target."

"But—"

I set my cup down hard, and leaned forward. "Help me protect Pilar. We must go slow. Respect their fear. It's the same as walking around a rattlesnake. He gives us fair warning. *Today* was our warning."

"The dark one, this Consuelo, said nothing to us, but she stared at Geraldo with . . . I won't call it love, more like a consuming desire, a cancer that won't let a person sleep, or eat, or think of anything else until the object of their adoration is inside their grasp or cut out of their body. I've seen that intensity on the faces of gamblers, on pimps, on mother cats hunting to feed their young."

"And the woman who shot Geraldo? That bullet was intended for my sister. Consuelo will not stop until she has her revenge."

"You think Consuelo controlled the madwoman, too?"

"Why did she appear at that moment? Consuelo has powers we can barely imagine. She dances with the devil, sleeps with his demons and captures souls with her love philters and amulets. I know. I've heard the young girls talk."

Monique stared at me unbelieving. "People will do just about anything for love," she said, her words slurred. "Oratoria?" She hesitated. "Pilar and Geraldo . . ." Her voice trailed off and Monique appeared innocent and unsure as she had when a child.

"To love a man is not impossible," I said.

"So I've heard."

"They had a fiery passion. Geraldo lived and died as he pleased." I held my cup aloft. "No old man's phlegmy death, cared for by his youthful paramour. To Geraldo, a hero's death." We drank again.

Pilar sat all night with her husband. In the morning, a steady stream of people arrived, bearing food and their condolences: rough men from his ranch and ours; the widows and orphans he had helped over the years; the merchants; a young lieutenant from the American army; assorted lawyers; the curious; the hungry; and the professional mourners who showed up at all funerals of note. La gente could not stay away, even if they wanted to. They expressed their sorrow to Pilar and backed away. The Americans hovered near her, solicitous of her health, worried over the financial pressures bearing down on her slender shoulders.

One lawyer offered his condolences, and then launched into his real reason for coming that day. "Don Geraldo expressed an interest in buying more land." The people quieted to hear better.

Pilar's face turned hard. "He didn't mention it to me."

"Well, he probably didn't want to worry your pretty little head, but several pieces have become available."

"Available? No one wants to sell their land," Pilar said.

"Turns out it was never theirs to begin with. They don't have the right titles." The lawyer chuckled. "Folks need to learn the new ways, and speak proper English. They can't expect to come out ahead if they don't talk right."

Pilar squared her shoulders. "They have grants from the Kingdom of Spain, and from Mexico."

Another lawyer piped up. "Well, now, señora, that's the problem. Don Geraldo had the right idea. I helped him register his land with the American government. But—"

Pilar pulled me aside. "Get them out of here," she said. Tiny beads of sweat dotted her forehead, and a crease had appeared between her eyebrows. "I want them out now!" She waved her arms wildly, as if she were shooing away ducks.

The Americans shook their heads. "She's overcome with grief," one said.

"Hysterical," said another.

They had been hired by don Geraldo to protect his interests. But to la gente, it appeared as if this old family favored the American occupation. The lawyers had no reason to think they were unwelcome, but many of la gente fled, thinking Pilar meant them.

"She needs to sleep," I said. Monique slipped her arm through Pilar's, and my sister leaned into her.

With the wealthy widow's absence all the self-important people faded away, leaving only the hungry and the truly sad. The latter had the good sense to take their grief with them, and once the food was packed for the former, they gratefully left, as well.

I checked on Monique and Pilar. They lay together in Alma's room, their heads touching, their hands tightly wound together. They slept in the same position the next night, and the night after, and Pilar did not return to her old rooms. When Alma came home, she could take over Geraldo and Pilar's bedroom and bath.

We buried Geraldo in the Sandoval cemetery on Christmas morning. "He wanted to be near me," Pilar said.

Monique remained with us. Stinky visited when he could, and we celebrated the New Year, 1847, together. The snow fell, cushioning our existence. Word reached us the American soldiers were marching north to quell another rebellion.

Later, we learned a mob of Indians and New Mexicans in Taos had climbed on Governor Bent's roof and dug a hole in it to gain access to him. Inside were his New Mexican wife and her sister, Mrs. Kit Carson, along with several children and servants. Neighbors, a French Canadian and his wife, helped them by cutting through the adobe wall to allow the women and children to escape into the adjoining dwelling. The mob broke into the house, and shot Governor Bent with arrows and with his own pistols. Not yet finished, they took his scalp, stretched it on a board, and flaunted it all over the town.

Wading through deep snow, Colonel Price and 353 soldiers encircled Taos Pueblo, where the rebel forces took over a mission church. The small army overcame the much larger resistance and the snowdrifts turned red with the blood of soldiers and insurgents. They held a trial, the rebel leaders accused of treason. Many, Americans and New Mexicans alike, believed that fighting in defense of your homeland was honorable. The arguments flew back and forth: the rebels were executed.

The year played out. La gente once again nodded respectfully to us at church, accepted our gifts of medicine and food, took our cash loans, and crossed the street with dread when we approached. The people were worried about losing their land, but the talk in town was that the Sandovals would most likely end up richer. After all, we spoke English and Geraldo had not fought on the side of the rebels.

Monique opened a gambling hall, and began to stay in town more often. Pilar stopped riding, except to the family cemetery. The war with Mexico ended, and in 1848 New Mexico became a territorial outpost of the American government. Our future was now coupled with that of the United States. Yet our language and the superstitions of our people did not change.

If anything, they intensified.

26
Pestilence

"We have to go to Willy! He's in danger."

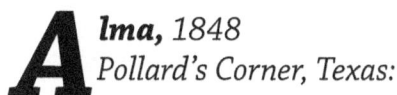

lma, *1848*
Pollard's Corner, Texas:

I REMAINED IN Texas, wearing black, writing in my diary. Soldiers and rangers returned home daily proclaiming Texan victories. The Pollards were in deep, lingering mourning. They had no son returning.

They wanted mine.

And Texas still wanted Santa Fé. Willy turned three in the spring of 1848 when Santa Fé County was established. It included all the area of New Mexico claimed by Texas. So the Texas legislature felt it was natural to ask Congress to recognize its ownership, and give it permission to organize the county.

Bertha acted triumphant. "You go back to Santa Fé now, sugah, and you'd just be going to the farther reaches of Texas," she said. "Might as well stay to home. Keep the family together." I had no immediate plans to leave Pollard's Corner, although Pilar and Oratoria remained in my dreams. In them, a happy Pilar had found love and traveled away from home. A strange dream, since Pilar loved Santa Fé, and insisted she would never leave. And my father, once a frightening and foreboding presence in my dream life, was now completely absent.

I took up the general practice of medicine at Shug's side again, and Bertha began to visit Willy more often. She always arrived at Eva's after I left in the morning, but made sure she was gone before I got home. One day in peak summer, the sun in a cloudless sky that never dried anything out, but only heated up the wet in the air, I returned home to find Willy and Pinkie gone.

Eva paced the floor, agitated to the extreme. "Bertha floated in here like the Queen of Sheba, packed him up and off she went! Said it was high time her grandson saw how the Pollard's lived. Said you wouldn't mind, that you had plenty to occupy your mind here in town." Eva's medicine and an empty glass sat on the table. She followed my eyes there. "I was feeling poorly. Otherwise, I would have gone along. As it was, I had to insist she take Pinkie."

I had been meaning to travel to their home for some time, but always found an excuse not to go. Hesitation was no longer part of my plan. Bertha would surely take over my life, and Willy's, if I didn't take immediate action. Although late in the afternoon, I hitched the horse to the carriage myself, and threw a few things into a valise for the stay overnight. At the last minute, I grabbed the black bag Shug had given me, identical to his own medical kit.

When I first saw the man, I was traveling fast on the flat lands well outside Pollard's Corner. In the distance a meandering dot crossed from one side of the road to the other. As I drew closer, he took on his human shape, walking drunkenly. He collapsed at the side of the road. I pulled up next to him, listening intently, even sniffing the air. Caution was the byword, as many strangers passed through on their way to California and the gold there.

I put the pistol Shug insisted I keep in my medical bag in the pocket of my dress, and got down from the carriage. Still on full alert, I grabbed my water bag and headed for the man. He sweated profusely, and mumbled to himself. I poured water on a cloth, and wet his lips. His hands shot up and grabbed mine. He pressed the cloth hungrily to his mouth while his eyes opened wide, revealing a lackluster blue surrounded by a sea of yellow.

He began to gag, and wrenched himself upward to heave black vomit onto the cloth he still held. *Yellow fever*, I thought, and backed away without thinking. He grabbed my hand again. "Don't leave. 'Snothing…just need to rest." He lay down, shivering, though the day was still hot as the sun slanted downward.

"I won't leave. I'm going to get you a blanket out of the carriage." No response from him. I wondered where he had come from, dressed in city fashion, like a flashy undertaker in a black suit, but with a fancy brocade vest. He stared at the darkening sky when I laid it across him. "Big wide yonder. Queens. Four beauties in a row. What a day that was!" He sighed, his breath dank, ending in a wet gurgle like a well run dry, his eyes fixed on the sky above. I pressed them closed.

I knelt next to him, unsure what to do. I couldn't lift him, but didn't feel right leaving his body exposed. The mosquitoes grew heavier as darkness fell, and I needed to act quickly. I went through his pockets, and found a letter addressed to Mr. Melvin Lee Edwards c/o the Hotel Sonora, New Orleans, Louisiana. A canceled steamboat ticket showed passage from New Orleans to Matagoras, Texas.

"What brought you to Pollard's Corner, Mr. Edwards?" I asked the night. I rolled him into the brush at the side of the road, and covered him.

The Pollard's were sitting down to supper when I arrived. "Mama!" Willy ran and leapt into my arms. "There's new kittens in the barn. I saw the last one come out. Can I keep him, Mama? Can I? *Can I?*"

"When they stop taking milk from their mother, you may have one." Willy gave me a big, wet kiss, and squirmed out of my arms to return to the table.

"Boy never saw a live thing born," Poppa Pollard said. He softened his tone, gesturing toward a chair: "L.B. made fried chicken, just the way you like." Bertha Mae kept silent, hands folded primly on her lap, her eyes unreadable behind her spectacles.

I held back saying anything about Mr. Edwards. "I'm hungry as can be." I forced cheerfulness into my voice. "I'll wash up in the kitchen."

L.B. was squeezing lemons. "Sit yo'self down, girl. You looking beat." I hugged her, and she patted me between the shoulder blades, then stood back to take a closer look. "City life doing you good. How *are* thangs?" I knew she meant Shug. She smiled big, her overlapping tooth charming me the same as always.

"Shug and I are still working together, L.B." Her eager expression prompted me to say more. "And, as you can see, I'm still wearing widow's weeds. Even beginning to like them."

"Umm-hmm. Well, thangs do take time. B.B. all for it now. You and Shug. She afraid you gonna hightail it back to New Mexico."

Pinkie walked in carrying a load of washing. "Miz Alma! Is we going back in the morning? Won't be too soon for me. Miz Bertha all bent outta shape cause Miz Polly supposed to come by, but she never show up." Since leaving the Pollard homestead, Pinkie had found her voice, and become quite a talker. "Been a widah for less than a year now, but she brought back a new man wit her." Pinkie giggled. "A fancy man she done found in New Orleans. A gambling man, I hear tell."

A shiver crisscrossed up my spine, like a rivulet of sweat running in the wrong direction. It stopped when it reached the back of my neck where it held me in its icy grip. My throat tightened, and I reached up involuntarily to massage it, grabbing the corner of the table for support with my other hand.

"New Orleans!"

L.B. was at my side immediately. "Hush up, Pinkie! Miz Alma don't wanna hear nothing bout Polly. You sit down now, Miz Alma. You actin' like you seen a ghost."

"Did she send word? Say why she wasn't coming?"

"Polly never showed up. She do that when a man involved. Came back from New Orleans wit him and some other folks she met there. Been holed up at her place ever since. Surprised you ain't heard talk of it."

Polly and I had parted ways long before she'd received word that her husband had died in the war. I'd heard she'd moved to New Orleans, but not of her return to Pollard's Corner.

"I hear tell they been partying up a storm," Pinkie put in.

L.B. shot her a sharp glance, and handed me a glass of lemonade. "Drink this up." She sat across from me, all business now. "What this be about, Miz Alma?"

I retrieved Mr. Edward's letter from my pocket, laying it on the table between us. It was a well-kept secret L.B. could read. She'd been taught by Bertha herself, although some Texans discouraged such an act.

L.B. squinted down the length of her arm. "Says here this belong ta Mr. Edwards in New Orleans."

"I found it on a dying man lying by the side of the road on the way here. He vomited blood." L.B. didn't react. "I think it's yellow fever," I whispered.

"Sounds like. Don't have ta die from it, y'know. Plenty folks get through." She thought for a moment. "Probably should head up ta Polly's place in the morning. Neighborly thing ta do. Folks'd understand if you was ta stay here, or run ta town and fetch Shug."

The next morning, the decision was made for us. A loud pounding at the front door thundered through our sleeping household before dawn. Willy, next to me, slept undisturbed. I tucked the covers around him, and crept out onto the dark landing.

Poppa Pollard was already on the stairs. He held a candle in one hand, and pulled his suspenders up on his shoulder with the other. "Hold yer horses." Before he lifted the bar locking the door he shouted, "Who's there? Friend or foe?"

A wobbly voice answered from the other side. "It be me, suh, Miz Polly's nigger. Linus my name." Poppa Pollard removed the bar to reveal a reedy Negro boy of about fifteen, his pant legs ending a good six inches above his bare feet. "Miz Polly in a bad way, suh. She asked if Miz Bertha and L.B. could come and check on her."

"I'll go," I said.

L.B. and I packed up the carriage with everything we'd need. She'd lived through many yellow fever scourges. I'd only read about them. I left instructions for Pinkie to return to town with Willie, and once there, to contact Shug regarding Polly.

Willy had not awakened when L.B. and I were ready to leave. He slept on his back, softly snoring. My kiss on the forehead ruffled his sleep. He sighed the sweet breath of the young, and turned on his side. Taking the chance he might awaken, I whispered in his ear, "Mama loves you." He slept on. I brushed the hair away from his forehead, and kissed him again. He did not move.

Nervous about leaving, I gathered my things, and moved to the door, trepidation in my footsteps. From behind me, I heard again the choking death rattle Mr. Edwards had made. Whirling around and running

205

to Willy's side, I found him unchanged. Same position. Same mellow breath. The same.

No one greeted us when we arrived. Linus had ridden in the back of our carriage, and he came around and took hold of the horse. "They took sick. The rest taking care of 'em, or run off scared," he said. He led the horse to the barn. L.B. and I entered a quiet house.

I'd never been to Polly's home, a structure far more elaborate than any other in Pollard's Corner. The central hall had a high ceiling with a crystal chandelier hanging from it, and a staircase leading up to the bedrooms. We were heading upstairs when a girlish titter stopped us.

We exchanged glances, and followed the sound to the kitchen where a bedraggled woman in a nightdress dipped her fingers into a jar of strawberry preserves. Brownish stains dotted her gown, and she smelled vile. She ignored us and stuck two fingers into her mouth. Then she looked up to the ceiling, as if listening for sounds overhead. Turning her head shyly away, as if she'd been caught stealing, she held the jar out to us.

"They're all dead," she said. Her hand shook, and she shivered. "I don't want to go back up there."

L.B. took the jar from her. "You sit right down here, Miss, and I'll fix ya up wit some coffee. We'll find ya another gown. There's bound ta be a shawl round here somewheres."

I left her in charge of the woman, and went upstairs, opening one bedroom door after another. They were empty except for two. A naked man sprawled across the floor in one, his head encircled by a black halo of vomit. I covered him with a blanket.

In the other, Polly lay in her bed, her arms stretched out alongside her. In one hand, she held her tortoiseshell brush, and in the other, a mirror. Her golden hair was loose and framed her face. Its delicate tendrils spread along the pillow, as if a vine grew from the bed intent on encapsulating her. Her eyes were open.

Except for a tiny rivulet of brown sputum trailing down the corner of her mouth, she appeared perfectly composed. Only the radiance was missing. I brushed my fingertips across her eyes to close them. They wouldn't stay completely shut, giving her a tipsy expression.

"Got to have it your way even in the end, don't you, Polly?" I pressed the lids back up. "Oh well, you were never one to shut out the world." I wiped her mouth with the corner of the sheet, and covered her face with it. Before leaving the room, I found a few nightdresses and extra blankets for the woman downstairs.

L.B. took them, nodding sadly when I whispered about Polly. I headed out to the Negro shacks. Linus wept outside one of them. "My grandma dead. T'others are nowheres to be found."

I patted him on the shoulder. "I'm sorry for your loss, but you're the only man around here now. We've got to get these people in the ground quick. We can bury your grandmother first. Can you get started on that?"

"Yes'm, I'll get right to it."

I went back to the house and found sheets to sew up shrouds. We weren't going to have time for coffins. I'd told Pinkie to head straight for Shug, so with luck he would be here in another three or four hours. After getting coffee down the woman, and settling her in the parlor, L. B. joined me in the kitchen.

"Who is she?" I asked.

"Name's Omie Beard. Say her husband upstairs. They singers on the steamboat. Friends wit Mr. Edwards who she say wuz married ta Polly. She say Polly in the family way, bout to deliver. Mr. Edwards, he on the way into town to fetch the midwife."

I corrected her. "He was heading to town to get Shug."

"Omie say no, Polly want her friend, the midwife." L.B. pursed her lips.

"I didn't examine her." It was my turn to gaze upward and listen. "Will you come with me?"

L.B. uncovered Polly. "She do look peaceful, don't she?"

We folded the blankets back farther, revealing the rise of her stomach, and the blood-soaked mattress. The baby had not made it out. I pulled her lips apart. She'd bitten her tongue during labor. Polly had not died of yellow fever, but in the agony of a difficult childbirth. She'd had time to think about her options, know she was going to die, and get ready for it.

A few household servants and field hands trailed in during the burials. It took convincing, but I persuaded Linus and a few others to ride out and bury Mr. Edwards. Exhausted, and worried that Shug hadn't arrived, I headed into town.

Shug was not at his home, and when I got to Eva's, Pinkie was there, but Willy was not. "Miz Alma, they keeping Willy ta the house. Miz Bertha say you wouldn't mind." There was no conviction in her voice. "I headed direct fa Doctah Smart, but he wasn't ta home, so I came on here." She wrung her hands and stepped from one foot to the other.

Eva sat in her rocker, knitting. "Bertha ain't happy lessen she's a thorn in someone's side. Used to be mine. Still bear the scars."

Too exhausted to feel much more than annoyance, I said, "It's not your fault, Pinkie. I'll run out and fetch him tomorrow early." Turning to Eva, I asked, "Did Shug leave a message, by chance?"

"Stopped by. Says there's a fever at the docks." She rocked back-and-forth, undisturbed by the news. "Bout time for yellow fever. Hot, wet summer and all."

"All the summers are hot and wet here," I said.

"This one's different. Cain't put my finger on it, but it was a summer like this when I took sick with the fever."

"You've had it before?" I went over and knelt at her knee. Thinner and more wrinkled than ever, all the life in her emanated from her shining eyes. "How'd you pull through?"

"Ain't no cure. Some folks just luckier than others." Seeing my disappointment, she added, "My Ma fed me chicken broth diluted with corn liquor. And not this fine drink I take today, but the good, old-fashioned kind that moves down your throat slow and thick. Always believed that's when I developed my partiality t'it." She winked.

"Speaking of which, I think I'll have a bit of your medicine tonight." I told her about Polly, and the others.

"Well, now," she said. "The old pestilence has come again. Let the battle begin." She raised her glass in salute.

208

I heard the misaligned trudge of his walk as he approached our front door while I lay in bed, trying to sleep.

"Shug," I whispered to the darkness, sitting up and throwing off the sheet. My feet touched the floor, my senses in joyful, full alert. I ran down the stairs and opened the front door, pulling him inside the house. I pressed into his arms and kissed him.

With his back against the door, Shug opened himself to me as if starved, and my kiss his sustenance. He whispered against my lips, "A short separation now-and-again may be worth it, if you promise always to welcome me home this way." He ran his hands up the sides of my thin nightdress, the material no barrier to his hardness. We'd never been this close, enveloped in the quiet and darkness, no somber widow's weeds to serve as reminder I'd been another man's wife. He pulled my hips toward him, forcing me to widen my stance to maintain my balance. Maintain my own pleasure.

"Who's there?" A soft light intruded from Eva's room.

"Shug's here," I called back, turning my head toward the faint glow, but keeping my hips stationary, unwilling to break away.

"Hold on. I'll make coffee." Whereupon she started her morning hacking and throat clearing.

We kissed again, and I stepped away from him, a sudden chill invading the bond of warmth we had created between us. "I've been up all night. And I have to go back," he said, sounding exhausted. Dawn pinked the windows and I could see his weary smile. "I'm going to need your help today. I've quarantined the wharf area."

Shug recounted his activities over the last twenty-four hours, as Eva and I made breakfast. "Five people have died, and a few others are teetering on the edge. I've had reports of isolated cases farther south, along the river. I'm not sure if they're related, but I want to avoid a traveling epidemic. And panic." In the growing light of morning, he finally showed his age. Puffy bags hung below his eyes, and the creases on either side of his mouth had deepened.

"It's probably best if Willy stays out at the Pollard's then?" It didn't feel right not to have my son with me, but I was frightened to have him so near this illness.

Shug nodded, placing a hand over mine. "We don't know what causes yellow fever. Keeping the patient comfortable and isolated seems the most we can do. I think L.B. would send for you if a problem arose, but it wouldn't hurt to send Pinkie back out there."

My stomach was jittery, my breathing shallow as I finished packing a few of Willy's favorite things: books, toys and clothes. Pinkie walked in, surprised to find so much hustle and bustle. Her lodgings were in the back of the property, and she was usually up first. She wasn't happy to be returning to the Pollard's, but kept quiet about it. Before she got in the carriage, I placed my hands on her shoulders. "If a problem arises, illness, with Willy or anyone else in that house, you come get me. I don't care what Bertha says or does, you find a way out. You hear?"

Shug and I headed for the docks, a notorious and overcrowded area where ramshackle buildings teetered on the edge of collapse.

"Alma, I didn't want to say anything over breakfast, but you need to be prepared for what lies ahead." He pressed his lips together, the muscles in his jaw visible. "The wharf is filthy to the extreme."

Outside town, in the direction of the river, was a junction of three roads: one led to Pollard's Corner, the other two to the smaller towns, upriver and downriver, that were not easily accessible to the larger boats. Though orders had been left to stop all traffic into and out of the area, the armed guard posted there waved people onward as they fled, their worldly belongings in carts, or carried on their backs. The guard was surprised at Shug's outrage. "More people died during the night, Doc. If they wasn't showing signs of the fever, I was letten 'em go. Tain't right to lock up well folk with the sick!"

"They could have the fever inside them. It doesn't show until the fourth or fifth day. *No one* is allowed to leave! *No one* is allowed to enter! Necessities should be left here. I'll send for them. Do you understand?" The man's bearing was defiant, but he nodded once.

Our destination was the series of identical row houses where the dockworkers, itinerant laborers, and their families lived. Almost every family had someone completely down or showing signs of the illness:

violent pains in the head and back, yellowing in the whites of the eyes, rapid pulse accompanied by nervous irritability, a dark coating in the middle of the tongue, the edges appearing raw. Some had a fever so high they experienced hallucinations; others had arrived at the fatal stage of black vomit.

We went from house to house bringing what little comfort we could: advising chicken broth laced with corn liquor, plenty of water, the patient restrained and kept covered, though it was hot and humid, so that he might sweat the fever out. I made mint, chamomile, elderflower, and lovage teas. All known to break fevers, now rendered useless in the onslaught of this disease. Often, we were called back to a home we had previously visited, where they had exhibited only headaches and nausea, but where now the tenants were dead or dying, seized with convulsions or vomiting the ominous black bile.

We left one dark hovel and Shug paused to take a deep breath. The sun was low, that misleading time of the day when it hangs motionless, then hurtles toward its end. Scurrying toward us, his towhead a beacon in the fading light, was Pete Beider.

"It's Mama, Dr. Smart! She's down with a fever!"

Shug's face reflected calm, but I could see his exhaustion, and his sorrow.

"It's in the town," he said.

We packed, and sped away in the buggy, but slowed as we passed the crossroads: no one was there.

Inesita lay in bed, her rosary clutched between her hands. "I go to join Henry and my little ones," she whispered to her husband.

He raised her hand and kissed it. "No, no, my Inesita, your children are here. We need you here." But her mind was made up.

The disease cut a feverish swath through the Beider family. The bakery closed when the illness seized the eldest daughter, Mary. And then Alice. And Pete. Finally, only Gustav Beider remained, his huge baker's hands lying useless in his lap.

Shug wrote letters to all the surrounding communities begging them to send their doctors. He wrote, and I wrote, until the mails stopped, and our plague-stricken community was quarantined. We tended the sick and dying almost nonstop. Every other moment, I longed for Willy, still at the Pollard's. We heard nothing from them, and I took that as a good sign. They would surely send for us if the illness spread there.

Three weeks passed in such a manner. Shug and I tended the ill, our nostrums ineffective, but the sight of us providing relief, it seemed. We survived on little sleep, often collapsing fully clothed in our beds without supper, only to be called to the next emergency in the middle of the night.

One morning, having been allowed to sleep a full six hours, I awoke with a start to a day in full light. I had time for a wash, and a welcome change of clothes, then joined Eva in the kitchen where she assured me there had been no urgent messages. It was ten o'clock in the morning, but a fine breakfast awaited me.

"Something's different. Can't put my finger on it," I said between bites of bacon. A cock crowed, answered by several others, their voices proud and distinct, as if they were breaking the quiet of dawn. Rooster's crow all day long, but their salutes are barely noticeable above the sounds of city life.

"It's the quiet," Eva said. "Town's deserted."

The general store had closed. No able-bodied men were around to unload provisions at the docks, and only uninformed boats arrived now. Scarcity became a new concern. Fear began to grow that we would have famine, as well as pestilence. Before the mails had stopped, we'd received news that one place after another had shut us out. Rumors spread that the boats arriving at our city would soon stop, thus closing yet another means of escape. Panic set in. People did not want to be trapped in a city turned charnel house.

A pit was dug on the edge of town. The silky sound of shovel in earth, and the creaking drays hauling the dead to their final resting place, were thunderous in the eerie silence of the town. The miasma blanketed Pollard's Corner, but still I heard nothing from my in-laws.

Two weeks later, Eva, Shug and I sat together solemnly eating supper. "Things lightening up?" Eva asked Shug.

He stared at her, chewing his last bite slowly. "There were fewer deaths this past week. Summer's not over yet." He swallowed hard.

"Well, hells bells, if it comes, it'll come. Celebrate the little victories, I say!" Eva poured a shot of brandy into our water glasses. We joined her in another round until it became evident that Eva was well into her cups, had probably begun celebrating in the early afternoon.

I settled her into bed, and returned to the kitchen, where Shug had begun to clear the table, humming a little tune as he did so. We reached for the same plate, crossing our thumbs.

He said aloud what I was thinking: "If there are no emergencies tomorrow, how do you feel about fetching Willy? It's too quiet around here without him."

"Oh, Shug! Yes, please! At first light?"

He drew me to him and kissed me lightly. "Anything your heart desires, Alma. What did you have planned for this evening?"

"Plans? I haven't made plans in weeks. I guess I'll wash my hair since I finally have the time." I laughed, and Shug smiled.

"Can I help?" He removed a pin from my hair. A heavy lock loosened, a weight lightened, so that now the rest of my head felt captive, wrapped in a stylish vise of my own design.

"Take them all out," I said. Each pin removed was an airy release. Tilting my head back, I shook it to loosen the hair further. Shug brushed his lips across the exposed curve of my neck, slipping one arm around my waist, the other into the tangle of my fallen hair. His lips moved up to my ear, then swept across to my lips.

"Get your soap and towels, I'll heat water," he whispered against my lips, but did not let me go. We kissed in the kitchen until I lost track of time, was unaware of space. I was drunk on kisses, dizzy with his mouth on mine.

He released me, smiling shyly. "Go on now. Get your necessaries." I still hadn't descended back to earth. He placed his hands on my waist, and turned me away from him. "Scoot! I'll finish here. You might want to put on a duster so we don't ruin your charming black dress."

My hair hung to my waist like a young girl, and I skipped up the stairs the same as one. I whirled around my room, flaring my skirts and swinging my hair, stopping when I caught a glance of myself in the mirror. The image reflected the girl I was: twenty-one and in love.

I washed, gave myself a talcum powdering, and stepped into a clean chemise. The thin cotton reminded me it had been a little more than one month since the night Shug and I had embraced in the darkened parlor. The memory awakened hungry pleasure centers in my body. Hunger denied for so long it grew sharp, akin to pain, but called pleasure, nonetheless.

Four years had passed since my escape to Texas as a young bride. In my first year of marriage, I had opened like a desert flower, and my husband deceived me. In my second year of marriage, our child was born, but my husband left for war. In my third year of marriage, my husband died, but I had begun to fall in love again. No rebellion against parental dictates separated me from Shug. He treated me like an equal. We were friends and Willy adored him.

I gazed at my reflection in the mirror, and decided.

Carrying my toiletries rolled in a towel. I swept into the kitchen, my nightdress flowing as if caught by an errant breeze. Shug stood by the stove, staring absently at the pot of water.

"A watched pot won't boil," I said.

His momentary surprise at seeing me in nightclothes was replaced by understanding, and desire, and love. He reached for me. "Are you sure?" he asked.

"Completely, and for the first time in my life."

"Miz Alma!"

I sat up with a start, staring into the dark corners of the room for L.B.

Shug slumbered next to me, his sleep unruffled by this call in the night. We were still in town. Five more days had passed since we had decided to retrieve Willy from the Pollard's, our plans waylaid by a resurgence of the fever. We had fewer new cases, but more relapse by those considered recovered. We returned to days filled with calls on the sick and dying. But in the evenings we spent stolen hours of exhausted rapture in each other's arms, the healing salve of love renewing us for the next day's battle.

"*Miz Alma!*" A fervent whisper in my ear.

"L.B.?" I answered, getting out of bed and going to the window, where a moonless night cast no shadows. "L.B.?" I called again, fear rising in my throat.

"Alma?" Shug's sleep-clogged voice this time. "What is it?" He joined me at the window, and hugged my trembling body.

"She's not here, but I heard L.B. We have to go to Willy! He's in danger."

We rushed off, leaving a note for Eva. If we encountered no problems, we would arrive at the Pollard's shortly before sunrise.

"I should have gone for Willy long before this. Six weeks is too long for a three-year-old. I'll never forgive myself if something has happened to him. My poor baby!"

Shug held both reins in one hand, and patted my knee. "Alma, you're jumping way ahead of yourself. Calm down now, sweetheart. I'm sure they would have sent for you if there was a problem."

"This was the message, Shug!"

"We're not too late. We've responded immediately." I searched his profile for reassurance. He glanced my way, giving me what I wanted. "We can deal with whatever awaits us."

The Pollard homestead was ablaze with lights. Dozens of candles must have been lit in every room to make it such a beacon in the night, a lighthouse warning of hidden shoals. Poppa Pollard met us at the door, unsurprised to see us. He nodded wearily in greeting.

"Willy?" I searched his face for tragedy.

"Asleep in your room." I ran up the stairs, but heard him whisper to Shug, ". . . in the parlor."

Willy's little-boy sweat and sweet exhalations permeated the room. His window was shut, making the room hotter, and he'd kicked his covers off. I opened it to the night air, the false promise of a cool Texas morning on the pink-tinged clouds, offering no hint of the burning day to come. He slept deeply, not stirring when I crawled into bed beside him, kissing his ear, and stroking his hair. His hair was damp, his skin hot. Bertha distrusted night air, but I had always slept with the window open. Even in the dead of a Santa Fé winter, the window would be left open a crack. The frigid air seemed clean, as if it brought renewal.

I picked up his hand, studying the minute perfection of it. He had a mosquito bite on a knuckle. He'd scratched it in his sleep, drawing blood. I sat up, and began a thorough examination of my son. He had a few of the usual childhood bruises and scrapes on his lower legs, and more mosquito bites healing over, but otherwise he appeared well fed and fit. I listened to him breathe, finally rising, expecting I would run into L.B. and Pinkie setting about their chores.

I stood on the landing outside Willy's room and listened. It was too quiet. Smoke from all the candles suffused the house. It made everything appear unreal, as if seen through the gauzy veil of a dream. Whispers floated up the stairwell on the candle vapors, and I followed them to the parlor.

Shug and Poppa Pollard stood side-by-side at the door as I passed through, concern etched in the lines of their faces. Bertha sat on a chair in front of a table piled high with flowers. Her arms were crossed on the table, her head buried between them, shoulders heaving as if she were sobbing, although, at first, I heard no sound from her. Her derringer lay next to her. I glanced back at Poppa, my eyebrows raised, questioning.

"She's been threatening to use it," he said, adding, "it's not loaded."

His lips moved, but I could barely hear him. All at once sound reached my ears like thunder.

"Mama! Mama!" Bertha pleaded between anguished sobs, and I saw what my heart wanted to deny. L.B.'s body lay on the table surrounded by wildflowers.

I reached out to her as if to wake her. I'd seen more death in the past two months than in my entire life, but there had been no room for tears. I couldn't fathom the cold I felt when touching my friend. My gaze traveled around the bier of flowers set up for her. "She was my first friend in Texas," I said, the tears finally arriving. I kissed my fingertips and touched them to her lips.

The warmth of Shug's body next to mine shocked me back to the here-and-now. "It was her heart, Alma. She didn't suffer."

"When?"

"Last night. She held on for a bit. Poppa said she asked for you."

Bertha's loud sobs ceased, and she stared at me, her eyes hate-filled. "That's right. She was mine, but it was *you* she wanted."

Poppa rushed over to her. "Now B.B., you know that's not true. L.B. had last words with you. Come on now, you need some rest." He had an arm around her, trying to guide her away from me. Poppa had shrunk since the last time I'd seen him; his skinny body was no match for her. She shook him off with a proud shrug, and he took a step back to steady himself. I turned to Shug and that's when the blow fell.

She caught me on the cheek. "You've taken my family away from me, you Mexican whore!"

Shug grabbed her before she could strike again. "Alma, get the laudanum out of my bag," he yelled over his shoulder.

"They're all dead!" Bertha screamed, arms flailing. Shug and Poppa managed to wrestle her to the floor. "I've got no one."

After handing the vial to Shug, I retreated to a corner. Shug stroked her hair. "Beautiful Bertha, quiet down, sugah. I want you to drink this. There, that's a good girl." Obediently, she swallowed the draught. "There now," he said, "I want you to go to bed now. Get your rest." He glanced at Poppa, and they helped her to her feet. She seemed to have forgotten I was in the room.

Bertha patted her hair self-consciously. Her Southern-belle airs came to her rescue, and she batted her swollen eyes at him. "Doctah Shug, please check my little boy before you leave."

The fever subsided in Pollard's Corner, so I stopped making calls with Shug, preferring to remain at home with Willy. My son had been well loved out at the ranch. He had grown, and had added to his vocabulary: 'pigheaded' would make him fall on the floor laughing. Every toy became a 'varmit,' that was either 'lousy,' or 'clean-as-a-hound's-tooth.' His visit had been a good one, and he had happy memories of it. Willy was full of stories about cats and cows, chickens and pigs, and the horse his Grandpoppa taught him to ride. It was a boy's life, and one I would never have denied him. My fantasy of family life was all-inclusive: happy mother and stepfather-to-be, perhaps a brother or sister for Willy in the future; happy grandparents, a child of their blood to watch over in their dotage. A fantasy.

Shug spent nights he wasn't working with me. If Eva was surprised to find him so consistently at the breakfast table, she said little, but advised us one morning that it wasn't written in God's book a woman had to wait a full year to remarry.

"Better wed and a baby on schedule, than a widah-woman in an all-fired hurry," she added, looking pointedly at Shug, then at me. So we had begun quietly to discuss our wedding date. Soon, we agreed. Not soon enough, for I felt I was already pregnant. Still, I said nothing, resisting the inevitable involvement of the Pollards. We couldn't ignore the founding family of Pollard's Corner, nor the grandparents of my son. A true Sandoval, down to the core, I ignored the wisdom of my predecessors who promised humility could forestall disaster. Where were the memories when I needed them?

The weather cooled and I awakened dreaming of pies. Not Providencia's poisoned delicacies, but L.B.'s delicious recipe for apple pie. I covered my widow's weeds with a white apron, and rolled out pastry dough. Willy played outside, visible from the window, but I monitored him by listening to the steady stream of orders he issued to Sam, a stray dog who had adopted us.

"Stay there, you lousy varmint, while I round up these chickens." Whereupon, a busy cackling of annoyed hens sounded above Willy's laughter, and the barking of Sam, who couldn't resist a hen round-up. His barking changed from high-pitched yelps to a guttural warning.

"Momma!" Willy shouted. The inflection different, not meant for me, but for his grandmother.

I ran to the kitchen door to see Bertha squatting next to Willy, hugging him. Bertha was bereft of her former beauty. She'd lost weight, and her hair was stringy and uncombed. She must have squeezed Willy too hard, because he tried to pull away from her.

"You've turned him against me! Like you did with Bill."

"Bertha, I'm happy to see you. So is Willy. Come inside and join us for some pie." Her expression frightened me, as did her white-knuckled grip on Willy. He squirmed, trying to pry her fingers loose from his arm. Feigning normality, I took a step closer.

She laughed. "Your pies? Bill told me about your pies. Old family recipes, aren't they?"

Willy began to whimper and call to me, "Mama, Mama!"

I moved closer, glancing around for help. "Bertha, where's Poppa?"

As if my question had let the air out of her, she crumpled downward, her skirts billowing around her. She still held Willy. "Poppa? Well, Poppa died," she said matter-of-factly. "In his sleep, the lucky bastard. Not like his sons. Or my mama. Or me." And with that, she pulled her derringer from a pocket in her dress, and hugged Willy close to her. Cheek-to-cheek.

They were cheek-to-cheek when she raised the pistol to the side of her head. I reached out, my fingers spread. A small, muffled pop the only sound. Not a mean sound.

Bertha fell sideways onto Willy. An errant wind blew the skirts of her dress up over them, so that I uncovered my baby, found my son beneath layers of crinkly taffeta. Their blood mingled on the ground.

My beautiful boy was dead.

27

Abogado

"You dress like a man, but you are a woman alone. They are soldiers."

Pilar, *1848*
Santa Fé:

"Los abogados estan aquí. The lawyers are here," Oratoria said.

She'd found me sitting next to Geraldo's grave. I nodded. Didn't move.

"You have ignored them long enough. There is business to attend to." She strode toward the hacienda without waiting for a reply. I followed because I had nothing better to do, hadn't ridden a horse, read a book, or been into town in weeks. I entered the kitchen. Oratoria sat at her desk, bent over a diary.

"They are in the library," she said, not bothering to look up.

The men stood. I waved them down and took the seat behind the heavy mahogany desk Geraldo had brought over from his ranch. An hour passed, and another. They finally left, tipping their hats on their way out. Oratoria came in, sat across from me, and waited for me to tell her what they wanted.

"Geraldo bought land for Monique's boardinghouse before he died," I said. "It's been vacant for so long someone offered to buy it. I said no. We'll build Monique's boardinghouse." I pointed to drawings on

220

the desk. "He left detailed instructions on how to handle just about everything. He thinks . . . he thought . . . I can do it, that I can handle the business."

"A confidence well-placed," she said.

"With the help of lawyers and money and more lawyers. He even has lawyers in the States, in their Capitol city of Washington. He'd already written to them about registering our land grants."

"Registering?" Her eyebrows shot up. "We have the official documents from the King of Spain, from Mexico, and the Church, all recognizing the Sandoval grants."

"Americans aren't Catholic and they don't have kings. They've won a war with Mexico. Land was the prize. You know how that works. You explained it to me and Alma dozens of times."

"New rules?"

"New thieves, new bribes, and a never-ending supply of lawyers." I picked up a small batch of letters tied with string and held it in the palm of my hand, bouncing it gently, as if weighing its importance. "He also thought the lawyers might be helpful in any dealings with Juan. These are letters from him to his father." I tossed the packet toward her, and picked up a single sheaf of paper. "And one new one. Sent to me through the attorneys."

"Geraldo has included him in the will, of course?"

"He left all the property in Mexico to Juan, several mines and two ranches," I said. "A home in Mexico City. Part interest in several shipping companies. But the Quintana hacienda and all Geraldo's property in New Mexico and in the banks in the States are mine. It reverts to Juan if I leave no heirs."

"Juan disputes this?"

I rubbed my forehead. "He wants permission to visit his father's grave."

Oratoria stood. "He must not return to Santa Fé."

"He's on his way." I exhaled, resigned to dealing with Juan. "An arrow in the back would serve him right, but he got lucky and ran into an American military convoy returning north. He's safe with them, and they send riders ahead with dispatches and messages. According to my lawyers, Juan gambles with the soldiers and is a great favorite of the Americans."

Oratoria picked up the letter and read it. "The marriage Geraldo arranged for him has produced two sons, but his wife died soon after the birth of the youngest. He regrets his past youthful misdeeds. He begs your indulgence in this personal matter." She let the letter fall back to the desk. "He'll cause trouble."

I felt it, too. Juan had savaged my best friend when she was still a child. He'd changed her life forever, and now he was on his way back to Santa Fé. "This won't be good for Monique."

Oratoria leaned over me. "He will go to Consuelo, his milk mother, venom-fed from the demon's teat. Together they will conjure—"

I held up my hand. "Geraldo left a small bequest to her, to be levied with my permission. I gave it." Oratoria collaped into a chair.

"For once you're speechless," I said. "Well, hear the rest. Consuelo has taken up with an American lawyer. With money and a new love, she's forgotten the Sandovals."

"Humph," my sister said, and left the room.

I turned my attention to the design for the boardinghouse, eager to get back to work. While waiting for me to follow through on Geraldo's plans, Monique's maids had arrived, and she'd opened a gambling salon and put them to work as dealers. Her establishment soon competed with all the others entertaining soldiers and travelers. Already one of Monique's maids had married a soldier, and more maids were on their way to Santa Fé. Monique stayed in town most of the time now. I missed her company very much.

General Kearny had appointed more Americans to governing posts in Santa Fé. He ignored the Church, but entertained the ricos in Santa Fé. Keeping the Church out of government business was fine by me. That, and his war against the Indians.

The Navajos in the northwest and Apaches to the south continued to steal our sheep, cattle and horses. Our men stood guard in the torreón to protect the hacienda, but unprotected merchant caravans arrived each week in Santa Fé. Death and loss with them could affect trade. The Americans sent battalions to protect the frontier, and they recruited more regiments. They promised volunteers 160 acres of land in exchange for one year of military service. More soldiers arrived, and it seemed as if thousands of men roamed the streets of Santa Fé. Monique needed the boardinghouse more than ever. I tucked the plans for it under my arm, and headed for the stable.

"Where are you going?" Oratoria asked.

"Town. I've got to see Monique about the boardinghouse."

"About time."

Over the door of Monique's saloon hung an American signboard that read, *The Lucky Strike*. Gambling houses were usually named for their owners, so her business stood out already. Soldiers, a priest or two, children, and a few local women filled a big square room. Rugs covered the dirt floors, and tables for cards and roulette were packed tightly together. Cigarillos hung from everyone's lips, and the billowing smoke clouded the mirrors around the room. Above the small bar hung a painting of a nude woman. A boy scurried through the crowd exchanging polished brass spittoons for the dirty ones.

"Pilar!" The smoke parted and Monique walked toward me, smiling, dressed completely in white, her dress and bearing out-of-place, yet completely at home in her gambling hall. She kissed me on both cheeks.

"I'm ready to start building," I said, and held up the plans.

"I knew I could count on you. Let's look at them over here." She led me to the bar and we rolled out the drawing, pinning it down at the four corners with shot glasses. The men crowded around us, offering advice.

"What do you think, doña Pilar, about the giveaway of our land to the soldiers?" one viejo asked. "Where is the land supposed to come from? I will tell you where. From us." He thumped his chest with his fist making the sound of a ripe watermelon.

Before I could answer, another viejo spoke up. "My cousin hired an American lawyer to save his land, but it took much silver to do it. More than my cousin had. The lawyer took the land as payment." There were nods and grumbles around the room.

A man I didn't know spoke. "My wife and sister and daughter wash the soldier's clothes. They are paid a wage, not with slops from the kitchen or hand-me-down clothes from the patrón."

"And you lose their wages here," his drinking-buddy said. Some of the men laughed; a few looked guilty.

A soldier, drunk and filthy, staggered back from the bar. "You're just the new niggers in town. White woman'd get twice what your women get paid."

"Get him out, Diego," Monique said. Her barman and a few of the other men shoved the soldier out the door.

Roberto, whose family had worked in our orchards for generations, stepped up to the bar. "My family works the Sandoval land. It is rich and black and has water. Our bones are in the land, niños y abuelos, babies and grandparents. The land is theirs *and* ours. If the Sandovals lose, we lose." Roberto turned his worried face to me. "You dress like a man, but you are a woman alone. They are soldiers."

I squeezed his shoulder. "Your place is safe, Roberto. Our land is safe, I promise you."

"The ricos never have to worry," another drunk said. "They have the world in their pockets. They never lose." Angry, deep-throated agreement rumbled through the room.

Just as quickly, it changed to an appreciative drone. Heads swiveled to a fair-skinned redhead sauntering into the room.

Monique waved her over. "Charmaine, I'd like you to meet my friend, Pilar."

Her hands were dry and soft, her eyes blue, but not so soft.

"Marry me, Charmaine!" a man shouted.

"No, choose me!" another yelled.

She ignored them all, and focused her full attention on me. "I bet you get your share of proposals." She tilted her head toward the men in the saloon. "They talk about your family. I hear there are no men alongside the Sandoval sisters."

The men were quiet, listening. The subject of marriage irritated me, but I managed to say. "I had a happy marriage, and I'm no gambler." A few of the men nodded their approval.

Monique cleared her throat. "Charmaine doesn't always think before she speaks. Not everyone has come to Santa Fé with the sole purpose of finding a rich husband." She turned to her. "And you shouldn't go around announcing it."

"Well, some of us can't afford to be so choosy," she said. "I can watch the saloon now, if you two want to leave."

"Are you hungry?" Monique asked me.

"I could eat a steer."

"Diego, my hat, please." The barman reached beneath the counter and removed a large hat decorated with flowers and ribbons, and even a nesting bird. Holding it with a single fingertip from either hand he placed it gently on the bar, and stared at it as if it might hatch an egg. Monique pinned it onto her head. The men around us gaped. I did, too.

"Where'd you get that thing?"

She smiled into a mirror at me. "Charmaine brought it with her. It's the latest Paris fashion."

"Are you French, Charmaine?" I asked.

"Only when I need to be," she said, laughing.

"Well, don't let my horse see that hat," I said. "She won't know what to make of it, and there's nothing more skittish than a horse that's seen something new."

The men laughed and picked up their cards. Monique ignored them, and hooked elbows with me. "A new restaurant opened, but first I need to stop at Scolly's."

Scolly ran the best general store in town, and always had a good tale up his sleeve. I wanted to put off telling Monique about Juan for as long as possible and hoped Scolly would stall her.

We strolled along the dusty street, avoiding stray pigs and goats. "I swear, every time I come to town there's a new storefront." We got to Scolly's Store, and after finding out he wasn't around, I leaned against a post supporting the portal outside while Monique did her shopping.

"Señora Quintana?"

An American, not so old, and dressed in a black suit stood at attention beside me. He held out his hand, and I shook it. "Pleased to meet you ma'am. I'm Jack Bleakman, attorney-at-law. I made the offer on your land here in town."

"How do you do, Mr. Bleakman. Sorry we couldn't do business. I have plans for that land."

"Yes ma'am, so I hear. This town needs more fine accommodations. My fiancée took a liking to the location. She runs a tailoring and leather goods business, although once we're married there'll be no need for her to work."

"Are you speaking of Rosa? She must be feeling much better. My sister sent over teas and rubbing compounds, but she . . . well, I'm happy to hear about your marriage plans."

"Oh no, not Rosa. She's not doing well at all, but Consuelo takes good care of her. My fiancée, Consuelo Benavides? You're acquainted with her, of course, since you arranged for the bequest." He lowered his voice and moved closer to me. "As her lawyer, I'm privy to such matters. In fact, if you're in need of counsel, I'm at your service."

"I'll keep that in mind, Mr. Bleakman."

He leaned in more. I could smell his hair oil, and would've taken a step back, but the post was behind me. "Santa Fé is growing fast," he said. "It's exploding with opportunities for a smart investor. I've got a few ideas—"

"Jack!"

His head snapped up. Consuelo Benavides stood in the doorway to Scolly's. She'd abandoned her usual loose skirts and blouse in favor of a blue gingham dress cut in the American style. She appeared vibrant, far different from the lovesick woman who'd pursued Geraldo.

Mr. Bleakman moved away from me. "My dear, you know señora Quintana. We were speaking about . . ." His mouth grew slack, his words lost. Consuelo glowered at her beloved. I was happy someone else was the recipient.

"We all know one another quite well," Monique said, coming up beside Consuelo. "Mr. Bleakman is a frequent customer at The Lucky Strike, and always speaks highly of his fiancée." Monique smiled at everyone.

Consuelo ignored her, and found a new target. Me. "Up to your usual tricks? You won't find this man as easy to steal as the last one!" Her voice rose and a few passersby paused to listen. "You'll have to be satisfied with helping the Americans steal land from the people."

I took a deep breath. "What—"

Mr. Bleakman went to her. "Dear—"

She held up a hand to stop him, but stared at me. "I don't want to hear your excuses for robbing la gente!" She whirled on Monique. "And you! The high-and-mighty madama with her nest of Anglo whores. Our girls are not good enough for your trade?"

Monique laughed, tilting her head back. "If I hired a few good Catholic girls, or even a few bad ones, you'd blame me for their fall. I only hire experienced whores." She examined Consuelo with a slow sweep of her eyes. "You're older than most, but you'd qualify."

The blood drained from Consuelo's face. La gente scurried past us: the women pulled their rebozos over their heads, the men tilted their sombreros back and smiled.

Consuelo regained her composure. "Come," she said to her fiancé. They left without a backward glance.

"Oratoria'll love hearing about this," I said.

"She probably already knows."

Inside the smoky restaurant, I pulled the chair out for Monique, and nodded to a few men eating their supper. They touched the brim of their hats and kept on chewing. I heard the word rico.

I dusted crumbs off the table, took out my handkerchief and folded it into a tight square, and then unfolded it. I made a point of saying hello to people I knew. I kept busy doing this so I wouldn't have to tell Monique the bad news.

She grabbed the handkerchief I was about to fold for the tenth time. "What is it, Pilar?"

The words tumbled out of me, "Juan is on his way to Santa Fé."

Monique slumped in her chair, as if I had knocked the wind out of her, her face blanching, but just as quick she straightened and pulled her shoulders back. Color returned to her skin, florid and hot, like an overripe peach. She pulled a fan from inside her sleeve and batted it back and forth. She sat there, fanning and fuming, for a long time.

"When?" she finally asked.

"In the next couple of weeks, depending on the usual hazards of the road. He wants to visit his father's grave."

"Which is on Sandoval land," she said, accusing. I'd never seen Monique so angry, and it made me uneasy, as if I'd invited Juan to return home.

I spoke, slow and steady, the way I do with a high-strung horse. "I'm sure he'll go back right away. He has nothing here, and two sons back in Mexico."

"No loving wife?"

227

"Dead."

We stared at each other. The cook brought our steaks, but neither of us lifted a knife to begin.

"There's no legal way to keep him away, but his letter is respectful . . . if he comes near you, I swear I'll—"

"Do nothing, Pilar," Monique said, her voice hard and angry. "Do you hear me? Do nothing. I'm no longer thirteen years old. I can take care of myself."

I stayed in town the next two weeks, getting the construction under way, but also keeping a wary eye out for strangers. Regiments rode in and out and wagon trains continued to cross the prairie to Santa Fé. It had been so long since I'd seen Juan, and there were so many new men in town, I wasn't sure I'd recognize him.

A new day and a new caravan blew into town, chock full of Texans to judge by their talk. A steady wind had been a cool companion, but it picked up speed as the teamsters herded the caballada into the overflowing corrals at the edge of town. The dust devils circled, and the canvas covers of the wagons bellowed in and out with a solid whop whop whop.

My eye caught the flaring black skirts of a widow woman. She was dressed in the cinch-waisted style of the Americans, her skirts flapping with the wind like a crow about to take flight. She wore no hat, and her dark hair was pulled into a severe knot at the nape of her neck.

I could see the grief and loss we widows carry in the curve of her back. A man in a wagon handed a black satchel down to her. Her hand and the side of her face were fair. She turned in my direction, walking with her head bowed, as if she were studying the ground.

"Alma?"

She raised her desolate eyes to mine, eyes so burdened with sorrow that all I could do was take my sister into my arms and rock her. She let me hold her, dropped her satchel, and hugged me. She patted my back as if to console me.

We stood in the middle of the busy road, but the hubbub and odor faded around us as we took stock of each other. She was too thin, her skin drawn tight over her cheekbones. Alma examined my calloused hands, and raised one to her cheek. She cupped her face with it. "Pilar," she said, "you've grown up. You're a beautiful woman." I restrained a whoop and a desire to whirl her around.

"Take me home," she said, with a smile so sad my heart hurt. I borrowed a buggy from the stable, tied my horse to the back of it, and sent a note to Monique. Alma said nothing more, and I tried to make the ride home as gentle as possible, avoiding ruts when I could, and asking no questions.

The gate was open and Oratoria stood by the kitchen door. The way she clutched her rebozo conveyed excitement, and the corners of her lips twitched, which meant she was wild with joy. I blew out air, relieved to be home. Oratoria took Alma by the hand and led her to the bedrooms. As always, I trailed them.

"This is Pilar's room," Alma said, hesitating at the door, and looking back to her old room, which I'd taken over.

"No longer," Oratoria said. "It belonged to Pilar and Geraldo, but she moved into your room after his death. Come, I've made a bath for you."

"My Geraldo? Don Geraldo?"

"Much has happened since you left. He gave his heart to Pilar and she received it. Come, let me tell you about the gift you gave to your sister. Let me tell you about a happy marriage."

Alma glanced at me, and I nodded. I saw a spark of curiosity, and knew for a moment she'd forgotten her past. She'd risked her life and her heritage in her escape to Texas, and she'd come home without husband, child or friend.

Just as Oratoria had predicted, Alma was ours again.

28

The Sandoval Widows

"Drink your witches' brew, the Devil will
have his due, Mama and baby make two."

**lma,** *1848*
Santa Fé:

"Mama!"

My eyes snapped open, my body on alert, waiting for the call to
come again.

It never did. Only in my dreams and only that one word. Willy's
sweet voice sounds as if he is next to my pillow, so close I can reach out
to him.

Awake, resolute grimness settled on me like fine dust as I contem-
plated the vast, never-ending day that awaited me. Oratoria insisted I
travel with her to deliver herbs and medicines to the sick. She'd seen
my medical bag, peered into its dark cavern of useless wonders, and
seen the meager tools Shug and I had used for delivering babies. She
didn't understand why I refused to visit expectant mothers since a good
partera, midwife, was always in demand. I trudged from this task to
that with her, trying to exhaust myself, but sleep eluded me.

Oratoria left the diaries of the Sandoval widows at my bedside, hoping I'd find solace in them. The stories that interested me were of the

230

Sandoval women who had buried their children, the babies born too soon or not long lived, or the unformed children who had withered in the womb, their small deaths known only to the mother. A few chose to die with their babes, seized while laying-in or taking care of the job themselves later.

Fecunda Sandoval bore eleven children and all survived but the last. Overcome with that one loss she leapt from a bridge, her pockets weighted with stones. Manuelita Sandoval lost her husband and three children in a flood. She remarried immediately and set about replenishing her brood with determination. Manuelita could not so easily replace her children. Her womb refused to finish what she had begun and each birth ended in a half-formed fetus. In desperation, she stole two children from a servant and fled into the wilderness where savages took them captive. No one heard from her or her kidnapped children again. Apolinaria Sandoval boasted of her children's many talents. When her lover married his mistress, she fed Providencia Sandoval's poisoned pie to her husband and all six of her gifted children. She wrote in her diary as she watched them writhe in their little beds. She told them she would be with them always. Then she cut her own throat. Her blood still dots the pages.

The Sandoval mothers took action. Rarely were they satisfied merely to exist, to go on, as I have. Once, at dawn, I got out of bed and dug deeply into the one chest I had resisted opening since my return. I pulled out Willy's christening gown, and buried my face in it, breathing deeply. A soft creak behind me drew my attention away from his beloved scent. Oratoria stood there, holding a candle, her graying hair already wound in braids.

"The bouquet of flesh remains?" she asked, her voice a soft murmur in the pinking dawn.

"A hint," I said. "Enough so I don't forget."

"You had a child," she said to herself.

"Yes," I said, as if a question had been asked.

"You have inherited the memories for a reason," Oratoria said. She took the gown from me and folded it away in the bureau. She gestured to the chest. "Are there more?"

"Some toys. A book. I didn't bring all his belongings."

She unpacked these and sat them out on the shelves, talking softly the whole while. "You and Bill married?"

"Yes."

"He died in the war?"

"Yes."

"But you no longer loved him?"

"I had a lover."

She stopped and looked at me, appraising. I covered my midsection protectively with my arms.

"You're with child?"

"I haven't bled since . . . since my son died." I cupped my hard, little mound of a stomach with two hands, as if presenting it to her. "It's been four months."

"Have you felt movement?"

I shook my head.

"Lie down," my sister said. She lifted my nightgown, and examined my breasts, pressed gently on my stomach, lifted my legs onto the bed and spread them. She felt inside my hollow womb searching for a sign. I began to cry.

"Nothing," I said.

She lowered my nightdress. Shook her head. "Your lover—?"

"I ran away. The heat and death in Texas suffocated me . . . took everything I had." I rolled onto my side and drew my knees up, and let my sobbing consume me.

Oratoria sat next to me, her weight creating an incline that drew me to her. She stroked my hair. "He'll follow."

I shook my head fiercely. "I left him."

"He *will* follow." She let her hand rest on my shoulder. "You're holding your blood inside, Alma, gestating your sorrow, congealing your guilt. You seek to swell your heart with the excess, so your pain will never leave. The memories are no longer alive in you." Her voice sounded strained. My sister's cheeks and neck were wet with tears. "You've lost your sense of direction, but children are coming to us. The Sandoval widows will have heirs."

I'd never seen Oratoria cry. My tears dried at the sight of hers.

She put me to work expanding our herb garden. Along with buttons and fabric, and pots and pans, the wagon trains also brought an assortment of seeds, bulbs, and cuttings of various medicinal herbs. Immigrants carried many from their home countries, and nurtured them in the States: several varieties of tomato; a morning glory vine resplendent with red and purple blossoms. Golden seal, an herb used by the Plains Indians and collected by the immigrants on their journey west, had healing properties. These transplants consumed me: I became obsessed with their survival in New Mexican soil. I worked tirelessly, digging the earth with my bare hands at times, and falling into bed exhausted each night.

Two weeks sped by, and one afternoon Oratoria came to the garden where I knelt pulling weeds. She held out her hand. "Come, Ortega's wife is in labor. Twins, I think, more than I can handle alone."

I brushed the hair back from my forehead with the back of my hand, and squinted up at my sister. She took a step to the right and blocked the sun, its light diffused into a halo around her brown face. I laughed. "You look like Our Lady of Guadalupe," I said. "All you need is a cloak of stars."

"Humph," she said, her expression adamant. I gripped her small hand, the fingers blunt and strong, and followed my sister to the birthing.

Ortega's wife was young, and huge with babies struggling to be born. Oratoria gave her a tea of cardo santo to speed the birth. I massaged the mother's groin with oil and spoke softly to her. The oil and massage would help stretch the birth canal so that cutting the perineum would not be necessary. I told her she had done good work creating these babies, and I knew she'd be a fine mother. I told her that her children would bring joy and tears into her life, but the joy is what she would remember.

"You have children?" she asked between spasms.

I hesitated, held my breath. My hand stopped moving, and the young mother tensed up. I began the gentle massage again, and sighed, my breath a long letting go of memory. "Yes," I said. "I had a beautiful child. He died when he was three."

"You'd have another? Even though—"

"Without hesitation," I said.

I eased the first baby into the world. What I'd feared experiencing was not painful, but filled me with bliss. I didn't want to let go when her mother reached out for the child.

The second baby made an appearance, and a third. They surprised us—happy father, mother, grandparents, and parteras. I felt as if I'd been delivered. Delivered from what, or into what I wasn't sure, but the experience had changed me.

I felt strange: dizzy, sweating, frightened. I went outside for fresh air. The rapture of the night sky overwhelmed me. I stretched out on the ground, and stared up for so long the sky seemed to swallow me. The stars flashed, speeding until they became streaks in the sky. Arcs of light moved, almost as if they were playing a celestial game, a grand scheme of a game meant only for me to see. Something unraveled inside me. The tight coil I'd held in my chest loosened and my burden of grief and misery spiraled out and traveled upward to the heavens.

I'm not sure how long I lay there, but the next thing I heard was the hooting of an owl. I hadn't witnessed this cosmic event alone! It was the exclamation point at the end of a sentence, the applause at the end of a performance, and it gave me permission to live again. That night, I began the life of a curandera in earnest.

Not many doctors traveled to the frontier, except the ones assigned to the military. 1848 wore on, and with the large influx of people to Santa Fé, I kept busy setting bones, mixing herbal elixirs for upset stomachs, easing coughs, soothing arthritic joints, along with my midwifing duties. I tended the maids at Monique's boardinghouse. A few came here suffering from various female complaints. Since I'd been home three more had arrived. One had barely unpacked when she received a proposal of marriage, accepted, and was whisked off to one of New Mexico's mining towns. I'd had the pleasure of meeting Charmaine. She shook her head at my widow's weeds and offered advice: "You'll never catch a man wearing black every day."

Most of the maids were grateful to leave the life, but a few found it difficult to change. They needed to prevent pregnancy, and the sea sponges Pilar still imported from New Orleans found a home with them.

Pilar had been staying in town with Monique, so I was surprised to see her ride in early one morning.

"One of the new girls is sick," Pilar said. "Can you check on her?"

"It'll take me a minute to get ready. Ask Pedro to get the carriage."

I double-checked my medical bag and grabbed a tortilla on my way out. Pilar stood next to the carriage holding the reins. "You're not coming?" I asked.

She flicked her chin toward the corral. It held a beautiful roan stallion tossing its mane and stamping its hooves.

"He's feisty," I said.

"I'm breaking him in today. I'll stay the night, and ride him again in the morning. Tell Monique I'll see her tomorrow."

Monique waited in the hall, pacing and wringing her hands while I examined the new girl. "She's had a miscarriage," I said. "She's anemic, but appears otherwise healthy." Monique nodded absentmindedly. She didn't appear to be listening. "The bleeding has stopped. You don't need to worry."

"Juan's here. I didn't tell Pilar."

I knew the full story by now: of Geraldo and Pilar, of Monique and Juan, of Consuelo, whom I'd never met, and of Oratoria and my father. And my sisters knew about me and all I'd left behind in Texas. We were well-versed widows.

Monique took my hand. "Come with me?" We left by the kitchen door and walked through the narrow alley that lay behind the boarding house and the buildings next to it. We came to the backside of her gambling hall.

"You're about to see the world through the eyes of a courtesan," Monique said. "A trick I learned from my stay at the Maison Carondelet in New Orleans. I commissioned a copy of a painting there, a painting both beautiful and useful." She held her finger to her lips. "We must be silent."

Monique unlocked the door and we entered a small storage room. Wooden boxes filled with bottles lay on the floor. Shelves along three walls were stocked with aguardiente, distilled from cactus, and the more expensive liquor Monique imported from the states. The remaining wall was bare, except for the door leading to the saloon, and a small, wood panel high up on the wall. I could hear the gamblers on the other side. One voice overrode the others: "Raise you twenty," he said.

"You already owe me two hundred. Pay up, Juan."

"The Quintana land is worth two thousand times what I owe you. When the estate is settled, you'll get your money," Juan said. "Eh, Charmaine, my beautiful redhead, my pelirroja, more drinks for my compadres."

Monique stood on a box and slid the wood panel, quietly and carefully, to the side. She peered through two small holes, got down, pointed at the box. I stepped onto it and looked through the peepholes; Juan sat at a table with three other men. He'd grown from slender youth to bulky man. Charmaine circled the group in her languid way, leaning over the men's shoulders and serving them drinks. When she reached Juan, he grabbed her hand. "Stay with me, for good luck."

She stood behind him, her hand on his shoulder, and tapped it restlessly. I recognized a repetitive pattern. I mouthed, "Cheating," to Monique.

Monique nodded.

The man sitting across from Juan spread his cards in a fan shape. "I win," he said.

"Ay, cabrón!" Juan slapped down his cards, and overturned the table, sending glasses and cards flying.

"Don't get angry, compadre," the winner said. "You've got plenty of money to pay your debts." A smattering of laughter rang through the room.

Juan dragged Charmaine by the elbow over to the bar. He shook her and shoved her into a chair. He scowled at the men sitting there until they moved away. Charmaine and Juan were less than two feet from where I hid.

He lowered his voice to a ferocious growl. "I told you five taps for a full house."

"He didn't have a full house when I served him," Charmaine said.

"That fucking thief! He cheated."

Charmaine laughed. Juan grabbed her hair, bending her head back. He stood over her, the muscles in his face tightening. The room grew silent. "That's right, mi amor," Charmaine said, her voice low, seductive. "He cheated better than us." Her tongue slid out of her mouth, almost touching him. She licked her lips.

He released her, and laughed with no sound, his shoulders jerking spasmodically, almost as if he were having a fit. Dice clicked, men coughed and laughed, and all the normal sounds of the gambling hall returned.

She rubbed Juan's back. "We'll have to learn to cheat better. What's a few hundred gold pieces? You can buy and sell every man in here."

Juan raised his head and stared into my eyes. "Yes," he said, pensive. "Strange how that whore looks right into your soul."

Charmaine followed his stare. "That portrait came all the way from New Orleans."

Juan turned to her. "Shall I see you tonight?"

"Tonight, and every night."

I'd seen enough. Monique and I went out into the alley again. I waited until she'd locked the door. "They stared right at me," I said, incredulous.

"They can't see you. The painting on the other side is of a nude woman, and my customers rarely focus on her face."

"Were you in the saloon when Juan arrived?" I asked.

"I saw him first and got out. I've been watching him."

"Come back to the ranch with me."

Pilar left the corral when she saw us drive through the wide gate of the compound. She helped Monique down from the carriage.

Oratoria came to the kitchen door. "He's here, isn't he?" she said.

"I'd begun to think he'd changed his mind, or took an arrow in the chest," Pilar said.

"I had to leave," Monique said. "I can't stand breathing the same air as Juan."

"Did you shut the place down?" Pilar asked.

Monique shook her head. "Then he would know I was in town. I left Diego in charge."

"What about the boardinghouse?"

"Charmaine will contact us if there's a problem." Monique sounded worried.

"You don't trust this woman?" Oratoria asked.

"She was helping Juan cheat at cards," Monique said. "They're intimate, but I didn't tell her about him. It's hard for me to talk about what he did." She glanced at Pilar. "Maybe there's some thirteen-year-old left in me, after all."

"She seemed to handle him fine," I said.

Monique leaned against Pilar. "More girls are arriving soon. Charmaine will let us know when they get here. Can you check in on them, Alma?"

"I'm in town at least once a week," I said. "Are the guards still posted at the boardinghouse?"

"They have orders to protect the girls, but I don't think Juan will bother you."

The following week another letter arrived. This one came directly from Juan, asking permission to visit his father's grave. All four of us were in the kitchen. Monique spoke first: "She can't meet him alone."

Pilar said, "He won't try anything. I'll be fine."

"I'll go with you," Oratoria said.

None of us warmed to that idea.

"What about me?" I asked.

"Can you handle a gun?" Pilar asked, not exactly kidding.

"Take two men with guns," Oratoria said.

Monique flicked her thumb at Oratoria. "That's why she's the boss."

Two of our men rode a few horse lengths behind: close enough to protect us, but far enough so my sister felt comfortable. "I don't want them breathing down my neck."

Pilar and I met Juan at the crossroads to lead him to the Sandoval cemetery. "Doña Pilar," he said. "Doña Alma." He bowed his head, but didn't acknowledge the men behind us. He got off his horse. "I'll drive the carriage for you."

Pilar said, "If I'm going to ride in one of these things, I'm going to handle the reins."

Juan smiled crookedly and got back on his horse. "You still have spirit, doña Pilar. I didn't understand it when I was a boy. I like it in a woman now."

Pilar glanced at me, said nothing. She flicked the reins and we started at a leisurely pace. Juan rode beside my sister.

"I have two sons," he said. "They resemble my father. I'm sorry he didn't have the chance to meet them. He loved children."

"Did he?" Pilar said, staring at the road ahead.

"He always said he wished I'd had brothers and sisters. I'm sure he wanted children with you. Perhaps with a younger man that joy will come to you. A large family makes a solid foundation for the future. My poor children have no mother."

Pilar snapped the reins, jolting the horses into a clop. "They have you. I'm sure you need to return to them soon."

"Soon," he said. "How were my father's last years? It must have been difficult caring for an old man."

"Geraldo was never an old man," Pilar said, her voice soft. "There's the cemetery."

Juan tied his horse to a fence post. "Would you care to join me?"

"You've traveled a long way to pay your last respects. I'll leave you to it." She whipped the reins, but Juan grabbed them, stopping the team.

"You are cold, doña Pilar. I guess I should have expected it. But, we are family now, and I hope to get to know you better. I think my father would have wanted this." I could hear our men closing in behind us.

Pilar jerked the reins away from him. "Don't lie to yourself, Juan." Her head was turned away from me, and I saw her neck flush red. "There's nothing here for you but your father's bones." Our men surrounded Juan.

He glared at Pilar, and then lifted a corner of his mouth in a one-sided smile. "As you wish. You may need a man's help in the future. Ugly rumors are whispered in town about you and your sisters. They say one sister married her father and murdered him. They think it strange my father favored a barren young wife over his male heir." He didn't leave me out of his appraisal. "Forgive me, doña Alma, but la gente find it odd you cater to whores in town. The Sandovals grow rich at the expense of the people. Trouble is brewing." He moved away from the wagon and licked his lips. "I offer you the same protection as my father."

"En boca del mentiroso, lo cierto se hace dudoso," Pilar said. She snapped the reins hard and we took off.

I said, *"From the mouth of a liar, the truth is doubtful?* You sound like Oratoria."

"He's got a lot of nerve, suggesting on the cemetery steps he could replace his father and then trying to scare me. I know another good one for that pig. ¡Cuando andes en la silla, maneja bien! Hiiyah!" Pilar stood in the buggy, urging the horses to move faster. Her hat blew off and her hair streamed out behind her.

The buggy rattled over the rough road faster than it was meant to go, and I held onto the side thinking about my sister's words, *when you're in the saddle, ride.*

Pilar was gearing for a fight.

The lawyers reported on Juan regularly; he did not act or sound like a man in a hurry to return to his life in Mexico: he gambled and lost heavily, drank a great deal, boasted of his wealth and property in Mexico, and of his prowess with women. Charmaine wrote to Monique that a wealthy widower with holdings in New Mexico wooed her.

"Does she mean Juan?" Oratoria asked. "He has nothing in New Mexico, except Consuelo."

"He's a blowhard," Pilar said. "I wonder what she'd do if she knew Juan owns nothing here. If she wants him, she's going to have to move to Mexico with him."

"Perhaps she's found a man wealthy enough to suit her taste," I said.

"Even Charmaine has better judgment than that," Monique said. "I hope," she added, not sounding convinced.

A few days later, another letter arrived, asking again for permission to visit his father's grave. Pilar wrote back that she would tell her men to allow him access to the cemetery "this last time before your return to Mexico."

"He knows the way," she said irritably.

Two more weeks passed. Juan's presence in town upset all of us. He stopped asking permission to come onto Sandoval land. Pilar's energy and optimism waned. She didn't sleep well. I heard her return from a night ride early one morning, and found her in the kitchen cleaning a rifle.

"I rode past the cemetery and saw a light. He was there again, and he wasn't alone. He had Consuelo with him. She'd thrown herself across the grave." Pilar set the rifle aside. "It was the strangest sight, Alma. Consuelo wept and pounded the ground while Juan held a candle. She was dressed in black. She looked more like a widow than I ever have. I don't understand it, this living in the past." Pilar studied my black dress. She scratched her head, a show of uncertainty for my sister and the beginning of a question. "La gente say your love for your husband must be great for you still to dress as a widow. They seem to think you know a lot about love?"

"La gente gossip and make up stories to explain anything new or unusual. As for Consuelo, I've never met her. But dressing as a widow to grieve for a man who scorned you, and in the secrecy of night, *is* strange. Maybe Oratoria is right—"

Pilar waved my words away. "Don't start with the magic and the witch talk. Juan is my main worry. No telling how often he's come onto our land." She let out a frustrated breath. "I'll get the lawyers to warn him off."

Another week passed and Juan showed no signs of leaving. Monique remained with us, sharing Pilar's room. She stayed in touch with Diego, and occasionally Charmaine. Late one morning, I found Pilar in the kitchen stuffing her saddlebags with gold.

"Juan?" I asked.

She pointed to a letter lying open on the table.

Doña Pilar,

You have two grandsons, señora Quintana. I would like to return to my father's ranch, my childhood home, and bring my children here. When may we meet to discuss this matter?

With respect,
Juan

"He can't pay off his gambling debts," Pilar said. "His entire inheritance was owed before his father died."

"Your lawyers—"

"Say Juan's debtors have followed him here because he told them his father's New Mexican wealth would be his. He needs money, and I'm going to offer it to him if he'll leave. All he has to do is sign a document saying he'll never return."

"Will you see him?" I asked.

She hesitated, unusual for Pilar. "There's more. I told you his wife is dead." She looked at me. "The word from Mexico is she was beaten to death."

"He's a monster," Oratoria said. She stood beside me. I'd not heard her enter the room.

"That's what his father called him," Pilar said. "I want him gone."

"Don't see him," I said.

"Maybe a different tactic is required," Oratoria said. She looked over at the diaries on her desk.

Pilar smiled for the first time in weeks. "Maybe a little Pious Pie is what Juan needs."

Another Sandoval secret had been revealed. I wanted to laugh, but Oratoria's stern expression squelched it. Now she knew that when we were barely out of girlhood, Pilar and I had disobeyed her and read all the forbidden journals on her desk. She looked first at Pilar and then at me.

"Providencia's recipe provides too slow a death for one such as Juan," Oratoria said. "But I'm happy to learn you've taken an interest in baking, Pilar." My sister had the good sense not to smile.

"She'd rather beat Juan with the rolling pin than roll out pie crust," I said.

Pilar hoisted the saddlebag onto her shoulder. When she stood, her knees buckled. She focused on the blazing sunlight drenching our patio, and I knew she wanted to be out in it.

"Please don't see Juan," I said again.

"I won't, unless I have to," she said, dreamily. She shook it off. "I'm going to ride into town to see the lawyers." Her clenched jaw made her face hard. "I'll have them make it clear to him this is my only offer. Juan signs and leaves with the money, or he'll leave without the money. I'll have him run out of town, carried out in a box, if I have to!"

My scalp tingled from Pilar's words. And from the deadly intent in her eyes. Tight and dark, all the animation usually there now focused in a pinpoint of hate.

"He gambles most of the night, and leaves with Charmaine around midnight, but I want him out of Santa Fé now," she said. "They have to get him to sign before he leaves the saloon for the boardinghouse."

I kept my voice calm. "Take some men."

"I make this ride alone all the time."

"I need to visit the new girls. Meet me at the boardinghouse."

Pilar nodded, and took off, riding hard, her saddlebags bulging with gold. I'm not sure how much she had with her, but surely it was enough to keep a moderate man happy for the rest of his life, with plenty left over for his children.

I checked my medical provisions. Under them lay my pistol. I ran my hand over the cool metal, and took a measure of comfort. One of our men rode behind my carriage as I set off for town.

About halfway there, a horseman overtook us. He was an agitated father-to-be. He had been to the hacienda first, and Oratoria had sent him after me. I turned off the road, my guard trailing me, and followed the frightened man to his wife's bedside. I had done this hundreds of times, and I had all my supplies with me.

Five hours passed. Even with the help of the father, it was a difficult birth, and the child was born with a clubfoot. I opened the door of their one-room adobe, and inhaled the clean mountain air. The light of the fading day had a pinkish-violet hue. Even in summer, the day closed earlier in the mountains than in the desert. The muscles around my neck and shoulders hurt, and I stood in the doorway kneading the tension out of them. Mother and father wept in the room behind me. The husband had broken a chair when he saw the child.

Down the curve of the road, a light moved steadily toward us. For a second, I wondered if it might be one of the rolling balls of fire many had seen. La gente said they were witches on their way to a meeting. My guard stood at attention beside me. The clackety-clack of wagon wheels reached me. It was the coach lamp of a buggy. Oratoria and Monique pulled up.

"The road into Santa Fé is busy tonight," I said, and squinted at the trail behind them. "You came without any men?"

"They're waiting at the crossroads," Oratoria said.

"Do you think you should be in town?" I asked Monique.

"Oratoria thought we should all be together."

The father stood in the doorway, and I went to him to say I would stop by tomorrow. Behind me, night wings whipped through the air, and a mouse squeaked once, followed by the victory song of the owl. The father heard and crossed himself.

"A bad omen," Oratoria said.

Which one, I wondered?

We arrived at the boardinghouse around 8:30. I remembered one of the girls was celebrating her birthday at the cantina. They were probably all there. Pilar would have left a note if she had been to the boardinghouse and gone. I sent my guard to the cantina to look for Pilar, and made myself comfortable at the kitchen table with a book. Oratoria and Monique drove to the lawyer's house. I'd read a few pages when I heard a high-pitched wail from upstairs, followed by a woman screaming. The clock read ten to nine; I'd heard no one enter the house.

I reached for my medical bag, but I'd left it in the carriage. Outside, a desert wind came up and whipped my skirts. The street was empty, but I felt as if I were being watched, and jumped when a tumbleweed crashed into me. A man's boot at the corner of the building caught my eye. The shrill call of crickets pierced my thoughts and on a rooftop behind me an owl hooted.

"Enough of this," I said to myself. I took the gun out of my bag and walked toward the boot. The wind faded as suddenly as it had begun and the crickets stopped their chorus. The only sound was the crunch of my footsteps.

A guard posted there had kicked the boot off. A whip lay next to him, the end of it wrapped around his neck. I looked up at the boardinghouse. A thin light wavered behind one curtained window.

I whirled around, feeling as if someone stood behind me. The street was empty. A heavy metallic smell hung in the air, like the scent of a lightning storm on its way. Another wail from inside jolted me into action, and I ran up the stairs. The sound of a woman sobbing led me to a bedroom at the end of the hall.

"Please, no, no, *no*! I'll do anything," the woman said.

A man laughed, a low *heh heh heh*. "Prize bitch of a whore. Thought I'd marry you."

I opened the door. Charmaine sprawled naked on the bed, her arms and legs tied to the four ends. A naked man knelt between her legs, the sweat on his back gleaming in the candlelight. He made a slow three-quarter turn toward me. Juan. He held a small knife, and a wet lopsided grin on his face. I saw what he had been doing to her and acid filled my throat: he'd sliced a harlequin's diamond pattern into her chest.

My stomach jittered, that old feeling announcing the memories, but instead of tensing to ward them off, I welcomed their company. I remembered the compliant Sandoval women who came before me, who had finally had enough of whatever life had served up to them. I was not frightened. I was not alone. I could kill this man if I had to.

I pointed the gun at him, and tried to keep it steady. "Throw the knife down."

He slid off Charmaine, leaving a bloody smear on the sheet. Juan held the knife lightly between his thumb and two fingers as if he had been practicing a demonic calligraphy on her. He took a step forward, and I pulled the trigger. He grabbed his arm, dropping the knife, but staggered toward me, still smiling. A moan from the corner distracted me. Pilar lay on the floor covered with blood. She tried to get up and more blood gushed from a gut wound.

Juan threw himself at me, knocking the gun out of my hand. He spun me around and wrapped his good arm around my head, squeezing it between forearm and biceps.

"I'll crush your head like a pumpkin, you Sandoval witch!" Wet with blood from his wound, Juan smashed my nose with his hand, covering my mouth, and cut off my air. I was about to faint when he slid his hand down to my neck.

"Delicate," he said.

His hand dropped and he pinched my breast, twisting the nipple. I dug my fingernails into his arm. He tightened his grip on my head, and turned me toward my sister. Pilar tried to push herself up again. He dragged me over to her, and still holding me tight with one arm, kicked my sister in the stomach with his bare foot. Pilar passed out.

"Thief!" Juan screamed at her, his breath hot and sour. "You've gotten what you deserve."

He bunched my skirts up in front and clawed at my groin. Thrusting his pelvis into my backside, he sang in rhythm to his movements:

"Drink your witches' brew, the Devil will have his due, Mama and baby make two."

He let my skirt drop and pulled my head, still cradled in the crook of his other arm, to the side. "Mama knew Pilar would come. That she'd try to buy me off." I could feel the muscles in my neck straining. "Should I twist your head off now or after I fuck you?"

Juan whirled me around again and shoved me onto the bed across Charmaine, who whimpered. I tried to sit up and he punched me in the face. Blood thundered in my head, and the room spun. A chorus of loud breathing hummed around me—mine, Charmaine's beneath me, Juan's, Pilar's, and . . . and someone else. I moved my head slightly and saw a woman standing in a corner of the room. She looked toward the door and my eyes followed hers.

Oratoria stood there holding a shotgun. Monique was beside her. She held a gun with two hands.

"Monique," Juan said.

She fired and he crashed against the wall behind him.

Monique ran to Pilar.

246

"Don't move her," I said. I pushed myself up, but hesitated until the room stopped spinning. Oratoria grabbed a blanket from the bed and pressed it into Pilar's wound. Footsteps pounded the stairs and our men rushed in. They stopped in the doorway for an instant. Then one cut Charmaine's bindings. Another went to Juan, who tried to stand.

"Leave him!" I shouted. "Get more light! Go to the fort. Tell them the Sandovals need the Army doctor. Bring me my bag. We need boiling water and clean sheets."

Oratoria wrapped Charmaine in the bloody sheet. Charmaine looked around the room as if she were searching for someone. She settled on Juan, still trying to crawl his way up the wall to stand.

Oratoria and I lifted Pilar onto the bed. She was conscious, but weak. "It was a trap," she said, and fainted again.

"She tried to stop him from hurting me," Charmaine said, "but the bastard was ready for her."

The men rushed back with water and more light. We undressed Pilar and washed her wound as gently as possible. She went in and out of consciousness while I examined her.

"We have to keep her warm," I said. Monique sat beside her, holding her hand. Oratoria had already taken a buckskin from my bag and begun scraping the carnaza, soft fluff, from the inside of it.

A man screamed behind us, a deep-throated animal wail.

Juan knelt in front of Charmaine again, holding something, but *she* had the knife in her hands and pointed it at him. Blood covered her face and hands.

The gun! He has the gun.

I ran to grab it away from him, but it wasn't my gun he held. Blood spurted from his groin in the rhythm dictated by his dying heart. His naughty-boy smile now perplexed, he presented his organ, as if it were a precious gift.

I took a step back.

"Come near me and I'll cut you again," Charmaine said to him.

"Mama?" he said, and looked around the room as if he were lost. He collapsed, curled in a fetal position. I didn't need to touch him to know he was dead. Charmaine still held the knife in front of her. She stared at him as if he might attack again.

"He called for his demon mother," Oratoria said.

I pointed to the corner. "Did you see the woman?"

Oratoria shook her head.

"The woman!" Charmaine began to weep. "The woman," she said again.

I took the knife from her. "Did you see—"

"Jesus, Mary and Joseph, what happened in here?" A young doctor, new to the frontier, surveyed the chaos. One of our men returned with several candles. "Well, at least we have plenty of light," the doctor said, a bit more jovial than necessary. He went to Juan first, but I stopped him.

"He's dead. This is the patient, Doctor." I led him to Pilar. "He used a knife. I think he nicked the small intestine. The uterus is torn."

"You're a nurse?"

"I have some medical training."

He rubbed his hands together, and lifted the clean sheet we had laid across her pelvis. "Hold the candle closer." He peered inside my sister. "You've put the scraping from buckskin in her wound to stop the bleeding. I've heard of that Indian trick. Does it work?"

"It can."

"I saw a wound the same as this at the Boston hospital where I studied. A prostitute ripped up by a dissatisfied customer." He started to smile, but seemed to notice for the first time my widow's weeds and swollen face. "The patient is a friend?"

"My sister."

"Married?"

"Widowed."

"Children?"

I shook my head, already knowing where he was leading.

"Sepsis is the problem, no matter what we do," he said.

Pilar's eyelids fluttered, struggled to stay open.

"Alma," she said, so softly it sounded like a sigh.

29

Pride and Prejudice on The Frontier

"They are the Sandoval witches!"

 **O** *ratoria,* *1848*
Santa Fé:

SANDOVAL BLOOD HAD been shed.

I caught my sister's blood on a whore's blanket, and was thankful for it. No mother I, but I felt a mother's agony watching my Pilar suffer. The love that surrounded her was pure: it flowed out of Monique, and Alma, and me. Almost tangible, it cushioned her like a feather pillow.

She opened her eyes and found Alma. "Doctor Sister," she said, like a whisper in a dream. She slept again.

Alma had felt inside Pilar's wound. She'd closed her eyes, and I knew her ancient memories, those secrets of the old Sandoval blood, guided her fingers. It was as it should be. The sun and snow of New Mexico had toughened Pilar, and her will to live was strong. That and the Sandoval luck would see her through.

She restored order to the crowded room, her first commandment the removal of Juan's body. Our men carried him out.

Ortega came into the room. He touched the brim of his hat, a short-cut the Americans used. Alma probably would not notice. "The sheriff is here," he said. "A man has been killed at the hands of a woman. La gente demand justice." Sweat gleamed on Ortega's skin in the dim light of the hall. He turned his head and coughed wetly.

"There is more," I said.

A sharp intake of breath rasped at the back of his throat, the beginning of a wheeze. "Juan was well-liked in the taverns. The people are calling for someone to be punished." He stuffed his hands in his pockets. "I am sorry, señora, the crowd is hysterical. They want revenge."

"Revenge for Juan?"

"For everything in their lives," he said.

"Our men are armed?"

He pulled his shoulders back. "We will stand by you."

"When we get home, I will make you an ocotillo tea for your throat."

Alma nodded when she saw that I'd finished with Ortega. "I'll be outside if you see any change in Pilar," she said to Monique. A slight inclination of Monique's head told us she'd heard, but her eyes never left Pilar.

I could hear the murmur of the crowd as we descended the stairs. Monique's maids had gathered in the parlor, and whispered among themselves. They stood when we entered, holding one another's hands. A sisterhood had formed.

They stared at Alma, their doctor, with concern. "Your face," one said.

Alma raised a hand to her swollen eye and nose. "Nothing's broken. Juan attacked Pilar and Charmaine. The army doctor is tending Charmaine. She'll be fine." She clasped her hands in front of her, the knuckles turning white. "Pilar is hurt badly. Monique is with her now."

A few torches, bobbing like fireflies, were visible through the thin curtains covering the windows. Alma drew one aside and looked out. The girls peeked over her shoulder.

"There she is, the black widow," a woman yelled outside.

"Murderers!" another shouted. A rock sailed through the window, shattering the glass. The girls scooted to the other side of the room.

"Don't come outside," Alma said to them. Monique's maids cowered behind our men, trembling birds cornered in their own nest.

Four of our men went out first, standing two and two on either side of Alma and me. Juan's naked body, covered with a blanket, had been placed on the street in front of the boardinghouse. About twenty people–men, women and children–had assembled. More were rushing down the dark street to join the throng. With each addition a hoarse whispering arose. They raised arms, pointed first at Juan and then at Alma and me. New people pressed into the pack, and worked their way to the front, pushing others aside. The group constantly churned, growing and oozing its way closer. One woman in front smiled drunkenly at me.

"Doña Oratoria," she said, a familiar slurring of her words sparking my memory. Antonia Mora, whose five children I had delivered, had been uproariously drunk when her last child was born. A shrunken mass of humanity gasping its first and last breath, it had been poisoned in the womb by its mother's excesses.

"Antonia," I said.

She nudged the drunk man next to her with her elbow. "This is my friend, Edmundo." They swayed as if standing in a boat, each trying to steady the other. "Doña Oratoria delivered my babies, and her sister," she pointed her lips and flicked her chin at Alma, "tends the gringa whores."

"Puta," a woman shouted, as if on cue. "Es una mujer más puta que una gata." She's more of a whore than a cat. The women quickly took up the call of whore, it being their second favorite slur after witch. It rippled through the assembly, a waning echo as it reached the farthest corners of the mob. Yet another sisterhood was born.

Alma squeezed my hand and I could feel the heat of her body as she leaned closer. One eye was closed completely, but with the other she stared defiantly at the crowd.

Antonia and Edmundo were pushed aside. New people appeared, their torch lit faces flickering, malleable, each one mighty with the strength of the horde. Individuals lost their uniqueness and each person became the same as the others. I didn't recognize anyone, but they all knew the Sandoval widows. They laid our fairy tale histories at our feet, and random voices shouted our predilections to the stars:

"She married her father and poisoned him to get all the money."

"We've lost our land and they've got more than ever!"

"They are all thieves and murderers. That is how the ricos get their money."

"Why would they need so many lawyers if not to cheat us?"

"They have no santos in their home. Not one."

"The other one is unnatural, wearing pantalones, riding horses at night!"

The young father whose child Alma had delivered that day appeared, weeping and drunk.

"She was at my home today. She made my wife drink her poison and my son was born deformed!" Women prayed and men shook their heads. Surely, God would not allow such children to be born. The cause had to be on this earth. A midwife who had disobeyed her father and run off with a Texan was easy to blame.

"She killed Juan in a jealous fit," someone else shouted. "Hang her!"

The young father raised his hands in supplication to Alma. "My child!" He turned to the crowd. "Hang her!" He crumpled in a ball, sobbing.

The sheriff, an Anglo appointed by the military, came forward, followed by his deputy, a local. The sheriff touched the brim of his hat, " 'Scuse ma'am, are you señora Sandoval?"

"They are the Sandoval witches," a man yelled. The crowd repeated it, the accusation picking up force. The pack edged closer.

The sheriff loosened the straps of his pistol. "Step back." He motioned with his hands. When they did not move, he glanced at the deputy. "Tell them."

"Pase para atrás," the deputy said. La gente did not obey, but they stopped moving forward.

The sheriff turned back to us.

"I am señora Sandoval," I said. "This is my sister, Mrs. Pollard."

He flicked his head toward Juan. "He's been shot *and* cut looks like."

"I shot him," Alma said. "He stabbed my sister, and cut up another woman. The army doctor is upstairs with them."

The wind came up strong and hard. The men grabbed their hats and the women hugged their rebozos tighter. A grievous wail swept over and around us. Wretched with loss in their own lives, the mob searched for the source.

252

"¡La llorona!" the people said, crossing themselves. The weeping woman, the story goes, killed her own children and cries evermore for them.

Her keening began again and la gente parted creating a narrow corridor down which a woman crept. Covered from head to toe with a black rebozo, she stumbled and fell. A thin Anglo man followed and helped her up. Her shawl fell from her head, and Consuelo Benavides collapsed to her knees before Juan's body.

"His mother," the deputy said.

I stepped in front of my sister. "Consuelo— "

"Consuelo?" Alma said. "This is the woman I saw in Juan's room. She was there when he tortured Charmaine, when he threatened to rape and kill me!"

Consuelo shook her head. "My son—"

"He is not your son," I said.

"He was mine!" Consuelo appealed to the congregation behind her. "I was not a mother but the milk came to me. For him the miracle came. My blood milk fed him."

Several women wept. Murmurs of pobrecita ran through the group.

"You were in the room," Alma said. "You watched. You didn't try to stop him."

Consuelo reached for the thin Anglo man, who took her hand. "You lie. I was with my Mr. Bleakman—"

"I saw you, too," a soft voice behind me said. Charmaine, stooped and pale, her face battered and her hair still matted with blood, clutched a blanket around her body. Monique's maids held her upright.

"La Charmaine," several men said. Their voices revealed disbelief that this bedraggled woman was the majestic redhead from the Lucky Strike.

Charmaine pointed at Consuelo. "You were there! He turned to you before he cut me. If you're his mother then Juan is a son of a bitch!" She spat on Juan's body.

Consuelo leapt at Charmaine. The sheriff caught her arms, but he could not quiet her. "Whore! You led him astray."

"Juan drank like a fish and gambled like a fool," one of the maid's said. A rumble of assent, deep in the throats of men, arose in the throng. They had all seen Juan in the taverns, and with his pelirroja.

The sheriff handed Consuelo over to Bleakman. She fell to her knees again and whipped the blanket off Juan. La gente surged forward to get a better view.

"The witch cut his cock off!" someone yelled.

Castration had to be the work of a devil, the men said, outraged. The women wept for the mother to see her son mutilated. The focus of their attention went from Juan to me and Alma and back again.

Consuelo stood and pointed at Alma. "The devil and his witches did this dark act."

"Bruja," a vieja shouted. "¡Bruja! ¡Bruja!" The mob took up the sing-song chant again. More torches were lit. The sweat on a hundred faces gleamed. An egg hit the building behind us. The sheriff and deputy pulled out their guns, yelling at the crowd to move back. The roiling swarm continued to push and shove for a better view.

Consuelo stroked Juan's hair away from his forehead. "You would have done anything for me," she said, tenderly covering the lower portion of his body. She raised her arms to the people, beseeching them, "The Sandovals took my family from me!"

"I did it!" Charmaine shouted. "I cut it off because he did this to me!" She shook off the girls supporting her and opened the blanket to reveal her naked body. Juan had sliced a nipple off, and her breasts and stomach were crisscrossed with stitches. Blood oozed from every wound. A host of women covered their mouths. The men looked away, and back again.

"Pilar tried to save me! He stabbed her! He said he would slice off my breasts and fuck me with his knife. Alma shot him before he finished."

Consuelo rose to her feet. "Lies—"

Charmaine raised a black and blue arm, shaking visibly, and pointed at Consuelo. "You saw. You were there!"

"She was a *mother* to him," I said, disgusted. "*See* what she created."

"Not even a whore deserves this," a woman shouted.

"He deserved to have it cut off," another woman yelled. Others nodded their agreement and scowled at their husbands. The men backed away. They urged their women to follow with soft words.

The army doctor came downstairs and wrapped Charmaine again in the blanket she'd thrown off.

"You need to rest. I'll come up and check on you before I leave," he said. Charmaine and the other two girls went inside.

"What's the condition of the other woman?" the sheriff asked the doctor.

The doctor, though young, seemed to recognize a dangerous situation when he saw one, and spoke to the people as well as to the sheriff. "Doña Pilar was beaten and stabbed in the gut. Her sister here patched her up good, and she might pull through. But, she'll never have children."

Alma and I bowed our heads. Hearing the words pressed the air out of me. Murmurs of lo siento flowed from the people. The ability to bear children was a gift, and to have it denied by such a brutal attack was an outrage.

The Americans had come and New Mexico no longer belonged to the people. Their lives had changed forever. A whirlwind of loss and retribution circled around us seeking release. Blood had been shed: a whore had been mutilated, Juan had been castrated, and a Sandoval sister doomed to a barren life if she should live. It was enough.

"Déjalos solos," the women said. Leave them alone. The sisterhood had spoken. They would hang no Sandoval tonight.

A calm breeze stirred the skirts of the women as they began to drift away. La gente continued to squabble among themselves, the rise and fall of their words fading, and disappearing into the wind. They carried Juan's body to the undertaker, and Mr. Bleakman dragged Consuelo away.

"There's no proof she was in the room," the sheriff said to his deputy. "Just the word of his victims. I think the culprit is on his way to the undertaker." He and the deputy tipped their hats and left. The army doctor went to check on Charmaine and Pilar. Alma and I were left standing in front of the boardinghouse. Only one person hurried down the street toward us: Padre Lopez.

"At last, a representative of the Church," I said.

He wiped the sweat off his forehead with a handkerchief and stared at Alma. "I came as soon as I heard. You've been beaten? Is Pilar hurt?"

"Upstairs," Alma said, and laid her hand on the Padre's arm. "Her wounds may be fatal."

"She needs last rites?"

"I doubt she'll let you perform them," Alma said.

"Tell her it is an exorcism," I said. "If she says she prefers to keep her demons, we will know all is well."

The corner of the padre's lips twitched, replacing the beginning of a smile. I remembered that mannerism from his youth. He was trying not to cry.

He shook his head. "Pilar's heart is pure. She does what she wants. She always has, and I'm not going to be the one to change her." He went inside.

Alma sighed. "What now?"

"The bruja rides the wind south," I said.

"You don't really believe Consuelo is a witch, do you?" Alma asked.

I licked my finger and held it up. "To the south," I said. "To Juan's motherless children in Mexico. Where else can she go?"

30

The Secrets Foretold

"Graves will litter the Santa Fé trail. There'll be orphans."

**ratoria,** *1848*
Santa Fé:

It was Pilar's own contrary decision to return home.

"I want to see my horses," she said, wrapping her arms across her chest defiantly. "I have work to do."

We had all neglected work at home to remain by Pilar's side. Monique set a tray with food I had cooked on the table next to her bed. "It's only been three weeks and you slept for most of the first two."

"Are there tortillas?" Pilar asked.

"I made them an hour ago. They should still be warm," I said.

Pilar unwrapped a dishcloth folded around two tortillas and slathered butter on them. "Yesterday, doña Juliana visited and warned I'd get fat eating these and then I'd never find another husband," she said between bites. "She just happens to have a worthy nephew with six motherless children in mind. I had to pretend I was about to faint to get her out of here. More viejas will visit if I stay in town. They have nothing better to do than arrange marriages."

"Marriage worked for you once," I said.

"Once in a lifetime," Pilar mumbled, her mouth full. "Where's Alma? Is her lover on his way?"

Alma walked in carrying a fresh pillow. "I felt my ears burning and rushed back to hear the gossip. Lean forward." She plumped the pillow behind Pilar's back. "Yes, Shug is on his way to Santa Fé. The letter was mailed over a month ago, so he could arrive at any time." She blushed.

Pilar laughed. "You're pleased, aren't you?"

"I'm very pleased."

"Well, if you get married, it should satisfy the people for a while. What time is it? Stinky should be here soon and I'm ready for his lecture on the lives of saints." Pilar smiled devilishly and rubbed her hands together.

"You torture him with your sacrilegious remarks," Alma said.

Pilar smiled. "Why must one lose a body part to be considered saintly? A saintly life should be a life well lived. Simply dedicating your eating, drinking and fornicating to the greater glory of God should guarantee sainthood. We're put on earth to live and to live gloriously."

"The gospel according to St. Pilar," I said.

Monique uncovered a bowl of steaming soup and blew on a spoonful of it. "St. Pilar loved often." She held the spoon under Pilar's mouth.

My sister gazed at Monique while she sipped her soup. "St. Pilar loved deeply," she said, and wiped her mouth with the back of her hand. "I want to go home. I miss my horses."

"St. Pilar should mind her doctor," Alma said, "and the doctor says no riding. I'd prefer it if you didn't ride for another six months—"

"Six months!"

"Pilar," Monique said, her voice trembling, "please be good."

"Be good, St. Pilar," Alma said.

"Be good or else," I said.

"Or else?"

I reached for the last tortilla on her tray, but she grabbed it first. "Not the tortillas!" Pilar scanned our faces. "I'm outnumbered."

We returned to the hacienda with Pilar's promises to stay off the horses. I oversaw the household and continued my history of the Sandovals; Pilar did the books, checked in on the ranch hands, and took the carriage into town to visit Monique; and Alma resumed her midwife duties. We were the Sandoval widows, rich beyond calculation, educated beyond reason, and happy to be well and whole. We were content and satisfied . . . and restless in the night.

Alma cried out in her sleep more than once, and Pilar got up in the middle of the night and passed sleepless hours cleaning rifles or mending harnesses. Disturbing dreams were usual for me; I found them intriguing rather than frightening. The morning after our dream-laden nights, we would eat our breakfast and speak amiably about the forthcoming day, never acknowledging our yawns or shadowed eyes.

After one such night, Alma and I stood on the hill watching Pilar groom a chestnut mare in the lower corral. The mare's foal ran circles around them returning often to nurse.

"Pilar's strength is growing," I said to my sister. She did not answer, but stared off into the distance. Alma had the glassy-eyed expression I remembered well: she was in the grip of her memories.

"Ambrosia Sandoval, 1648, grew fat and strong on mare's milk after her mother died," she said in a monotone. "She helped her father in his horse trading. Indians killed her when she was sixteen."

I nodded, recalling the diary entry written by Ambrosia's father.

Alma took a deep breath and continued. "Martín Sandoval, 1719, bred his stallions to be racing champions. Before each race, he soaked the leather bit in the urine of a mare in heat. Pilar Sandoval, 1885, rode her stallion in the night and leapt for the moon . . . dying . . . "

My sister stared into space, her eyes unfocused, her lips parted. She had gone forward in time. This was new.

"Alma?"

"It's 1848. We're in 1848!"

Foot-stamping and heavy breathing drew our attention to Pilar climbing the slight rise. "She's the sweetest thing, covered me with kisses when I gave her an apple." Pilar wiped her neck with a kerchief, smiling wildly with the joy of her contact with the horses. "What's going on? Have you two seen a ghost."

I tilted my head toward Alma. "The memories." I took her arm in mine and led her into the house.

"I'll make tea," Pilar said.

I sat at the table with Alma. "You remembered the future. The diaries say it happens. Don't worry."

She shook her head and whispered so Pilar would not hear. "It's too great a burden. I don't want to know the future. I saw Pilar die. She was tricked! We all were . . . will be."

"Will be what?" Pilar asked, as she set the table and poured our tea. "I feel so great. I'm really itching to ride." She caught Alma's grief stricken expression, and rushed to say, "But I won't."

"Padre Lopez is coming to supper tonight," I said, trying to divert the talk away from horses and riding and memories.

Pilar nodded. "He's upset over new dispatches from the Vicar General. The Church wants to reorganize and needs someone in Santa Fé to run the parishes. There's one too many priests with wives and children to suit them. They don't trust anyone locally, not even Stinky."

"They'll send a priest from Durango?"

Pilar shrugged. "Who knows? They could send a Frenchman for all I care. What's—"

Alma pressed her hands to the side of her head and squeezed her eyes shut.

I touched her shoulder. "Don't be frightened. Is it the French priest? I've seen him in my dreams, too . . . a French priest who comes to Santa Fé and builds a grand cathedral. I've seen the plaza filled with Anglos, more gringos than the people think possible."

"Yes," Alma said.

"More wagon trains will arrive and illness will follow in their wake. Graves will litter the Santa Fé trail. There'll be orphans."

"Yes," Alma said, weakly. "I've seen them."

Pilar cleared her throat, serious for once. "I didn't want to say anything, but my dreams–"

"You've dreamt the same things?" I asked, surprised.

"About the French archbishop, yes, and the cathedral." She crossed and uncrossed her booted leg, scratched her nose, peeked up at us.

"Tell us the rest," Alma said.

Pilar didn't hesitate. "In my dreams, there's an old, withered woman who makes charms. She makes dolls that look like us—"

"Consuelo?" I asked.

Pilar shook her head and hunched her shoulders. "I knew you'd think that, which was why I didn't mention it. Didn't you tell Geraldo the diaries said our bloodline would diverge? That you were the first, but not the last?"

I glanced at Alma, and chose my words carefully. She had a lover traveling West to claim her, and I knew she wanted more children. "Geraldo said marriage produces a new mixture. It strengthens the blood."

"But the diaries predict a new direction," Alma said, flat and unemotional.

Pilar sat up straight. "Well, that explains a lot. I don't know who the doll maker is, but they're meant to be us except for two. Two children. Both Anglos."

"I saw their faces," Alma said, her voice filled with wonder. "I saw them."

"*Our* children?"

Tears flooded Alma's eyes, but she was smiling and nodding. "Children," she said. "The Sandoval heirs.

The End

1

First, We Were O'Reillys

June 22, 1865 Mother passed on. We wrapped her in one of her best quilts and I stitched it closed like I'd seen her do for Ben.

THAT BRIEF DIARY entry was all I wrote the day my mother died 62 years ago. Plain dry facts, the same as the high New Mexican desert we were lost in. Those dry words are still awash with emotion for me. My daughter never wanted to hear the old stories. Her mind was made up. About me. About the Sandoval sisters. Her experience of them was not mine. She'd never been lost and abandoned on the trail to Santa Fé.

We played next to her grave for two days. Then, the food gave out. With only a bucket, a blanket to rest on, and my diary, we walked farther from the campsite, not looking back very often, and then not at all.

No memory of our former life in Missouri, nor the faces of our parents, entered our thoughts. It was as if our gestation had been on the trail.

Our birth was yet to come.

The Sandoval blood was not destined to flow into new generations . . . by chance or by choice. Who knows? Our arrival at their doorstep was taken in stride, as if expected.

Their blood was not our blood, but we became Sandovals, nonetheless. They could not let us go. They were set apart, and so were Phil and I.

We played with the other children and eventually flirted with them, but we were not the same. Our Anglo last name disappeared and we became the Sandoval children on every legal document of that time, but we were not la gente. We were the children of the Sandoval witches.

The community would not forget the old blood.

To my early writing group readers Jill Smolinski and Candy Deemer, thank you for your patience, helpful critiques, and encouragement. Aimee Bender's classes lit the writing spark for me. Claire Carmichael gave me meaningful praise at my darkest moment, and she had brilliant ideas for structuring this novel. Garrett Quintana fostered my early ambition. My deepest love and gratitude goes to my husband, who pursued me when I needed it the most.

www.ingramcontent.com/pod-product-compliance
Lightning Source LLC
Chambersburg PA
CBHW021955170626
46808CB00001B/161